A.W. BOARDMAN

THE TWO HORNS OF THE MOON

The Life of Harry Hotspur

First published by Amazon 2020

Copyright © 2020 by A.W. Boardman

All rights reserved. No part of this publication may be reproduced, stored or transmitted in any form or by any means, electronic, mechanical, photocopying, recording, scanning, or otherwise without written permission from the publisher. It is illegal to copy this book, post it to a website, or distribute it by any other means without permission.

This novel is entirely a work of fiction. The names, characters and incidents portrayed in it are the work of the author's imagination. Any resemblance to actual persons, living or dead, events or localities is entirely coincidental.

A.W. Boardman asserts the moral right to be identified as the author of this work.

A.W. Boardman has no responsibility for the persistence or accuracy of URLs for external or third-party Internet Websites referred to in this publication and does not guarantee that any content on such Websites is, or will remain, accurate or appropriate.

First edition

ISBN: 9798574802021

This book was professionally typeset on Reedsy. Find out more at reedsy.com

For my Family

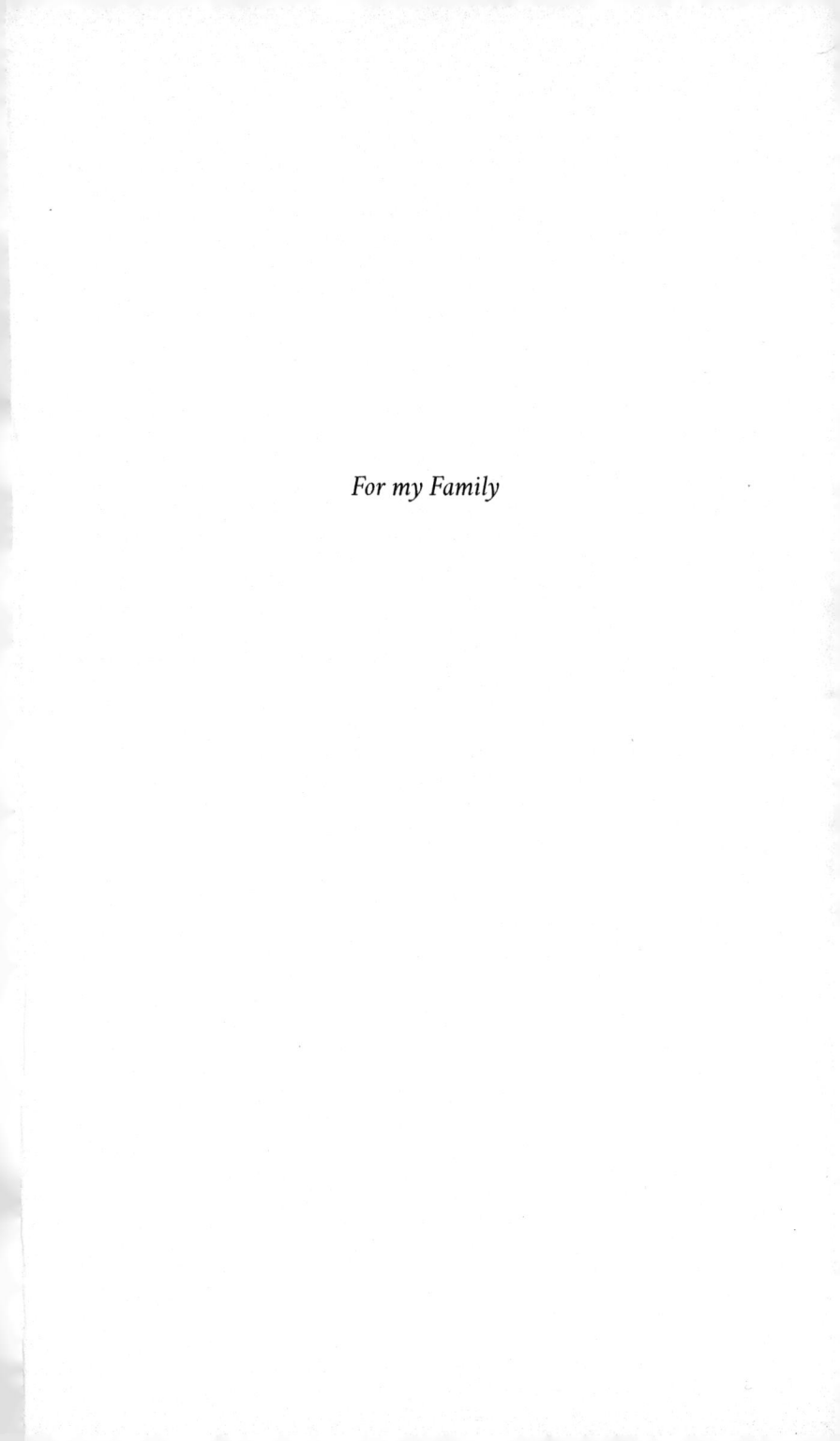

…and by his light did all the chivalry of England move. To do brave acts. He was indeed the glass wherein the noble youth did dress themselves.

WILLIAM SHAKESPEARE

Contents

Foreword		iii
1	Kyme 1461	1
2	Leconfield 1373	6
3	France 1373	17
4	London 1377	29
5	Berwick 1378	39
6	Alnwick 1378	50
7	Lyliot's Cross 1381	61
8	Scotland 1385	73
9	Westminster 1386	85
10	Radcot Bridge 1387	96
11	Borders 1388	105
12	Saint Inglevert 1390	122
13	Wigmore 1392	135
14	Périgord 1395	146
15	Kenilworth 1397	156
16	Gosford Green 1398	165
17	Warkworth 1399	173
18	White Friars 1399	182
19	North Wales 1399	193
20	Borders 1400	202
21	York 1400	215
22	Wales 1401	224
23	Homildon Hill 1402	236
24	London 1402	247

25	Bamburgh 1403	255
26	Cocklaws 1403	264
27	England 1403	277
28	Hateley Field 1403	287
29	Battlefield 1403	298
30	Shrewsbury 1403	308
31	Kyme 1461	317
About the Author		328

Foreword

The framework of this story is true. Most of the characters who knew Harry 'Hotspur' Percy were real people who had feelings, faults and diverse ambitions that shaped our history. Some were tyrants, some brutal killers. One was a kingmaker. Another was a powerful woman whose family's dynastic claim to the throne was her obsession. Very few names in *The Two Horns of the Moon* have been fictionalised, and all hopefully bring to life the epic sweep of events that transformed Britain in the late fourteenth and early fifteenth centuries.

The narrator of this story was also a real person; a soldier, spy, and later a writer who rode with Hotspur into battle on at least two occasions. His chronicle, written in English, is a work of poetry, and I have used this and other contemporary documents as a foundation on which to build a story primarily written to entertain as well as inform.

In 2003 I was fortunate enough to publish my third non-fiction book, *Hotspur: Henry Percy Medieval Rebel,* for The History Press. In it, I traced the known facts about Hotspur's life, the Britain he knew, and his daring rebellion of 1403. But during my research into the 'real' Sir Henry Percy (or *Haatspore* as the Scots called him) it soon became apparent that here was a story that deserved to be fictionalised. Why? Because a non-fiction account of Percy's life could never hope to capture the real-life character that, for me, literally leapt off the page. To write a fictional biography of Hotspur would be too non-academic, I thought. But the more I wrote about him, the more I wanted to portray the real man, and I soon discovered why.

My real interest in Hotspur is far more personal. And through extensive research, I now know that Henry Percy probably suffered from chronic anxiety or a form of ADHD that surprised contemporaries but failed to tarnish his celebrity. As for me, 'creating' Hotspur has been a distraction and sometimes a cure for far less volatile symptoms of anxiety that many of us face in our lives today - so this book, in a way, is a catharsis.

In it, I have tried to illuminate the past, and although our ancestors spoke, acted and thought differently to us, I hope I have done Hotspur's story justice without resorting to too much colloquialism. Retrospectively, Shakespeare was probably very close in his own dramatic portrayal of Harry Percy in *Henry IV Part 1*. However, even he could not know the real Hotspur or appreciate some of the facts about his extraordinary life.

Andrew Boardman
2020

1

Kyme 1461

'When the battayle was stryken of mykell myght'

Shadows from the past haunt my bedchamber. It is Saint Mary Magdalene's eve once more, and in my mind's eye, hunched figures roam the battlefield near Shrewsbury.

Overhead a blood moon is waning, and the sky is starless. Thousands of dead bodies cleave together in tangled heaps. Pale, lifeless faces stare blindly skyward in contorted agony, and riderless horses bolt into the distance. The cloying stench of death fills the evening air, cries from the dying torture the living, and in a ditch at the edge of a field of peas lies a naked dead body mutilated beyond recognition.

His horse carried him beyond the great heaps of dead sprawled on Hateley Field, and even the dutiful heralds have failed to identify him. Here the man met death alone, despite a rebel soldier's feeble attempts to resurrect him. The soldier remained with the corpse for hours, avoiding capture, but in the end, he covered the body with brushwood and summoned enough courage to report his findings to the king.

In the shadows, I see King Henry, the fourth of that name, rebuke the rebel soldier for opposing him. He knows other insurgents are waiting to test his kingship and fears this might not be his last battle. Loyal subjects are becoming difficult to find in England since he usurped the throne, and even Henry's closest allies doubt the kingdom will ever be secure again. Confusion and uncertainty reign in each man's mind and I see the shattered remnants of the royal army gather as the king, closely guarded by his household, follow the rebel soldier into the night.

In my mind, I hear a clarion call to arms announcing Henry's arrival on the battlefield. The young Prince of Wales rides ahead of his father crying out 'God save the King!' to warn everyone of His Majesty's approach. Each soldier echoes the cry. They fall to their knees as Henry passes, and those men who are not wounded, follow their sovereign across the fields they have so recently fought over. Soon thousands of exhausted levies and their lords converge like cattle, eager to gain assurance that the battle is over and their commissions are ended. But all now depends on the dead body in the ditch and the king's willingness to pardon the rebel soldier for his crime.

King Henry, bloody and weary from fighting, fixes his gaze on his wounded son and waves the heralds away as they try to pass him scrolls estimating the dead. Henry is worried about the stray arrow that has badly mauled the right side of the prince's face. He knows he needs a surgeon urgently before the wound becomes infected. But the Prince of Wales is adamant that no one is safe until the traitor is found, and he will not be stopped from identifying the body first.

When the prince dismounts, he pushes the rebel soldier aside like a common criminal. He only sees branches covering a body, and his heart quickens as he lifts them to reveal what is beneath.

'Is it him?' asks the king.

No answer comes from the ditch, and the king crosses himself.

Henry is grief-stricken, but the prince shows no remorse for the corpse and pokes it with his sword. He frowns at his father's weakness and kicks the body causing the rebel soldier to lurch forward.

He crashes into a wall of guards, and they seize him before he has a chance to protest.

'Dies nostri!' shouts the Prince of Wales raising a fist. 'Victory!'

There is a halfhearted cheer from the army, but most soldiers who are close by are unsure what the discovery means. They refuse to believe that the rebel leader is dead and despite their loyalty to the king, each man measures the prince's elation against the reaction of the highborn prisoner closely guarded by Henry's bodyguard.

The Earl of Worcester is not bound to his horse by ropes, but by a great reputation, and when he stares forward refusing to grieve for the body in the ditch, or himself, the king becomes annoyed.

'And by his light did all the chivalry of England move,' cries Henry, as memories replace all traces of ceremony. 'See how chivalric virtue has been killed by foul ambition.'

There is silence as years of friendship pass between the two men. But Worcester remains stone-faced, glances at the body in the ditch, and shakes his head.

'His spur is not cold yet.'

'You lie!' cries the Prince gazing at the corpse and its arrow-destroyed face.

'He lives yet,' snarls Worcester, 'I saw him ride away.'

The prince looks to his father for support, who instead calls upon his confessor to sing *Te Deum* to ease his soul. Henry is grieving, but now even he doubts his son's words. Despite the ordeal of battle, he secretly hopes his former friend escaped the field. And as the voice of his confessor stills the air, the young prince kicks the body again out of spite.

'But Harry, he was your friend,' says the king dismounting quickly.

'No friend of mine—'

The prince aims another kick at the corpse. His anger is too much for him to bear, and I see the rebel soldier break free from his guards aiming to charge the prince down.

There is a scuffle as the king protects his son. More guards seize the rebel soldier, and this time he is tightly bound like a young goat.

'He was a traitor, and like all traitors was executed,' says the prince eying the rebel soldier confidently.

King Henry avoids the quarrel and passes his son the queen's favour to staunch the blood coursing down his face and neck. He helps the prince from the ditch, and when they see the wry smile on the rebel soldier's face, the past comes alive in an instant.

Above them, the blood moon casts a parting amber glow on the crumpled body in the ditch, and in a dark corner of my bedchamber, I weep bitterly. Shadows fade in my bedchamber, and once again, the past is consigned to history. It is almost dawn, and before heaving myself back into the present, I see a fading vision of the prince who turns and strikes the rebel soldier across the face with his gauntlet.

I was that rebel soldier.

2

Leconfield 1373

'At nyne yere he shalle to the felde I sure'

My name is John Hardyng, and to clarify my place in this history; I am not born yet. But, long before I joined the Percy household men spoke of my master's life and how his fame grew out of a need to be the perfect knight. They told me of his reckless youth, his inner demons, his overbearing family, and as for his later deeds, I bore witness to these when I became his squire and shield-bearer at the age of twelve years.

For most of my youth I lived at Leconfield in Yorkshire, and even today the manor house is a fair place worthy of the Percy family who built it. A deep moat surrounds its limestone walls, a fine barbican gate welcomes the weary traveller, and many other chambers, including a great hall, enclose a spacious courtyard where my father taught me archery. But only one small corner of Leconfield Castle was special to my master, and I remember him returning to it many times to gain solace when life became difficult to bear. The little library, known as Paradise, served as a schoolroom for the Percy family in those days, but young Harry Percy was no scholar. In his world, there was only one book in Paradise worth reading, and even now, I can recall him showing me its contents when I was young and impressionable.

Esperance en Dieu were the words inscribed in gilt on its cover, and my master would always translate the meaning of the motto no matter how many times I saw it.

'Hope in God,' he would shout, trying to curb his stammer, 'and never f-f-forget it.'

And I never did.

It was the old *Perci* watchword, but despite his passion for its meaning Harry Percy was no philosopher or poet. The family motto was his ancestor's battle cry, and he was more suited to riding fast, shooting straight, and pursuing a military career rather than thumbing through the humanities or divine scripture. Instead, my master doted on stories of chivalry and only took an interest in Latin or French texts to learn how men made war and became *grand chevaliers* to earn a living.

To match this singularity of mind, Harry made sure his body was physically fit. His chief henchmen at Kenilworth told me that my master was more attuned to fighting than most boys of his age. He could run fast, wrestle, and lift large weights using muscles in constant use on the training ground. Unlike most of his other trainees at the castle, Harry was also well versed in grown-up weaponry too. He could swing a two-handed sword with ease, shoot a war bow like a trained archer, and run several courses in the lists against adult opponents. Even at the age of nine years, he was a stronger and much more agile warrior than some of his father's ale-soaked men-at-arms. But, as for formal education, the only book in Paradise Harry ever read with any interest was the one inscribed with the Percy motto.

All of my master's forebears had lived in the north of England since the Conquest, and a Percy had continually ruled there since the days of Algernons Percy who had served King William, the first of that name, during his harrying of the north. Thereafter, Yorkshire became Percy's titular kingdom, and south of the River Trent every Englishman knew that the family provided the only real bulwark against the Scots who were forever active on the border. In particular, Harry identified with his ancestor's battles against the old enemy. And whenever he thumbed through the old leather-bound book of his ancestors, he often paused at a specific page to read it aloud to anyone who might listen.

He would draw his sword and imagine his forebear, another Henry Percy, at the head of his retinue killing any Scot that set foot over the border. Sir Henry fought like a lion said the book, and despite his diminutive size, the whole kingdom of England was saved by his feats of arms.

Harry's voice always raised a full octave whenever he read from the book, and his speech on these occasions was never plagued by that annoying hesitancy of his life that others copied later. Enthralled by the chronicler's words, he never thought to question war as a youth nor the mentality of those who made a living from it. He knew from the book in Paradise that a knight could make a vast amount of money from capturing nobles in battle, and that his father had forged his lordship of the north not only by the letting of Scots' blood but also by taking lucrative ransoms.

But money and fame was not the only thing on Harry's young mind. In his world, there was more to war than killing or prisoners. Chivalry was the intangible code that consumed his daily thoughts, and he often visited the places where his ancestors had fought to try and unravel its secrets. Here in the field, and the little library at Leconfield, my master contemplated what life might be like as a *grand chevalier*. And soon his craving to learn the arts of chivalry was so all-consuming that his every waking hour echoed to those knightly skills that many thought unnerving in one so young.

But long before I was born, it was not in England or Scotland where the brutal realities of the age first touched Harry's life. And he told me afterwards that the death of his cossetted youth began one day while he was reading his favourite book in Paradise. The excitable footsteps climbing the tower staircase heralded the approach of a russet-haired youth who one day would be king. And when the door was flung aside, my master's hand went instinctively to his dagger.

'What…are you a scholar now?' said the youth.

'Do you w-want a fight?' said Harry.

'No, you would beat me, and besides father's here so would not allow it.'

Harry closed his family history. 'So, will he let you g-go?'

The russet-haired youth gazed at his friend through the dancing shafts of northern light streaming through the arrow loops. 'No, next season I will go to France, God willing. But I wanted to see you before you leave.'

'Then old Gaunt has agreed?'

'Father's in the yard waiting for you.'

The youth called Henry of Bolingbroke frowned at his friend's casual acceptance of such a great adventure. As the eldest son of John of Gaunt, Duke of Lancaster, he too desperately wanted to go to France. But as yet he was a closely guarded asset that his father dared not cast into the hazards of war.

'Richard's here too,' said Bolingbroke, casting his eyes to the floor. 'I had to share a horse with him—'

'Does he w-want a fight?' said Harry.

Bolingbroke smirked. 'No, you know how he is.'

'Is he still being g-groomed by your f-father?'

'Richard might be king sooner than you think.'

'Ha, then you should be g-g-glad,' said Harry lurching forward and clipping the back of his friend's head. 'When Richard is k-king old Gaunt will have to obey him.'

'Richard's no king. You know that,' sneered Bolingbroke.

'Ah, but he has the r-r-right.'

'Richard's a peacock!' spat Bolingbroke.

My master drew his dagger, and before his friend could say another word, a flash of swift-moving steel cut through the shafts of light between the two boys. 'Sure you don't w-want a fight?' said Harry pressing the cold blade against his friend's throat.

'I speak the truth Harry, Richard's a *bougre*, I saw him once… doing it!'

Bolingbroke slipped under Harry's arm. 'It's not like when we used to all play together at Kenilworth. Now King Edward is old, and the Prince of Wales is near death, soon Richard will wear the crown.'

'You mistrust everyone,' said Harry lowering his dagger.

His friend smoothed back his ruffled hair. 'Richard's feeble-minded too. What kind of a king is that? A king must be strong-willed to earn the respect of his subjects—but now you must go, Harry, before father scolds you.'

My master clipped the back of his friend's head again and easily avoided Bolingbroke's fist as it swung loose in the air.

'Even you would make a better king,' said Bolingbroke grinning.

'Esperance en Dieu!' yelled Harry, who had already sidestepped the door and leapt the first angle of the stairwell.

'May God keep you safe my friend...'

It was a typical exit by my master, but it was how God had created him. And he told me numerous times he was never comfortable in anyone's company for long. Harry could always feel the spirit of his ancestors setting him on. Rekindled by the glowing words he had just read in Paradise, he was ready to take his place in history just like all the other Percys before him. His great-grandfather had risked his life to save England, and now it was his turn to shine.

In the courtyard his horse was being saddled, a servant was loading his armour and weapons onto a cart, and even though he was only nine years of age, he had the feeling that his life was about to change. All his nervous habits, including his annoying stammer, the chattering voices in his head, and his rashness of mind were about to be cured, he thought. But the House of Lancaster had not finished with my master's schooling yet. The ties that bind great families together are too strong to be cast aside so quickly, and a great bulk of a man in a thick quilted aketon jacket barred Harry's way to his horse.

Richard of Bordeaux's lean, elfin-like figure clung to the giant's heels, and as usual, Harry became the butt of his other friend's jokes.

'Harry's in t-t-trouble,' mocked Richard cowering in his

uncle's shadow.

Richard's frailty craved constant attention. But his sickly blonde complexion hid a sly craving for affection. He had been wet-nursed and brought up in France by a flock of doting women, and the famous man casting a long shadow across him encouraged the future king to do as he pleased.

As all men knew in those days, John of Gaunt was the richest man in England next to King Edward. He was accustomed to all the finer things in life, including food, wine, fine clothes, and above all, the pleasures of whoring. He carried with him a lifetime of battle scars, several carnal diseases, and lately, a nasty bout of intestinal worms. But beneath the grand title of Lancaster and his wanton excesses, few men knew the real Gaunt other than him being the king's third son and incredibly ruthless. Most men trembled in Gaunt's presence, he was a consummate hater of the French, more than double the size of Harry or Richard, and today he had one last thing to teach my master before he shipped to France.

'Where you going stutterer?' said Gaunt, blocking Harry's path.

My master froze as Lancaster assumed his full height.

'F-France my lord.'

Gaunt was fearsome to behold, especially for a youngster of nine years. But today his barber had shaved off the famous whiskers that always gave him such a ferocious appearance. His sable locks were basin-cut too, and Harry immediately realised it would not be the king or the Prince of Wales that would lead the English army to France. Even he knew that Gaunt's new haircut meant he would command in person, and there was no doubt in his mind that he was ready for a brawl.

'You're late,' said Gaunt, stopping another of Harry's feints with the flat of his hand. 'Your father has already shipped, so make haste or I'll shove that stutter down your insolent throat!'

This time Harry ran into Gaunt's aketon and was quickly thrown aside.

'You worthless little shit heel! Has my money been wasted on you boy? Haven't you learned anything from my henchman?'

Richard laughed. 'Only how to s-s-stutter!'

But when my master sprang back onto his feet, Lancaster raised an eyebrow. He was impressed; even more so when Harry drew his dagger.

'Good!' shouted Gaunt, scratching his inflamed backside. 'I see my money's been well spent on you after all. Now strike Percy, goddamn you, strike me dead or I'll make you wipe my itching arse.'

At that moment Bolingbroke appeared in the courtyard. He knew Harry's impulsiveness would someday lead him into trouble.

'Father!' he called out, hoping to divert attention away from his friend.

'I told you no,' said Gaunt eyeing his son with contempt. 'You and Rich will stay here until I return from Aquitaine. And mind you watch your manners, especially you Rich, the Percys don't allow—'

'Sacrilege with animals,' mocked Bolingbroke edging closer.

Richard stared innocently at Gaunt. 'No, I didn't, he made me do it!'

'You lie,' said Bolingbroke. 'I saw you with that white hart—'

'Enough!' Gaunt glared at his son. 'We have yet to see what

Harry will do with his blade. Now strike Percy, or your father will have one less son.'

Harry crouched low, ready to launch himself at the giant. His training took over, his palms dried instantly against the leather-bound hilt of his dagger, and the discipline taught in Gaunt's castle urged him to strike quickly, without mercy.

But this time everything was different.

Gaunt was not some expendable levy at Kenilworth paid to spar with him, he was the king's son, a good friend of his father, and Harry knew that to injure Gaunt would be unthinkable. The flood of doubtful thoughts would have made any other youngster run for his life, but Harry was not any other youngster. He was a rash feverish child that had already made up his mind to stab Gaunt deep in the crotch or somewhere just as painful.

However, the fight did not last long.

And when the bright summer's day turned into premature night, my master knew he did not need to fear for Gaunt's life. When Harry pounced on Lancaster, he was cast easily aside and smashed squarely in the jaw. A kick in the balls felled him to the ground in a cloud of dust, and once disarmed he was beaten senseless, not by Gaunt, but by repeated kicks from Richard egged on by his uncle.

Gaunt held Harry in place. 'Harder! Harder! Put the boot in, show him who's master!'

Richard began to cry like a baby but continued to obey his uncle, striking Harry this way and that until his foot began to burn.

The bullying meant nothing to anyone, apart from young Bolingbroke who turned his head away when blood started to flow. Not even Harry's father, who was a powerful man in his own right, would have raised an eyebrow against his son's beating. It was all part of a young knight's training. First, a noblemen's son was taken hunting to see animals bleed. Then he was sent to war to see men bleed. It was no different for Harry, and he only survived crippling injuries because Gaunt knew from experience how far to go.

But all this was only a prelude to Harry's life as a page.

Instead of riding to France lance in hand and mounted on the new palfrey given to him by his father, Harry found himself thrown into one of the many arrow wagons on its way to the south coast. By late evening the next day, my master's horse was missing, and he could only wonder who in Gaunt's army had seized his harness and weapons. All he knew was that the humiliation of it all was far worse than the savage aching in his ribs. Gaunt had provoked him, but it was Harry's demons that made him strike. He told me years later; he should have sought to avoid the beating and not challenged a man who feared no one. My master said he was a slave to his recklessness, and he had paid the price of his affliction by going to war in a baggage cart.

The hog-nosed driver said not to worry, they would reach the Cinque Ports in a few days and from there they would board a ship to Calais, England's one sure foothold in France. He bragged that he was a veteran of the French wars, of Crecy and Poitiers. He assured Harry he would soon see the kind of battles that had made England great, and that they would quickly profit from ransoming wealthy French knights who had nothing better to do with their time.

But none of this talk satisfied Harry, and with good cause. Gaunt's latest campaign would be a different kind of war, and unlike any Harry had ever read about in Paradise. History would call Gaunt's expedition the *Grande Chevauchée,* but men who were there called it the Great Disaster. It would be a sad continuation of the long-losing war with England's greatest enemy, and where my master would experience the worst atrocities humans can inflict on their kind.

3

France 1373

'Hys wapyns alle in armes to dyspende'

And only now did he know how dead bodies stank; only now could he describe what defenceless men, women and children looked like after being mutilated and burned beyond all recognition. There was no honour in this kind of killing, thought Harry. It was murder, a crime against God, and he decided to block such thoughts from his mind.

His father had not told him what to expect during a *chevauchée* or 'ride' through enemy territory, and the reality for a young boy was shocking. The devastation was not comparable to anything my master had witnessed before, and the random slaughter carried out by the English, and their Breton allies verged on madness.

Gaunt's ruthless campaign of burning and pillaging every French province the army passed through was matched only by English soldiers thirsting for blood. Innocent victims of the 'great raid' lay unburied for days. No one was left alive to dig graves, so bodies rotted, or were eaten by animals, where they fell. Women and young girls were ravaged and killed by gangs of men-at-arms, and their children were either murdered with them or left to perish in the ashes and rubble of their former homes. Civilian deaths and the destruction of property was the price that Charles the fifth of France paid for a Pyrrhic victory. And when the *noblesse* of France refused to fight in the accepted manner, the English rampage became more ungodly.

The deadly work of the English war bow at Crecy and Poitiers was still recent history in French minds, and the Constable, Bertrand du Guesclin, considered fighting such battles again madness. So instead the French picked at Gaunt's beleaguered army like meat on a bone and soon it became a skeleton of its former self. The French knew where best to strike the invaders to cause the most damage, and this, above all else, was the only thing that impressed young Harry Percy amid his daily revulsion. Out of sheer stupidity, the English became victims of their actions, and soon Gaunt's army was starving to death while the French became jubilant spectators to their downfall.

Subjected to this new form of warfare, English soldiers degenerated into wild animals, and it was a lesson that Harry's father decided that his son should never forget. In his mind, he thought the shock of such brutality and hardship might curb his son's rebellious spirit. It was an absurd thought, but one the Lord of Alnwick wholly condoned. Percy had seen such atrocities many times before in France, and now his first-born son was to be force-fed the same medicine. But my master told me years later that the strain of the campaign was so great that every day he threw up more than he ate.

To add to Harry's woes, his overzealous father had a henchman called Thomas Crackenthorpe, and his loyalty to the Percy family was unquestionable. His indentures of service went back several generations, and his complete devotion to the Lord of Alnwick was absolute. Crackenthorpe was a lean man with a long-healed war wound that caused his right leg to cast outward as he walked along. He could not run, but then a man like Crackenthorpe did not need to. He feared nothing, he was ruthless and cruel, and before long the Lord of Alnwick ordered him to take young Harry Percy out on a typical English raid to further his education.

As always the French village chosen near the southern border of Périgord was of no strategic value to the English. Food was scarce even for the local peasantry, and when the Percy raiding party arrived there, the rustic hovels surrounding a market cross seemed deserted.

'Smoke them out,' ordered Crackenthorpe to his men. And following his instructions, the humble village was soon in flames.

Dogs barked as a bell tolled in the distance, and a wailing noise suddenly consumed the surrounding countryside. Cries from sick and infirm villagers burning alive inside their flaming homes made Harry's horse rear savagely. And when he saw Crackenthorpe pushing the terrified peasants back into the inferno, he decided to ride off and play no further part in the murder.

However, Harry told me later that he wished he had taken another road, or galloped back to England, to avoid the guilt of what happened next.

At first, my master was comforted by the serenity of a forest clearing where the villagers had built a small wooden church. Birds were chattering in the trees, the wintry sun was beating down on his upturned face, and for once the world felt far removed from the destruction and wanton carnage of the *chevauchée*. However, the sight of English soldiers destroying winter crops in the fields soon disturbed Harry's brief solace. It was a process that was second nature to the English by now and if nothing else it would mean the French villagers would starve when spring came.

A sad smoke-filled stillness drifted through the trees and into the clearing. The nearby village crackled and burned into the azure sky, and soon Thomas Crackenthorpe sought out Harry to show him that chivalry and mercy meant nothing to Englishmen who had mislaid their humanity when they set foot on French soil.

By this time, a young priest had emerged from the wooden church, and he shook his staff at the invaders in the fields. My master thought for a moment that the soldiers might observe his sanctity, but sadly there was no mercy in English hearts that day. When confronted by a barrage of religious fervour Crackenthorpe limped over to the priest and threw him to the ground.

He immediately straddled his struggling victim, first holding his arms, then his legs unable to control the cleric.

'Hold fast!' said Crackenthorpe trying to catch the priest's flailing hands.

His men gathered to help their master, but he ordered them away, screaming, 'Get the boy you arseholes!'

The priest's crazed attack on Crackenthorpe continued. His strength seemed inhuman, and when one of the English soldiers seized Harry's bridle, my master fell heavily to the ground. Winded by his fall, he tried to rise but was too slow for the Percy soldiers who collectively dragged him over to where Crackenthorpe was struggling with the priest.

Harry's heels ploughed a deep furrow in the ground.

'Non, non, pas d'épargner l'enfant!' cried the priest incensed at Harry's involvement.

But the priest's words were lost on Crackenthorpe who ordered his men to drag my master over at knifepoint. It was as if his Percy lineage had been set aside until the ordeal was over, and all Harry could do was to obey Crackenthorpe's orders, or risk being killed by one of his father's overzealous men.

In the end, my master fell before the priest in a state of shock.

'Hold his arms damn it!' spat Crackenthorpe.

'Ne bouge pas!' pleaded Harry several times seizing the priest's wrists. *'Ne bouge pas*...be still...'

My master was in floods of tears, but when the priest saw his plight, he stopped struggling. Only the blood pounding through the cleric's veins reminded Harry that he was still on Earth. His mind had escaped into a different realm where the memory of his ordeal would plague him for a lifetime.

Crackenthorpe grinned and moved his weight back onto the priest's legs. 'Aye, we only want vittels don't we master Harry? Only vittels for the lads.'

My master nodded in agreement, thinking there was a legitimate reason behind the henchman's words. But just as Harry thought his ordeal was over, Crackenthorpe produced a blade from his belt and stabbed the priest in the abdomen several times. It was a ruthless and calculated attack by the henchman. And as dark stains multiplied on the priest's robe so his resistance weakened and his pulse slowed in Harry's clenched hands.

In the end, the cleric stopped moving. He moaned and searched out my master for help. *'Aide moi...Jesu...'* he pleaded.

But my master told me that all he could do was look away. He had pissed his breeches as any child would, and the coppery-sweet smell of blood and urine numbed his mind and body into a grateful acceptance. The attack seemed to last an age, and by the time Crackenthorpe had finished his butchery, Harry threw up several times on the ground much to Crackenthorpe's delight.

But the henchman had not finished my master's tuition yet.

With added vigour, he stood up, gathered the priest's fallen crook and placed it through the ringed handles of the church door. Next, he ordered his men to gather some brushwood and ferns from the nearby forest and stack them around the wooden church.

Then Crackenthorpe gave Harry a flaming torch to set the building alight.

It was only then that my master saw that all the villagers were inside.

'Now, make your father proud, Master Harry,' said Crackenthorpe breathing heavily. 'Make him proud of you, and I'll not tell him you pissed your pants.'

Harry backed away, and Crackenthorpe winked at his men. He was secretly pleased with my master's decision not to participate in the atrocity, and when screams erupted from within the church, my master knew God had abandoned them all.

'Now we have them,' cried Crackenthorpe setting fire to

each bundle of bracken piled against the church door. 'Like deer in a buckstall!"

In a few moments, the smoke consumed the cries of the villagers inside. And as the main timbers caught fire, Harry ran to his horse, feeling that his head might burst if he stayed any longer. He had seen a small girl staring through one of the church windows, and he called upon God to save her from the madness. But even the girl's screams did not stop the English. And when Harry looked again, Crackenthorpe was pissing on the dead priest's body without a thought to God or humanity.

The screams of the trapped villagers stayed with my master for the rest of his life. It was just one raid among many during Gaunt's unholy war, but it afflicted Harry's mind in perpetuity. His body was never still thereafter, and he developed tremors that aggravated his wayward speech and anxious nature that no leechcraft or learned physician could remedy. Crackenthorpe considered he had done the Lord of Alnwick's bidding by permanently curbing Harry's wilder side. But the ravages of that day near the Dordogne River had the opposite effect. Harry's parting words to his father's henchman were the last he spoke to anyone for days.

'Do you not f-f-fear God?' said Harry as the raiding party rode into camp that night.

Crackenthorpe's voice matched his detachment. 'I only fear one thing in this life,' he said pleasantly.

Harry lifted his head hopefully.

'Aye, only one thing,' repeated the henchman.

Harry waited for Crackenthorpe's reply and wondered. But in the end, he was confounded by the obvious. The henchman pointed to Harry's father, the Lord of Alnwick, who was waiting for them to return.

'He's my only master,' said Crackenthorpe, 'and today I have done his bidding.'

After hearing the henchman's words, Harry never acknowledged him again. He never mentioned the raid on the village to anyone, nor the atrocities committed there, and soon he became numb to the dreadful monotony of the *chevauchée* just like everyone else in Gaunt's army.

Harry's confessor told him that evening, 'The Lord said it is forbidden to kill unjustly, and therefore all murderers, no matter what their rank, should be punished for their crimes.' But now my master knew the scriptures lied. Those words did not apply to men who killed in large numbers, to the sound of drums and trumpets, or to men who had lost their faith in God.

And the next day God's judgement blew a new curse on Gaunt's beleaguered ranks in the shape of deepest winter.

The army was already down to half strength. Thirty thousand horses had been lost or eaten climbing the highlands of Auvergne. Soldiers were deserting like sheep before a cull and on entering Aquitaine snow began to fall. The Breton contingents had gone home long ago, and now the English army was alone, strung out in ragged knots for over twenty miles. But even these setbacks failed to stop John of Gaunt. He drove his men on relentlessly, mostly on foot, refusing to admit defeat, and when even Gaunt's chief captains began to question his competency as a leader, desperation gave way to feelings of mutiny.

Soon an intimidating silence fell over the English ranks, and there came a day when death from disease and exposure became more commonplace than combat.

'Fear not my friends,' said Gaunt trying to rally his troop's spirits, 'for when we return to France, we shall see fields littered with quartered helmets, shields, swords and men split through the trunk to the belt.' His words verged on the prophetic, but in truth, everyone knew that the French would never fight the English on equal terms. 'I tell you I have no such joy as when I hear shouts of victory and the neighing of riderless horses,' raged Gaunt. 'Next time we'll ride in blood, my lords. So, let no man of birth think of anything but the splitting of heads and arms. From this day on talk not of chivalry, but that a dead Frenchman is worth more than a live prisoner!'

The bitter wind rolled over the frosted fields as Gaunt's words fell on deaf ears. 'Yes, think not of chivalry my friends,' he mumbled. 'Put in pawn your castles and towns, for when we return to France again, Charles will not be begging for his ransom, but his worthless life!'

'Think not of chivalry?' said Harry to his father, who was riding alongside him. My master had not spoken for days, but the continuing slurs against the one thing in the world he could hold on to hammered another nail through my master's heart.

'I've heard him dismiss chivalry many times before boy,' grinned the Lord of Alnwick taking a sip of wine Crackenthorpe had robbed from a monastery. 'My lord of Lancaster is only quoting the troubadours.'

It was true Gaunt knew his Occitan poetry well. But Percy was also well aware that any discord in the ranks was punishable by death, so he was quick to put his hand over Harry's mouth to silence him.

'What say you Lord Percy, will we not break a few lances yet?' said Gaunt turning in his saddle.

'Well Highness, as I see it we have taught the French a valuable lesson that they'll never forget.'

Gaunt reined in his horse. 'And what lesson is that my friend?'

The Lord of Alnwick smoothed his forked beard over his breastplate and tried not to heed the hunger in his gut. 'I say that it is the French who are unchivalrous my lord and that by this rule they are not worthy of our lances. They refuse to fight honourably, so by computation, I say they are all bastard warriors who defy the codes they founded in the days of Charlemagne.'

Hearty laughter came from the Percy contingent.

'Well said Percy,' said Gaunt nodding agreeably. 'At least one man has the bollocks to question me.'

Again there was silence in the ranks. But when Gaunt's squire fainted and fell from his horse each man feared he might be next. Even more so when the English banner the squire was carrying fell and sank into the muddy road.

Gaunt ordered one of his men-at-arms to dismount and retrieve it.

'He's dead Your Highness,' said the soldier turning over the squire's body.

Gaunt was furious. 'What of it? Retrieve my banner you shit heel!'

It was a sign of desperation that everyone understood. There was no honour in defeat, and every English noble knew that Gaunt had been defeated by arrogance and overmighty thoughts of grandeur. Even Harry's father was sick of his vainglorious friend. But like all English nobles, he was powerless to act. He knew that great power was useful and that someday he might need that power himself, so he decided to humour Gaunt instead of challenging him.

But young Harry Percy did not applaud Gaunt or his father. Unlike other boys of his age, such as Bolingbroke or Richard of Bordeaux, my master found it difficult to lie. His face was always a direct give-away to the truth, and he considered Gaunt a stupid and unchivalrous man. In his mind, God had punished the English with a fitting defeat, and when he broke loose yelling, *'Esperance!* Harry's demons were released.

'And where's he going?' shouted Gaunt.

'He needs to shit my lord,' replied Harry's father covering for his son again.

The Percy retainers laughed despite their griping stomachs, and Thomas Crackenthorpe shook his head as Harry's speeding figure disappeared into the snowy waste. The Lord of Alnwick had hoped campaign life would curb his son's strange nature. But there was no profit in breaking a deranged horse, and he was fast becoming afraid of what kind of Percy he had sired.

As for Harry, he told me that he raced his horse at breakneck speed until the English army was no more than a thin grey scar on the horizon. The biting wind stung my master's face, the swiftness of his horse raised the hackles on his neck, and the world rushed by like a loosed arrow. Speed matched his character. He imagined himself back in the north of England where he could breathe and chase the roe deer across the border hills. He pretended he was with his great-grandfather fighting the Scots, saving the kingdom. It was a pleasant childhood fiction that involved hewing branches from trees, chasing a wild boar across a frosted meadow and leaping ditches; that is until his horse collapsed from sheer exhaustion and he fell from the saddle.

And there he lay gazing at the featureless sky.

He desperately wanted his life to change; to someday become embellished with the chivalric deeds of his ancestors. But now he knew that quest would be difficult to achieve in a world inhabited by men like Gaunt, Crackenthorpe, and even his father, who used chivalry to commit murder.

He was alone with his demons once more, and he later told me that a small part of him died in France that day. The countryside spoke to him, and it said that when he was fully grown, he would be a hero, but at a price that might cost him his sanity or his life.

4

London 1377

'Of fayttes of armes and chyvalrye'

It was the feast day of Saint George, and it should have been the proudest day of my master's life. At the age of thirteen years, Harry was knighted along with Henry of Bolingbroke, Richard of Bordeaux, and his two younger brothers Thomas and Ralph Percy. To the blast of trumpets and choristers, the lavish ceremony at Windsor Castle had been one of the most well attended of the year. Garter knights, the nobility, the clergy, had filed into the little chapel to observe the investiture. And even the frail King Edward had managed stir from his sickbed to touch each recipient with his great sword *Curtana* before wobbling back to his throne.

But Harry had fainted during the accolade and stumbled from the chapel.

After weeks of leechcraft and purgatives, it was no wonder my master was so weakened. Family physicians had proscribed water, a bland diet, barley rather than wheat bread, fish instead of meat in the hope of curbing his demons. They said his bodily humors suffered an excess of fire over water. But all of these remedies and potions did little good; the demons still chattered away in Hotspur's head, and he was fearful that he might succumb to them again at the sumptuous feast given by John of Gaunt later that evening.

As expected, the guests at the Savoy Palace that night included most of the nobility staying in London. Geoffrey Chaucer, the poet, was also present at the great banquet along with several Lollard knights, who all enjoyed Gaunt's protection given his acquaintance with John Wycliffe, the theologian. Also present at the Savoy was a host of other English gentry including Sir John Neville, the Percys chief rival in the north, and Harry's famous uncle Sir Thomas Percy who had rarely been seen at court since being ransomed from the French three years earlier.

Thomas's ransom had cost the crown a vital castle in France, but this was nothing compared to how much territory Charles the fifth had clawed back from the English since Gaunt's failed *chevauchée*. Now only Calais, Bordeaux and Bayonne remained English possessions, and worse still, the ailing Black Prince had recently died of dysentery leaving only Richard of Bordeaux, a minor of eleven years, to succeed to old King Edward's throne.

'Woe to thee oh land when thy king is a child,' cry learned men when a boy is expected to do a man's job, and Richard Plantagenet was certainly an heir who men thought might gain power before he could sire children. Minorities were bad for kingdoms and king's prey to the will of ambitious nobles. King Edward was still in power, but the reversals in France had placed a heavy burden of tax on the country. The poor were starving, and John of Gaunt had not only been blamed for his incompetence abroad but also for the way he had quickly emptied the king's war chest at home for no reason. The Savoy still bore the scars of a break-in by a London mob, along with the Percy's Aldersgate home that suffered by association. But even this had not stopped Lancaster's blinkered quest for power.

As for Thomas Percy, he had purposely kept well clear of his elder brother's outspoken affiliation with Gaunt. Thomas was his own man, a great soldier, statesman and lawyer, but above all, he was a shrewd politician who could often predict the future with great clarity. Thomas, always conscious of his higher right shoulder, was not suited to great feasts or the company of women and therefore, his presence at the Savoy that night was somewhat unusual. However, my master told me later that his uncle was there to know his elder brother's mind. He needed to know where the Lord of Alnwick stood with Gaunt so that he would not be disadvantaged if the great duke fell from favour.

But as usual, that night the Lord of Alnwick was drunk with self-preservation and Thomas had to plough a deep furrow to release his brother's innermost secrets.

'Look how they all suckle before Lancaster,' smirked Thomas staring at a group of women surrounding Gaunt. 'I think your master craves a different kind of realm to that of Castile and Leon!'

The elder Percy was perusing the great hall looking for his son Harry. 'And Lancaster will have the English crown one day,' he said, taking another cup of wine from a servant. 'Did you see the king today, he could barely lift his sword, and

Richard, well what can I say…'

'A child cannot govern England,' said Thomas.

'No, but a child can be governed—have you seen Harry?'

Thomas shook his head. 'Mark my words, Lancaster will be the ruin of us all if we are not more prudent.'

Percy fingered his beard, a sure sign that he was worried. 'Gaunt has his faults brother,' he said at last, 'but as long as we are wise and prudent, we'll survive the storm.'

Thomas's body language betrayed all the deep feelings of a wounded man. His tightly folded arms concealed a brooding resentment that yearned for revenge on the whole world. He had never recovered from his humiliating capture by the French at Soubise, and his predominantly black robes and lank lice-ridden hair portrayed the carelessness of a man in permanent mourning.

'France is lost thanks to Lancaster,' continued Thomas, 'but how long will it be before the French are rowing up the Thames and throwing gun stones at the Tower?'

Percy pulled his brother closer. 'I'll have the earldom of Northumberland first Thomas. Then I can sleep soundly in my bed. Those Neville bastards are getting too cock-sure of themselves. Look how they strut the floor like roosters at feeding time.' He pointed at Sir John Neville in particular who was now cupping his hand to whisper in Gaunt's ear. 'They lick the arses of anyone who throws them a morsel of power,' added Percy. 'Ah, Harry…come here boy and greet your uncle.'

My master had come out of hiding for only one purpose. He admired his uncle Thomas and was looking forward to hearing stories of chivalry, a love he always enjoyed as a child. But against all his efforts of control, Harry's restless nature made it difficult for him to stand still that evening. Memories of France were still raw in his brain, and all day he had failed miserably to adopt the poise of a newly dubbed garter knight.

Thomas's brow furrowed when he saw his nephew's agitated state. 'Do you want a piss lad?' he said jokingly.

'That's got worse,' said Harry's father, 'he barely stands still for more than a moment these days.'

Harry took out his dagger and thumbed its glistening blade. He had quaffed several cups of wine to calm him, but even now his mind was fraught with visions of being pursued by unknown assailants.

'So, tell your uncle about your journeys in France boy,' said the Lord of Alnwick still eying Neville in the great hall.

Harry shook his head and bit his nails savagely.

'See, he's dumbstruck,' continued Harry's father, 'sometimes I wonder what will become of him. All he cares about is riding like the wind and killing my horses.'

Thomas nodded thoughtfully. 'I've seen that restless nature before brother. Learned physicians say some wounds never show on the body but bleed in the mind. What did you see in France lad that offended you so much?'

My master continued to study the blade that mirrored a face he hardly knew. He was yearning to learn more about chivalry from his uncle, but also to escape into the north. His muscles tried to restrain the demon working away in his gut. He thought he might faint again and his body broke into a cold sweat that drenched his doublet.

'By all the saints,' crowed his father, 'speak boy!'

The Lord of Alnwick was notoriously indifferent to all things of a sensitive nature. But at that moment he spotted Gaunt laughing with Sir John Neville, and he rushed into the hall to break into the conversation.

Thomas grabbed Harry's arm. But Harry lurched away and cut the air between them with a sweep of his dagger.

'*Je me rends!*' exclaimed Thomas raising his hands in submission. 'I only wanted to congratulate you on your knighthood Harry, and give you a little token to match your new spurs.'

Harry thrust out the dagger until his uncle backed away.

'Here, take this,' said Thomas carefully trying not to upset his nephew, 'it was mine once.' He fumbled inside his purse and unfolded a small silk lance pennon decorated with gold thread, precious stones and three *lions passant*. 'This served me well in France and Spain,' he said.

Harry snatched the pennon from his uncle's hand.

'Yes, it was a good talisman for me at the battle of Najera and in my captivity, but I have no use for it now I am back in England, so keep it, it's yours.'

Harry quickly folded the pennon inside his doublet. 'You used to tell me g-good stories uncle.'

Thomas smiled. 'I'll tell you another about chivalry if you'll let me. One that you may not have heard yet, certainly not in France anyway.'

Somewhat against his nephew's will, Thomas beckoned Harry out onto the ramparts that overlooked the Thames. A full moon cast slivers of quicksilver across the swelling currents fermenting far below them and a flock of wild geese skimmed the southern shore on their way to the sea. Thomas said to me once it reminded him of hunting in the flatlands of the Humber with his friend Sir John Chandos and he began to relax in his nephew's company.

'You remind me of someone I lost many years ago,' he sighed, 'someone who I held dear and lost in the blink of an eye. Tell me, Harry, how well do you know your *Chanson de Roland?*'

Harry shrugged his shoulders.

Thomas grinned. 'I take it you know the codes of chivalry that Roland lived by?'

Harry shook his head.

'Lancaster herald must have taught you something at Kenilworth!'

My master took a deep breath. 'Fear G-God and his church…serve your liege lord in valour and f-f-faith…protect the w-weak and defenceless…live b-by honour and for g-glory…r-r-respect the honour of w-women…'

Thomas sighed. 'Good, although that impediment of yours has got much worse since we last met.' He stared at his nephew's awkwardness. 'Tell me, do you have night terrors Harry and think that someone is hounding you?'

My master was surprised at his uncle's admission. Dark thoughts flooded his mind again, and like one of the whirlpools swirling in the Thames far below them, a shimmering image of his experiences in France was conjured up out of the depths to haunt him.

'What did you see in France that made you so changed?' continued Thomas following Harry's vacant stare. 'I'll wager you saw nothing of a chivalrous nature during Lancaster's failed *chevauchée?*'

Harry took a step back from his uncle.

'No? Then I'll wager his methods made you question the code. You see lately I too have abandoned chivalry. It has become more fleeting to me than…than those marsh geese over there…'

In his vision, Harry saw his most treasured book in Paradise crumble before his eyes and the image of his great-grandfather destroyed along with it. He let out a mournful groan of disappointment, and Thomas knew he had found common ground.

'Ha, I thought so,' he said. 'You too mourn the passing of true and *parfaite* chivalry. If you had seen the sack of Limoges, you would say so too. Thousands of innocents killed for no reason. Sometimes I believe there is only ambition left in the world—'

Harry thrust out his dagger. 'No!'

'Then what about that village in France you pillaged?'

'I do p-penance for that...every day!' raged Harry, pushing his uncle between the stone crenellations.

Thomas was shocked by his nephew's strength. 'God may absolve you of the sin,' he said, struggling back onto his feet, 'but what of the night terrors? Believe me, Harry, I know what you suffer. I have the same dreams.'

My master fixed his uncle's stare. 'Then I w-will be the light of chivalry, and men will w-wish they were me.'

'Ha, now that's a thing I would pay to see,' said Thomas throwing his nephew a sly grin. 'I hope to marvel at your chivalric splendour one day,' he said, avoiding the dagger trembling in Harry's fist, 'but for now, think on what I have said. I may need that sharp blade of yours one day.'

Thomas glanced at the feast inside the Savoy and noticed that his peeved brother was returning from yet another heated conversation with Sir John Neville. 'Sometimes methinks your father is at the root of all our troubles,' he moaned. 'Look how the Percy lion cowers before his keeper.'

The embarrassment on the Lord of Alnwick's face was unmistakable. He was wringing his hands together like a washerwoman. And judging by his worried look, he had been made to look a fool in front of Gaunt. It was not the first time, and he called out for his brother's help as he skulked away into the shadows.

'Put away the blade,' groaned Harry's father watching his brother go. 'What did you say to him, boy?'

'You told him...about F-France.'

The Lord of Alnwick let out a great sigh. 'Aye, and why not? God knows how you'll deal with the Nevilles when I'm cold in my grave. I rue the day I ever married your mother, and now you too aim to disappoint me with your stuttering ways and talk of chivalry.'

'Uncle said chivalry is d-dead.'

'Well he should know, he wears it like a cloak every time it pisses down with rain. Tomorrow he'll think it shines like the summer sun. But we'll need more than chivalry to deal with the Nevilles boy. With Gaunt's help, they aim to shit in our midden and claim it as theirs—'

'*Esperance!*' cried Harry rushing over to the parapet.

As always my master's blood raced at the mention of his mother's family, and he climbed onto the battlements thinking to jump into the swirling Thames. But instead, Harry leapt between the stone crenellations, arms outstretched like a great bird of prey, and dropped onto an embrasure below.

'No! No!' cried his father tearing at his hair.

He had not seen where his son had landed, and Percy's commotion was so loud and fuelled by an excess of wine that he lost control. He rushed over, thinking to save his son's life, and peered over the wall wailing like a bereaved woman. The noise caused a ripple of concern amongst Gaunt's guests, women screamed, guards were called, and some thought the

Lord of Alnwick had gone mad as he yelled Harry's name.

'Harry! Harry! No…please God…' he screamed into the night.

And for a moment there was a fearful notion that Percy's first-born son had drowned. But when my master emerged at the opposite end of the terrace unscathed, his father's concern changed to full-blown rage.

'Come here, boy!' he yelled, noticing Gaunt's guests were staring at him. 'Look to your place. You do me no honour with your silly Neville ways…'

It was the ravings of a man who had a distorted love for his son and an insatiable loathing for his dead wife's family. And when the large crowd departed back into the great hall, Gaunt and Neville stood together open-mouthed, gazing at the two Percys, unable to comprehend the antics of so great a northern family.

5

Berwick 1378

'So went he then to Berwyke wythout delaye'

As in all the chivalric writings of war, a newly dubbed *chevalier* had to win his spurs, and this by association had to be verified on the field of battle. It was assumed that the recipient was not a knight at all until he had drawn blood. But Harry told me that winning his spurs was a personal affair and that I must seek out others, like my lord Umfraville, if I wanted to know the truth.

The town of Berwick, situated on the north bank of the River Tweed, was always a contended port in those days. And soon after Harry's father achieved his ambition to become the Earl of Northumberland, the Scots, commanded by George Dunbar Earl of March, began pillaging the borderlands contended by both kingdoms. It was a test of Northumberland's might to subdue the old enemy, and predictably John of Gaunt ordered his closest friend to secure the east march for King

Richard who had now succeeded to the throne on his father and grandfather's deaths.

With the old order swept away, the new king summoned the Percys to act as their ancestors had done before them, but everyone knew it was John of Gaunt who commanded the Lord of Alnwick by achieving his much sought after title. Harry's father could now sleep soundly in his bed, he said, but out of respect for Lancaster, he had to succeed against the Scots to seal the bargain. Becoming warden of both marches towards Scotland was Northumberland's next obsession, and to his credit, he managed to secure a permanent peace treaty with Dunbar instead of emptying the king's purse.

However, like all border treaties, local raiding soon shattered the fragility of life, and early in the young king's second year on the throne, the Scots launched another attack on the east march, this time aimed at the town of Berwick.

When occupied by the English, Berwick was the key to Scottish invasion. English armies were supplied from its port, and high walls protected the town on three sides against the lowland influence of the earl's of Douglas and March. The castle was permanently garrisoned, and Berwick's browbeaten population had endured a long history of sieges. In English hands, the town was the administrative headquarters of English-occupied Scotland. But when the Scots managed to seize it, they always celebrated the capture as a mark of territorial pride, or *fay,* that threatened English rule and the king's credibility.

Berwick's castle had been rebuilt several times over the years, but in those days its defences had become so badly in need of repair that a band of Scots, led by Sir Alexander Ramsay, had no trouble crawling inside through a hole in one of its walls. They killed the warden, Sir Robert Boynton, in his bed, and issued a warning that his wife and sons were to be held hostages, provided that the Scots received a ransom of three thousand marks within a few weeks.

It was clear the Scots were testing the Earl of Northumberland's power to raise the north against them. They expected a swift English response to free Boynton's family, and it was not long in coming. As the heavens opened with a month of spring rain in one day, the great earl, along with Harry and a thousand men-at-arms, crossed the bridge over the River Tweed. Ramsay knew the English outnumbered him, but once again, it would be the shedding of blood that would shape Berwick's fate, and it seemed the Scots were more than happy to do this despite their numbers.

Soon an impressive array of siege engines had surrounded the castle ready to pound its walls with stones and fireballs. Two days later the earl's largest trebuchet smashed through the barbican gate, and when a portion of English men-at-arms rushed forward to attack, the Scots were easily repulsed.

The Earl of Northumberland watched every move of the battle from the vantage point of a small knoll above the castle and town. He was drinking wine with his henchman Crackenthorpe, and Harry's strong right arm was holding a shield above his father's head to shelter him from the rain.

'Look, we have the barbican and drawbridge now master,' said Crackenthorpe pointing to a swarm of Sir John Heron's men who were carrying all before them.

'Let's have at them then, before we all drown. Sound trumpets, *avaunt!*'

The earl drained his cup, tossed it into the grass, and drew his father's sword. *'Esperance en Dieu!'* he cried.

It was what my master had been waiting for, and before his father could say another word, Harry slipped his shackles and charged towards the bridge that spanned the gully between the town and castle. Spurring his horse hard through the driving rain he aimed for the beating heart of battle. But he was too late. Despite his speed of approach, the English had already won the barbican gate and before him was a wooden bridge that, like most of the fortress, was in a bad state of repair. The rain had soaked its timbers and bodies were strewn randomly across its length, making it difficult to cross even for a foot soldier.

But Harry understood nothing of what lay on the other side of the barbican, and he emerged from the inner gate at speed over the bridge without a thought to his safety. Fallen bodies sped beneath his heels and new rowel spurs. His thundering approach could not be halted. And before he reached the inner gate, his horse slipped and tumbled end over end into the abyss below.

As he fell from the saddle, Harry was left hanging by a thread.

Taking into account the weight of his harness, it was a miracle he survived. One of his arms had hooked on the drawbridge chain of the main keep, and he thanked God the metal roundel attached to his couter had snagged on it. He had only lost his sword and helmet in the fall, and when he heaved himself back onto the wooden platform, he was thankful that no one had seen his charge.

The main fighting had moved to the inner ward of the castle by now, but a longhaired Scot who had been concussed under a pile of dead bodies was waiting for Harry to rise, and when he did so, he threw an axe at my master's head.

As the weapon wheeled in the air, the Scot seemed to realise that his victim was only a youngster. For a moment, he extended his hand in vain, but then he was more shocked by where his axe had landed. Harry had somehow caught the haft of the weapon as it spiralled through the air and now he had the opportunity of throwing it back; and what is more, his father and Crackenthorpe were riding through the barbican gate to see him do it.

'Ha, you have him now, Harry!' shouted Northumberland excitedly.

It was true, the Scot was trapped on both sides of the bridge, and the earl could not help raising an eyebrow at his predicament. As for Crackenthorpe, he too was captivated by Harry's situation. He happily reflected on his former pupil's cowardice in France and how his master and household knights emerging from the barbican might witness him piss his breeches again.

'That Scot can either take that axe like a man or learn to fly like a bird,' said the earl peering into the abyss below him.

Crackenthorpe grinned. 'Aye master, a chance for Harry to win his spurs I think...'

But Harry told me later that he had already decided on the most chivalrous thing to do. He had recognised the heraldry on his victim's jupon, and when he lowered the axe to concentrate his mind and stammer, everyone was puzzled.

Meanwhile, the longhaired Scot placed his hands squarely on his hips, puffed out his chest, and waited for the youngster to strike. He was ready to die for Scotland, but even he was taken aback by Harry's indecision.

'What name have you,' said Harry at last.

The Scot smoothed back his sodden hair and frowned.

'Alexander Ramsay o' Dalhousie, what of it?'

And it was at this point that Harry remembered his history. He knew from the book in Paradise that his great-grandfather had captured a Ramsay at Neville's Cross and he decided that this would be his first step on the ladder towards chivalric fame.

'Then submit your s-sword to me, R-Ramsay,' said Harry unhappy that his concentration had wandered.

The Scot furtively glanced at the deep gully below him and laughed. He thought to jump, but after seeing horses and bodies broken on the rocks, he unbuckled his belt and let his dagger and sword fall to his feet. *Je suis votre prisonnier,'* he said in a bad French accent.

Northumberland clapped his hands. He was amazed at his son's foresight and the fact that a great deal of money could be exchanged for Ramsay's life. When he raised his fist, there was a great cheer from the Percy household behind him. However, one man was furious. Thomas Crackenthorpe felt betrayed, and he stood up in his stirrups, shouting, 'Kill him! Kill the Scots bastard!'

'No, he has the right Thomas.' said Northumberland still elated.

'But he has no mettle master, no mettle…' mumbled Crackenthorpe.

Northumberland's back straightened. 'What's that, what's that you say?'

'It was the same in France master…I told you…'

Northumberland's face turned a deep crimson. 'You look to your position,' he snapped. 'Harry is my son and heir!'

'But master I—'

'God damn you, Thomas, look to your place!'

Crackenthorpe knew he had gone too far, and he was so shocked by his behaviour that he was speechless.

'If you value your indenture,' exclaimed Harry's father, 'you will think about what I have said this day.'

Crackenthorpe bowed to his master and urged his horse across the drawbridge. He had never spoken out of turn to Northumberland in his life, and Harry told me later that everyone on the bridge was shocked by his lack of respect. So much so, that they failed to see a dark shape crouched behind Berwick's walls.

A lone Scot's archer had Crackenthorpe in his sights. Beyond the gatehouse, he knew his comrades were defeated, but he was still looking for an easy English kill. And from an archer's point of view, the lanky henchman plodding towards the gatehouse was the perfect target to skewer with an arrow.

But Harry thought the enterprising Scot was aiming his bow at his father and the guttural cry that echoed back from the walls told everyone on the bridge that someone had dealt with the danger. Harry's axe had split the archer's skull in two, and even Crackenthorpe marvelled at the miracle throw.

When the archer fell silently from the ramparts, Northumberland stared in disbelief, and everyone watched as the body cartwheeled through the air, then smashed like an egg on the rocks below.

'Now you're a Percy,' cried Northumberland watching his henchman skulk beneath Berwick's portcullis. 'Now you have won your spurs boy.'

Harry's capture of Sir Alexander Ramsay brought an end to the siege. But the man killed on the walls that day failed to meet Harry's high ideals of chivalry. Even though the Scots were his blood enemies, my master only considered the archer's death a matter of self-defence. He was amazed to feel no trauma or guilt in this type of killing, and when Crackenthorpe realised how wrong he was about my master, he felt his indenture and career slipping through his hands.

Later that evening, there was much feasting in the castle, and as usual, everyone was drunk at the Earl of Northumberland's expense. It was as if the siege had never happened, and Harry's duty was to entertain his prisoner Ramsay. Luckily Sir Robert Boynton's wife and children had been set free after the siege, or the mechanics of chivalry might have dictated a different outcome for Ramsay and his men. But as soon as his prisoner was suitably drunk, Harry decided to excuse himself in his usual spontaneous way.

But Ramsay caught him by the arm. 'So, how old are ye Haat spore?' he slurred.

Harry frowned. 'Haat-spore?'

'Aye, ye on that bridge sporrin' haat.'

Harry shook his head. 'My father says I k-k-kill too many of his horses.'

'Gud fling of the axe though,' exclaimed Robert Umfraville who was a little older than my master at the time.

Harry quickly changed the subject and poured Ramsay more wine. 'Have your men b-been well treated R-Ramsay?' he said bored with the festivities.

'Aye, yer man with the wee totter is looking tae them,' he spluttered.

Harry nodded, but then his anxiety spiralled down into confusion. '*Crackenthorpe...*' he whispered to himself.

'So, tell me how old are ye?' repeated Ramsay. He was willing Harry to say he was older than he looked.

But Harry had already gone. The mention of the man with

the limp had brought all the old memories of France flooding back into his mind, and he had the feeling that he had been made to look a fool.

Outside, a thunderstorm was raging. Large pools of rainwater flooded the inner-ward of the castle, and Harry saw Crackenthorpe's tall ungainly shadow looming over a workman's trench near the north wall. A heavy iron grill had been placed over a pit to carry out repairs, and under it, ten of Ramsay's men were huddled together up to their necks in freezing water.

The deluge was draining into the trench from all four corners of the courtyard, and Harry immediately knew that Crackenthorpe had purposely devised the torture for his pleasure. Some of the Scots had already drowned in the pit as Harry ran forward yelling. He could see the survivors were desperately clawing at the iron grill to escape the flood. But it was the blank look on Crackenthorpe's face that angered my master most. He had seen it many times in France.

'We don't want any stragglers on the march,' said Crackenthorpe as Harry ran at him. 'Your father's orders—'

Harry unsheathed his dagger.

'Your father told me to look after them, and that's what I'm doing—' said the henchman as he was hit by what seemed like a charging horse.

Ramsay and Umfraville ran from the keep, and the Scot dropped the cup of wine he was holding. Ramsay saw his men drowning in the pit, but Umfravaille was confused as to why Harry was attacking one of their men. He watched in amazement as my master, dagger drawn, lurched at Crackenthorpe's throat, cutting it through like a freshwater trout. A second cut in the same place ripped open the henchman's windpipe, and when Harry cast him aside, a great gout of blood sprung from his gullet.

Harry showed no mercy, and all the dreadful images of France surged though his blade as he stabbed Crackenthorpe just like the priest who had tried to protect his innocence. It took a confused Ramsay several attempts to pull Harry off, and even when my master was helping the Scot remove the iron cage trapping his men, my master was so consumed by what he had done that his hand repeatedly jerked with overuse.

Umfraville tried to calm him and carefully removed the blade from his bloody hand. He was having difficulty understanding why Harry had attacked his father's henchman, and Ramsay was equally confused about why the English were fighting among themselves.

'Mah men need help Haatspore,' said Ramsey urgently.

Harry's mind seemed to be somewhere else. 'I'm not Hotspur,' he said dreamily, 'I'm Sir Henry P-Percy.'

'Yer Haatspore now, or I'm not Ramsay o' Dalhousie,' cried the Scot, helping his men out of the trench.

Harry nodded and took Crackenthorpe's legs. He dragged the body over to the pit, took a large stone from beneath the walls and fastened it to the henchman's belt with a length of workman's rope.

'So, how old are ye then Haatspore?' said Ramsay, paying no attention to my master's deadly work.

Harry remained silent, and when the last Scot climbed from the pit, Harry tossed Crackenthorpe's body into it. His strength seemed magnified by the task in hand, and as the henchman's body sank into the watery grave, Harry watched the oily slick of blood follow it down to hell.

'Thirteen...thirteen years,' said my master looking up.

'Ah ye sure o' that?'

Umfraville nodded his head in agreement. He was still staring into the trench and could not believe that the Earl of Northumberland could have sired such a rash offspring. The freezing Scots stared at Harry throwing more rocks into the pit. Between them they could have overpowered my master easily now he was exhausted, but as chivalry dictated, they filed into the castle to await their fate.

'Get them meat and vittels,' shouted Harry after Ramsay.

'Ah will,' said Ramsay thoughtfully, 'and ah will mind this day tae the Douglas.'

'D-Douglas?'

'Aye, he's mah master,' bragged Ramsay turning away.

Robert Umfraville later told me he could hear the Scot begrudgingly telling his men who had saved them as they crossed the courtyard. Ramsay was careful to pass over how Harry had captured him on Berwick's drawbridge that day and failed to mention my master's real age. But when Harry's father eventually released him from captivity some months later, Ramsay was true to his word. He told Sir James Douglas the truth about young 'Hotspur' and how he differed from his father the earl. A truth that was lost on Douglas yet stayed with Ramsay for the rest of his life.

As for my master, Crackenthorpe's death did not purge the past from his mind. He had won his spurs but had not avenged the guilt born in France. And that night, as he held a vigil in the castle chapel and swore Umfraville to secrecy, he vowed to sleep soundly without a host of demons raging in his head. But revenge brings no one true peace, or a good night's sleep, only the fear that the past can never be buried.

6

Alnwick 1378

'His father purposed had Mortimer hys coronoment'

Hotspur spent his infant years at Alnwick Castle even though he was born on the road to York whilst his mother was trying, at his father's request, to return post-haste to the family seat in Northumberland.

Alnwick was, and is now, the most prestigious seat of the Percys, and whenever Harry found himself there, he told me how his anxiety increased tenfold when he rode up to its sprawling magnificence. It was a fear that was tangible. A reminder of the past and how his mother and father had always been at each other's throats. The constant bickering that began when his mother's family, the Neville's of Raby, were mentioned to his father in conversation always aggrieved Hotspur as a small child. And he spent most of those early years bearing it in silence. The situation should have eased when his mother, Margaret Percy, formerly Neville, died suddenly in childbirth. But my master's insecurities continued despite the grief that ripped through the two families.

The outcome was inevitable, and the split final. The Percys soon alienated the Nevilles, and the two houses gradually became rival powers in the north.

However, Hotspur, as the Scots now called him, was convinced that the ghost of his dead mother still haunted the northern fortress, and this is one reason why he avoided Alnwick at every opportunity. He was more at home at Warkworth or Bamburgh where his father's narcissism failed to resurrect the Neville threat. He was even happier when he accompanied his mother to Leconfield during her *mensis horriblis*; a condition that was similar to my master's demons. Namely, his need to be impulsive and over-anxious regarding all things trivial or unknown.

A lack of understanding by the Earl of Northumberland meant that the Nevilles and Percys were always at odds over Margaret's state of mind. Spies were everywhere, warning against even the smallest whiff of scandal. And when Hotspur's mother died followed by his aunt, Maud Percy, the final link between the two houses was severed making the antagonism between Percy and Neville unresolved and more permanent.

Even as I write this history, English noblemen are warring over their hard-won lands. They are all feudally insecure by nature. But in Hotspur's day, the status quo in the north was continually challenged, especially by Sir John Neville, who had been openly courting John of Gaunt and the young King Richard for many years. John Neville was looking for an earldom himself, and he was determined to hammer a firm wedge between the Earl of Northumberland and his benefactor Gaunt to get what he wanted. Thus far, he had failed, but he was a determined man who loved his family, and this was the main reason why Hotspur's father was obsessively insecure.

As for Hotspur, he had never argued with his estranged in-laws. Sir John Neville was his maternal uncle and his son Ralph Neville was Hotspur's age and had always been ready to oblige him with 'a fight.' However, landed insecurities meant nothing to my master compared to his newfound quest for chivalric perfection. So when he was ordered back to Alnwick before Christmas in the second year of King Richard's reign, Hotspur knew that he would have to face the same tense atmosphere he had experienced as a child.

It was snowing when he arrived at the main gate and unusually, his father was waiting for him at the guardhouse. He was warming his hands on a brazier outside, and his shoulders were heaped with snow.

'Christ knows why the Scots call you hot-spur,' he said irritably, 'you fail to impress me with your timeliness. I'll wager a hundred marks you forgot yourself again, just like your mother used to...'

My master was exhausted. He had been in the saddle since dawn, and it was well known to any northern traveller, and his father, that the Berwick road was treacherous and fraught with danger in the winter months.

'That nag is blown boy,' said Northumberland adding insult to injury. 'You've pushed it too hard as usual.'

Hotspur dismounted without a word and patted his steaming horse on the neck.

'Come on, don't dawdle!' said his father urging him across

the inner-ward.

As always, my master knew when to speak and when to keep silent in his father's company. He was covered in mud, and all he wanted to do was bathe, eat meat and fall asleep. But this night it seemed his father had other plans for him. He was pulled and pushed through the castle like a pet dog, and when my master noticed servants had lit fires in every chamber, he concluded that his father had important guests; he just hoped to be excused their company and that they would depart early next morning.

'Your face is too clean Harry,' said Northumberland pushing Hotspur up the staircase towards the great hall. 'Here, this will suffice…'

The earl scraped his hand on Hotspur's armoured leg and smeared a great lump of animal dung across his son's face.

Hotspur lurched away, a reaction that always followed when anyone touched him without permission.

'Now make haste boy!' said his father giving Hotspur another push towards the oak doors that concealed the great hall.

My master became anxious and froze. 'Who's in t-there?'

'You'll see, you'll see. Now best foot forward boy, and mark this: stop playing the fool, think before you speak and lose that infernal stammer, or Crackenthorpe's wife will get to know who slew her husband at Berwick.'

Hotspur gazed at his father, who thumped his fist against his son's breastplate. 'And if you ever act on your own accord again boy, I'll renounce you. Crackenthorpe's death will cost us dear, so there's no Christmas presents for you either this year.'

Despite his shock about Crackenthorpe, and that Robert

Umfraville had betrayed his confidence, Hotspur was confused by his father's seasonal remark.

'No p-presents? I don't need p-p-presents,' he said, failing to hold back his anger.

'In the way of ransom boy,' added Northumberland. 'The price of Ramsay's freedom will come directly to me in lieu of lost earnings.'

Beneath his grubby exterior Hotspur's gut churned. He knew there was no use arguing with his father and all the old feelings of insecurity and overbearing authority choked him to death. He could hear his mother's ghost arguing his case, and now he understood that his father's threat was part of a much wider undisclosed plan. Even the dishevelled look of a dutiful son acting far beyond his years was a ploy to woo whoever was cossetted behind the great doors towering above him. The only certainty was that his father's guests were not called Neville.

Inside the hall, the long dining table was set in silver for dinner, and two men were warming their hands on a blazing hearth. The tallest man was dressed in a fur-trimmed gown under which Hotspur could see an ochre surcoat impaled with azure bars. Sir Thomas Percy, also dressed in furs, was the second man outlined by the fire's amber glow and judging by the grubby state of their riding boots they had been out hunting in the earl's deer park.

Northumberland bubbled over with smiles as he pushed his son forward. 'Here he is my lords!' he said slapping Hotspur on the back.

Hotspur threw his uncle a forced smile.

'Been playing in the mud again, Harry?' said Thomas straight-faced.

'Protecting our heritage brother,' corrected Northumberland. 'Now Harry, I want you to greet the king's new Lord Lieutenant of Ireland. My lord Mortimer this is my first-born son Henry, lately called Hotspur by the Scots on account of… of his…'

'His prowess in the saddle?' said Thomas.

My master bowed courteously to Mortimer and extended his hand.

'I've heard of your feats of arms at Berwick, Harry,' said Mortimer ignoring his hand and warmly embracing him. 'For one so young, you certainly seem to be made of the right stuff.'

Hotspur bowed.

'But then you've never fought the Irish have you?'

'Not yet my lord,' interrupted Northumberland, 'but I have made arrangements for Harry to join you in Ireland and there he will learn from the Mortimers how to fight the shag-haired kern!'

'Do not be so scornful of the Irish my lord,' said Mortimer, 'the kerns are fiercer warriors than the French and the Scots conjoined. They slit more throats in the dark than we do in open battle.'

Northumberland laughed. 'I doubt that my lord, but I will bow to your wisdom and bid my son report on their craftiness when he returns to England.'

'I'll make sure he is well educated,' said Mortimer raising an eyebrow.

Northumberland bowed and immediately became the grand host. 'Come, my lords, cast off your gowns and refresh yourselves…'

Northumberland clapped his hands, and a servant appeared with a tray of wine.

'Harry prepare for dinner,' he said, 'you look and smell like a pigsty. And put on the azure jupon with *fleur-de-lis*, there is someone else I wish you to meet.'

Even now, I marvel at how the destiny of others can change by the slightest misfortune. For my sins, I am a great believer in fate, and after dinner that night, I fear my master's life changed forever. After feasting on a lavish banquet of swan, jellied pies and a great deal more wine, the conversation inevitably turned to Northumberland's favourite subject - the Neville family.

Hotspur tried to eat quickly and excuse himself, but he was in too much trouble to interrupt his father. Northumberland could not be swayed from mentioning the Neville threat. And by the end of the conversation, the earl became so aggressive that he slapped the flat of his hand on the table displacing several silver goblets and plates. 'Yes, my lord Mortimer, they are nothing but sheep-farming bandits. We have always been at odds with them, and now John Neville aims to strip me naked by befriending Lancaster to get what he wants.'

Hotspur heard his dead mother's admonishing reply echo back from Alnwick's thick walls. But this time his father's argument stuck in his throat like the northern pie he had just eaten. There was no self-assured feisty woman to joust with anymore, and Mortimer threw the earl a polite nod to cover his embarrassment. But Thomas Percy was on hand to rescue his brother as usual. He had heard every argument about the Nevilles a hundred times before, and it became clear to everyone present that Northumberland was hopelessly drunk again.

'But have no fear my Lord Mortimer we still have the balance of power in the north,' said Thomas trying to ease the tension.

'Ah, but Neville wants an earldom,' said Northumberland finishing his wine, 'if not from Gaunt, then from the king who will follow the will of his bedfellows.'

'I thought you were Lancaster's oldest friend,' said Mortimer with a sly grin.

'Gaunt's power over Richard is waning my lord. His decisions are being constrained daily by his council. Lancaster has many enemies. The commons hate him you know. His palace was burned down in the riots, and he needs all the friends he can muster.'

'The commons are never happy when they are overly taxed, my lord.'

Northumberland waved his hand dismissively. 'Yes, but the Nevilles will stop at nothing to injure me and—'

'But John Neville is a good soldier,' said Mortimer stiffly, 'would he not be useful in our forthcoming enterprise?'

'Never! That man covets my crown.'

'Your crown, my lord?' laughed Mortimer. 'Are you Richard's heir?'

'My brother means his northern crown, my lord,' said Thomas Percy irritated by his brother's outburst.

'And now they have obtained a license to fortify Raby Castle!'

'We have many fortified castles brother,' said Thomas trying to restrain his anger. 'Neville has one great seat in the north. I agree with you, my lord Mortimer; we should keep our enemies close. Let Neville have the west march, or an earldom if he desires. He'll have to come cap in hand to us for manpower if the Scots raid Westmorland in spring.'

Mortimer grinned at Hotspur who was hiding behind the

great swan's leg he was eating. He could see the impatience in my master's eyes and stood as if to seek relief at the privy. The conversation ended abruptly, but as Hotspur edged over to the hearth also hoping to be excused, he heard a shrill cry that disturbed him. It came from somewhere beyond the hall, and when the conversation turned into whispers, his thoughts returned to why his father had summoned him back to Alnwick.

He knew from his obsession with heraldry that, like the king, Mortimer's son was a Plantagenet and therefore in line to the throne. Still, he had no idea why the head of the Mortimer family had invited him to Ireland. That is until he felt a small hand pulling at his richly embroidered jupon.

A little girl barely half his size was craving attention, and her small face flushed red with embarrassment as Hotspur brushed her away. Her hair was plaited in the Irish fashion, and when she ran over to Mortimer, she flung her arms around his waist. She protested at being rejected by my master. But soon the girl's innocence provided a refreshing diversion from the dour politics as a minstrel appeared at the door and she began to dance and skip to the beat of an Irish *bodhrán*.

Each revolution of the hall avoided Hotspur's presence and her carefully arranged steps multiplied until everyone, even my master, fell silent mesmerised by her purity and grace.

A round of applause followed the dance, and when Mortimer coaxed the little girl back to Hotspur, she stared at him, this time, demanding praise.

'What thinks you of my daughter Elizabeth?' said Mortimer to my master.

As usual, Hotspur was uncomfortable with the question.

Girls were not his regular pastime, but when he saw his father's face stiffen, he soon remembered the threat about Crackenthorpe's wife.

'So what thinks you?' repeated Mortimer.

'She dances like…like a y-y-young hawk, my lord,' said Hotspur.

'Ah, spoken like a true soldier,' laughed Mortimer. 'A rough and ready description, but I have spoken to your father, and I trust you know that our two houses are to be united?'

Hotspur was more puzzled than ever.

'A dowry has been set,' continued Mortimer, 'and I wish you to join me in Ireland where you will be wedded to Elizabeth. Then, God willing, we will both restore order there for King Richard.' Mortimer took Hotspur's hand and shook it. 'Welcome to my family,' he said glancing at Northumberland.

The earl's face was beaming with joy.

'God be praised!' he said, taking Hotspur's hand and thrusting it into Elizabeth's to seal the bargain.

It was a cold calculated business, but now the Percys were royally connected to the late king in more ways than one. As well as being associated through marriage to Edward's third son, this newfound connection through the king's second meant that any male heir of Hotspur's would have a better claim to the throne than Lancaster. It also meant that, if King Richard remained childless, or died then a Mortimer could, if named, ascend the English throne with Percy help.

All three men in the hall knew the computations of this particular heredity conundrum were endless, and that fate could take a hand at any time. But child kings were bad for the kingdom, especially if they were vainglorious, spoilt, or had a scheming uncle like John of Gaunt who coveted the throne. A powerful ally against men like Gaunt who might oppose the Mortimers long lost claim to England was sound politics. And as for the Percys, the Mortimer connection meant support against the Nevilles; and that was good enough for Northumberland.

Hotspur and Elizabeth were the price of that ambitious plan. Thomas Percy was equally pleased, and as for my master his answer, as always, was to acquire a fresh horse and ride back to Berwick that night. He knew he must marry a girl of seven against his will, but five and twenty years later no one could foresee how she would play a significant role in shaping his life and causing strife in England.

7

Lyliot's Cross 1381

'That wyth our two bodies we maye cease all debate'

An ancient stone crucifix marked the favourite meeting place where the English and Scots met to settle their disputes. Another fragile truce was in place on the border, and by the time Hotspur arrived at Lyliot's Cross, the two duellists were armed and ready to fight for their lives.

A great mist had descended on the Shire of Roxburgh during the night, and two pavilions could be seen beyond the wayside marker. In the heavens, a pale yellow sun battled with the elements, and a strange heaviness descended on what soon would be a place of fierce and final judgment.

Fleeting shadows moved between the tents. Groups of men stamped their feet against the chill air. Everyone present was there for a reason. The duel had gone far beyond a local dispute between two men who had a personal grievance, and for this reason, there were no uninvited guests to the gathering, apart from a group of crows perched on a nearby fenced-off enclosure.

Hotspur had sought out the crossroads with his usual haste. He knew the border country well enough by now and was wearing full plate armour in case he had to remind some renegade Scot about the truce with his lance. He also knew his warlike appearance would cause a stir. But that was his intention. He wished to appear a pageant of heraldic devices rushing to fulfil his father's duty, and even the two duellists were impressed when the sun suddenly broke through the mist and stars of refracted light burst forth from Hotspur's armour.

Sir John Neville was the first to greet the vision with a friendly wave. 'So now the great earl sends his son to do his job,' he called out cheerfully. 'Has the Lord of Alnwick forgotten his duties as March Warden?'

Hotspur acrobatically dismounted from his horse before it came to a halt and threw Neville a scroll bearing his father's seal. 'My father is at p-p-parliament, my lord, and has bid me to act in his p-place.'

'Very well, good to see you, Harry, it's been a long time.'

Neville's son Ralph stepped forward and shook Hotspur's hand in a kindly but forceful way. 'Do you w-want a fight?' he grinned.

'After this combat, if your f-f-father agrees to it,' said Hotspur sensing movement behind him.

'Haatspore!'

The two Nevilles were startled by the cry, and when Sir Alexander Ramsay left his companions, they both went for their swords.

'Harry, do you know this man?' asked the elder Neville.

Ramsay circled Hotspur twice and tested the quality of his new harness by pulling at each leather strap and plate in turn. 'Sae this is what ye bought with mah ransom eh?' he joked eyeing Neville.

Harry said nothing, knowing his father had used the ransom elsewhere.

'They'll be noo ransoms today, Haatspore!' added Ramsay.

Neville set his teeth. 'I think we should be about our business,' he said, ending the conversation abruptly. 'Has everyone produced safe-conduct letters and have oaths been sworn?'

Ramsay puffed out his chest. 'Aye, let's see it done!' he said.

The sour look on Neville's face spoke volumes of his hatred for the Scots, and the two combatants were asked to draw near. Neville and Hotspur would act as chief judges to their quarrel and my master bid the two men recite their names in turn.

'John Chattowe esquire,' said the Scot.

'Sir William de Badby,' shouted the Englishman. 'I'll have your head for breakfast Chattowe!'

Hotspur placed himself between the two men and prevented Chattowe from swinging for the English knight with his mailed fist.

'You're a lying Scots whelp just like your wife!' continued Badby.

Hotspur calmly stood his ground and ordered Badby to behave like a true knight or suffer the consequences. Standing apart from the quarrel, Neville was unimpressed. He had judged many such combats before and quickly read from a scroll setting out the pair's grievances that a Berwick court had failed to settle.

According to the statement, Chattowe's wife had falsely accused Sir John Badby of raping her, and the fact that such men as Ramsay and Sir James Douglas thought otherwise made the accusation even more severe. Lesser crimes could spark border wars, and Badby's close friendship with John of Gaunt, through his family ties with John Wycliffe, had raised the stakes. Badby, a Lollard knight, protested that Chattowe's wife had led him on before crying rape, and when the crime of perjury was brought before the Berwick judges King Richard and King Robert of Scotland had become involved. Gaunt and Douglas would not let the affair rest, and when the two kings finally consented to the matter being settled by a duel to the death, Lyliot's Cross was chosen as the place for combat.

As always in such delicate matters of border law, it seemed only Chattowe's wife and her attacker knew the real truth behind the crime. But both the accused and the accuser were under no illusions of what lay before them. They knew one of them would die that day. There was no other possible outcome. And when the two men were ready to do battle, their 'seconds' escorted them to the fenced-off enclosure from which the crows sensibly took flight.

The assigned area for the duel was sixty feet square, and two chairs draped in black velvet had been placed inside. Once seated, a priest admonished first Badby then Chattowe and after crossing themselves, the two men stood up, servants removed their chairs and handed them their shields.

Hotspur now searched each man for talismans asking both Chattowe and Badby the same question before he began the task.

'Do you r-r-renounce the aide of magic in the name of G-

God?'

Both men replied 'Yes' in unison, although when Hotspur searched Badby, he found a string of small finger bones sewn into his jupon.

My master recalled some years later that Badby was sweating like a pig as he removed the relics. He stank of beef stew, and Hotspur asked him to reject the talismans on pain of death, which he promptly did. The Englishman was a portly man with a large red nose and a purple scar dividing his face. He was carrying a lot of additional weight and was keeping a keen eye on the leaden sky, hoping for another glimpse of the sun. Chattowe, on the other hand, was a lean rat-like creature with a shaggy mop of red hair. He had a lilt in his step, was at least ten years younger than Badby and the Scots crowd cheered him on with patriotic fervour as he took up position in the enclosure.

In addition to their shields, the two men wore similar armour and carried the same weapons. They had a short poleaxe, sword and dagger, but by the time Hotspur vacated the enclosure Badby had gained an unforeseen advantage. As the sun burst fully through the clouds, the Englishman shuffled like a crab to put it at his back. It was a cunning move. The sun was now in Chattowe's eyes, and my master would have intervened, had Neville not signalled for the duel to begin.

'Faites votre devoir! Faites votre devoir!' cried Neville.

And in the dull silence of that damp and misty morning, the two duellists advanced towards each other wary that this might be their last day on Earth.

Using the sun's glare to his advantage, Badby hit out at Chattowe smashing his shield with his poleaxe. The Scot yelled out. The force of the blow had broken his wrist, and another swipe from Badby's weapon hurled his protection to the ground. However, Chattowe was an agile creature and young enough to launch a counter-attack of his own. With his axe, he stove in Badby's helmet before the Englishman had a chance to raise his shield and a trickle of blood appeared on Badby's aventail, which made the Englishman back off in a daze.

He had little time to inspect the wound but judged it was not severe. He had fought in many battles in France, and when he recovered from the shock, he stove into the Scot with his shoulder, cutting downward into Chattowe's thigh with his axe at the same time. Then it was blow-upon-blow amid the dancing moorland light until a great mist of breath joined the natural fog that swirled overhead.

This particular type of combat carried no rules other than to kill the opponent by whatever means possible. And Chattowe's main hope was that Badby would tire soon enough. Today the price of a mistake was death. The fight was to be pursued *à l'outrance* 'to the bitter end', and all methods of attack were allowed to test the case in question and end the dispute to the satisfaction of the court.

Both men were now bloodied, but not seriously injured. The light on the moor continued to flicker and change shape as they bludgeoned and smashed open each other's armour with their poleaxes until the hafts broke. Then they used their swords like blacksmith's tools exploiting gaps between metal plates and forcing them open. They grappled and wrestled until their weapons locked and their stale and coppery breaths made them gasp. They threw each other hard against the wooden enclosure. They broke fingers as they fought, and in the end, they used their daggers wrestling each other to the ground like fighting cocks.

But like crazed animals, both men soon tired, and when they crawled away from each other breathless and leaking blood, there was a lull in the fighting.

Leaning on the barrier, Hotspur followed every move the two men made and sighed despondently at their skill with weaponry.

'I hear your father has shunned Lancaster,' said Neville taking a cup of wine from his son Ralph.

Hotspur was shocked by the interruption and continued to stare at the two duellists recovering on the ground. 'I have b-b-been in Ireland, my lord,' he said.

'Then you should know your father is out of favour. I now have Gaunt's ear since the recent troubles in London, which is why I stand here for him to judge this combat.'

'I have b-been—'

'Ah yes,' said Neville, 'congratulations on your marriage Harry and my sympathies on the untimely death of your father-in-law. Mortimer was a good soldier.'

Hotspur had not seen his child-bride for three years now, and Mortimer's death had been suspicious, even though most men believed he was killed in battle against the same Irish kerns he respected so much.

'Rumour has it that the king still favours the Mortimers as his heirs,' continued Neville trying to break Hotspur's will again. 'When their children are old enough to wear a crown, that is!'

'That's more than I k-know.'

Neville knew his nephew was being typically evasive. He knew politics was beyond his reasoning, but he was content to pass away the time with small talk. He had known Hotspur since childhood and that he was much like his mother in temperament. She too had a wild and distracted nature, unlike her husband Northumberland, who Neville hated, and had not seen since the death of his sister.

'I do hope we might ride together one day Harry,' said Neville, 'and I know young Ralph wishes it with all his heart.'

Ralph nodded, and my master was about to speak, but movement in the enclosure interrupted the conversation.

This time the two duellists raced headlong at each other. Daggers swooped and probed the gaps between their shattered armour. Blood sprayed from their weapons, and those watching took a few steps back from the fence to avoid the gore.

'Yes, I hope we can be friends one day Harry,' said Neville unmoved. 'The marches are becoming a perilous place, and we will need to share the burden between our two families. That damn Scot over there, and his master James Douglas, will not rest until both our Houses are destroyed, and they have independence.'

Hotspur's eyes momentarily strayed from the fight and he saw Ramsay wink at him from the opposite end of the enclosure. 'You will have my s-s-support if you ever need it, my lord,' said my master pleasantly.

It was a crucial point in the duel, and Ramsay knew it. Badby was exhausted, and when Hotspur's attention turned back to the fight, it seemed Chattowe had gained the advantage. Badby cried out, and everyone thought that the Englishman was finished. He lay panting and defenceless on the ground, and Ramsay winked at Hotspur again. But then another yell caught everyone by surprise. This time it was Chattowe who was writhing in agony. A large bloody hole had appeared in the top of his head, and Badby stood over him looking victorious.

The English knight had picked up Chattowe's broken poleaxe and smashed the spiked into his skull. Hotspur had missed the fatal blow, but he was not alone. Neville had been distracted by two riders approaching from the east, and one was a woman.

'Stop this! Stop this!' cried out a genteel voice as they drew near.

Even Badby lifted his head to see the commotion, and when Neville helped a Carmelite priest to ease a frail young woman from her saddle, he lowered his axe.

All could see the woman's hair had been roughly shaven off. Her chemise was covered in rotten food, and cut ropes could be seen hanging from her thin wrists. The priest tried to shield her from Chattowe's fate, but it was no use. Screaming wildly, the woman broke free, and when she attempted to leap the fence, another cry of agony came from the enclosure.

Blood was gushing from between Badby's legs, and when he lifted his jupon, he realised something was missing. With one final gasp of life, Chattowe had managed to reach under Badby's broken mail and sever his genitals.

Hotspur seized the woman as she almost fell from the fence. He held her close, and her hands clawed at him to be set free. She bit into his hand, struggled fiercely, then my master drew his sword and rushed forward with her into the enclosure.

Hotspur could see that Chattowe was already dead, but the woman and priest had clearly come to Lyliot's Cross to protest, and the Scots thought so too.

'Whatever she...says is...a lie!' shouted Badby attempting

to staunch his blood pooling into the heather.

'Let the p-priest speak!' cried Hotspur eying Ramsay. The Scots had just crossed the fence into the enclosure and Hotspur took up a defensive stance in front of Badby to halt their advance. He could see a renewal of border hostilities was only moments away unless he or Neville could settle the matter to everyone's satisfaction.

Neville drew his sword and urged the priest forward.

'This woman is the innocent victim of your carnal lust John Badby,' said the Carmelite pointing to the sobbing woman in Hotspur's arms. 'Now confess your sins Badby, or I will let you die unshriven.'

'I have…no fear…of death priest!' gasped Badby cowering before him.

'This woman is Chattowe's property, and she has already confessed to being violated by you Lollard knight.'

Badby cried out for his squire to help him, but Ramsay prevented him from entering the enclosure with his sword.

'Behold her my lords,' continued the priest. 'She has been outlawed by her own parish for a crime she did not commit.'

Hotspur tried to hold Chattowe's wife fast, but she struggled free and threw herself over her husband's dead body.

'The law says she should be punished,' said Neville to the priest. 'She lied, so Badby is in the right.'

'She's a harlot…the whore led me on…' wheezed Badby.

Hotspur kept his eye on Ramsey who had taken another step closer with his men. 'Then confess Badby, said my master, 'and a surgeon will tend y-your wounds.'

The Englishman knew he was slowly bleeding to death, but he also knew that the law of both kingdoms was on his side now he had won the duel.

'Confess and God will forgive you,' said the priest, hoping that Badby's admission of guilt would invalidate the woman's perjury.

'Burn...in hell!'

At the opposite end of the enclosure, Ramsay ordered his men to draw their swords and form a line.

Hotspur crouched beside Badby. 'Are you r-ready to meet your G-God?' he whispered secretly.

'I am a true...follower of Wycliffe...and will not submit to that false priest.'

'Then s-s-submit to me as a true k-knight,' said Hotspur.

'What good is that?'

'Do your t-teachings not say that every p-person is his own p-p-priest?'

'Then...I confess to myself,' said Badby growing weaker. 'Now make haste...close up my wound before I bleed...to death!'

Neville overheard Badby's last words and stepped forward eying the Scots. 'As you can see Ramsay the matter is concluded.'

But Ramsay held onto Badby's squire. 'No, its nae over yet!'

The Scots closed in on Badby intending to finish him off. But they were too late. My master had already pivoted on his heels and with one cut severed the Englishman's head from his body.

Everyone was dumbfounded, and the shocked stillness in the air was only broken by the sobs of Chattowe's wife still grieving over her husband's lifeless body. Hotspur took her hand intending to lead her away, but she refused his help. The scene was so tragic that no one dared question my master's judgement.

As for Neville, he was speechless. He was unsure what action to take against Hotspur if any. The duellists were both dead, and the only loser was Chattowe's wife who urged Ramsay's men to take up her husband's body and deliver him back to Berwick.

Everyone knew my master had averted a border war that day, but only John Neville knew if Badby's death could be the price of peace.

'God knows you have gone too far today Harry,' said Neville at last.

But my master ignored him and galloped away into the thinning mist.

Hotspur said to me years later that God had served justice on Badby that day at Lyliot's Cross. The English court was in the wrong, and that Badby was, without doubt, guilty of raping Chattowe's wife. And although Hotspur later swore an oath in court that he could not remember his actions with any clarity, he said that an unknown hand had guided his sword. But secretly he told me that his demons made him act against his wishes. The voices spoke persuasively to him that he should not follow the codes of chivalry any more, and that Roland, Charlemagne's champion, would have acted the same way.

Had it not been for another unknown voice in his head, my master said he might have gone mad with indecision. The more assertive voice said to follow God, respect true chivalry, and bring about an end to all wars and needless killing with truth and honour. His only question was how he might accomplish this quest against an unjust world and the many demons that laboured within him.

8

Scotland 1385

'To Edynburghe hys corage to fulfyll'

While taking part in an invasion of Scotland by the king, Sir Richard Scrope of Bolton had seen a strange thing. As Edinburgh burned and the English army plundered the town, Scrope was shocked to see another knight had stolen the arms displayed on his shield. This knight was called Sir Robert Grosvenor and amid the atrocities of the siege the two men found time to argue about who had the right to bear the charge *Azure, a Bend Or*.

Meanwhile, Hotspur had seen enough of yet another Gaunt led disaster. The English pillaging spree reminded him of France, and he had already decided to ride back to Berwick if the Scots, like the French, did not submit to open battle. Predictably English soldiers had reverted to what they knew best in enemy territory. And when my master saw the ravaging of Edinburgh was against all he believed in, he thought the dispute between Scrope and Grosvenor was a far more chivalrous cause to follow.

Richard Scrope was one of the Earl of Northumberland's retainers, and he demanded of Hotspur that his father the earl should help him settle the dispute in person with the king. Grosvenor, on the other hand, was not so well supported, or tolerant of authority, and he decided to challenge Scrope to single combat to save his family honour. For both knights, nothing else mattered, but my master suggested that in place of a duel a remedy might be sought with the king and his heralds at Holyrood where a great encampment had been built to entertain the English nobles when they tired of bloodshed.

King Richard, then aged eighteen years, was looking to end his minority early. His spoilt and fragile nature had not changed much since he and Gaunt had beaten up Hotspur at Leconfield. But physically Richard had developed into a tall Plantagenet much like his dead uncle Lionel, Duke of Clarence. In his ermine robes and fashionable clothes, Gaunt's protégé looked every inch a king despite being skin and bone beneath. His ochre-coloured hair had reddened with age and his round, usually flushed face, was pasted with white lead makeup to hide countless blemishes. Richard carried himself like a ghost on his heels, hardly touching the ground as he walked along, and he spoke with an air of majesty that was quick to change and display profound evil.

Hotspur knew all the king's eccentricities better than most. Richard had favoured him and lauded his many achievements in contrast to Bolingbroke who he still hated with a passion. Richard had recently appointed my master Warden of the East March, making him a wealthy man in his own right. He had followed his adventures with the Teutonic Knights in

Lithuania and had protected him from blame when a holy crusade against the anti-pope failed in Flanders. In short, Richard had become Hotspur's patron and admirer. He could see my master's star was in the ascendant, he identified with his flaws, and when all the nobles at Holyrood turned to greet my master, the young king felt a surge of recklessness and pride in his presence.

However, after greeting his childhood friend with an affectionate nod, Richard resumed his oration to the nobles who had been summoned to hear a council of war. What to do next in Scotland was being discussed in earnest, and that evening the king was determined to end his minority by stamping out his uncle's fire for good.

A great crowd of courtiers surrounded King Richard who was seated on a richly decorated dais of flowers. The smell of perfume overawed the stink of sweaty soldiers, and the king eyed Gaunt with contempt as he spoke about the army's excesses in Edinburgh.

'Yes uncle, but I decree that my soldiers are not here to satisfy your distractions,' said the king with an assured grin. 'In truth, I tire of this unsavoury pillaging. Are we pirates my lords? Does this not go against all the precepts of true chivalry?' He eyed Hotspur as he spoke. 'I say we are in error, and so we have decided not to pursue our interests in Scotland one moment longer. Tomorrow we shall ride south back to Berwick and then on to my palace at Sheen where we will endeavour to restore our flagging spirits.'

There was an uncomfortable silence in the pavilion as Gaunt marshalled his thoughts and edged closer to address the king in private.

'Stop there!' said the king extending his hand.

Only the striped and richly ornamented drapes overhead could be heard billowing above the assembled nobles.

'But...but this is not the way Your Majesty,' said Gaunt at last, 'we must persist if we wish to exact homage from the Scots. To retreat now would court disaster. I will break their will any day now, in truth I can feel them breaking—'

'No uncle, we will retire to Berwick.'

'But I have never retreated from the foe Your Majesty.'

Richard rose from his throne and inhaled the scented cloth he always carried with him. He stepped forward and fluttered it like a flapping bird before his uncle's stern face. 'Oh, I venture you have fled my lord, once or twice to my reckoning.'

'No, Your Majesty, I have always pursued my enemies to the last. Even in France, when all seemed lost.'

Richard laughed and winked at his councillors grinning behind him. 'Ha, next you'll be wanting to plunder my treasury again uncle and vex my good people of Kent!'

Gaunt's eyes fell on the king's favourites. 'I will not be blamed for the Kentish rising Your Majesty,' he said carefully. 'Those taxes were levied by your Chancellor, not I. You forget yourself, Richard, I too was punished by the commons when they burned my palace of Savoy.'

Richard took up his sceptre and angled it fiercely at his uncle. 'Ha, yes my lord, that was when you fled into the north, and I had to deal with the mob myself.'

'I was forced into seeking refuge, Your Majesty.'

Richard leered at his uncle. 'Ha, then you did retreat!'

Gaunt knelt and held out his arms in submission. 'If I have offended Your Majesty I will happily go—'

'Yes go,' said Richard eying his favourites.

'And leave you to that shit-stirring viper!' raged Gaunt

pointing to Sir Robert de Vere who had whispered something in the king's ear.

'Yes, go to Spain. Go to your mock kingdom,' shouted de Vere confidently taking the kings hand.

Gaunt laughed. 'What? Am I to be banished, Your Majesty?'

'Don't play the fool with me uncle,' said Richard. 'If you tire of England go cool your ardour in the ample bosom of that Castilian cow you call your wife!'

Gaunt froze and marvelled at how quickly Richard had turned on him. It seemed the old understanding between mentor and pupil was over, and when de Vere whispered again to the king, Gaunt removed his leather glove.

There was a sharp intake of breath from the nobles as Gaunt stepped forward to confront the man who had wooed his way into the king's trust, and it took his son Bolingbroke to restrain him from challenging de Vere to a duel.

'I'll have that shitten-turd, or I'll die trying...' said Gaunt under his breath.

His younger brother, the Duke of Gloucester, came to his aid quickly and proudly stood as his second. But instead of acknowledging Gaunt's challenge, de Vere took Richard's arm, and everyone bowed as they both spirited away.

It was a miracle that the king had not officially exiled Lancaster from England and Hotspur saw his friend Bolingbroke protesting bitterly to his father and Gloucester. Both men were seething with rage. Gaunt was breathing heavily, his face was pockmarked with red patches, and Bolingbroke knew his father could do nothing while the king's favourites ruled England. It seemed as if the bond between Lancaster and the king was slowly unravelling before his eyes and with a heartfelt nod to Hotspur, Bolingbroke left the pavilion embarrassed.

As for the assembled nobles they broke into whispering factions.

The Earl of Northumberland was at his son's side in an instant. 'Good God!' he cried. 'That rebuke could have fallen on us, Harry. If I had not been so prudent lately with Gaunt, it might have.'

Hotspur frowned as his father peered over the nobles and gentry. He had ignored the presence of Scrope and Grosvenor during the commotion between the king and Gaunt, and my master tried to get his father's attention again.

'What's that boy, what do you say?' said Northumberland distracted. He was eying Sir John Neville talking secretly with Lord Clifford, and Hotspur followed his father over to them along with Scrope and Grosvenor who still carried their identical shields.

The two knights were fast losing patience, and my master now realised that the dispute was hardly an appropriate issue to bring before the king or his father under the circumstances. Both petitioners were angry with Hotspur, and the comedic effect of their matching shields was evident to everyone present as they pushed through the crowd eagerly seeking a resolution.

But it was Scrope's patience that broke first. He thumped his shield proudly, and everyone in the pavilion was startled by the noise. 'I wish to protest against this affront to my family, my lord,' he shouted to his master Northumberland. 'My reputation has been tainted—'

'I think I have precedence my lord Scrope,' interrupted Grosvenor, pulling Scrope back by his collar, 'I will have this matter resolved now or in the field.'

Grosvenor threw down his gauntlet, and Scrope picked it up.

'I have borne these arms since the Conqueror,' said Scrope thumping his shield again, 'and no one will part me from them!'

Scrope felt confident that his lord and master Northumberland would intervene. If he could only get preferential treatment as one of the earl's oldest retainers, then there was a chance that the case might be settled without resorting to a duel that he might not win. But as usual, Northumberland was fearful of the Neville shadow hanging over his northern dominance. 'My lords, you will both have your satisfaction,' he said, still distracted by his rival who was now shaking hands with Lord Clifford. 'Leave me be my lords, and I will put the case before the Marshal of Arms. We will gather witnesses, and I will see that your quarrel is settled in a trice.'

But the duration of the subsequent chivalric trial would last longer than any man thought possible. Even Scrope and Grosvenor had decided that spilling blood could only settle such a case; and so did the man who had been listening and stalking Hotspur since his arrival in Scotland.

'Wait, Percy!' shouted the stranger.

But Hotspur lost patience and stormed from the tent.

The man's coal-black eyes and long swept-back greying hair gave him the look of a hermit or religious fanatic. But his knightly appearance and the red dragons on his breast said otherwise. Anyone could have mistaken him for a French knight with his fine armour and richly decorated jupon, but Hotspur ignored his presence until the stranger seized his bridle and stopped him from riding off.

'I r-ride south,' said my master warning the stranger with a dismissive flourish of his sword, 'and I will not be s-s-stopped.'

'I'll ride with you,' said the stranger.

Hotspur shrugged his shoulders, and he detected a familiar lilt in the man's voice. 'Do you w-want a fight?' said Hotspur.

'A gallop would be more beneficial to my nature,' said the stranger.

'First man to B-Berwick then,' said Hotspur reaching for his purse.

The stranger frowned and called a servant to bring his horse. 'That's a day's hard ride, isn't it?'

'This g-g-gold coin says I beat you r-r-red dragon.'

'My name is Owain ap Gruffydd.'

'Ah, a man of W-Wales—'

'Na…Tywysog Cymru ydw I,' snapped the Welshman grinning.

Hotspur failed to decipher the Welshman's last words, but he knew Owain Glyndŵr by the heraldic beasts flying on his jupon and decided to make him regret his offer.

As for Owain, he knew Hotspur by reputation and was fascinated by his rise to fame. He was the complete opposite of my master. Coming from a wealthy Welsh family linked to the mystical Prince's of Powys, he had made it his business to study English customs, their laws, and those politics that might further his cause. He was a cautious man, but dangerous too, and worse, he had a prophetic plan for his nation that would soon see borders crumble and a country alienated. Even though he knew Hotspur would win the wager to Berwick, Owain knew that by the time they reached the border town he would know the famous Hotspur better than himself.

But the two riders failed to reach Berwick without stopping.

They ran into a band of Scots knights galloping the other way, and Hotspur immediately couched his lance under his arm, set his teeth, and warned Glyndŵr to stay back while he dealt with them.

Without warning, and much to Glyndŵr's surprise, my master charged at the lead horseman along the narrow causeway across the marshes. It was a typical reaction by Hotspur even though he was outnumbered. I saw it many times in my life, and his lance sent the first Scot hurtling down the high bank into a sea of yellow gorse bushes.

Hotspur, still mounted, reined in his horse and prepared to charge again. Half the remaining Scots were now attacking Glyndŵr and half were waiting for Hotspur to turn on them. But when my master saw one of the Scots hurl himself down the bank to help his comrade, he decided to take on the remaining two men by himself; that is until Hotspur found his arm was a useless piece of meat.

Clumsily wielding his broken lance, he tried to correct the downward angle. But after realising his shoulder had been disjointed in the charge, he dropped the weapon and drew his sword with his left hand.

Glyndŵr yelled out, 'Rescue! Rescue!' when he saw my master wheeling his horse down the road towards him. The Scots were now attacking him on two fronts, and if my master hoped to break through, the two soldiers that barred his way had to be dealt with first.

It was a risk against fully armed men-at-arms, but the notion only lasted a moment in Hotspur's mind, and he charged the wall of steel and horseflesh without a thought to his safety.

He had already anticipated what the Scots might do, and

when an axe slammed into his shield slung over his back, he swung back into the saddle and took another glancing blow on his shoulder before speeding between them. The last blow was savage, but it returned feeling back to his arm, and as he charged towards Glyndŵr, he threw his sword at one of the Scots tumbling him from the causeway.

Now with only his shield for protection, he handed-off another attacker while Glyndŵr crashed his horse into a third leaving the Welshman stunned at my master's wildness. However, the force of Hotspur's last charge was impossible for any man to correct, and when his horse reared up uncontrollably, it too tumbled from the causeway into the bracken below.

Glyndŵr now thought he was a dead man. The gorse had swallowed up my master, and he was alone against the remaining Scots. But thankfully the branches saved Hotspur from breaking every bone in his body. It was a humiliating way to end a good fight, recalled my master years later. But when Glyndŵr cried out for mercy and Hotspur found he was stuck fast in the thorns they both knew there could only be one outcome now Scotland was burning.

However, the Scots leader had other ideas. My master recognised the torn stars and 'bloody heart' badge on his breast and that he was more than a casual enemy.

'Ah should murder ye young Percy,' said the Scotsman frowning, 'but then there would be noo one else worth fighting on the border!'

'You should k-k-kill me Douglas,' said Hotspur struggling to get free of the gorse. 'I would fight you if this b-bracken would let me free.'

'Ramsay o' Dalhousie told me about ye,' said Douglas. 'Ye

are the Haatspore he fought with at Berwick methinks.'

'Then you should k-kill me, my lord.'

Douglas took a deep breath and peered into the evening mist rising above the marshes. He savoured the sweet northern air perfumed with bracken and sighed. 'Nae, not today, this is nae a good place to die, even for a Percy.'

'Then r-r-ransom me, my father will—'

'Its nae yer father's gold a'm wanting either,' said Douglas.

'Then what do you w-want?'

Douglas helped my master from the tangled gorse. 'Like ye a'm wanting a name,' said Douglas searching Hotspur's mind. 'Are ye nae wanting a good epitaph o'er yer sepulchre laddie?'

'My name is P-Percy...' said my master, confused.

Douglas shook his head imperiously and gestured for his men to release Glyndŵr who rode off, not looking back.

But my master could tell something else was on the Scotsman's mind. He told me he could not place it. It was something intangible, religious even, and only present in a man who had reached a crossroads in his life.

'So, tell me,' said Hotspur, 'w-what do you wish for?'

The Scot paused for breath, and my master waited for him to answer.

'Immortality...' he whispered.

And it was at this point my master secretly reached for his dagger.

But Douglas ignored the threat and threw back his head in triumph. 'Aye, ah would gladly die like William Wallace or the Bruce if men sang o' mah name hereafter.'

Hotspur had never met Sir James Douglas before, but he had learned from others that he had a strange dour manner about him. Douglas spoke of death glibly as if he craved it, he was a ruthless man like all his clan and had a hawkish, brooding determination that was strangely unfamiliar to Hotspur. My master knew the Douglas's were respected by the lowliest of their tenants to the King of Scotland and everyone hailed James a great fighter, a noble landowner in his own right and a powerful claimant to the throne. However, that day on the causeway Douglas's retainer Sir Alexander Ramsay had inadvertently saved my master's life, and this helped Hotspur curb the demons inside him that urged to grant Douglas his dying wish.

Instead, Hotspur saw in Douglas a kindred spirit who walked the earth forever hoping to be something more than mortal, and when they both emerged from the sea of gorse, my master bowed to the Scot and thanked him for his life. Rivulets of blood were beading on Douglas's forehead from his fight to be free of the bracken. A sprig of thorns had tangled in his raven black hair and when he spoke to Hotspur in a kindly, but determined way, my master thought he resembled an image of Christ he had once seen in a Lithuanian church. And like Christ, my master concluded, James Douglas wished to be equally well remembered.

9

Westminster 1386

'A worthy knyght, and of ryght noble fayme'

The quest for personal honour in an unjust world is never easy to achieve, and there comes a time when a man must become his own hero.

The French were threatening Calais and rumours had quickly spread that their new king, Charles the sixth of that name, was about to land an army on the south coast of England. But to Hotspur, the promise of yet another fight with the French was not enough to fulfil his high expectations of chivalry. He was bored with skirmishes, border duties, and the persona of being a dutiful knight. He perceived there was no honour in it, and lately, the parting words of James Douglas near Edinburgh had been the only thing on his restless mind.

Just a few months earlier, my master had beaten back the French in Picardy until no one else was left to oppose him. Then he had swapped his horse for a ship and had almost been killed while attempting to relieve the siege of Brest singlehandedly. Hotspur even forced the French king to contemplate a truce with England such was his notoriety as a soldier. King Richard called him his greatest knight, but still, my master was not satisfied. And now to make things worse, he and his brother Ralph had been ordered to repel an expected French invasion near Yarmouth, which might further bore him, but satisfy his many admirers at Richard's court.

Soon Hotspur's uncle Sir Thomas Percy had to eat his words about his nephew's quest for chivalric fame. Now many Englishmen wished to emulate my master. Courtiers and knights were mimicking his slight hesitation of speech and were even dressing like him so that they might in some small way share in his celebrity. Even chroniclers were asking for interviews so that they might better understand the history he had made. But there was still a great hollow space in Hotspur's life. And he once told me that although he had enemies who might end that life at any moment, he too, like the Earl of Douglas was desperately chasing a higher ideal; something that might bring him peace from the demons that still plagued him at night.

However, unbeknown to my master a much more significant storm was gathering to test his notoriety and even he was unprepared for what Henry Bolingbroke would tell him in confidence when he arrived at a frosty Westminster in late November of that year.

In the abbey refectory, the Scrope and Grosvenor trial was continuing with no sign of a verdict. Various witnesses had been called to give evidence in the case, including John of Gaunt, the Earl of Northumberland, Henry Bolingbroke,

Hotspur, Glyndŵr and even Geoffrey Chaucer had been asked to speak about who had the right to bear the contended arms *Azure, a Bend Or*. Thomas Walsingham, the celebrated Saint Albans chronicler, was also present at the famous trial and Hotspur was itching to leave having already collapsed from another bout of what one of his father's physician had termed - *anxietetum*.

Gaunt presence, as usual, loomed large over the trial and in the antechamber where everyone had gathered after the morning session. He had not yet left for Spain at the king's bidding, and most nobles agreed that he feared that the king might seize his assets if he did. Hotspur's father, as usual, was quizzing Lancaster about how the Nevilles figured in Richard's plans and there was a tense closed-in feeling in the chamber that no one else felt more than my master. Gaunt was sat in a high-backed chair constantly fidgeting due to another inflammation below the belt. He kept interrupting Northumberland's questions, reminding him about the vultures now encircling the crown, and of how Robert De Vere was really a woman and should be publically executed for leading the king astray.

Owain Glyndŵr was stood on his own looking out of place in the grand company of Englishmen. He was listening intently to what was being said and as usual, measuring the mettle of those who loomed large in the room. As for Hotspur and Bolingbroke, Walsingham had cornered them, and Chaucer was scribbling away at a table occasionally eyeing up my master with a view to his latest tale.

But when Sir Thomas Percy blustered into the antechamber, everyone could tell that something was wrong. Northumberland had seen the same fraught look on his face when things were beyond his control, and Gaunt knew Percy had been working on an undisclosed legal matter for him for some time; although no one in the chamber, apart from Northumberland, knew that the secret 'appeal' verged on treason.

'Something needs to be done,' said Thomas carefully closing the door behind him. 'The king has just made Robert de Vere the Duke of Ireland.'

'I say we kill him!' exclaimed Gaunt stiffening in his chair.

'If we do that, my lord, the king will have our heads. Best we appeal lawfully to His Majesty in the law courts.'

Northumberland made a sign to his brother that the conversation should take place elsewhere.

'The king will never spurn his bedfellow,' said Gaunt, ignoring the warning.

Bolingbroke laughed. 'De Vere is the white hart to Richard's hind!'

Hotspur glanced at Glyndŵr. He was heading for the door, and my master also took a step towards it, hoping to be excused. The talk of treason and court appeals went against the grain with Hotspur, and it was only when a clerk of the court appeared through the door that the outspoken conversation ended abruptly.

'Thank Christ,' sighed Gaunt turning to the clerk, 'is the case adjourned?'

The clerk bowed. 'Yes, my lord.'

'Then we go to Spain to claim a crown.' Gaunt rose stiffly and shook hands with Northumberland.

'But what of John Neville my lord, how can I resist him with you gone. If the king grants his earldom of Westmoreland—'

'You have power enough to constrain him, my lord. Come, Harry,' said Gaunt throwing his fur gown over his shoulders, 'there is no room for me in this shit-tip of a country anymore.'

But Bolingbroke stood his ground. 'I think it best I serve you in England father.'

'He may be right my lord,' exclaimed Thomas Percy, quickly taking the sting out of Gaunt's anger.

'Now what?'

Thomas continued. 'If you both leave for Spain, God knows what the king and de Vere might do...'

There was silence as everyone took in the gravity of the situation. And in the close confines of the antechamber, the stale air became heavy with expectation - especially for Hotspur who stumbled towards the door.

'This is no time for a piss!' growled Northumberland. 'Sit down boy!'

Hotspur felt for his dagger. He was sweating profusely and began to pace up and down like a caged lion. Thomas Percy saw the desperation on his nephew's face and took Gaunt aside, hoping to free Hotspur before he killed someone. He whispered in Gaunt's ear secretly and something he said so shocked the duke that he embraced his son Bolingbroke and prepared to leave.

'Thomas is right,' said Gaunt opening the door, 'you will need to protect our inheritance here, or peacocks like de Vere will steal it from us.' Gaunt then pointed at Hotspur, 'and you will help my boy do it...agreed?'

Hotspur was breathing heavily and said nothing. He was trapped by the demon chatter inside his head and thought he was about to die.

'Look after my boy, I said!' repeated Gaunt sourly.

My master sheathed his dagger, summoned up enough strength to open his eyes, and nodded in agreement.

Northumberland shook his head and followed Gaunt from the chamber, leaving everyone feeling vulnerable by what they had just witnessed. But the tirade was not over yet, and as Percy's appeals to Gaunt faded down the corridor, Bolingbroke clipped Hotspur playfully across the head.

It was what they used to do as children, but this time my master lashed out and put Bolingbroke up against the wall.

'Take care B-Bolingbroke,' snapped Hotspur.

Glyndŵr grinned as he left the antechamber. 'I know why the Scots call him Hotspur. Like an unbroken mare, he needs restraint.'

'He is the perfectly devoted, youthful, and completely honest model of English chivalry,' enthused Walsingham already supplied with a wealth of notes for his forthcoming history.

'Yes, the perfect knight,' added Chaucer gathering up his papers.

Bolingbroke was still struggling. 'By all the saints Harry, let me free!' he choked.

'Let him free,' growled Thomas Percy.

Hotspur eased his grip on his friend and waved everyone away, but as the door closed behind Chaucer the inner fire heating my master's spurs still burned with a vengeance. Hotspur had released the demon on Bolingbroke, and when he released his grip on his friend, he fell to the floor exhausted.

'I'm...d-d-dying!' he gasped.

Thomas was quickly at his side. 'No, breathe slowly Harry, it will pass.'

'I need to talk to Harry alone,' said Bolingbroke.

Percy nodded knowingly, and when he left the chamber Hotspur rushed to open the stained glass window.

'I had a presentiment last night,' said Bolingbroke ignoring another of Hotspur's sudden convulsions.' It came to me in a dream, and I awoke in a cold sweat, fearing for my life. I conjectured that Lancaster was destroyed. All my family were put to death, and my son Harry and all his sons thereafter paid dearly for our hatred of King Richard.'

Hotspur gazed at the wintry clouds glowering over Westminster Palace. It reminded him of the day in France when he had fallen from his horse, and he suddenly felt weak, embarrassed and insignificant.

Bolingbroke took him by the arm. 'I will send for my physician Harry.'

'Does he speak of t-treason too?'

'Although I think our king is the worst king in Christendom,' said Bolingbroke, 'I fear his ministers more. Even now they have Richard dancing to their tune at his palace at Eltham. He elevates them to positions of power they are not worthy of and leaves the old blood of England out in the cold to die like starving dogs.'

'The king is our k-king,' replied my master wiping his brow of sweat.

'And I may need your sword one day to prove it Harry,' said Bolingbroke. 'God knows how long my father has tried to steer Richard away from those who seem older and wiser than he. Men like de Vere. All his woman-like friends are frowned on by God, you know.'

Bolingbroke produced a scroll from his gown and smoothed it flat on the table where Chaucer had been writing.

'Look here…do you believe in destiny, Harry?' he said, pointing to a representation of his shield on the parchment. 'It's clear to me what would happen if Richard dies without issue.'

Hotspur followed his friend's finger as it traced a crooked line down his leafy family tree. 'See, my father is next in line then I,' he said confidently.

'I hear R-Richard has chosen Mortimer instead.'

Bolingbroke waved his hand dismissively. 'My grandfather appointed Lancaster to succeed him if Richard should die or could not sire an heir. And the latter course seems likely, don't you think?'

Hotspur shook his head. 'The king will a-announce the Mortimer claim in the coming p-parliament.'

'Good God, do you know that for certain?'

'My b-brother-in-law Roger Mortimer is to b-be named,' said Hotspur.

'But he is not worthy—'

Bolingbroke heard cheering coming from beyond the palace, and he peered through the window sorrowfully. A great crowd of people had gathered beyond the gates of the palace, and soldiers with polearms were pushing them back.

'But you will take my side Harry if I need you, my friend?' said Bolingbroke.

'Against anyone w-wishing to harm our k-king.'

'But he's not worthy of the crown!'

'And I am a soldier.'

Bolingbroke sighed. 'God knows what his ministers are planning against us…your father too! And I'm not the only one who is like-minded.'

'Gloucester, Arundel, Warwick and Mowbray p-p-perhaps?'

Bolingbroke was surprised. 'You are well informed for a soldier Harry. Yes, I will join them, and with your uncle's lawful petition to appeal the king in parliament, we will rid

England of corruption.'

'And w-what will your father say?'

'He will approve,' said Bolingbroke. 'Your uncle Thomas has told me what is lawfully right and best to do, and anyway, my father's destiny lies elsewhere.'

'And my d-destiny is to go f-fight the French,' moaned Hotspur gathering up his sword and gown.

Bolingbroke laughed. 'I doubt they will come against you Harry.'

But as was his way, Hotspur was out of the door before his friend could mention the heavy taxes that were being levied by the king to defend against the expected invasion. Money was the last thing on my master's mind, and when Thomas Walsingham saw him rushing towards the gatehouse, he was determined to catch him.

'You do chivalry great honour my lord,' he said breathlessly following Hotspur as best he could in his monk's habit.

'I do?'

'Yes,' said Walsingham, 'England adores you, and I can make you immortal in the chronicles if you let me.'

Hotspur stopped. 'Immortal? I've heard that saying once b-before. But b-believe me, Thomas I'm not that f-f-famous.'

Walsingham pointed to the crowd. 'Tell that to the commons. Look, my lord...'

By now thousands of cheering Londoners were swarming beyond the gatehouse, and when Hotspur tried to push through them, he had no choice but to stop and take their adulation.

Seeing his brother Ralph, he thrust his fist aloft. *'Esperance Percy!'*

The crowd cheered. The Mayor of London had come

to wish them both good luck against the French, and my master forgot his demons. Women kissed Hotspur's hand and robes. Beggars and poor children scurried forth and prostrated themselves at his feet. Husbands left their wives and rushed eagerly to serve him against the French. And even Walsingham was pushed aside as Hotspur's admirers increased and Ralph gathered in their horses before they were crushed.

'Christ's blood, where have you been,' spat Ralph, as a merchant's wife gave Hotspur a bunch of flowers.

My master threw a few coins into the crowd to part the sea of people.

'In future, you can get a groom to hold your horse,' continued Ralph, 'if he can keep up with you that is!'

'You're my g-groom brother.'

'No, not I,' said Ralph, 'I have other plans, and anyway our father's too tight-fisted to pay me. Go get a squire to look after you.'

'I'd r-r-rather look after myself.'

As the two brothers mounted their horses, the crowd pressed in blocking their escape. Their mounts reared and bucked wildly, but some of the citizens refused to let go of Hotspur's reins and bridle, and this included a bedraggled hermit who clung to the leather straps as though his life depended on it.

Fearing that the crowd might crush the man, my master reached down for his purse and tried to appease the hermit with money. But when he saw the glint of silver in Hotspur's palm, the man spat on it. My master winced at the grey slime clinging to his glove, and it was only after seeing black scabs in the hermit's hair that he lurched away.

But my master was too late to escape the hermit's presence, and as Ralph tried to free them both from the surging crowd, the hermit hissed an ominous warning through his yellowing teeth:

> *'The blood of the Percys shall manure the ground,*
> *At Berwick, the lion's last trumpet will sound,*
> *Two millstones will encircle his noble frame,*
> *And men will soon forget his name.'*

Hotspur wiped the soothsayer's spittle from his glove, but when he looked again, the hermit had spirited away like the chill breeze.

'What's that you s-s-say?' said Hotspur, still consumed by the man's words. 'What say you of B-Berwick?'

Ralph was perplexed. 'Have you had too much wine again brother?' he said, handing-off a citizen who tried to snatch his purse.

Hotspur was searching for the hermit. 'Did you n-not see him?'

'I only see no way out of these thieving crowd!'

But, as I write here at my desk, and think myself well rid of those far off times, I often think that some things are not so easily explained away. There are more things to this world than flesh and blood, and I believe that the curse uttered that day at Westminster did more harm to my master than any weapon could ever do.

Years later, Hotspur told me that he believed nothing would ever come of the hermit's prophecy. However, from that day on he vowed never to steer a course near, or visit, the northern town of Berwick.

10

Radcot Bridge 1387

'With battayle stronge, at Radcot Brygge he toke a hand'

The stone bridge over the Thames River was blocked. Bolingbroke's men had partly broken it down, and now sounds of battle filled the still air. The king's men pushed and shoved to gain the opposite bank, but so far they had failed to make any headway against the army of those nobles now known by King Richard as the hated 'lords appellant'.

The north bank of the crossing was crammed with soldiers commanded by the king's man Sir Thomas Molineux, but Bolingbroke's small force was managing to hold them off due to the narrowness of the bridge. The fight was developing into a stalemate and to Bolingbroke's annoyance the cry of *'Esperance en Dieu!'* was nowhere to be heard above the din of battle. His friend Hotspur was always eager for a fight, but without his support on the northern bank of the river, Bolingbroke began to see visions of the headman's axe looming over his rebellious head.

Weeks earlier Bolingbroke had done the unthinkable, and with others of like mind, he had appealed the king in parliament accusing several of Richard's closest friends of deceit and misusing the king's power. Gloucester, Arundel and Warwick were the chief movers of the petition, but when they all refused to appear before the king at the Tower, fearing for their lives, they escaped into hiding.

Unsurprisingly Richard had already called upon his favourite Robert de Vere, now Duke of Ireland, to march south with an army to save him. And although the appellants could not see his banner flying over Radcot Bridge that day, everyone knew who was in overall command. The stakes were high, but the truth was that de Vere was a coward and now Sir Thomas Molineux was the only one who stood between the appellants and the king's security in London.

It was a mainly bloodless fight, and even Molineux's loyalty was fickle in the push and shove to gain control of the bridge. Seeing no support, his men soon became mutinous and when the crossing became a death trap, Molineux, along with several of his followers, jumped into the freezing water hoping to save their lives.

As they did so, a huge cheer went up from Bolingbroke's men, and this cry increased when a mounted force attacked the royalist rear. Those that could fled from the bridge, although most of the fugitives appeared to be getting away far too easily for Bolingbroke's liking. The striped banners of Mortimer were everywhere, and as the royalists fled in all directions, only their leaders floundering in the water remained to be captured.

Molineux, the Constable of Chester, was a man of great influence in his shire, but now he was just a man trying to save himself from drowning. Clutching at the reeds and sedges that lined the Thames River, he was easy prey for Sir Thomas Mortimer who had ordered the rear attack on the king's men and was bathing in the glow of victory. After dismounting from his horse, a cheer went up from his men and Mortimer shouted for the constable to come out of the water or he would order his archers to make a hedgehog of him.

'If I…come out,' spluttered Molineux freezing to death, 'will you save…my life?'

Mortimer grinned and shouted, 'I'll make you no such promise Molineux, but either come out now, or I'll give the word to shoot.'

The constable saw Mortimer's archers loading their war bows on the riverbank. He realised his comrades had either drowned or drifted down the river and there was only one other way now to save his life.

'Well then…if you're adamant,' shivered Molineux, 'suffer me to come up…and let me try and match you…or some other knight…so I might die with some honour.'

'Agreed,' said Mortimer holding out his hand to the constable. He had just seen Bolingbroke urging his horse across the bridge, and with Hotspur's men riding from the other direction, his thoughts turned to how he might prove himself worthy of their notoriety.

But Mortimer's helping hand was the last thing the constable felt on Earth. As he clambered from the river, Mortimer stabbed him several times in the top of his skull, and he fell to his knees dead. Mortimer's toothy grin matched the shocked look of surprise on Molineux's face, and his head was still leaking blood like a sieve when Hotspur and Bolingbroke rode up.

'He wished for a duel Harry,' laughed Mortimer kicking the constable's body into the river, 'what do you think of that?'

Hotspur massaged his chin thoughtfully. 'Did you a-agree?'

'No, of course not Harry,' replied Mortimer.

'That's a p-p-pity,' said Hotspur, 'I was hoping to see a g-good fight today.'

'He deserved to die. I hooked him like a fish,' laughed Mortimer wiping Molineux's blood from his dagger. 'And like a fish, I threw him back in the river!'

'You should have given him quarter Mortimer,' said Bolingbroke cynically. 'The king will hold it against your family.'

'I'm my own man, and my family will have the crown one day with or without the king's help. What do I care for chivalry...or you Lancaster.'

'So he did challenge you to a duel,' said Bolingbroke reaching for his sword.

Mortimer shrugged his shoulders and was about to mount his horse when my master seized him by his mail collar.

'Do you w-want a fight then?' he asked politely.

Mortimer shook his head. 'Elizabeth wouldn't like us fighting Harry. Besides we're family and on the same side.'

'But Elizabeth's not h-here and knows n-nothing of chivalry.'

Bolingbroke covered up a sly grin. He knew all about my master and his hate of unchivalrous men.

'So, do you w-want a fight?'

'Ha, you're jesting with me Harry,' laughed Mortimer.

'I never jest,' said Hotspur. 'What d-do you take me for, a

f-f-fool?'

Beads of sweat appeared on Mortimer's forehead, and his face drained to the colour of sour milk. 'Now I know you're fooling with me,' he said, watching Molineux's dead body floating down the Thames.

Hotspur's eyes narrowed. 'So, you do think me a f-fool?'

'No, I didn't mean to—'

'Perchance you t-think my speech f-foolish then?'

Mortimer shook his head quickly. He knew Hotspur's temper was unpredictable, and he felt the sour taste of bile rising in his throat.

'I have the g-greatest respect for y-you Harry,' he said uncontrollably.

'There, d-did you hear it?' said Hotspur to Bolingbroke, who was trying not to laugh. 'He mocks my s-s-speech!'

Mortimer went down on one knee. 'No, please—'

'What in God's name is so f-foolish about me?'

Hotspur drew his sword.

'I-I have no words…please…'

'Then s-say your confession!'

Hotspur thought he knew all his wife's family well. His late father-in-law had been a true warrior and a respected man in Ireland, but the cold-blooded killing of Molineux threatened my master's high ideals of chivalry, and he could feel his chest tighten at the thought. Mortimer was guilty of murder in his eyes and, even though Elizabeth was still a stranger to him, Hotspur was determined to find out what kind of man Sir Thomas Mortimer was.

'*Préparez-vous à defender votre honneur!*'

'What?' cried Mortimer.

'Defend your honour!'

'And that of your family,' added Bolingbroke slyly.

Hotspur cried out and spun on his heels. 'Hold your tongue B-Bolingbroke, or I w-will cut it out.'

Bolingbroke held up his hands in mock submission and stepped back.

'Now Mortimer p-prepare to d-defend yourself.'

'No, Harry, think of Elizabeth...' Mortimer's words failed him, and he prostrated himself in the grass pleading for his life. He didn't want to die. He declared he was only an illegitimate child who never knew his mother, that his elder brother was dead and that he was the only one taking care of Richard's nominated heir. He even shit his hose before Hotspur let him scramble away across the water meadows.

Bolingbroke laughed until he burst. 'That beats any fight we ever had at Kenilworth!' he said, shaking his head. 'I wonder, would you have cut my tongue out?'

Hotspur gazed at Bolingbroke confidently, and then he offered him wine from the flask he was carrying.

'Thanks Harry,' said Bolingbroke.

'For w-w-what?'

'For the wine and for lending me your sword today, I knew you wouldn't fail me. Only de Vere and Richard to deal with now.'

'De Vere is d-dead,' breathed Hotspur. 'I found his horse and armour in the r-river a league from here.'

Bolingbroke took a mouthful of wine and savoured its sweetness in his parched mouth. 'That's good news, my friend. We will see them all in hell before the year is out.'

'We?'

'Ha, you're not going to say you're only a soldier again are you, Harry?'

'You know my w-worth.'

'Is that why you let Molineux's men go free? I saw Mortimer's ranks open up and let the king's men through. I take it was you who gave the order?'

Hotspur folded his arms. 'I have no quarrel w-w-with trueborn Englishmen.'

'One day you will have to show your true colours, my friend.'

Hotspur stared through Bolingbroke's words to a place far beyond the Thames River. He was conjecturing a time in the future when all wars would cease, and only champions would compete for crowns and kingdoms. 'If I ever have to choose sides it w-will be a b-b-black day for England,' he said.

'Nonetheless, we must purge the king's government, Harry. We are all in danger of losing our lands and titles, even your father.'

'Be careful B-Bolingbroke, lest you incite civil w-war.'

'If we do nothing all our lands will be forfeit to the crown. You saw how quickly Richard turned against my father in Scotland.'

'Then he should be more p-p-prudent—'

'Like your father, eh?' spat Bolingbroke. 'I thought he and my father were friends. Now Northumberland treats him like a stranger.'

Hotspur took up the reins of his horse. He had seen the Duke of Gloucester, Warwick and the rest of the appellants crossing the bridge and he was not used to gloating over victory. 'You k-know why my f-father is aggrieved with G-Gaunt,' said Hotspur sourly.

'Your father abandoned him in the north.'

'Think again.'

Bolingbroke had forgotten that my master's youngest

brother Thomas had lately returned from Castile in a lead coffin and he lowered his head. 'Does he still blame my father for your brother's death?'

Hotspur cracked his reins together.

'Spurring away again, my friend?' said Bolingbroke.

'I never run,' replied Hotspur. 'You s-s-should know that...'

Bolingbroke tried to stop my master and apologise, but Hotspur's speed matched his well-known nickname, and his friend soon disappeared from view.

My master explained to me one day that it was his unswerving allegiance to the king that caused him to spirit away at Radcot Bridge. But in my humble opinion Hotspur was more aloof. As a neutral observer and a champion of chivalry, he had no master. The sword had temporarily dulled royal power at Radcot Bridge, but unbeknown to the lords appellant Hotspur had lied about Robert de Vere's death. My master had allowed him to escape with his life to appease his conscience and code of honour.

But in the next few weeks, a seed would be planted in England that only a few years later would purge the kingdom of its leading nobles. After Radcot Bridge, everything changed. Gloucester and his followers, aided by the Earl of Northumberland, mediated a compromise with the king who was now indefensible. Rumour had it that Richard had tried to enlist French troops against the appellants and he realised that resisting their demands was useless. But if the king and his councillors thought they had escaped blame, they were wrong. At a gathering of parliament the following February, the appellants made sure Richard was hamstrung by culling his household of all his closest supporters; most were executed or exiled for life, while others ran for the shadows.

Thereafter Richard burned for revenge, especially so when he received news that his lover Robert de Vere was alive but dared not return to England. As a result, the king swore never again to be a slave to parliament or his nobility, and as for Hotspur, he returned to the north where he remained in the king's trust, chiefly due to the saving of de Vere's life at Radcot Bridge.

The power of the appellants now ruled in England. But their involvement in what became known as the Merciless Parliament would only be the start of Bolingbroke and Hotspur's troubles with King Richard.

11

Borders 1388

'At Otturborne as chronyclers dyd tell'

Lord James Douglas made a promise that he would join the Earl of Fife's great army then assembling in the west march of Scotland. But instead, Douglas raised his standard in the east and on Saint Oswald's day he and his army began to burn and pillage the north of England.

Douglas's desperate quest for independence and renown caused widespread panic south of the border, which, despite his promise pleased his master, the Earl of Fife. The earl was happy to let Douglas cry havoc in the east while he and the main Scots army attacked Carlisle in the west. The diversionary tactic would serve to test the resources of both English march wardens at once, and send a message to King Richard that the Scots would not submit to being ruled.

But unbeknown to Fife, there was another plan formulating in Douglas's mind aimed at Newcastle where Hotspur was lodged with his brother Ralph. The Earl of Northumberland, as prudent as ever, had decided to remain at Alnwick to frustrate the Scots escape route back across the border. He hoped that his son might destroy Douglas by bringing him to battle before he attacked, but like their allies the French, the Scots army proved elusive yet again, and soon everyone was looking to Hotspur for a miracle.

As fate would have it, I was in Hotspur's retinue when he received news that the Earl of Douglas and his army were heading for Newcastle. I saw the Scots army arrive below the walls of the town and heard Douglas issue a challenge to Hotspur that he could not ignore. In those days Hotspur always saddled his horse personally even though three squires were in his pay. However, on hearing Douglas's challenge, my master was so eager to arm that he left Thomas Felton, his most trusted squire, to prepare his best horse for battle.

I was only a page at the time but, despite being only young, I can remember that day like it was yesterday.

I had been apprenticed to Thomas for five years, him being Sir John Felton's only son, and was fortunate to be taught by him the ways of a squire, although sometimes I was forgetful. Thomas beat me regularly but said that if he failed in this important task, then I would not be hardened to combat when the time came. Thomas always looked to my every need and even bandaged my wounds when his beatings went too far. He was also a good fighter for his age and like a lot of us employed in the Percy household he worshipped Hotspur like a god.

'I would gladly die for that man,' he said, picking up Hotspur's saddle and placing it on his best courser's back.

The fiery animal bucked savagely. It was agitated more than

usual that day, and I passed Thomas the bridle and reins to try and restrain the gelding's temper.

'Not yet!' he said, slapping me across the head.

I stood back, careful to not cross him again.

'Yes, if I face the Scots today,' he continued pleasantly, 'I would rather die with Hotspur than surrender to the likes of James Douglas.'

Thomas seemed to relish the thought of battle and the possibility of dying young, whereas I thought myself more of a scholar than a soldier. Felton was dreaming of a time he could give his life for my master, where I was hoping for a long life avoiding the hazards of war. Not that I was a coward, God knows I have fought for my life many times since those far off days. However, thinking back, I would put my prudence down to loving life rather than ending it for no good reason. I revelled in the thought that I was lucky enough to be born studious, whereas Thomas was brought up to violence from the day he was born. And it was this common trait that proved to be the difference between us in the days ahead.

However, daydreaming of battles and service was our ruin that day. We had to saddle Hotspur's horse urgently, and when Thomas's father appeared at the stable door, he disciplined his son for wasting time. Hotspur was known for his intolerance, and those who served him had to keep up with his every move or be dismissed out of hand. To serve under him could be both a delight and a curse, and this time in the rush to girth his excited horse Thomas failed to check that the animal's cinch was secure under its swollen belly.

There had been some skirmishing before the town walls that day, and at the west gate my master was waiting for his horse eagerly looking out for Douglas so that his challenge might be met on equal terms. Hotspur and his followers, Sir Matthew Redmane, Sir Ralph Lumley, Sir Robert Umfraville, Sir Robert Ogle, Sir Thomas Grey and Sir John Felton, were all in favour of trying to weaken the Scots resolve first. Either that or they hoped Douglas would simply bypass Newcastle loaded with booty and thereby provide an easier prey for the Earl of Northumberland further north. But my master, against all the advice of his captains, was determined that there was only one way to stop the Scots. And after he mounted we watched him from the battlements prepare for a desperate duel with the man who wished for immortality.

Douglas saw my master coming at a tremendous speed and met his charge halfway between the walls and the Scots camp. The ground was perfect for Hotspur, and he picked out his target with his lance point with ease. With the 'bloody heart' emblem of Douglas in his sights, and a gradual slope adding more speed to his attack, he churned up a great dust cloud in his wake almost as if his horse's hindquarters were on fire.

We heard the resulting collision echo like a thunderclap above us, and everyone tried to get a good view of the fight on the walls so that they might see Douglas fall and his army thrown into panic.

From where Thomas and I were standing, we could see that my master's lance tip had lodged directly in the centre of Douglas's shield. Thomas Percy's gifted lance pennon was attached to it, but as for the rest of Hotspur's lance, it had shattered into several pieces, and these lay with him on the ground. The force of the collision had shunted my master back against his saddle, tearing loose the cinch and buckle that was supposed to hold it in place. And when the fog cleared Thomas Felton's mistake spiralled towards him and hit him squarely in the gut.

He sprung back on his heels as if hit by lightning. We saw that my master had been thrown from his horse twenty paces back up the slope. Hotspur's horse was bareback, and beside me, Thomas buried his head in his hands. He tore at his hair madly, and when he saw the saddle and cinch cast randomly on the ground, his exasperated cry seemed to last forever.

We saw Douglas shaking his head disappointedly. He cantered over to Hotspur and prodded the broken saddle with his lance, then he reined in his coal-black horse and removed his helm. It was only many years later that my master confided in me and told me what words passed between them.

Douglas laughed at my master, sat winded on the ground. 'Ye better get yerself a fresh groom Haatspore,' he said. 'That saddle o' yours is nae worthy o' yer valour.'

'It's not…over yet,' exclaimed Hotspur gasping for air.

'No, this is nae a good place tae die,' replied Douglas removing Hotspur's lance tip embedded in his shield. 'But ah will take this pretty pennant o' yours and see it fly over mah castle at Dalkeith.'

'You'll n-never leave…England with it,' replied my master.

'Come an' take from mi then!' roared Douglas leading him on.

The Scot wheeled his horse and waved the captured pennon above my master's head like a trophy. Each time he lowered it, my master tried to retrieve it, and Douglas taunted him with more talk of immortality and how Hotspur would never achieve it.

The whole Scots army cheered their champion as Hotspur collapsed from the sheer embarrassment of seeing Douglas circling Newcastle's walls taunting the garrison with shouts of independence. We all stared at Hotspur sprawled on the ground, especially Thomas Felton, who was transfixed to the spot. It seemed his whole world had stopped turning, and within an hour of retrieving Hotspur's concussed body, the Scots had dismantled their camp and were following their loot-laden wagons across the Tyne River back to Scotland.

We all praised God that my master was still alive, but Thomas Felton fled and hid away in the deepest dungeon he could find. His mistake destroyed him, and when Hotspur recovered that evening, Thomas expected to be flogged by his father. But it was not to be. Instead of apportioning blame to a minor, a council of war involving all the northern lords took place to decide on what to do next. A messenger had arrived saying that a relief army led by the Bishop of Durham was a day's march from Newcastle, but everyone knew that by then the Scots would be safely home in Scotland. Hotspur naturally demanded urgent action. Douglas had tainted his honour, there would be more bloodshed due to his failure, and he was raging about the loss of his uncle's pennon. His demons told him to act, and none of us doubted that Hotspur might have ventured across the Tyne alone to meet the Scots had not everyone agreed on a general pursuit.

The next day our exhausted army arrived at a place called Otterburn in Redesdale an hour before sunset. I was not allowed to go with the army on account of my age, but Thomas Felton was determined to redeem his lost pride, and he foreshadowed Hotspur's march embracing a death wish. That morning his father had disowned him for his mistake and when I saw him secretly leaving Newcastle by a sally port in the walls his face was deathly pale and filled with a deep-seated longing to right the wrong he had done.

My master told me that there were two Scots camps at Otterburn, one somewhere above the valley and one near the bend in the river. It was getting dark, the setting sun was grazing the tops of the trees that bordered the parched moorland to the east, and overhead the sky was becoming overcast and purple with clouds threatening the approach of night. As darkness rolled in, everyone knew there was no time to waste even though the English were tired from forced marching. To delay would ruin the element of surprise, chided Hotspur. Therefore he decided on an immediate attack even though he had no idea what dangers lay in front of him to the north and east.

The only visible Scots camp was the one hugging a bend in the river. Servants were preparing food, and their smoking cook fires billowed into the still air smelling of pig fat and blood. It was a perfect situation for the English, even though the main Scots army was nowhere to be seen, and Hotspur ordered Sir Matthew Redmane, his chief captain, to attack while he sought out Douglas high on the moor.

Sir Ralph Percy smiled. He differed greatly to my master in every way and was a heavy-set knight who looked more like his father than his athletic brother. Whereas Hotspur was fair like the Nevilles, Ralph was dark-haired and gaunt-looking like the Percys. His mood was always frivolous rather than anxious, he spoke of Jerusalem and far-flung lands in the east and that day he wore the best harness and weapons money could buy.

'Douglas is a better man than this brother,' said Hotspur gazing nervously at the bleak heather-strewn moorland.

Ralph's eyes widened. 'I do believe Douglas did you a great favour at Newcastle. Either that or that buffet from Douglas brought you to your senses.'

Hotspur stared at his brother.

'Your stammer has gone,' explained Ralph.

Hotspur ignored his brother's words.'Redmane's got the bit between his teeth,' he said, hearing a blast of horns raise the alarm in the Scots camp.

'He needs reining in,' snapped Ralph, applying his spurs.

Hotspur seized his brother's bridle. 'No, not yet, they're only varlets tending the baggage. Keep y-your eyes open for Douglas.'

Redmane could be seen pursuing the Scots fugitives along the bend of the river. His men were cutting down the cooks, servants and grooms like sheep, while a few other tried to protect the camp. Hotspur urged his horse forward a few paces and then stood up in the stirrups. He sensed movement in the heather and thought he saw campfires in the woods to his right. The sun was about to set, and a strange silence descended on the moor.

'Douglas is here. I can feel his p-p-presence,' groaned Hotspur.

'Ah, I was mistaken,' said Ralph realised his brother's speech impediment had returned. '*Haatspore's* himself again!'

'We should embattle the men, my lord,' shouted Sir Robert Umfraville, who had spurred his horse from the rear.

Hotspur nodded, and Umfraville gave the order.

But before the English trumpets could sound the alert, there was a fluttering of bird's wings in the distance. Hotspur heard a rattle and scraping of metal. Shouts of alarm sprang up from the English scourers on the far right, a discord of noise split the air, and before anyone could react, the main Scots army rose from the heather like a herd of beasts and crashed into the English flank. Their bristling spear points shone like stars as the sun finally set in the west, and when the ragged English line buckled against overwhelming odds, Hotspur saw the terror in his brother's eyes. It was a trap, and my master had run into the jaws of it.

Some of Hotspur's men were still arriving on the field and rushing to bolster the English ranks, but the damage had already been done. Douglas's army, alerted by Redmane's attack, had issued from a higher unseen camp. They had slipped through the dense woodland like a herd of wild deer and emerged from a shallow fold in the land. Now they had the advantage, and the onset of night added to the confusion and panic in Hotspur's bewildered army.

Men were cut down. Others sped past Hotspur in a rush to escape the massacre. Friend and foe became indistinguishable as the uncertain glow of moonlight replaced the certainty of day. The advancing Scots schiltron pushed all before it like some unstoppable barbed monster. A trickle of fainthearted Englishmen yelled 'All is lost!' Loose horses galloped away into the darkness. A cry went up 'Rescue! Rescue!' and Hotspur launched himself at the fence of spear points to try and stem the tide. Ralph followed his elder brother's lead, and with the help of others, the English somehow managed to push Douglas's men back up the slope.

But it was not enough.

The English soon faced the onrush of yet another phalanx led by a Scotsman wielding a huge battle-axe, and the English line broke again. Blood sprayed in all directions as weapons hammered down crushing flesh and bone. An abundance of bodies and severed limbs fell in the heather. Their owners either died instantly or fought on disabled by their injuries.

Hotspur's men were being hacked to death mercilessly, and the axeman called Thomas Swinton was only stopped when a cry went up from another part of the field that Douglas's standard had fallen.

The battle stopped for what seemed like an age. The savagery slowed to a snail's pace, and at that moment, Hotspur turned to see his brother stood bolt upright staring at him. He was perfectly still, mouth half-open. He urged my master to help him, and Hotspur broke off from the fight only to be shocked by the amount of blood seeping through a knee joint in his armour. One of Ralph's greaves was overflowing with gore and Hotspur ordered one of his men to help him quickly remove his brother's leg harness.

Umfraville ran over too. 'Douglas's banner has fallen!' he urged Hotspur breathlessly. Then he saw Ralph's injury and stared back at the masses of men moving towards them. A Scots spear had torn a ragged hole through the back of Ralph's leg. His kneecap was displaced, and as my master caught his brother as he fell, Umfraville tore his jupon open to tie it around Ralph's thigh.

On the English left, the battle stopped momentarily. Douglas's standard had vanished into a mass of bodies, but Hotspur was determined to stay with his brother despite Umfraville's news that there was still a chance to win the battle.

'We need to finish them, or we'll all die here!' exclaimed Umfraville.

He pointed to a new attack slowly forming into a bristling wedge of spears. The Scots were yelling wildly into the twilight, and Hotspur hung his head, knowing that his foolish pride and preying demons were the cause of everything.

'Go…go now…' said Ralph barely able to speak.

'We will be overrun if our line breaks again,' pleaded Umfraville.

Hotspur got to his feet. 'Forgive me, brother—'

Ralph waved him on, and Hotspur set his teeth against the nagging realisation of his stupidity. He knew the battle was lost, and his only thought was killing Douglas. There was no other way to save his brother's life.

On the other side of the field young Thomas Felton had thrown himself into the fight too. He had killed for the first time in his life, and his victim had been James Douglas. The Scot had received mortal wounds from several English blades, but Felton had been the one who killed the Scots leader outright. He had no idea who he was, such was his crazed mind, and in the uncertain light and onrush of battle, no one knew for certain who was alive or dead. Those close to Douglas saw him fall along with his standard-bearer, but another knight in his retinue raised his banner and with an arousing cry of 'Douglas! Douglas!' the Scots aimed at their master's killer.

Amid the cauldron of carnage, Thomas thrashed about him wildly between the prodding fence of spears, screaming desperately for honour or death. He swung his axe, splintering a handful of spears like matchwood as they thrust towards his body. But when Thomas saw more replace them, he knew the sand in his hourglass had run out. The last thing he saw was Hotspur and his father trying to break through to him. They knew the reason for his fit of rage was partly their fault. Tears were rolling down Sir John Felton's cheeks as his son disappeared from view, and at that moment he realised that his final words to his son had been an angry reprimand to make haste with Hotspur's saddle.

Thomas made one last effort to break through the wall of bodies to his son. But it was no use; the Scots knew the English were beaten. The tide of battle turned, and had it not been for Umfraville, who had already spirited Ralph to safety, Hotspur could have been killed in the rout.

It was all over.

Despite fighting courageously, the English ranks soon broke, and Hotspur, along with a Sir Robert Umfraville and a few of his men, found themselves trapped in a marshy hollow beside the twisting River Rede which gave the dale its name.

Breathing heavily into the damp night air and exhausted from their brutal work, the English knew their lives were now hanging in the balance. Ralph Percy was still alive, but he was weak through loss of blood, and my master had no choice but to bandage his wounds and plead for mercy. The remnants of the force that entered Redesdale only an hour before had been reduced to a few loyal followers, and what remained of the English army was in full retreat back to Newcastle.

'Get your men to safety R-Robert,' said Hotspur to Umfraville.

Umfraville shook his head when he saw my master was shaking.

'No, Harry—'

'Go now, or there w-will be more b-bloodshed.'

Umfraville waved his men across the river and into the night. 'I will go tell your father.'

Hotspur frowned. 'Yes, tell him, you're g-good at that!'

My lord Umfraville told me years later that he left a part of his soul at Otterburn that night. Hotspur's words cut him to the core. The past flashed before his eyes, and a broken promise at Berwick Castle to a younger Harry Percy lived and breathed again. Looking back, he saw Hotspur stood alone, tending his wounded brother in the grassy oxbow of the river. He was crouched demoralised under his tattered Percy banner. And when he threw down his weapons before the advancing Scots they seemed determined to rush him in one final onslaught of spears.

But one man stood in their way of the slaughter, and Hotspur thanked God he was called Sir Alexander Ramsay.

'Mah master is dead,' shouted Ramsay to the advancing Scots phalanx, 'but this Haatspore saved the lives o' mah men at Berwick and ah will nae see him murdered.'

There was a contemptuous growl from his blood-hungry comrades peering like wolves out of the darkness.

'The Percys are our mortal enemies,' called a knight named Montgomery. 'We want blood an' will nae abide being ruled anymore.'

'Let's hae at them!' shouted another knight called Maxwell.

A howling cheer went up from the Scots ranks, and Montgomery pointed to their burning camp. 'Even our baggage is brent Ramsay now stand aside!'

Ramsay placed himself between Hotspur and Montgomery and juggled a bloody axe from one had to the other.

'Stand apart or I'll hae at ye both,' he said.

The assembled Scots could have overpowered Ramsay easily, but when the Earl of Moray arrived with a line of torchbearers, everyone fell silent. The whole army bowed their heads in unison. Some knelt in silence, and the army parted to let the procession through. Moray appeared a broken man, and he was even more displeased to see an argument raging between his chief captains. He pointed to the soldiers carrying Douglas's dead body draped in his blood-spattered standard, and every Scot crossed themselves at the loss of their famous leader.

Some Scots burst into tears so great was their grief.

'Let there be an end tae this now,' said Moray holding his hand aloft.

Montgomery pointed at Hotspur and his men. 'Ramsay wants to save them m' laird.'

'He haes the right tae ransom,' replied Moray.

'Montgomery can hae mah share if he wants it,' said Ramsay, 'as long as Haatspore an' his men are freed.'

At the mention of this, Montgomery's anger seemed to cool, and Maxwell whispered something in his ear.

'Sae be it then,' said Montgomery shaking Ramsey's hand. 'Sae be it.'

Moray saw a calm acceptance grip the two Scots, and contented with the bargain the earl resumed his mourning behind Douglas's body.

Soon a horse was provided to carry Ralph Percy away, and Ramsay helped my master lift him into the saddle.

'Douglas said tae me this was a good day tae die,' said Ramsay at last.

Ralph moaned, and Hotspur comforted his brother as best he could, but all he wanted to do was escape into the night. His other brother Thomas was dead, and as my master gazed at the mounds of bodies strewn randomly in the heather, he realised Ralph could have easily become one of the many bloated corpses sprawled before him. Soldiers clawed miserably into the darkness. They cried out for help, for water, and some pleaded with their comrades to put them out of their misery with a friendly dagger across the throat.

Sir John Felton emerged from the night bearing his dead son in his arms. He was weary from carrying the weight and stared blindly forward as a Scots spearman prodded him into captivity.

'Was it a good day to d-die Ramsay?' said Hotspur watching Felton's ghostly progress.

'A good day for us Scots.'

'And your master? He once told me he w-w-wished for immortality.'

'Then he haes it,' said Ramsay curtly. 'When last did yer hear o' a dead man winning a battle eh?'

Hotspur's eyes were still on Felton's slow progress across the battlefield. 'I see only death,' he said, hanging his head in prayer.

'Aye, but the bards will sing o' Douglas long after we're both dead.'

Hotspur shook his head as a Scot lead Ralph away to seek a surgeon.

'No good will come o' yer grieving Haatspore,' warned Ramsay. 'Men will sing o' this day for eternity.'

Hotspur's face was blank and demanded no further intrusion unless it was to somehow turn back the clock.

'Anyhow am needing a dram,' said Ramsay handing Hotspur over to his captors. 'Mah debt to thee is paid Haatspore; we'll sae no more about it.'

Years later, my master said that the fight at Otterburn was wholly his fault. He said that Douglas tested his chivalric pride and that he was blinded by demons who refused to let him see sense. But he also said that Douglas had planned the encounter right from the start. He knew my master would try and retrieve his precious pennon and fall into his trap. And as for his untimely death, Douglas had finally got his wish. He would go down in history and become immortalised in the chronicles.

As for the English, there were no winners at Otterburn, and far away from Redesdale, the English defeat shocked the kingdom. The king paid three thousand pounds to free Hotspur from captivity, and there were questions as to why the Bishop of Durham's army had failed to arrive in time to save the day. Some asked if Hotspur acted rashly, while others praised his bravery. And when Sir Robert Umfraville returned to Alnwick bringing news of his my master's capture, the Percys were overjoyed for a different reason. The Earl of Northumberland knew he would have to pay some of the ransom to free his two sons, but Douglas's death was worth every penny of it. In all seven thousand marks were delivered to Montgomery and Maxwell leaving Ramsay to count his losses, but not his pride.

Everyone agreed it was a small price to pay for the return of England's hero although some saw Hotspur's defeat as a chance for advancement. On the English side, many men thought his star was waning, and if the truth be known, my master was a different man after the battle. He was rarely seen in England for the next few years, and despite his notoriety, the fight at Otterburn affected him greatly. He had seen men die miserably out of honour, or for an insatiable desire to prove their worthiness. His brother had been disabled for life, and he never recovered the use of his left leg. Even Hotspur's precious pennon, given to him by his uncle Thomas Percy, had been lost forever and it never flew above the ramparts of Douglas's castle of Dalkeith.

For all these reasons, Otterburn was a blow to Hotspur's

notions of chivalry, and he would have to live with the memory of the defeat for the rest of his life. I was only ten years old at the time, and when I learned of Thomas Felton's death, I paid the ultimate price. I became Hotspur's only squire knowing full well that my master knew I too was guilty of his poorly placed saddle.

12

Saint Inglevert 1390

'To Saynt Inglyvert came, where justes were mayd and tournyment'

Hotspur took up every challenge offered to him in those dark times. He cheated death at many tourneys all over Europe. His mind was lost in violent competition, and his quest for the chivalrous ideal was pursued to the utmost, but never realised in any meaningful way.

He rarely spoke. His language was the lance and sword. And when he jousted, he was reckless beyond reason. He laughed in the face of death as if he wished for it to take him like Sir James Douglas. It was a terrible thing to see, and by the time I became Hotspur's *écuyer du corps*, his extreme activity made me fear that I would not be in his service for very long.

However, because of his prowess in arms, there were only two instances where I ever saw this self-loathing might kill him. The first was at Saint Inglevert, near Calais, and the second was in London at Smithfield where the odds against his survival doubled by a near-fatal injury received at the former competition.

King Richard revelled in tournaments; especially the sumptuous feasts and flirting that accompanied them. He doted on Hotspur's successes, and apart from Henry Bolingbroke's involvement, who he had reason to hate more than ever, Richard was besotted with the jousting fraternity and its sporting celebrities. Hotspur's exploits, and even his defeats, were the talking point of the age. And at Smithfield, on Michaelmas Day, the king organised an extravagant gathering of over sixty English knights so that they might split lances in honour of his queen Anne of Bohemia. Contestants came from all over Europe, and my master was reunited with Henry Bolingbroke who was, by this time, a famous jouster in his own right.

This was the second time Hotspur could have lost his life, and because he had to carry his lance left-handed due to an injury sustained in France, he was unhorsed by a lucky strike to his helm. He fell unconscious for two days at which time the king himself visited his bedside in a state of worry. I was also in attendance, along with Bolingbroke, when he finally recovered and a surgeon told my master that his tournament days were over. Hotspur screamed out that 'Goat-Face' had taken away his manhood: Goat-Face being the nickname of the French knight who had deceived the English at the famous jousts of Saint Inglevert in the spring of that year.

And it was here that my master cheated death trying to prove a matter of chivalric fraud. We had travelled to Saint Inglevert from Calais taking advantage of the latest truce between England and France, and on this occasion, three French knights had challenged all comers to a 'joust of war' over thirty days. The English had been the first to answer the call to arms, and everyone agreed it would be the greatest tournament ever held in Europe. Over forty knights and squires would compete with the French, and the three challengers, Sir Jean le Maingre, known as Boucicant, Sir Renaud de Roye and Sir Jean de Saimpy were all adamant no one could beat them. When he heard this boast, my master wished to dispose of all three French knights at once in the name of chivalry. He was in the peak of fitness and as fearless as the Percy lion wrought on his shield. But so too was his friend Bolingbroke, who was also determined to be first into the lists against the most famous knight in France.

Called Boucicant, or as my master called him forever after, 'Goat-Face', Sir Jean le Maingre was a stocky, thick-necked knight with powerful shoulders and arms that had become hardened to the joust. His raven-black hair was always shaven back to a small tuft at the top of his conical head, his dark, brooding eyes were shaped like the two slits in his visor, and most men feared his presence, not only in the tilting yard but also on the battlefield.

All the French knights had agreed to run five courses against their opponents, and if one of them was injured or killed, then the two others vowed to fight on to the last man. Before the tourney, John of Gaunt had urged every knight in England to take part in the joust, including his son Bolingbroke. He could do no other, despite still having political misgivings about his son's safety it was a matter of prestige in the absence of war. Matched against the French knights, Gaunt hoped his offspring would rise above the rest and prove that he was worthy of his family name, not only in the lists but also as a contender for the English throne.

Close to the main arena at Saint Inglevert, the heralds hung shields on a nearby spruce tree, and challengers stepped forward to select who they would ride against with blunted or sharpened lances. Most of the contestants picked to ride with sharpened lances and after three days of feasting the jousts began in earnest. The Earl of Huntingdon and Sir Thomas Mowbray, the latter Bolingbroke's fellow appellant, appeared in the lists twice against the French but despite their bravery, they failed to unseat Boucicant, de Roye and de Saimpy. So too did a host of other opponents who could not believe the three French knights stayed in the saddle. The French seemed invincible, and they made short work of seasoned jousters like Thomas Clifford, Lord Beaumont, Sir Peter Courtenay, John Golafre, John Russell and Thomas Swynford. German and Bohemian knights could make no headway either, and by this time no one else would dare run courses with the French, not even with blunted lances.

However, appearing cowardly was worse than death among the jousting fraternity - and next, it was the turn of Bolingbroke and Hotspur who were more than eager to compete against the French. Their pairing with Boucicant and de Saimpy was evenly matched, said my master, but this time the two Frenchmen had decided to change the rules. They petitioned the English to face them over ten courses rather than the agreed five, thereby increasing the chances of mortal injury.

When news of this change reached my master, he was with his friend Bolingbroke along with Thomas Mowbray, John Beaufort, Courtenay and Swynford who were, through injury, slumped in chairs in the English arming pavilion.

'Ten?' gasped Bolingbroke amazed at the new rules.

Mowbray shook his head, crying out in pain as he did so. 'I tell you Bolingbroke; the French cannot be beaten. Some curse is upon us, my lords.'

'Or some evil spell has been invoked on their lances,' exclaimed Swynford, his whole body shaking from a previous encounter with Boucicant the day before.

Hotspur frowned and continued arming himself.

Courtenay and Swynford were severely bruised due to heavy falls or being rattled by lances in the lists. Swynford had lost consciousness after his fall. Beaufort had injured his right wrist, and Mowbray had been wounded when de Roye knocked off his helm. The leather straps holding it to his head had torn a huge gash in his throat, and this made even the slightest movement of his head agonisingly painful.

'They lose their helms and shields,' exclaimed Mowbray, 'their lances are shattered, they suffer blows to the body, yet they remain in the saddle.'

Bolingbroke turned to Hotspur. 'I'll not be dissuaded Harry, will you? No one will call me a coward.'

'Then be careful my lord,' warned Beaufort, Bolingbroke's half-brother. 'Rein in your horse at the last moment. You must lessen the blow.'

Hotspur was still cleaning his equipment and seemed to be preoccupied with other things. Beforehand he had sent me on an errand to spy on our opponents, and when I arrived back in the tent, I reported what I had found out in the French stables. I had acquired a bloody nose for my pains, but Hotspur rewarded me with a silver penny as I arrived secretly and whispered in his ear.

'I fear the F-French are d-deceiving us my lords,' said Hotspur after hearing my plea for caution. 'Their harness… here…and here…' explained Hotspur pointing to the metal faulds in his armour, 'it's b-bolted to the cantle.'

'What kind of trickery is that?' spat Bolingbroke his eyes widening.

'No witches spell for sure,' added Courtenay amazed at the revelation.

Bolingbroke picked up his helmet and lifted the tent flap. 'I'll not believe it, my lords, Boucicant is my friend.'

Hotspur's eyes narrowed.

'I can feel your thoughts, Harry Percy,' said Bolingbroke, 'but you are wrong.'

Hotspur turned to Mowbray. 'The course you r-ran with de Siampy my lord, d-did I see his saddle come off too?'

Mowbray nodded painfully.

I turned to my master, and all the memories of Hotspur's duel at Newcastle flooded back between us, especially the death of John Felton at Otterburn.

'What more p-p-proof do you need my lords,' warned Hotspur becoming agitated.

'If you fear them, Harry, then I suggest you return to England,' said Bolingbroke. 'No one will call me a coward—'

Hotspur lurched forward but stopped short of his friend's face.

There was silence in the tent until I stepped forward and addressed Bolingbroke directly. 'My lord, I saw de Siampy's saddle in the stables. It was torn in four places, and I found this fixed to the cantle…'

I held out a broken bolt with another shard of metal attached to it.

Bolingbroke eyed Hotspur coldly. Then he pointed at me. 'You would take the word of a bloody-nosed squire against that of a knight who has been on crusade to the Holy Land?'

My master had not seen Bolingbroke like this before.

'I'll prove you all wrong!' he continued.

'Then b-be certain you aim for the saddle, my lord,' called Hotspur after him.

But Bolingbroke was already on his way to the lists.

Outside the weather was perfect for a day of jousting. But by the fifth charge against Boucicant, Lancaster wished he had taken notice of my master's warning. After every course, we saw him quake in his saddle. Dazed by five direct hits to his helm and body, the partisan crowd cheered on Boucicant to finish the job. Their jeers and mocking chants echoed around the arena while the English spectators were stunned into silence. Their homemade banners lowered signalled yet another humiliating defeat, and they vented their frustrations by brawling with some of their French hosts.

On their part, the French released all their anger on the son of John of Gaunt - the architect of so many atrocities in their country. Tensions had been building up for years, and Saint Inglevert was far more than a friendly joust for them. It was personal. And in the end, Hotspur turned his back on the spectacle sickened by the apparent fraud that I had uncovered.

As the sixth charge was run and survived by Bolingbroke, I could tell Hotspur had sunk into a deep depression. He was gazing at his right forearm, checking the straps and bolts securing his metal vambrace. He inspected his gauntlets, and lastly, he picked up a nearby lance from the stand running a keen eye along its grip.

Another crash and moan from the crowd told us that Bolingbroke had survived yet another charge. But this did not deter my master. His depression turned into rage, and all the old feelings of his youth seethed inside him. It was the first time I had seen the demon that possessed him at close quarters, and after gazing at the heralds and officials blindly watching the fake contest, he bid me follow him back to the arming pavilion.

He was next in the lists against de Saimpy.

As expected, Boucicant was victorious against Bolingbroke, and his run of ten courses had left his opponent badly shaken. Hotspur's friend had miraculously survived the ordeal despite receiving a host of unseen head injuries that would affect him later in life. Dazed and trembling from repeated strikes to his body and head, he was helped to his bed personally by Boucicant who then re-armed ready to joust again.

Hotspur was relieved when he received news that his friend was still alive, but his next words to me seemed foolish and beyond reason.

He picked up his lance and turned my attention to the grip. 'Fix it t-t-to my arm Hardyng,' he said, shaking with rage.

'But—'

'Do as I say!'

I took a step back visualising the circumstances of a duel where both knights had abandoned the rules and could be smashed against each other like duck eggs.

'This is not chivalry John, now d-do it,' replied Hotspur.

I picked up a hammer and a handful of rivets. 'But you will be killed master.'

'Where is it w-written that we should r-run ten courses instead of four? Where is the law saying a knight should succumb to f-fraud? I know the r-r-rules Master Hardyng. Now get about your w-work.'

'Yes Lord,' I replied, knowing full well that my master's arm might be ripped from its socket if I did his bidding.

'I w-will only have one chance,' said Hotspur removing his vambrace.

I nodded and made several holes in the metal plate. Then I applied rivets to the lance and fixed it to the vambrace. I worked like a demon, knowing that to be late in the arena would mean forfeiture for my master.

'Make fast John.'

'There will be no mistake this time my lord,' I said, remembering my master's duel against Sir James Douglas at Newcastle.

I heard Hotspur sigh. He let out a halting breath of air that seemed to calm him. 'Yes, poor Felton,' he said sadly, 'I pray for his s-soul every day.'

'Then I will pray for you and that a French girth rips like an English one,' said I.

When my work was finished, Hotspur used all his weight to try and wrench the unwieldy lance from his arm. He bid me try and push it sideways from the grip, and when he was satisfied there could be no movement back or forth, I led his new black courser called 'Parzival' into the tent.

'God go with you master,' I said, passing Hotspur his helm.
'Believe me. De Siampy will d-d-drop like a stone.'

I checked my master's saddle and nodded. I had done my best, but when I escorted my master into the arena Boucicant, not de Siampy, was waiting impatiently at the other end of the lists.

There was no herald's warning or dropping of a flag to

begin the joust. Boucicant began his run as soon as Hotspur appeared and I saw my master dig his spurs into Parzival urging the animal to charge. It put him at a grave disadvantage. His horse reared, and I feared that Boucicant had already gained two lengths on him. Thundering down the lists at full tilt and with his lance lowered ready to strike, the sight of the French champion was chilling to behold. There was a collective gasp from the crowd as Hotspur tried to make up lost ground and an even greater commotion rose from every mouth when the two knights crashed together, and my master's helm flew high into the air.

Boucicant's lance shattered. A spray of blood leapt from Hotspur's face, and I feared he had been mortally wounded. The French crowd rose in unison and cheered their champion. Some of the English ladies in the stand screamed, so great were all our fears for Hotspur's life. However, as my master cantered to the end of the lists, we all saw he was only injured. A large fragment of wood had pierced his left cheek, and as he neared the end of the arena, he pulled the shard out angrily.

God was with him, I thought. But rather than retire hurt, Hotspur reined in Parzival and turned sharply throwing up dust behind him. With his unbroken lance still fixed to his arm and couched tightly under it, he thundered against Boucicant whilst the Frenchman was still retrieving a fresh lance from his page. The advantage was now with Hotspur, but everyone in the arena knew my master was bareheaded, and that one well-aimed thrust from Boucicant's lance could easily kill him.

The swarming crowd, the attendants, and even the studious heralds surged forward to get a better view of the next run. The English contingent chanted Hotspur's name wildly while

I secretly prayed that the Frenchman's cinch would break just like de Siampy's the previous day. However, both Hotspur and I knew that Boucicant's saddle had to be hit in the right place to dislodge it.

It was a tense moment, and the cries from the crowd were so intense that the usual crash of wood and metal was not seen or heard. I thought I saw Boucicant's horse lurch right and the wooden lists shatter like matchwood. But when more screams came from the arena and then there was silence, everyone could only wait for the dust cloud to settle to view the outcome of the charge.

It seemed like an age until a cheer went up from the crowd.

At the other side of the lists, I saw Parzival strutting about loose. He was whinnying uncontrollably, throwing back his great head in a rage and I rushed across the enclosure to catch his reins. Near the demolished fence I passed de Siampy and a French armourer tending Boucicant on the ground. He was conscious, but I could see that every effort was being made by his attendants to conceal his saddle before the heralds could uncover the fraud.

When I finally caught Parzival's reins, my master was nowhere to be seen, and his saddle was empty and smeared with blood. There was a commotion in the crowd near the pavilions to the right of the arena. Our contingent of knights rushed over in fear of Hotspur's life, and when I joined them, I thought my master was dead too.

One of the pavilions near the fence was utterly destroyed, and Mowbray and Swynford frantically searched the billowing canvas. They called out Hotspur's name several times, and his broken lance was the first thing we saw protruding through the wreckage. It was still affixed to my master's forearm, and I thought that whatever had occurred during the clash of arms, somehow he had been thrown a great distance.

'He's alive, I can hear him breathing,' cried Swynford.

'God be praised!' said Mowbray.

But then Swynford saw the fraud. 'What in God's name—'

Everyone frowned at Hotspur's forearm, and Mowbray caught me by the collar. 'Master Hardyng what is the meaning of this?'

Quickly explaining what Hotspur had asked me to do, Swynford concealed the undoing of my handiwork under the canvas awning as several pursuivants approached. But as I carefully removed my master's vambrace, I could tell his arm was limp and contorted beyond reason.

'When his lance broke on Boucicant's saddle, the violence of it lifted him to the heavens!' said Mowbray amazed. 'I saw it. He flew into the air...'

'The pavilion saved his life,' I added.

'I never saw the like of it before,' said Swynford. 'Maybe now the French might be punished for their crimes?'

But it was not to be. There was no inquisition court or trial after the jousts at Saint Inglevert. The English contingent of knights and squires, once suitably entertained, returned to Calais most still believing that the French had been faithful to the laws of chivalry. But my master and I knew Boucicant and his companions had been desperate to lift their country's spirits. They had kept the field for the promised thirty days without being beaten, and that was enough to please their beloved king who had lately succumbed to madness.

However, it was not surprising that after the English left France, the three knights were not challenged further. Rumours were rife of fraud, although nothing could be proven. The heralds were satisfied, and French chroniclers managed to censor the whole affair to preserve reputations and keep the fragile peace. Even Bolingbroke, once recovered, went on a crusade to Lithuania with Boucicant as if nothing had happened.

As for Hotspur, his next tournament at Smithfield in honour of Richard's queen was to be his last. His injuries sustained in France were great, and although he suffered no grievous wounds, he always suffered from a weakened sword arm, not to mention a renewed frustration in his beloved codes of chivalry.

Thomas Percy once said to my master that true chivalry was dead, and Hotspur now began to believe that it was not only dead but also buried in the dust and blood of Saint Inglevert.

13

Wigmore 1392

'And Mortymer hys mighty and greate estate'

By this time Hotspur's wife had aged twelve years. She had grown into a golden-haired beauty, and most courtiers who met her said Elizabeth rivalled all the angels in heaven. But despite her charm, my master was estranged from his child-bride and, as we all know, angels are not always what they seem to be.

Apart from their first meeting at Alnwick Castle, and occasionally in Ireland while serving her father against the kerns, Hotspur had almost forgotten his wife existed. Elizabeth had grown into a woman without him, and now she was her family's greatest asset, the Mortimer's were seriously questioning my master's absence and their contract with the Percys. Without procreation, the bond between the two families was not legally binding they claimed. There were rumours of a marriage annulment, and soon eligible men from all over England began to line up to prove Hotspur unchivalrous and his family unworthy of the Mortimer bloodline.

In response to this news, the Earl of Northumberland was furious.

'As a knight, Harry has to satisfy her and produce male heirs,' he said to his brother Thomas one day. 'Even physicians say that when a woman's womb is cold, it coagulates. Therefore it needs constant attention. If a seed is not provided regularly, Elizabeth could die, and then where would we be?'

Thomas Percy had never heard of such a theory, and for a moment, he felt physically sick.

'Yes,' Northumberland persisted, Harry must do his duty in the bedchamber, and it's your job to arrange it brother, or else…'

But all this scientific nonsense did not interest Lady Percy. She had grown up amongst scheming courtiers and was more used to wooing through politics than worrying about anatomic fermentations. For many years she had lived in the bleak peat-land castles of Cork, but when her father died in battle, and the Mortimer line became threatened Elizabeth assumed a more dominant role in the family. She became suspicious of others, especially King Richard, who she blamed for her father's death, and forceful enough to champion the Mortimer claim to the English throne. She took up residence at her family seat of Wigmore Castle in the rural hills of the Welsh marches and here she became a powerful noblewoman in her own right.

I learned many years later that Elizabeth had sworn an oath on holy relics to protect the Mortimer bloodline with her life. Despite Hotspur's unwillingness to see her, Elizabeth coveted his celebrity from afar, not to mention sharing the irony of her bastard brother's encounter with him at Radcot Bridge. She understood Hotspur's estrangement of her was due in part to his overbearing father, who had planned their arranged marriage despite my master's strange ways. A marriage annulment seemed best for both families she thought. But, as always, the power of the Earl of Northumberland loomed large over everyone's life. He was impatient for a grandson whose royal blood could provide England with a Percy king one day. The great earl knew succession in the male line was everything, and his son's indifference to Elizabeth threatened his northern dominance over the Nevilles. It was not acceptable behaviour for a Percy, said Northumberland, and in the end, he and Thomas Percy devised a plan to coerce his wayward son into fulfilling his marital duties.

Firstly, they had to arrange for his son to meet Elizabeth again, and secondly, they had to guarantee Hotspur would do his duty in the marital bed. The first part of the plan would involve the political expertise of his brother, Sir Thomas Percy. But the second part might prove more complicated, although not impossible said Northumberland, even if he had to supply the Percy seed himself.

After speaking to his brother, Thomas Percy assured Hotspur that a marriage annulment with Elizabeth was possible if both sides saw there could be no possible chance of union. But Thomas also had personal interests at heart. He was acting as a chief spy for his Lancastrian benefactors and wished to know how John of Gaunt might legally block the Mortimer claim to the throne. Roger Mortimer, Earl of March, was secretly eager to enlist Percy support against Lancaster. Also, his patience with Richard was waning. Mortimer's head was filled with thoughts that the king was plotting to reverse the late King Edward's wishes; namely that the Mortimers should succeed Richard if he should die or remain childless. Thus, in the end, both parties were eager to meet at Wigmore Castle, where Hotspur's marriage issues might be settled, and the fate of kings decided upon.

Hotspur told me his only wish was to gain freedom from Elizabeth to spite his father. But I knew this was only a feint. He had suffered many fits over the past year, and a surgeon had attended him due to an unspecified 'wound' that had softened his manhood. I knew by his temperament my master was beset with demons day and night, and when we arrived at Wigmore, I doubted that his wife, nor anyone present, could appease him.

That evening the Mortimers prepared a great banquet in honour of the Earl of March whose nomination as Richard's heir presumptive had caused a host of rumblings in England and France. Then aged eighteen years, Roger Mortimer was about to return to Ireland as the king's lieutenant within the month. He was an able soldier and firm administrator, but everyone said that his sister Elizabeth influenced his decisions. 'No one would ever have believed a woman could wield such power,' wrote some commentators at the time. However, Hotspur had sensed his wife's controlling influence at Radcot Bridge when Sir Thomas Mortimer had shit his breeches, and Elizabeth's name became an excuse for him to play the coward.

As for my master, his arrival at Wigmore just heralded another anxious bout of agitation that he wished to escape from quickly. Northumberland grudgingly accepted the position of a concerned father, and his brother assured him to keep to their plan and not to worry about his son's outbursts.

'One look at Elizabeth,' said Thomas confidently, 'would be enough to arouse Hotspur's impetuosity in 'other' regions.'

But Elizabeth's beauty was not her only asset, as the strange festivities at Wigmore would soon confirm. She had prepared the entertainment herself, and it was so lewd and grotesque that we were all shocked by its otherworldliness.

The spectacle began when a group of resident male fools and jesters acted out various sexual positions while unruffled troubadours sang quite ordinary verses of poetry in the gallery. Then one of the jongleurs called 'the farter' accompanied his wailing bagpipes with a selection of anal noises that everyone found hysterical in the extreme. It was as if all the playacting came from a darker, simpler age, more devilish than godly. All the costumes were overtly pagan in origin, but above all, I felt there was a menace in the air that was directly aimed at us.

The sudden appearance of an armed band of soldiers dressed as Irish kerns confirmed my suspicions. And when the 'crowned' king of the feast appeared dressed in ermine and greenery, he wasted no time in commanding a fake massacre of all the fools complete with severed limbs and pig's blood. One of the jesters was even wounded by a spear when the music became more frantic and out of control.

The actions of the kerns were ludicrous and dangerous, and it became clear to me that we were being served no ordinary wine in our cups. However, when a fairy king called a halt to the music, the fools scattered from the floor. Only the Irish kerns remained with their spears to attention, and in their green garb and shaggy red wigs they took on the appearance of statues as the hall was plunged into darkness.

A feeling of menace returned as each kern lit a candle they were holding and held it before them like a trophy. With their faces now lit from below, the expectation in the hall became even more alarming as a low moan from a strange wind instrument filled the stale musky air.

There was an awful silence as the pungent aroma of perfume made our heads spin. I felt weak and insecure. The incense filling the hall was intoxicating, and it was out of this foggy translucence that a sprite or fairy appeared for all to see scantily clad in the sheerest silk.

Her naked body swayed to the strains of the ethereal wind instrument, and when she began to frolic with the kerns, dancing around each one in quick succession, I saw my master's tension ease. This way and that, the sprite moved around the hall until we were all dizzy by the speed, agility, and lustfulness of the sprite's performance. Her strong legs wrapped around each of the unmoving kerns in turn, and each one submitted to the one-sided flirtation by blowing out their candles. We were all shocked by the girl's antics, and we wondered who she was under the rainbow mask. I guessed it was some mummer or guiser. A lady would never stoop so low as to show her nakedness in public, I thought. But when she blew out the last candle, and darkness returned to the hall, a hand appeared before my face, and my master was dragged from his seat.

I sprang to Hotspur's aid with my dagger drawn fearing some assassination attempt, but all I saw was my master's hand held aloft and the angry sprite's face staring up at me out of the darkness. Elizabeth had removed her mask, and when all the candles were lit again, she and Hotspur had disappeared as if by magic.

Thomas Percy pulled me towards him. 'My nephew does not need your help tonight Master Hardyng,' he said, raising a toast to the fairy king.

The king, who had now also removed his mask, was the Earl of March, and he responded to the Percys with a friendly nod. 'I will see to it that my sister desists from sapping your son's strength, my lord,' he shouted to Northumberland. 'We will need his speed in our coming enterprise methinks?'

'Have no fear of his virility,' replied the earl drunkenly, 'the Scots call him Hotspur for a good reason!'

Sir Thomas Mortimer, still burning with revenge from Radcot Bridge, was sat drinking by himself at the end of the dais.

'Elizabeth will kill him,' he mumbled, 'with God's help.'

The Earl of March ignored his half-brother sly remark and climbed onto the long table cluttered with food and drink. He strutted towards the earl kicking goblets of wine over, and when he crouched before Northumberland, he farted.

'I hear that you and your son have been ousted from your hereditary role in the marches my lord?' said Mortimer wafting the foul stench towards his guests.

'There is a truce in place, my lord,' slurred Northumberland pinching his nose. 'The Nevilles will only be caretakers of the border for a short while. The king has lately given my son full powers to command both marches against Scotland.'

'Good to know the border is in safe hands,' shouted Sir Thomas Mortimer from the far end of the table.

Northumberland noted an air of flippancy in the younger Mortimer's voice. 'More to the point my lord,' he said, addressing the Earl of March, 'I trust our two families can now have a greater bond of love and understanding?'

'Now I am King Richard's heir, you mean?' said the earl.

'In part,' interrupted Thomas Percy, 'but now we are all friends again we would also know your mind on the Lancastrian claim—'

Mortimer gagged and wine sprayed from his mouth.

'But Gaunt is out of favour now,' said the earl recovering. 'And his son Bolingbroke is more interested in crusades to the Holy Land than seeking the crown. Believe me, my lord the Lancasters are all living on borrowed time after Radcot Bridge. We Mortimers will have England, and if Richard goes against his grandfather's will, we will take it by force.'

'As you please my lord, but if my memory serves me well, some of your family were complicit in the appeal to rid the king of false councillors.'

'Some were more appealing than others,' replied Sir Thomas Mortimer, remembering the incident with Hotspur.

The Earl of March put on his fairy king crown and laughed. 'Make no mistake my lords the king knows who his loyal subjects are and who are not. We are many,' he bragged toasting the air with his cup of wine, 'and now we protect the Welsh marches and Ireland for his majesty. The Mortimers are everywhere, and so is our royal blood.'

A great cheer went up in the hall.

'And like Elizabeth, we breed like rabbits,' laughed Sir Thomas Mortimer, who threw his meal up on the floor.

Northumberland nose curled. 'That's true my lord, your father's prick was truly prolific I remember—'

'What's that? What did you say Percy?'

'Take it from me, Sir Thomas,' said Northumberland, 'being a bastard child is not a bad thing financially. I have many bastards who rob my purse!'

The Earl of March embraced his illegitimate uncle with a smile. 'Ah, but Thomas is loved by his family, my lord.'

'And he is a credit to you and the resilience of Mortimer line,' said Thomas Percy putting aside the story of his flight at Radcot Bridge.

'Yes, you Percys would do well to love your family more,' said the Earl of March with a smile. 'You northerners are all too frosty. You live too far away from the sun, and you will get no generous appointments from Lancaster. Unless you crave Catalan ones that is!'

Thomas Percy knew fortune's wheel was turning in favour of the Mortimers, but Richard's marcher lords could only be used to block Lancaster when conditions were favourable. Everyone knows that in the game of chess, a black knight can leap over a rank of pawns easily, and it seemed that King Richard was now yielding them up as sacrifices to protect his crown. The Mortimers were being weakened by the king ounce by ounce, and old King Edward's precedent was being ignored like it never existed.

But none had bargained on the female white lion of the Mortimer pride.

When Elizabeth had devoured her prey that evening at Wigmore, she took Hotspur's demons away with a single caress. When she kissed him, his breath became hers; when she mounted him, it was she who wore the spurs. Elizabeth had traded her shag-haired kerns for a man who would protect her honour and her family name to the death if need be. And throughout her dance Hotspur's demons had stopped chattering in his head. His whole being had yearned for her body, and now he had his lady, or as I saw it, his *Morgain la Fée* of Celtic and Arthurian myth.

Henceforth, I could only look to my master's horse, serve him at his table, arm him for battle and carry his banner as his trusted squire. For my sins, I felt I had failed him in some inexplicable way when, in reality, I was insanely jealous of Elizabeth. In short, I had vowed to protect him in battle, against all enemies, but I could never protect him from his wife.

That night I drowned in my grief, but in that delirium of wine and vomit, I learned a truth that I could never divulge to my master for fear of incriminating myself. After Sir Thomas Mortimer had emptied his stomach for a second time on the table, he sat beside me and whispered deceitfully in my ear.

'You're a bastard Hardyng aren't you?' he whined.

For my sins, I replied that I was.

'Then we are twins.'

I poured a cup of ale and toasted his good health.

'Bastards must be brothers, don't you think?' he said.

I nodded, and when my head dropped, it hit the dais hard.

'Yes, although our illegitimacy is held dear by society, it is secretly frowned upon by some who think we are weakened by it.'

'Weakened to...remain a squire,' I remember saying.

'We have to look to ourselves Hardyng—'

'Yes, and our masters' horses.'

I managed to turn my head, and a wicked smile met my drunken stare.

'Did you hear what your master did to me at Radcot?' said Thomas.

I nodded.

'I'll wager he has many enemies in England,' he continued. 'And now he jousts with my Elizabeth in her bedchamber.'

I laughed. 'Yes...for sure!'

Thomas laughed too and spat yellow bile on the floor. 'Yes, we bastard warriors are the bottom of the pile, but not for long, eh Hardyng?'

I nodded, and although I slid sideways into a puddle of wine, I heard Thomas continue to groan about Hotspur. He was speaking of the siege of Brest four years ago when my master's ship had been holed and sunk.

'Yes, that time I made him shit his breeches!' said Thomas.

But then I heard no more and all went black.

Next morning dawned cold and grey like my soul. I feared what I had said to Thomas the previous night might have compromised my oath of fealty to Hotspur. And as we left Wigmore Castle for the north, I said nothing of Thomas's attempt on his life as this might have led to more questions. Lady Elizabeth rode beside my master to York, and I followed dutifully behind them carrying his banner and listening to their romance flower into perfect love. It was the first time I ever saw Hotspur smile in his life. And, God help me, I wished his demons might return so that I could serve him as before.

I have never felt so low in my life, even though the balance of more significant events weighed upon us. The wheel of fortune continued to turn full-circle, and soon the questions were not of love or honour, but of how long it would be before the hated lord's appellants would suffer for their crimes against King Richard's bedfellows.

For the Percy and Lancaster families, the fight for survival was far from over. But in truth, all that had gone before was nothing compared to what was to come.

14

Périgord 1395

'I am not come to fyght sharpely, but to parley'

Nothing calms the disquiet soul better than a vigorous gallop. And Hotspur's remedy for his tormented spirit was to recklessly hasten against his enemies as if they were his demons. I never doubted his warlike courage in all the days I served him, but in my humble opinion, his real strength was not in his feats of arms, of which he was truly prolific, but rather in the way he overcame the many devils that plagued him every day of his life.

Chivalry also served to cure Hotspur's anguish, and it enabled him to carry on in the dark years after his decisive defeat at Otterburn. The field of battle, as I was soon to find out, was a hellish place to behold. Hotspur had told me how his brother had almost bled to death before his eyes, and how young hopefuls like Thomas Felton had died for respecting a dream of service that was largely unattainable. Most knights who attempted to reach for the chivalric ideal were doomed to failure chiefly because they were trained killers. The purist codes of chivalry naturally opposed this way of life; therefore, the knight needed to cleave to some higher cause to justify his actions. Some used religion to explain their blood-letting and war crimes, others said they were obeying their lord's commands, but Hotspur found some respite in the romance of chivalry and justice to explain his actions.

Lady Percy, in particular, helped my master realise this romantic notion of the code more than any other. And at least in the early days of their marriage, romance flourished in that a knight's whole purpose in life was to fight for his lady.

'He who defends with love will be safe,' I heard Elizabeth say to my master one day. 'And I will save you and protect you from harm with perfect love.'

I was just seventeen years at the time and had been in my master's service for a full five years. As his only squire, I had already shared in Hotspur's frantic life on the borders of England and with him and his lady on several diplomatic missions abroad by order of King Richard. However, while in Cyprus at the court of King James, I noticed a change in my master, and when he fell gravely ill, I feared the consequences. While ever Hotspur was active, he was content, but when he was idle, he suffered terrible physical strain and the real fear that every morning he was about to die. It was an ailment that even learned physicians could not cure; apart from bidding me rouse him at dawn every day with a pail of cold water, much to the displeasure of his lady who, I fear, never liked me.

However, in the sixteenth year of King Richard's reign

Hotspur was once more called upon to serve, if only briefly, nearer home. Because of his absence in France, John of Gaunt appointed him Lieutenant of Aquitaine for four years, and in the autumn of his last year in office, we sailed for Bordeaux expecting to enjoy more vigorous days in the saddle and fewer mornings armed only with a bucket.

But alas, when we reached France, there was a truce in place. And when we travelled east to the borders of Périgord, where our quarters would be for the next few months, we found the castles near Bergerac deserted. The longest truce between England and France was in place, and Hotspur wrote several letters to Gaunt to know the reason why he had sent him to such a remote outpost.

Gaunt never replied, and my master knew that he was not the only knight who was hamstrung by peace. Thousands of soldiers suffered a similar fate and the reasons for such a long truce were twofold. On the French side, King Charles had suffered another breakdown that challenged his furthering of the war; in fact, he considered himself so fragile that he might break like a pane of glass. And as for King Richard, his wife Anne had died recently, and he was eagerly looking forward to marrying Charles' six-year-old daughter Isabella for eighty thousand francs. Therefore the two kings found a consensus regarding the war at the expense of their unemployed warriors who would have to find work elsewhere.

My master was no exception, and as a result, he relapsed into states of deep depression and days of intense restlessness. He sent out letters to local French knights challenging them to single combat, but due to the treaty, none of his rivals ever answered his call to arms. Hotspur even turned out the meagre garrison one day intending to punish a band of brigands who were pillaging the countryside. But he was reminded by the Castellan of Bergerac that Gaunt had forbidden any such forays into France in fear that it might lead to a renewal of hostilities.

However, a more worrying fact was that Hotspur had begun to venture out into Périgord alone. The province was only a few miles distant, and his solitary rides along the Dordogne were becoming more frequent by the day. So regular in fact that one morning Lady Percy woke me early, furious that I should know my master's whereabouts at all times.

Elizabeth was already dressed for riding, and after casting off my bedcovers, she scolded me for not doing my duty as a squire.

'Did you rouse your master at dawn in the usual way?' she said, watching me struggle to cover my manhood.

I managed to shake my head and fumbled for a reply.

'Your master has ridden off again. His mind is as taught as a highly-strung bow, and we must find him quickly,' she said, heading for the door. 'Make haste!'

'Yes, my lady,' said I bleary-eyed.

'I fear that this child in my womb will have no father one day, and then you will be blamed you…you bastard.'

Elizabeth was more anxious than usual, and when I heard that she was with child, I dressed more urgently fearful of the consequences.

'If we do not find him today I'll have you flogged,' she added as I followed her into the courtyard. 'Do you understand me Hardyng?'

'Yes, my lady I—'

'Horses are ready and saddled. Now will you make haste, or do I have to whip you myself?'

Elizabeth had a fearful temper when aroused. But that morning, her worried expression and glaring eyes betrayed the look of a hunted animal. She was determined to ride with me despite my concerns, but this made me think that my master was in more danger than usual, so I armed myself well for the journey ahead.

We took the main road into Périgord intending to not stray from it. However, I knew that we could only hope and pray that my master had taken the same road. A gallop across country was more to his liking, although as soon as we crossed the border into France, we found out that he had followed the river instead. Lady Percy's fraught expression confirmed that the mangled corpse of a French soldier sprawled in the dust was probably her husband's handiwork.

'This is the way he came,' said Elizabeth.

A heavy weapon had crushed the dead soldier's skull, and his horse was lying dead in the meadow beyond. It was as if a madman had repeatedly struck the poor man over and over again for no other reason than mutilation, and I bid Lady Percy continue up the road while I searched the corpse and rolled it into a ditch.

Further into the province autumn's approach blew a squall of leaves into our faces. Winter was approaching fast, and the deeper we rode into Périgord, the more I feared there would be more senseless killings waiting for us. I knew what my master was capable of, and I soon realised that his great skill in arms was once again being guided by those chattering demons in his head.

And as we passed through a forest, my prediction was proven right.

The constant rustle of bare branches overhead hid the

moans of a wounded soldier propped against a tree trunk. He had been shot through the fleshy part of his neck with a crossbow bolt and was desperately calling out for help. The soldier was bleeding to death, and he pointed into the sea of ferns surrounding him crying out weakly. *'Va-t'en...Va-t'en... lion azure.'*

I repeated his words to Lady Percy as my native French was not good, and she urged me to mount quickly.

'God help us,' she said, 'my husband is possessed.'

And as I gathered the reins of my horse, I had a strange feeling there was an evil presence watching our every move. I felt the forest close in on me and drew my sword. The French soldier let out another cry, and it was only then that I saw two more bodies strewn in the bracken, their throats cut lengthways like stalked deer.

'Hardyng, make haste!' said Lady Percy urging her horse away.

I dared not be asked a second time, and after noticing that all the soldiers were dead, including the one beneath the tree, we both sped out of the forest into the rolling countryside beyond.

However, not more than a league later we found yet another dead Frenchman partially stripped of his armour. A crossbow bolt had also killed this man, but in difference to the soldier in the forest, his blood-stained heraldry marked him out as a knight. He still clutched his broken reins in his stiffened fist, and when we found his mount nearby, I found out that the attack on him had been so brutal that the neck of his charger had got in the way of the fight; its large, proud head had been severed with a single blow.

Now I knew Hotspur was lost in a raging fury. We both

agreed that the devil possessed him, and I bid Lady Percy take refuge in a small village nestling in a clearing on the other side of the valley. She was trembling with fear, and I could see that despite her hardiness she was not accustomed to such random bloodshed; when we arrived at the village, she began to retch so violently that I feared for her and the health of her unborn child.

Elizabeth told me her sickness would pass, but that she must rest. I bid a group of French women to look after her while I followed the road to try and apprehend my master; although God help me, I had no idea how I could reason with Hotspur when I found him. He had killed another six men on the outskirts of a nearby town, and it appeared the citizens had gathered to take their revenge.

Most of the townsfolk stood trembling near a small water mill close to where the soldiers lay butchered. One fatal slash with a sword had sliced each man's throat, and as I approached the slaughter, an eager hand seized my bridle. The man pointed to three other peasants who were busy dragging another body from the river below us, and to my horror, the large crowd moved to cut off my retreat.

I tried to converse in French with the man holding my horse, but failed miserably. By the way he was ordering other citizens around, I could see that he was a town official of some degree. And when he spoke to me, he did nothing to explain the carnage.

'*Cherchez-vous le lion bleu?*' he said gesturing wildly with both hands.

I partly understood his meaning and asked where the *lion bleu* was.

The Frenchman fluttered his hands away from him like a

flapping bird, and I gathered from it that Hotspur had escaped the way he had come.

'Le bon chevalier du lion bleu...nous a sauvés,' called the man after me, but all I could tell from his words was that he thought Hotspur was a good knight.

And the good knight had ridden back towards Aquitaine it seemed. He had followed the river instead of the road, and I found him watering his horse in the Dordogne's pebbled shallows. He seemed oblivious to my approach, although I felt sure he knew I was there. Despite his gory appearance, Hotspur was perfectly calm; a condition that I found hard to believe taking into account what he had done.

'I have come this w-way many times before,' he said, staring into the glassy river.

I carefully dismounted beside him. 'Lady Elizabeth wished me to ride with her master...to find you.'

Hotspur turned quickly, eyes glaring. 'Elizabeth?'

'She is safe master. I will take you to her.'

Hotspur nodded and waded into the river to wash his armour and face of blood.

'You thought me p-p-possessed?' he said.

'Lady Elizabeth thought you lost master.'

'She speaks the truth. The d-demon has returned.' Hotspur stared at me as if he had committed a great sin. 'I thought I had chased it away, but I was w-wrong.'

'Then we will fight it together master,' I said.

'I can f-feel it now urging me on...rattling my bones... making me spur away. I am cursed and have b-been since birth...'

Hotspur's voice grew hoarse. He tried to confess his sins as if I was some pardoner who could absolve him for money.

But in the end, he apologised and urged me to show him the way back to the village and his wife.

He explained that he had been following a band of *écorcheurs*. They were mostly bandits and unemployed mercenaries who were taking advantage of the truce and pillaging the countryside. The French had sent out soldiers to apprehend them fearful that the treaty might be violated if the mercenaries entered Aquitaine. However, most of these men were ambushed and killed. It had been these that Lady Percy and I had come across on the road and in the forest, and when Hotspur finally caught up with them, they had turned on him to their disadvantage. The *lion bleu* had been the town's saviour it seemed, and I heaved a sigh of relief knowing my master had not lost his mind after all. His numerous journeys into Périgord had not been in vain, but when we arrived at the village and met Lady Percy, I wished I had never brought him there.

Sometimes people are drawn back to places they once knew. Over twenty years had passed since Hotspur was last there, but he soon realised he had never really left the place. The villagers had built themselves houses, and there was a newly built stone church in the clearing where once there had only been ashes. The fields were once more filled with ripened crops waiting to be harvested, and it was here that my master re-lived his youth as though it was only yesterday.

Lady Percy comforted him as he broke down in tears before a simple cross that stood in the market place. A crowd gathered around us, and the guilt on Hotspur's face was plain to see. It was clear to me that he had been searching for the village since arriving in France, perhaps all his life, but now he had found it, it was too much for him to bear. He clutched at the stone memorial with both hands, bowed his head in silent prayer, and turned to the villagers as if seeking forgiveness.

But it was only after Lady Percy coaxed a young woman to my master's side that Hotspur recovered his bearing. And when she gave him a flower from the small bunch she was carrying, he knew instantly who she was by the wrinkled scars and healed blisters on her arms and face.

15

Kenilworth 1397

'Wyth all theyr frendes, the kyng Richard did expell'

John of Gaunt had taken no active part in any of the recent upheavals culminating in the battle of Radcot Bridge. However, when he returned from Spain after the Merciless Parliament, he was received by the king with open arms. Richard was humbled and heartbroken by the sudden death of his wife Anne, and now he looked to his old mentor Gaunt to remove his grief and seek revenge on his old enemies, the infamous lords appellant, who had robbed him of absolute power.

Richard's restoration would involve the murder, execution and banishment of some of the highest nobles in the land. But it took nine long years for Lancaster to exact Richard's revenge. The main reason being that the king still considered Gaunt's son his enemy. Bolingbroke had not only raised forces to stop royalists coming to Richard's aid, but he had also participated in the bloody aftermath of Radcot Bridge by making short work of the king's household. However, using Richard's vulnerability, Gaunt now saw a way out for his son by punishing others for the coup in his place, despite putting his younger brother the Duke of Gloucester in grave danger.

It was a dangerous and personal gamble by Gaunt, but the alternative was unthinkable now that Bolingbroke had dug himself an early grave. The Lancastrian succession hung in the balance, and the Mortimer claim threatened to trump their card. But unlike previous plots to further his ambitions, Gaunt was no longer a healthy man. Recent events, and his opulent lifestyle, had taken a dreadful toll on the duke's mind and body. He had retired ill from parliament, and whilst recovering at Kenilworth, his throne-like chair became his sick-bed where he sat looking deathly pale and near to death. The castle echoed to his constant moaning. And his belligerent demands for whores, despite his withered member, had alienated his new wife Katherine so much that she had taken refuge elsewhere with her recently legitimised Beaufort offspring.

Now, more than ever, Gaunt needed an advisor to help him save his son and title from the king's wrath. And in that role, his lawyer Thomas Percy proved an invaluable asset, despite the great cloud of uncertainty which now hung over England.

'Look after my son,' Gaunt kept saying to my master as we languished at Kenilworth waiting for something to happen. 'Swear that you will take his side Harry?'

Hotspur nodded. He was unaware of a plot gathering speed by the hour, and for the first time in my life, I saw how quickly great men like Gaunt could fall from favour, become childlike and dependent on others.

'I have little time left in this world Harry,' coughed Gaunt. 'It's not like the old days when I used to give you a clip round the ear.'

'You w-will outlive us all my lord,' said Hotspur forcing a smile, but remembering Gaunt's bullying at Leconfield long ago.

Bolingbroke remembered too. He was pacing the floor, only stopping now and then to gaze from the narrow arrow-slit windows dripping with rain. He was trying to see beyond the storm to a better time when life was much simpler.

'Where is he?' he mumbled slapping his hand against the wall.

'Who are we w-waiting for?' said my master.

No one answered.

'I'll wager he's been arrested,' said Bolingbroke at last.

The strained look that always accompanied Bolingbroke's black moods was much more pronounced than usual. There had been harsh words between the remaining appellants after the trial and execution of Arundel. Warwick's banishment for life to the Isle of Man had resulted in a family argument between father and son. And now Bolingbroke's anger simmered beneath the surface due in part to Gaunt's sudden lethargy. Only one man in England could ease Lancastrian fears now, and he was somewhere on the muddy road to Kenilworth.

I too felt uneasy in the gloomy chamber, and the unearthly chill in the air added to the rawness of the situation. The fire in the hearth had not been lit that morning, and all of Gaunt's servants had been dismissed under orders that only Thomas Mowbray, the newly created Duke of Norfolk, was to be allowed into the castle.

'You do not need to fear my son, nor you Harry,' said Gaunt weakly, 'others will fall in your place—'

'Fall? I've d-done nothing wrong,' said Hotspur amazed.

'You have not told him, have you?' Bolingbroke said to his father. 'Richard will not rest Harry until he has all our heads for Radcot Bridge.'

'You are all safe as long as I live,' croaked Gaunt, his face looking paler than ever. 'Now get me some more wine boy before I throw up.'

Bolingbroke's eyes rolled, and another long silence ensued as he filled his father's cup.

'So, where is he then?' said Bolingbroke. 'He should be here by now.'

Gaunt coughed. 'I told you, Mowbray will do our bidding, and the king will approve of it. Now go sit down and stop worrying.'

'But what if Richard changes his mind?'

Gaunt was about to reprimand his son again, but at that moment the door was thrown open by small hands. Everyone's head turned as two children blustered into the chamber, and after screaming wildly, they ran to Hotspur who received them with open arms.

The tension eased. 'Ha, the two little Hotspurs!' enthused Gaunt. 'By all the saints, there is hope for England yet.'

Lady Percy flustered in after the children and Gaunt's eyes rolled lustfully. 'And the beautiful Lady Hotspur too, what more can an old man ask on his deathbed?'

Elizabeth humoured Gaunt's lecherous smile, and she gathered up her children apologising for the noise. She was about to go, but barring her exit from the chamber was a man steaming with sweat. He removed his hat, loosened his wet cloak, being careful to not touch the old jousting scar on his neck.

Bolingbroke rushed over and seized Mowbray by the arm. 'Thank Christ! Well, what news?'

Mowbray frowned at Hotspur's children who were still reeling around the chamber at speed. My presence was frowned on too, but Bolingbroke's eagerness to get an answer from Mowbray saved me for the moment.

'Get out! Get out!' cried Bolingbroke urging the children away.

Hotspur raised an eyebrow, and his wife bowed following them out.

'So, what did Richard say?' said Bolingbroke folding his arms.

Mowbray stared at me. 'Say about what?'

Bolingbroke threw up his hands in despair. 'Christ's blood Mowbray speak! We are all friends here.'

Gaunt frowned at my master, and Hotspur gestured for me to leave the chamber.

For my part, I was glad to be free of the tension, and I only found out later that Mowbray was carrying terrible news direct from Calais of which he was then captain.

Of the former appellants, we all knew that the Earl of Arundel had been examined by Gaunt and executed for treason. Warwick had been banished for the same crime, and the Duke of Gloucester had been exiled in Calais awaiting trial. However, it was Gloucester's fate that everyone in the chamber was eager to hear about; especially Gaunt who, contrary to his plans, was numbed into silence when Mowbray disclosed what had befallen his younger brother.

Mowbray's news of Gloucester's death affected the whole

kingdom, including my master, as he too along with Bolingbroke and Mowbray had supported the appellants at Radcot Bridge. By his own admission, Mowbray was disturbed by the murder of Gloucester. However, his reward from King Richard had been a dukedom, and even Gaunt marvelled at Mowbray's ruthlessness.

Much later, in the reign of King Henry the fourth of that name, Hotspur told me that a man called John Hall, a valet of Mowbray's confessed, in part, to Gloucester's execution. However, he claimed that 'others' were involved in the crime and that he had become a scapegoat. These other men, Hall said, included great lords, two of the king's men called Searle and Frances, a knight named Colfox and some other menials who had all been sworn in to carry out the duke's murder in secret.

Mowbray's instructions were to take the Duke of Gloucester to the royal residence in Calais called the Prince's Inn, where, it was said, he would be safe and better lodged. However, once there, Searle and Frances escorted the duke to an upper chamber of the palace saying that it was the king's will that he should die immediately, at which point Searle allowed Gloucester a priest to hear his last confession.

After this, the king's men caused the duke to lie upon a bed. Then Searle and Frances threw a feather quilt over him, the sides of which Colfox and others held so fast that the duke could neither move nor breathe. John Hall, guarding the door, later told his examiners that he burst into tears. But when Searle and Francis were forced to lay on the duke's mouth to hasten death Hall disclosed that every man present began to regret their actions.

When Mowbray entered the chamber, he was amazed at

the outpouring of grief, but he comforted all the murderers saying that they would not be blamed for the homicide and that the duke had been too outspoken and dangerous to live long. He said that Gloucester had committed high treason and that they were only carrying out the king's orders. However, all these reassuring words fell on hollow ground once the conspirators returned to England. When Mowbray arrived at Kenilworth that rainy afternoon, Hall was already dead. He had been arrested, written a confession, and had been taken to Tyburn for execution. There his bowels had been cut out and burnt before him, his body had been hanged, beheaded and quartered so that the parts could be distributed at the king's pleasure; and this is how the one man who least deserved to die covered up the identity of the real criminals who were still at large.

Hotspur said to me that Mowbray did all this in full knowledge of King Richard, but he refused to believe the king was responsible. However, when my master emerged from the chamber that day, he was still unaware of the real truth of the matter. It would be the last time my master and I saw Gaunt alive, and through a gap in the open door, I saw the one-time great duke with his head in his hands recanting his sins to God. He whined to Bolingbroke how he would miss his brother Gloucester, and recalled how the Earl of Arundel had forgiven everyone before dying on the scaffold; that is except Gaunt whose name he tried to curse before his severed head dropped from the block.

Lancaster cried out for God to forgive his sins. He called for his confessor who never came. I heard his cries echoing throughout the castle, and from that moment on, his illness began to eat him away from the inside. We were all shocked by his outpouring of grief, but more surprised to see Thomas Percy hurrying along the corridor carrying a bundle of papers each bearing the king's seal.

'What's that infernal noise?' asked Thomas breathlessly.

My master shook his head. 'The Duke of Gloucester, he's d-dead.'

Thomas was struggling with the rolled-up documents he was carrying. 'Here take these Harry…I'm pissing wet through.'

My master frowned, and after asking what the papers were, he opened one.'

'These are p-pardons. Pardons for who?'

Thomas removed his coat. 'More than pardons Harry.'

Hotspur glanced at the wording on the documents. 'This one says you are the Earl of W-Worcester?'

'You should congratulate me Harry,' said Thomas taking the papers. 'You have all been pardoned by the king.'

Hotspur bid me follow him quickly away, but Thomas caught my master's arm as he passed. 'Did you hear me, Harry, you are pardoned for Radcot Bridge?'

'But I d-did nothing w-wrong at Radcot Bridge.'

Thomas grinned. 'You were guilty by association along with the lords appellant, but now you are at liberty to do as you please.'

'I will not be b-b-bought and sold like an old w-warhorse—'

'You mean like your friend Bolingbroke, the new Duke of Hereford, and Mowbray, the new Duke of Norfolk. Or perhaps you will tell Ralph Neville, the new Earl of Westmoreland he has been bought and sold too?'

For the first time in his life, Hotspur looked betrayed, and when he shook off his uncle's hand, he swept all the pardons from Thomas's arm.

As my master stormed off, I saw Elizabeth grinning from the confines of a small alcove. She shielded her two distraught children from the whirlwind my master created as he blustered by them.

'Titles can be d-d-done and undone uncle!' raged Hotspur lurching down the corridor.

'And so can you!' called Thomas collecting the fallen papers on the floor.

I followed my master dutifully. But looking back I saw Lady Percy stood over Thomas laughing. She kicked one of the pardons away and gloated when he had to scramble for it on all fours.

'My family will rule England one day,' said Elizabeth to him, 'then you will all be undone.'

Thomas sat stone-faced staring at Lady Percy's wry smile, and when Bolingbroke emerged from consoling his father, Elizabeth gave him a cold hard stare.

'Lancaster's days are numbered,' she shouted, pointing at Bolingbroke.

It sounded like a curse.

16

Gosford Green 1398

'At Coventree, in barres armed clene'

And so it all began. Seeds of doubt were randomly cast on the harrowed fields of England, and within a few years, former friends would become enemies embroiled in revolution and civil war. We were all caught up in it, and like discarded seedlings between the ridge and furrow, no one knew who would survive the crows.

Only a few months after King Richard had pardoned everyone for their wrongdoings at Radcot Bridge, Thomas Mowbray met with Henry Bolingbroke on the road from London to Brentford. Mowbray warned Bolingbroke of a plot by the king to revoke their pardons, and with good cause. Richard hated his childhood playmate, and when he left Mowbray rubbing his hands, he spurred on to consult his father at Kenilworth.

Gaunt rose from his sickbed and went to inform the king

of Mowbray's threat and slanderous language. However, Richard was preoccupied with dire omens and was increasingly suspicious of anyone around him. Even Gaunt, who had helped him regain the throne, was suspected of treason. The young king's mind was unstable, and he even thought the dead Arundel's head had somehow re-attached itself to its decomposed body to exact revenge on him. Richard also informed Gaunt that from now on he had decided to rule England absolutely and that by appropriating the wool subsidy, he would no longer need the consent of parliament, or his ministers, to govern the realm.

Gaunt was astounded, and went further by accusing Mowbray of his brother Gloucester's death in Calais, thereby fracturing the old bond between mentor and pupil for good. It was the end of Lancaster as far as Richard was concerned. Battle lines had been drawn, and when Mowbray received news of Gaunt's interview, he feared that the king would destroy him and the Lancastrian line in a fit of anger.

Bolingbroke's move to publically accuse Mowbray of treason made matters worse, and it was a challenge no one could ignore. The issue was immediately put before the Court of Chivalry to resolve. But when the duke's claim remained unsettled some months later, King Richard suggested that God's judgement should take precedence instead - namely that a joust to the death would take place where everyone's honour might be satisfied. The venue selected for the duel between the two dukes was Coventry, and in the autumn of that fateful year, all the eyes of Europe turned towards England; including my master and I, who rode from the north to support Bolingbroke and see Mowbray punished for his crimes.

Close by Coventry, a large open space called Gosford Green was set up with a tiltyard. It was a fine September day, and on Richard's orders, suitable festivities had been arranged in lavish tents and pavilions, chiefly to satisfy his French and Bohemian guests. However, when we arrived at the tourney, Bolingbroke was sat in his tent armed and alone. His father was elsewhere awaiting the king's arrival, and he was fidgeting with several talismans that he had removed from around his neck.

'I do not need these now,' said Bolingbroke, giving them to Hotspur. 'He tried to poison me, you know.'

'Now you can p-p-pay Mortimer back,' said Hotspur.

'Mowbray's good though, you know that?'

'You're b-better, my friend.'

Bolingbroke held out his hands. 'Look,' he said, his fingers trembling. 'Saint Inglevert's curse has returned. I would not listen to you, my friend, and for that, I am truly sorry.'

'Mowbray's not B-Boucicant,' said Hotspur, 'and the judges are s-satisfied there is no fraud. This time it w-will be man against man. A true contest of chivalry.'

Bolingbroke cleared his throat and stood up proudly, legs apart. 'I am Henry of Lancaster, Duke of Hereford and have come here to prosecute my appeal by combating Thomas Mowbray, Duke of Norfolk who is a traitor false and recreant to God, the king, his realm, and me,' he said confidently. Then Bolingbroke relaxed and sat biting his lip. 'What do you think?'

'Good enough, but you will have to k-k-kill Mowbray. You and your father will never be safe w-while he lives.'

'We're all in danger, Harry. Richard is more devious and corrupt than I ever imagined. He preens himself like a peacock while others fall into the dung heap of history. He is the author of all this deceit. Even you must see that now?'

'He is s-s-still our king,' said Hotspur, unable to control his feelings.

Bolingbroke threw his hands up in despair. 'God save us! He even conspires with the French king. Why do you think he's married that seven-year-old girl?'

'To make peace?'

'But you know that's impossible, Harry,' snapped Bolingbroke, 'the French war is unwinnable.'

'There is another w-way,' said Hotspur reflectively.

Bolingbroke took Hotspur by the arm. 'Yes, your way, I know...a more chivalrous way. If only knights could compete for kingdoms in the tiltyard instead of on the battlefield - like in the days of Charlemagne - then all would be well.' But the thought bypassed Bolingbroke's reasoning like a speeding arrow. 'Even your brother-in-law Mortimer would make a better king than Richard,' he said.

Hotspur's usual revealing face mirrored his wife's grieving that morning. 'I had w-word today from Ireland...' he said miserably.

Bolingbroke continued to arm himself.

'Mortimer was k-killed in battle a week ago,' continued Hotspur. 'Roger's infant son is your only t-threat now.'

Bolingbroke was unsure how to take the news. 'Ireland has always been a sad place for the English, my friend,' he groaned.

'So, you too think our k-k-king had a hand in it.'

Bolingbroke set his teeth, and as a trumpet sounded the call to arms, he reserved judgement. 'Pass on my regrets to Lady Percy, if she will accept my offer that is?'

My master nodded and passed Bolingbroke his helm. 'Aim not for the s-s-saddle today Duke of Hereford. Stick your lance in Mowbray's lying throat.'

Bolingbroke tried to smile. 'We...I mean my father and I... we conspired against Richard, my friend. I want you to know that if—'

'And my uncle?'

'It was the only way Harry, but we had no hand in Gloucester's death. That was the king and Mowbray's doing. And now the king is slowly killing my father too.' He paused for breath and called for his Bohemian valet to buckle on his sword. 'Richard and Mowbray are laughing at us, my friend. And if I die today, he removes another card from the pack.'

Hotspur's hand fell on the hilt of his dagger.

'There's no need for that, Harry. I'll kill Mowbray. But if I die, promise me you will look after my son Harry of Monmouth, God knows he will need your help if Mowbray escapes my lance.'

Both men embraced each other, and after a moment praying together, Bolingbroke and his valet rushed from the tent.

Once outside, Hotspur was careful not to draw attention to himself. He wore a cloak fearful of his celebrity and of what might happen if he too, like his friend, was singled out for punishment. Outwardly my master was the most confident and famous knight in England. He was confident that his friend would kill Mowbray on the first run of the joust. But now his future was more unpredictable than ever, and only one man could change that. Only Richard could foresee the future, and despite all his lavish preparations for the tourney, the king astounded everyone by putting a stop to the duel before it began.

As both dukes mounted their richly decorated horses and galloped towards each other, Richard threw down his warder.

Bolingbroke and Mowbray were stunned. The king had wielded absolute power to good effect, but what now? He had bypassed all the principles of chivalry, and with a flurry of trumpets, Richard retired with John of Gaunt to discuss the matter privately over dinner.

The waiting dukes spent two hours in the saddle while the king dined with Gaunt and his guests, and Hotspur pushed through the crowd to try and learn what was being said in the king's pavilion. He could hear heated words coming from beyond the canvas, but the king's Cheshire archers stopped anyone from entering the royal enclosure. Mowbray and Bolingbroke stared at each other, willing the joust to begin again. They sweated in their heavy armour, and it was only when a cry went up from somewhere in the king's pavilion that Hotspur knew the adjudication was over.

Old Gaunt's face was grey and beading with sweat when he emerged back into the arena, but the king nimbly jumped back onto the dais and addressed the waiting crowd.

'Remove your helmets and cast your lances aside dukes,' said the king returning finishing a cup of wine. 'We have decided that there is to be no more high-born blood spilt in England…so this is my will and sentence on you both…'

Richard produced a scroll of parchment with seals attached, and everyone waited with bated breath for his ruling. It was clear to all that the warrant was no afterthought. The wording was too long to have been fashioned during dinner, and after the king mumbled the legal preamble, he came to the charges and verdict that would decide the duel.

Only a flock of migrating gulls overhead broke the silence.

'You Henry Duke of Hereford, we banish from these shores for ten years,' said the king pleasantly.

A gasp came from the assembled crowd.

'And you Thomas Duke of Norfolk...'

The crowd gasped again.

'...you shall be exiled for life.'

When a riot ensued from Gaunt's supporters, Richard's Cheshire archers formed a wall to protect their king.

'This is my will and commandment,' shouted Richard over the tumult. 'Now see to it both of you, and let no men assist the said duke's to enter England lest they wish a similar fate, or worse, to befall them. This matter is now concluded.'

The two dukes removed their helmets and gazed at each other blankly. Then Mowbray threw down his lance and helm in a fit of anger. Bolingbroke was numbed by what the king had said, and both looked to John of Gaunt who sat impassive, broken, and alone beside his grinning protégé.

Richard and his entourage immediately left the dais. More festivities were arranged to entertain his French envoys, and part of the sumptuous feast was distributed to the people to cover the king's retreat. The whole tourney had been a sham, and when the furore in the crowd finally died down, there was an embarrassing silence in the lists. King Richard had ignored the rules governing chivalry, and for the first time in his life Hotspur was furious with him. He leapt the wooden barrier, closely followed by myself, and took hold of Bolingbroke's bridle. Mowbray was about to say something, but a savage look from my master put paid to that.

The once-proud Bolingbroke hung his head in prayer. 'God help us,' he said miserably wiping the sweat from his eyes, 'it would have been better if I had been run through the heart by Mowbray's lance.'

'You need to leave q-q-quickly, my friend,' said Hotspur.

Bolingbroke's glassy eyes followed Mowbray from the lists, and he drew his sword as if to charge him down.

'No, he's finished!' warned Hotspur.

'Give me back those talismans Harry. How did it all come to this?'

'What w-will you do now?'

'My children, my wife, God knows who'll protect them now. No one is safe.' The anger in Bolingbroke's eyes burned with an overriding concern for his family.

Hotspur could only marvel at how cruelly fortune's wheel had turned on his friend. 'Your father will k-k-know what to do,' he said.

'No, his power is spent, my friend. Don't you see?'

Bolingbroke waved his sword at Mowbray again.

'Forget him,' cried Hotspur, 'or you will be b-banished for life!'

'It's all about that white hart,' mumbled Bolingbroke savagely. 'You remember, I caught Richard with the poor creature at Kenilworth. I said I'd tell my father about what he did to it. Now he strips me of my country…'

My master let go of Bolingbroke's bridle. 'Go quickly, and G-God be with you.'

Hotspur struck Bolingbroke's horse on the rump, and I saw all our lives change in an instant.

'Keep out of the king's way, my friend,' shouted Bolingbroke spurring forward. 'I will need your help when I return to England.'

17

Warkworth 1399

'And to avoyde the realme without variaunce'

And Bolingbroke's return from exile was not long in coming. When John of Gaunt died suddenly in his sleep at the age of fifty-eight years, the wheel of fortune turned full circle in Richard's favour. Some said the Duke of Lancaster had died after receiving a poisonous and soon destroyed letter from his nephew the king at Leicester Castle. Others said it was simply the grief of his son's ten-year banishment that killed him. Either way, the giant's already decomposing body was consigned to a sepulchre without delay, and it was only when physicians examined it before burial that rumours of foul play were dismissed. The duke's constitution was putrid to the core. Even his genitals had rotted away after a lifetime of whoring and debauchery.

However, two days after Gaunt's funeral at Saint Paul's, King Richard took steps to destroy the House of Lancaster forever. Firstly, he commanded that like Mowbray, Bolingbroke's ten-year banishment would be commuted to life, and secondly, the king also made arrangements for increasing his wealth through illegal means - namely by appropriating the Lancastrian inheritance.

It was a bold move, and we were all shocked by it. However, this outrage came as no surprise to Bolingbroke, and when he received news of this in Paris, he began to make plans of his own to invade England.

Sir Thomas Percy, Earl of Worcester, who was still acting as Lancaster's lawyer and confidant, was predictably shocked by Richard's craftiness too. Although as always he was playing a longer game with the king then 'campaigning' in Ireland. Hotspur knew that his friend Bolingbroke was receiving letters from Thomas, who had contrived a plan that would suit the Percys and also protect them from the king's tyranny. Thomas's private, and dangerous correspondence with Bolingbroke had been continuing since his exile, but when a letter from Thomas arrived at his brother's castle at Warkworth, the Earl of Northumberland and Hotspur were both struck like a thunderbolt.

As his father read from the letter, my master burst into the great hall.

The newly built keep echoed to his measured footsteps, but his father was quick to take the sting out of his son's tail.

'Bolingbroke's got the bit between his teeth,' he said.

Hotspur folded his arms in defence.

Northumberland shook the letter in his son's face and read out loud. '...if you wish to raise arms against the king brother there will be no half measures,' he quoted frowning at Hotspur. 'And if you and Harry take Lancaster's side you will be committing treason and will be punished accordingly...'

My master threw his hands up. 'We k-know that—'

Northumberland glared at his son and read on silently.

'Is Bolingbroke coming b-back to claim his lands, or the t-throne?' said Hotspur.

'His inheritance, obviously.'

'What else d-does Thomas say,' said Hotspur pacing the floor.

'By all the saints, he says our sentences for not attending Richard in Ireland are still fresh in the king's mind. We should have been more prudent, Harry. Before we know it, those Neville bastards will have the north!'

Hotspur flexed his stiff right arm. 'Bolingbroke w-will not rest until Richard is d-dead, I know him.'

Northumberland nodded.

'He w-wishes the crown for himself,' continued my master, 'he told me so at Coventry b-before he left for France.'

'He needs our support first,' replied his father.

'I will not g-go against the king!'

'You will do as I say. We too have committed treason in Richard's eyes. Do you think he will forget that?'

'Thomas w-will know what to do.'

'Wait,' said Northumberland reading more of the letter. 'Thomas says...as you know brother I have supplied the king many ships, men-at-arms and archers for his journey to Ireland. So, if Richard tries to punish you or Harry for not attending him in Ireland, he knows he will lose my support. He also knows I will not uphold parliament's judgments to revoke Lancaster's rights of inheritance—'

'Then the king is d-d-determined...' mumbled Hotspur pacing the floor.

'Aye, but Thomas says Richard's pretended campaign to avenge Mortimer's death in Ireland will fail, just like others before it. He thinks Bolingbroke will return to England, reclaim his rightful title, and that we will both depose of the king between us. Thomas also says the commons will support us against King Richard and that young Mortimer should rule England in his place—'

'Never!'

'And if not him, Thomas says…we will see to it that Harry's son is crowned king and we will rule through him.'

Thomas's kingmaking plan burned into Hotspur's brain like a hot iron. It seemed to have a life of its own, and my master knew that once his uncle saw the future, his father would see it too.

'This is not the w-way,' said Hotspur, trying to control his temper.

'It's the only way, Harry. We must look to ourselves now. Even old Algernons is watching us. If we fail in this task, I foresee a dark time ahead for the family. We will lose everything and the Percys will become nothing more than merchants or tradesmen!'

'But the king is our master,' said Hotspur. 'We will all be judged by what we do when Bolingbroke returns to England, and I will have no p-p-part in uncle's plan.'

'By all the saints—'

'You f-forget I am a soldier father, and Thomas incites rebellion. It is unchivalrous to go against the k-king—.'

Northumberland brought his hand down on the table. 'You will do as I bid or I'll disown you!'

'Then be about it!'

'I will—'

'If you do, I'll t-tell the king everything.'

'You'll do as I bid,' said Northumberland slamming his hand on the table. 'I tire of your Neville ways...fainting off like a woman at bedtime and always wanting a piss or a shit when we have guests. Remember you are still a marked man for coming to Bolingbroke's aid at Radcot Bridge. Not even your cock-sure ideas of chivalry will remove that stain from the king's blacklist.'

Hotspur went for his dagger.

'And you are rash to the point of absurdity, always drawing your blade and killing my horses with your blasted spurring.'

'I've saved the b-b-border many times for you.'

'If your mother was here she'd—'

At that moment Elizabeth entered the chamber. She was badly dressed in some of my master's armour, and the comical sight and sound of her clanking towards Hotspur were in complete contrast to the tense mood in the chamber.

'What's this?' cried Northumberland taking Elizabeth's hand and kissing it. 'Are my son's wages not financing your wardrobe these days?'

'I've come to join your army, my lords.'

'Then curb your husband's temper first, Sir Knight, before he kills me with his talk of chivalry.'

Elizabeth took my master's arm, and Northumberland shuffled from the chamber shaking his head. 'Think on what I have said...' he mumbled to Hotspur as he left.

Hotspur felt a tightness in his chest strangle him. The demon was fighting to be free, clawing at his ribs, and he reached out for Elizabeth to save him. He told me later that his wife was the only one who could do this. But not this time, and before he hit the floor, he threw his dagger at the oak-panelled door closing behind his father.

The blade bounced off an iron rivet and hit the wall.

'Why are you...dressed...in my harness?' said Hotspur gasping for breath.

'I wanted to know how it feels to be you, my lord.'

'So...how d-does it feel?'

'Wearing it makes me feel like a man. Like I could do what women are not allowed to do in the world.'

'Take it off now—'

Elizabeth stamped her foot. 'But I will be naked, my lord.'

Hotspur got to his feet and kissed her roughly on the mouth. He glanced at the cold steel plates covering his wife's body and was momentarily distracted by the thought of the hard metal and leather straps against her soft flesh.

His shortness of breath eased, and the demon subsided.

'So, what do you w-want of me?' said Hotspur, pulling away from her embrace.

'As I said, I wish to join your army against the king.'

'To w-wear my helm, I would have to c-crop your p-pretty hair.'

Elizabeth's hand caressed Hotspur's thigh. 'I would do anything to put a Mortimer on the throne; you know that my lord.'

'You'll not seduce me this time,' said Hotspur. 'I will not be part of your w-web of deceit. And you should stop listening at k-keyholes.'

Elizabeth stooped down on one knee. 'Then I crave your mercy, my lord.'

'King's are b-born Elizabeth, not made, and that harness you wear, I w-wear it in service of King Richard, not the Mortimers.'

'But the Mortimer's are your family too.'

'G-God chooses kings, and I am chosen by the k-king to do his bidding. It is the highest honour a man can achieve.'

Elizabeth flung her arms around Hotspur's neck. 'Then my lord, do me the honour of your service too.'

My master escaped her embrace and began unbuckling her armour. 'I know Richard is a bad king Elizabeth, but with chivalrous d-d-deeds, I can make him see—'

'And what of your friend in France?'

'Bolingbroke? He hates King Richard. Not b-because of his lack of manliness, or even his bad g-governance,' he paused to kiss Elizabeth who now stood naked before him. 'No, Bolingbroke hates the k-king because Gaunt always d-d-doted on him like a son.'

'You men are all strange creatures to me,' cooed Elizabeth. 'Like animals, you tear each other apart in battle, then treat your enemy to a feast in their honour. Your knightly friends would even kill innocents to ensure their survival. We Mortimer's love our menfolk and children above all else in the world.'

'And I love you for it—'

'Yes, Henry and Elizabeth are loved like Mortimer children.'

'Then stop all this idle talk of crowns and k-k-kingdoms.'

'Your son could be Earl of Northumberland one day, and he will need protection from men like Bolingbroke,' said Elizabeth.

'I may not live that long.'

Elizabeth shook her head anxiously, and tears welled in her eyes.

My master's mind strayed to another time and place. 'Once, when I was in France, I had a p-premonition,' he said. 'I fell from my horse, and some d-d-demon told me I wouldn't live long—'

'I'll not let you go to Berwick…never!' cried Elizabeth.

'I will d-die nonetheless.'

'We will all die one day, so that's why you should approve of your uncle's plan. To put a Mortimer on the throne would secure our children's future? We are the true Plantagenet blood of England. Even the king condones Edmund is the rightful heir—'

'No, never!'

'Ah, is that because Richard is the anointed king, or is it Bolingbroke you fear?'

Hotspur pulled away from his wife.

'Don't you see my lord, Lancaster covets the crown,' snapped Elizabeth. 'Bolingbroke will not be content with his father's inheritance when he returns to England. He will want the throne.'

Hotspur frowned. 'So, you have been listening at keyholes.'

Elizabeth pouted and covered his hand with hers. 'What will you do then my lord?'

'I will make Bolingbroke p-p-promise that he will not usurp the throne. Richard is not an evil man. He has even p-protected Bolingbroke's son, while others might have k-killed him to secure the crown.'

'But he is a hostage, my lord,' cried Elizabeth, 'imprisoned in Ireland.'

Elizabeth stole my master's fur gown from his shoulders. 'Harry I love you dearly, more than my life, but oftentimes you only see what is written in that old book of yours at Leconfield.'

Hotspur pulled his gown over his wife's nakedness. 'That

old book does not speak to me anymore,' he said, shaking his head. 'And you need no armour to imitate a man. You think and act like a man, but dance like a little girl, and I love you for it.'

'See, your affliction has gone my lord. So, put your sword away for today, and we'll make more Mortimers and Percys in your father's armchair.'

'You will not change my mind,' said Hotspur kissing her neck. 'A Mortimer shall never rule in England.'

Outside the door, a hoary grey head pulled away from the keyhole. Northumberland nodded to himself, grinned and then returned his eye to the entertainment in the chamber.

Even when my master was at his lowest ebb, he never blamed anyone for the misfortunes that shaped that calamitous year. Even his wife, who I now blame for all that came after, was never privy to my master's real purpose in life or understood his strict adherence to chivalry. But then how could a woman understand chivalry unless she was brought up to violence from birth. A woman could only receive the benefits and protection of the code; or am I just sour in my old age, and even all these years later, regretful that most chambers have more than one door and keyhole to spy through.

As for Hotspur, he still firmly believed that chivalry might end wars for all time. But in those far off days, I thought the purest form of chivalry was peace. And when the new Duke of Lancaster came back to England in the summer of that year Hotspur was more determined than ever that he would challenge his friend. More than anything else, he wished to see if Bolingbroke was a true Christian knight or just a common thief.

18

White Friars 1399

'To Dancaster he rode full manfully'

Henry Bolingbroke first landed in England at Holderness in Yorkshire. But he was soon forced to ride from Ravenspur north along the east coast to find a safe haven where he could be more confident of Percy support.

My master and I had been tasked with raising men on the border. From there we scoured the Ridings of Yorkshire until fully mustered with archers and men-at-arms. Then we marched south towards the Don River, there to meet Bolingbroke's entourage who had been escorted from the coast by the Earl of Northumberland and many other nobles who had rallied to his cause.

The day was stifling hot, and when we arrived at Doncaster, we were surprised to be greeted by Ralph Neville, Earl of Westmoreland, who galloped across the bridge with an armed escort. We could see his large force encamped on the opposite bank of the river and Hotspur immediately rode out at speed to greet his cousin with his lance couched under his uninjured left arm.

Everyone was surprised by the challenge, but not Westmoreland who met Hotspur in a similar frame of mind. A loud splintering of wood told us that the winner of the contest was uncertain and Neville whooped with delight.

'That's a draw!' he said, throwing open his visor.

'Go again!' shouted my master wheeling his horse.

But Ralph lowered his lance. 'No, we must save ourselves Harry, for the coming fight.'

'Then match me w-with your sword.'

'My father was cross with you last time we met,' replied Neville as Hotspur rode past him. 'That Badby affair was a sad business.'

'That was years ago,' said Hotspur drawing his sword. 'Perhaps your father w-wanted a war with the Scots? Do you w-want a fight or not?'

Neville held up his hand in submission. 'My father wanted peace on the border, and between our two families, you know that. That's why he never pursued the Badby case any further.'

Hotspur bowed his head. 'I was w-wounded to hear of your father's death.'

The sad look on Ralph's face matched his newfound prominence as the first Earl of Westmoreland; a position his father had craved and worked tirelessly for but never achieved in his lifetime.

Ralph pointed at the town of Doncaster, partially obscured by mist. 'They are giving thanks to God for Bolingbroke's safe passage through England,' he said. 'But I fear a blessing at White Friars will not be enough. The Duke of York's army is marching towards us and then it will either be a crown for Lancaster or a quartering for us.'

Hotspur set his teeth. 'What d-do you mean a crown for Lancaster?'

'Bolingbroke's claim, what of it?'

'Make yourself plain R-Ralph, what are you d-doing here?'

'Not for money, that's for sure. Your father has the lion's share of that, and I'll wager you do too.'

'What d-did you say about a crown?'

'I want my share of the north when Bolingbroke becomes king.'

Hotspur shook his head. 'Then you have b-been deceived cousin.'

'What?'

My master turned in the saddle and signalled for our contingents to cross the stone bridge spanning the river.

'Harry, what do you know about this?' pleaded Westmoreland, 'I have a right to know—'

'I will tell you p-presently Ralph. Rouse your men and ride with me to White Friars,' exclaimed Hotspur releasing Neville's bridle. 'We must stop this.'

But despite my master's previous assurances from his father and uncle, there were men across the river that had their own ideas about where the crown should sit. The former Archbishop of Canterbury, a lofty prelate with a tearful disposition, was stood in the shadows of the white-stoned Carmelite priory. And as Northumberland and Bolingbroke emerged arm in arm from its ivy-adorned porch, the pale-faced prelate sat down in a shady alcove to rest.

'Harry!' yelled Bolingbroke rushing forward. He took my

master's hand warmly in his glove and glanced at Neville nodding agreeably. 'And you too Westmoreland. Now we shall prevail.'

A great cheer went up from the converging armies as Bolingbroke strode forward with his friends. And when he raised his fist above the sea of soldiers, more gathered to hear him speak. His power over them was plain to see. Stiffened banners bearing their lord's heraldic signatures waved emphatically in the still air, a forest of weapons endorsed each soldier's willingness to serve Lancaster, and Hotspur immediately became suspicious of his friend's intentions. Behind him, in the shadows, Archbishop Arundel cradled a gilt-edged reliquary in his arms, and Hotspur knew what holy purposes they served.

Bolingbroke detected the concerned look on Hotspur's face, and he knew from childhood experience that his friend had questions.

'I knew you would come Harry,' whispered Bolingbroke waving at the crowd.

The remark took my master back to his last meeting with his friend at Coventry, and it chilled him to the bone. But when Lancaster embraced Hotspur and kissed him on each cheek, my master detected Bolingbroke's greeting was more forceful than usual. There was an urgency in his eyes, and he kept a close eye on Arundel and the casket he was holding.

'Why the sad face my friend?' said Bolingbroke, still waving to his soldiers. 'Are you not glad to see me?'

'I would be g-glad if I knew your mind cousin.'

'My mind's made up now my father is dead. I told you at Coventry I would return to claim my right.'

Hotspur gnawed at his lip. 'And w-what is your right?'

Bolingbroke continued to wave. 'I've made assurances before God and sworn an oath on the holy relics Arundel is holding in his lap—'

'To not seek the crown?'

Lancaster's eyes never left the crowd. 'What do you take me for Harry, a liar? I told you, God has urged me to reclaim my inheritance.'

My master stepped back to let Bolingbroke address the army. He took his place beside the Earl of Westmoreland who urged Archbishop Arundel to join them on the raised terrace. I saw the prelate tremble when Hotspur drew near, and when Lancaster began to speak, he began to sweat like a roasted hog.

'Soldiers of the north,' cried Bolingbroke confidently. 'I have come into England to save it, and you, from tyranny. With God's help, we can win back England's freedom and see to it that the king never again steals our livelihoods and levies false taxes. I damn any man who fails to challenge those who wish to seize the property of any trueborn Englishman. By this action, the perpetrator commits treason against his people and deserves a punishment worthy of the crime.'

Another cheer went up, and Bolingbroke calmed the army with a wave of his hand. 'God will see that right prevails,' he continued, 'and be assured I will be in the forefront of all our battles if we have to fight against those that come against us. This is a holy cause and if any of us are called upon to die, then God, who sees and knows everything, will greet us in paradise in all his glory.' The army cheered him again. 'So come, let us all take a new oath of fealty. Let us do what is right and lawful to remove the king's false ministers and free England from bad governance. The time and hour are upon us, my friends...'

Archbishop Arundel stepped forward carrying the reliquary in his arms, and there was a collective rattle of weapons as the army knelt to take the oath. Hotspur, Westmoreland and I knelt too as everyone crossed themselves and repeated the archbishop's words. It was a call to arms that each soldier understood. And before we joined the Earl of Northumberland in the priory to give thanks to God for Bolingbroke's return, I saw my master shaking his head as if to be free of the words he had just spoken.

Archbishop Arundel was still faint and had to sit on the altar steps while a monk brought him a cup of wine. He was deep in thought, and his face was the colour of unbaked bread. Everyone knew his enforced exile following his appellant brother's execution had not been easy. It had taken a terrible toll on his health. But now there was something else worrying him that made my master uneasy and mistrustful of Bolingbroke and his choice of close confidant.

'So, does anyone know where York's blasted army is?' said Northumberland once the priory door was closed and barred.

'He's marching north,' answered Westmoreland.

'No, he's marching w-west to join the k-king in Wales,' said Hotspur.

Hotspur's father grinned at Neville's mistake.

'Ah, then we have time,' said Bolingbroke giving Arundel another cup of wine.

My master frowned. 'Time for w-what my lord?'

'To increase our power, what else? We must rouse others of like mind to our cause. Many nobles will be fearful of losing their inheritances too.'

'There are rumours you w-want the throne,' said Hotspur

flatly.

'I told you, Harry, I have sworn an oath on holy relics only to reclaim what is mine. Everyone in England knows that.'

'I know of no oath.'

Northumberland stepped forward, shaking his fist at his son.

'Swear again,' said Hotspur

Arundel and Northumberland stared in disbelief, and the archbishop buried the reliquary deeper within his robes.

'By all the saints, why does he have to swear again?' spat Northumberland. 'You cause me no end of trouble boy with your—'

'It should b-be no hardship father,' suggested Hotspur. 'My friend has b-but to lay his hands upon the reliquary and swear again. What d-do you say, Westmoreland?'

Ralph Neville shrugged his shoulders.

'Keep out of this Neville. I know your game!' snapped Northumberland.

Westmoreland's hand went to his sword.

'My lords, my lords, enough of all this bad blood,' said Bolingbroke, 'we are in God's house. We have re-affirmed our loyalty to each other and stifled our past differences with a common aim. This is not the time to quarrel among ourselves; we have a holy task to perform, and must all be of one voice.'

'I b-bear no ill will against you, my friend,' said Hotspur to Bolingbroke. 'But I fear others have misled you.'

'And who is that?' exclaimed Northumberland. 'I see only one enemy here—'

My master stayed Westmoreland's hand on his sword and pointed at the reliquary sat in Arundel's lap. 'Whose holy r-r-relics are in the casket my lord archbishop?'

Arundel quaffed another mouthful of wine. 'Why, the bones of Saint John of Beverley of course,' he said, 'the same that my lord of Lancaster touched after landing in England.'

'Then let me see inside,' said Hotspur

Arundel sat bolt upright. 'No, that's sacrilege!'

'Show me, or I will take my men back to their p-ploughshares.'

'Give it here,' exclaimed Bolingbroke reaching out to place his hands on the casket.

But as he did so, my master swept the box from Arundel, and everyone stared as three silver nobles tumbled out onto the stone floor.

Bolingbroke was distraught, unable to speak. And Northumberland stepped back into the shadows biting his nails.

Westmoreland picked up the shrine and examined it gazing at the archbishop. 'My men swore on a few coins?' he said. 'What kind of mercenary trick is this Bolingbroke?'

Lancaster's voice trembled with anger. 'Arundel, explain yourself,'

The archbishop's words were spiteful and to the point. 'The king deserves to die,' he said. 'Don't you see he will have us all killed if we let him live? He's a tyrant and holds council with the Devil.' The archbishop sighed and burst into tears. 'Forgive me, my lords, I know the Duke of Lancaster is a true and just man, but how could I let him swear to take back only his inheritance. The king has deceived us all. He made me lure my brother out of hiding under safe conduct only to have him beheaded like a common criminal!'

Bolingbroke was deeply troubled. He knew that the Earl of Arundel's death was his father's doing, but he could never disclose that to the archbishop. He had saved himself from Richard's vengeance at the expense of others. But Hotspur went further, and he bid me pass him a heavy bound bible from the altarpiece.

He held it before Bolingbroke.

'Swear that you have only come b-b-back to England to claim that which is rightfully yours,' said Hotspur.

'What?'

'Namely, the lands and titles that Lancaster p-previously held by right of King Edward the third. Swear it—'

'You have my word,' said Bolingbroke.

'Place your hand on the b-book.'

Everyone stared in disbelief at Hotspur's audacity, and Northumberland edged forward from the shadows gazing not at his son, but at Bolingbroke's hesitancy. Hotspur saw his father's hands were clenched tightly in prayer, willing Lancaster to take the oath with every ounce of penitence he could muster.

'This is all…madness…' laughed Bolingbroke nervously.

My master seized his friend's right hand and slammed it on the leather-bound cover of the book.

'Swear to G-God that you will not take the crown!'

'Harry you know that I—'

'Swear it, or I will d-disband my army!'

Now a look of hate swept across Bolingbroke's face, and he eased his hand back so that the palm barely touched the cover.

Hotspur drew it up and slammed it back down again. 'Swear!'

'You go too far!'

'Swear!'

'I swear that I...will not...usurp the throne!'

Bolingbroke's nervous admission echoed in the vaulted ceiling of the priory like a shout of defiance, and my master nodded agreeably. Northumberland heaved a sigh of relief, and each man looked to himself and measured what the oath meant to him personally. Even I wondered what might happen next.

In the end, Bolingbroke stormed from the priory closely followed by Hotspur's father. I saw Lancaster push the great earl away and rebuke him severely. Arundel's head fell into his upraised hands, and when he too skulked away, Westmoreland looked to my master whose breath had quickened as if he had run a race.

'Good God Harry, Lancaster has you marked now,' he said.

'It will not be the first...or last time...we have...not seen eye to eye.'

'You would go against your father, your family, to serve a tyrant? You know Bolingbroke covets the crown. He has no other course open to him now you must see that?'

'And you must...see we were all...about to be deceived.'

'You may have to fight Bolingbroke one day, Harry,' said Westmoreland gravely. 'He will have the throne by hook or by crook.'

'No, you are wrong, Arundel was behind all this...Bolingbroke needs my help, now more than ever. I will speak to the king...when he returns from Ireland...he will listen to me.'

'Then we must leave tonight,' said Neville.

Hotspur nodded and bid me to follow him. 'Get the men ready Hardyng...'

'If time is on our side, we can stop York joining the king,' added Neville watching Hotspur sink to his knees.

I gave my master a flask of wine to drink, and he gazed at the stone crucifix hanging behind the altar.

'Tell no one of this...' said Hotspur.

'What ails you, Harry?' said Ralph shocked. 'Have you seen this before Hardyng?'

I nodded, and Hotspur cast the wine aside. 'My mother... she suffered the same affliction...'

Ralph helped Hotspur to his feet. 'Thank God I'm not plagued by it, but my aunt...I remember she suffered from some affliction.'

'I need...I need my horse Hardyng...where's Parzival?'

Hotspur stumbled away not waiting for my answer and Ralph marvelled at his hasty departure. 'Good God, I had no idea Hardyng,' he said. 'I will pray for him.'

'A hard ride is a good healer, my lord,' said I, chasing after my master.

'I've heard time is a good medicine too!' I heard him shout.

But as we all know, time is a fickle master and a constant hindrance to those desperate to tame it. Even Hotspur's speedy exit could not overtake the multitude of events set in motion by Bolingbroke's landing in England. In a few days, many discontented nobles flocked to Lancaster's standard. The kingdom was hungry for change, and this urge went against all my master's notions of loyal service. He yearned to save his king and fulfil his sacred duty as a true knight.

But no one could halt the sand passing through the hourglass.

19

North Wales 1399

'And then the Kyng, at Flynt as was seene'

In the space of a few weeks, most men began to view Richard's rule with disdain. Most English nobles were fearful of losing their inheritances, and the Lancastrian army more than doubled in size by the time it marched west. In the end, only a few English towns, such as Bristol and Chester, remained loyal to King Richard. The few followers who landed with the king in Wales soon deserted his cause, including Thomas Percy, and he soon joined his elder brother and nephew then marching on Chester.

Their combined forces created a threat that the Duke of York could not ignore, and York's fickle army crumbled without a major battle. Thereafter fortune rapidly turned against the king, forcing him to take refuge in Conwy Castle where the Earl of Salisbury was his only supporter. With Chester still offering up strong resistance Richard might have hope for better times, but in the end, the town soon fell to Bolingbroke who ordered Hotspur to keep the peace while he and Northumberland rode into Wales to seek out the king.

Despite being hounded into a corner, Richard still refused to believe he was in danger. The king never lacked self-confidence when his mind was made up and always believed that his divine status was sacrosanct. During the past few years, he had learned to survive without his uncle, John of Gaunt, and his murdered ministers. He had quelled a peasant's revolt in London in the past, outlived major rebellions by leading nobles and was still more determined than ever to pursue an autocratic rule. He was a prince chosen by God to rule England, he said, and in this mood, Richard lacked no courage either, despite his lack of martial skill. However, when Hotspur received news in Chester that his father had captured the king in Wales, he became increasingly anxious. Bolingbroke's oath was only to purge Richard's government and chastise him, not arrest and imprison him. Therefore a little before the Feast of the Assumption, Hotspur and I rode hard for Flint Castle to ensure Lancaster's oath was not further violated.

Flint was, and is now, the first of an iron ring of castles protecting North Wales. Its grim millstone grit walls are so thick that they can resist most siege engines apart from bombards. Its massive round keep is impregnable. A wide moat surrounds it at high tide, and the castle's bleak uninterrupted outlook commands the coast, the Dee estuary and landward approaches into the Principality. Therefore, in those days, Flint was the gateway to Wales. However, when Hotspur and I arrived there on a cloudy and overcast Monday morning, there was a large army encamped within a bowshot of its walls. The castle looked like it was being besieged. And we were careful not to forecast our arrival as we clattered our horses across the drawbridge.

Among the nobles inside, the Earl of Northumberland was the least happy to see us, and he remonstrated against his son's desertion of Chester despite Hotspur's raging mood.

'What in God's name are you doing here boy?' he said shocked.

'Chester is subdued,' replied Hotspur confidently. 'Where is the k-king?'

Bolingbroke greeted my master with a forced smile. He was knawing his lip, and his agitation was aimed at Thomas Percy, who was calmly reading an old legal document that he held up to a lantern. Archbishop Arundel, who had recovered some of his confidence since Doncaster, moved between them deep in thought and everyone in the dimly lit corridor appeared annoyed.

The curving inner gallery was deserted apart from two guards who stood with polearms flanking one of the iron-studded doors. Flames from a brazier danced on the granite walls and the feeling that Flint was a prison poisoned my master's thoughts against everyone present.

Hotspur looking around repeated his question, but nobody answered.

Bolingbroke nodded beyond the guarded door, and my master approached the two soldiers who crossed their polearms before his face.

'Let me pass!' he said, unsheathing his dagger.

Northumberland pulled him aside. 'What do you take us for boy, murderers?'

'The king is well Harry,' assured Thomas Percy calmly, 'but

your father is right, you should be in Chester.'

'Westmoreland is there.'

'Neville?' gasped Northumberland. 'I hope you've killed all those Cheshire archers first, or Neville will retain them for his own.'

'Be assured father the town is subdued. And I have assured all the p-people that our king will soon g-greet them in p-person.'

'That will do no good,' said Bolingbroke taking Hotspur's arm. 'Richard is adamant and will not budge from his corrupt policies.'

Hotspur shook Bolingbroke off. 'Then I w-will know his mind myself.'

Bolingbroke sighed. 'He is irresolute Harry, believe me, his feathers are ruffled, but he still preens like a peacock.'

My master drew his dagger again, and everyone stepped back. 'Let me pass!' he said, threatening the guards.

'You go too far boy,' snapped Northumberland stopping him. 'I'll wager your mother dropped you at birth.'

Hotspur turned his blade on his father. 'I am Warden of the East March, and I will see my master the king.'

'Let him pass,' said Thomas Percy. 'God knows we have tried our best. Perhaps Harry can ease the king's mood.'

Bolingbroke waved his hand dismissively. 'Be sure his milk-white words don't sour you against us, my friend. I have already told him that I have come to help him better govern the kingdom, not take his crown.'

Hotspur flicked his dagger upwards, and the two sentries parted.

My master told me later that inside the great chamber, the king was squat quietly in a corner humming. His raw-boned knees were drawn up to his chest, he was wearing a simple linen gown, and his armour was strewn on the floor in pieces. It was as if a storm had gusted through the chamber and only Richard's gold coronet, balanced between his thumb and forefinger, remained unspoilt and symbolic of his high estate.

'Have you come to kill me Harry?' asked Richard quietly.

Hotspur sheathed his dagger.

'They ambushed me like I was a foreign power, my dear Hotspur,' continued the king almost in tears. 'But then I have always been a foreigner to Bolingbroke have I not? He never liked me because I was born in France and was different from everyone else. Now even you, my dear Hotspur, have deserted me. What is to become of chivalry now my champion has fallen from grace?'

'No sire, I w-will never—'

The king raised his hand. 'No, please, my dear Hotspur, I've heard enough lies for one day. When we were children, things were much simpler. Do you remember you were different in those days too? You always protected me. Always w-w-wanting a fight,' said Richard playfully. 'But will you fight for me now I wonder?'

'I will sire, but you must give B-Bolingbroke what is his by right.'

'If I give him his lands, he'll take my crown!'

'He swore an oath before God.'

'I heard about what you did at the White Friars...very funny...but Bolingbroke is a liar. They are all liars, even your father.'

Richard stood up quickly, regally placed the crown on his head and pointed an accusing finger at Hotspur. A change came over him as he spoke, and Hotspur said to me later that even he was scared of Richard's wild staring eyes.

'He who raises my people and rides to make war against me in my realm of England will be duly attainted and judged a traitor. You too are guilty, and I swear that whatever assurances I may give to Henry of Lancaster, someday I shall put him to a bitter and utter end for the outrages and injury he has done to us this day.'

'I have an army at Chester, Your Majesty,' said Hotspur.

'Then why have you not destroyed Bolingbroke already?'

Hotspur hesitated. 'And g-go against my father and uncle?'

'But I am your rightful king! Have they not told you how your uncle deserted me? How your father lied to me at Conwy and then ambushed me with a band of brigands? How they still assure me that I will be allowed to rule providing I give credence to Bolingbroke's inheritance? Don't they know that I know they will kill me and take my crown when my back is turned?'

The king paused for breath. Tears were welling in his eyes, and the crown was slipping from his hands.

'Yes, when we were at Kenilworth, it was much simpler,' he continued.' Was it always not so my dear Hotspur? Everyone said that Bolingbroke looked like a king, walked like a king, talked like a king and fought like a king. What about me? I am the son of Edward the Black Prince of Wales!'

Richard began to cry. He was becoming exhausted by his ranting, and after his last outburst, he squeezed himself back into the corner.

There was a moment of silence, and as the wind howled through the arrow loops, the king slithered down the wall into his previous hunched position. He gave out a long sigh. He stared into oblivion. Then, without warning, he threw

Hotspur the crown.

It clanged to the floor, rolled, and stopped at my master's feet.

'Take it and give it to him; I do not need it now. But remember I will still be your anointed king even if Bolingbroke decides to wear it.'

'Sire, if I can k-keep Bolingbroke to his oath, w-will you ride with me to Chester?'

'What then my dear Hotspur?'

'Chester will p-protect you sire, but you must restore Bolingbroke's inheritance.'

'But don't you see he's just like his father? Too overmighty to bow to a king, and he will be overmightier still if I give him back his lands and power. All I want is peace...peace in England...with France...the world. And Bolingbroke is his father incarnate, and I will see him without a head, or die in the attempt.'

Richard smoothed his thin russet beard into a point and placed his index finger on his cracked lips. 'I know what you did for Robert at Radcot Bridge, my dear Hotspur,' he said, 'that's why I let you live.'

'Then you must k-know sire I am no traitor.'

Richard's eyes closed. 'If I restore Bolingbroke's inheritance, you will keep your word?'

Hotspur nodded, and bowing to the king, turned to leave.

'And how is my dearest Robert?' asked Richard earnestly.

My master knew de Vere had recently died in exile. 'He is well sire...and—'

'You could never lie well Harry, unlike those men outside who wish me dead. That's why I will follow your banner and leave the rest to God and his angels.'

'Yes, Your Majesty.'

Hotspur was embarrassed by his attempted cover-up of de Vere's death, but he bowed again to the king and opened the door.

The king shook his head and began to hum again to himself. It was the last pleasant sound my master ever heard from Richard of Bordeaux, and he left the vaulted chamber unsure of the promise he had made.

Once outside, everyone rushed forward except Thomas Percy who listened to what Hotspur had to say from a safe distance. There was a point at which I thought my master was enjoying the power of knowing the king's mind. For once in his life, he commanded all his peers, and despite the king's paranoia and otherworldly notions of kingship, he was confident now that there might be hope for his sovereign.

'He will return w-what is yours,' said Hotspur to Bolingbroke, 'but we must convey him to Chester.'

'No!' cried Northumberland.

'We will all be murdered in our beds!' said Bolingbroke,

'Chester is ours, no thanks to you, my lord,' replied Hotspur casting Bolingbroke a sour glance. 'If your men had refrained from p-p-pillaging the town then you would not be so w-worried about your bedchamber.'

'That looting was Westmoreland's work Harry,' replied Bolingbroke.

'Yes, it was Neville,' interrupted Northumberland eagerly. 'All his men are cut-throats and thieves...'

Hotspur eyed Thomas Percy who had said nothing so far. 'I have done your bidding uncle,' said my master sourly. 'The king has agreed to restore Lancaster if he p-promises not to steal the crown.'

Thomas Percy nodded. 'Thanks, Harry. We would do well to march to Chester my lords,' he said bowing. 'England should see that their king still lives.'

Everyone was amazed at Thomas Percy's calmness. Everyone agreed to the plan as there was no other way the king could be moved involuntarily, and no one wished to inflame Hotspur's famous temper or feel his dagger at their throats.

As for my master, he thought that in the staunch royalist town of Chester, he could more easily protect the king and see that Bolingbroke kept to his word. However, some plans are simply words cast irreverently on the wind; and that same wind was blowing ever harder in favour of the new Duke of Lancaster.

20

Borders 1400

*'There ys no lorde that may defende you agayn
Scotlande soo well as he'*

As dawn broke clear and frosty above Roxburgh Castle, my master and I prepared for a hard day in the saddle. Hotspur said his farewells to his wife, and she reminded him not to be late for her celebrations that night. It was the feast day of Saint Valentine, and several northern lords were invited, including Ralph Neville Earl of Westmoreland who was riding from Pomfret to speak with Hostpur urgently.

Our journey that day would be a dangerous one taking us to the east coast and back, but Lady Percy seemed not to be concerned with our safety only our punctuality. Lately, my master had lapsed into one of the dark moods that prevented him from conversing or abiding anyone's company, and she hoped that a long ride might rid him of the many demons that troubled his mind ever since returning from Chester.

All of Hotspur's demons had re-surfaced because of Bolingbroke. The moment Hotspur and his father were dismissed from Chester, Lancaster had been acclaimed King of England by a consensus. Richard, still very much alive, had been imprisoned in fear of a rebellion to restore him to the throne. He had been forced to abdicate in favour of Bolingbroke and was sent promptly to the Tower where he languished in the royal apartments for months without a crown or kingdom. In short, Bolingbroke had broken his sacred oath made at Doncaster. He had lied to Hotspur and the Percys. And in his first parliament as King Henry, the fourth of that name, he wasted no time in legitimising his action by charging his cousin Richard with incompetency and treason against his own people. Bolingbroke's victory was complete but hollow, and in the same parliament, the Percys received great titles and appointments despite their feelings of betrayal. It was a whirlwind of change, and it angered Hotspur so much that he failed to attend Henry's coronation even though lavish robes had been specially prepared for him and his wife.

In gratitude for their help, the king granted the Percys control of both the east and west marches towards Scotland for the unprecedented period of ten years. All the family received generous grants, castles and annuities for life. The Earl of Northumberland was made Constable of England and was awarded two-thirds of the young Earl of March's inheritance. Hotspur, despite his fury at Henry's usurpation, was rewarded with the captaincies of Roxburgh and Bamburgh castles, the Justiciar of Chester, North Wales, Flintshire, along with many other garrisons that had become vacant. The king also granted Hotspur the entire Mortimer lordship during the minority of his young nephew Edmund. And as for his uncle, Thomas Percy, he became King Henry's right-hand man, the Admiral of England, and the king's Lieutenant of South Wales, receiving numerous other annuities as befitting his lofty position as Earl of Worcester.

The flood of Lancastrian generosity was so all-consuming and premeditated that it sickened my master to the core. It seemed that he was now associated with the dual crimes of perjury and usurpation, and as he spurred his horse Parzival over the River Tweed that frosty morning I became increasingly fearful of his mood.

In this disposition of mind, Hotspur was at his most dangerous, but what worried me more was that we had to cross the agreed border to carry out our marcher duties. This wild country was Scots territory, and, to add to my fears, Hotspur was still drunk from the night before. He was also carrying additional flasks of wine to sustain his flagging spirits during the journey, and I noticed that a grim rebellious nature had come over him that I dared not question.

It was never quiet on the border. Even in times of truce, there was constant cross-border feuding. Families raided and pillaged other families as a means to survive from one day to the next. But pickings were small. Due to continuous warring with England, the border was a burnt-out swathe of destroyed farmsteads, wasted croplands and unburied corpses. The sweeping hills, mountains and desolate moors were bereft of sheep, cows and livestock. The people huddled in clans or moved on to seek protection with great lairds such as the Scots march wardens who might punish their neighbours for them. Family warring and private feuding went back generations. It would never change. But we English were always considered the real foe, and against this threat, the Scots united in a common cause when it suited them to invade the north.

With his usual speed, my master despatched law and order against this ever-changing landscape of uncertainty, and in so doing, he lived up to his nickname of Hotspur in every way. His presence was even felt in areas beyond his jurisdiction, much to the annoyance of the Scots. And that day in February was no exception. We had a dangerous journey ahead of us to deliver arms and men to the beleaguered garrison of Fast Castle.

The east coast was a tough three-hour ride from Roxburgh, and along the way, we had to apprehend a small band of reivers who had been destroying farms on our side of the border. After conducting our business at Fast Castle, we had to ride south to Berwick, where Sir Robert Umfraville would hand over a vital witness in a border dispute. This court was in session at Norham Castle, from whence we had to return to Roxburgh, a further two or three hours journey, all before Lady Percy's Valentine's feast that night - or there would be hell to pay.

But the first threat to our itinerary was not a question of time or distance. It was the ominous sighting of a band of horsemen outlined against a gap in the hills. The riders seemed to be shadowing our every move, but for the moment presented no threat. There was a truce in place, and we hoped they would see sense. So, Hotspur waved us on, keeping to our side of the border, towards a place where our reports said the Scots reivers had encamped the previous night.

My master told us that the reivers had attacked a local farm near Roxburgh. They had carried away several chickens and three sheep belonging to a local family, but the real crime was killing the farmer and his wife, who was carrying their unborn child. This outrage went against the grain with Hotspur, and aside from his sense of justice, he had vowed to punish the murderers personally.

That day we were all mounted on good strong horses and our force comprised of fifty fully armed men-at-arms carrying additional weapons and horses to relieve the garrison at Fast Castle. Therefore, provided we could find the reivers, Hotspur judged the Scots would be no match for us. However, when we came across a group of grey monks near Kelso Abbey, we thought our mission was over before it began. The reivers had ridden north, the monks said, so were out of our jurisdiction. But Hotspur soon found out there was a flaw in the monk's story that everyone had overlooked and we lingered a while so that we might know their mind.

At first, my master addressed the monks with reverence. He asked one of them why monks of the Trionensain Order were so far from their enclave. Did they want an escort back to the abbey perhaps? He told them that the reivers might come back and would not discriminate between who they killed or robbed. The eldest monk said that they were simple friars out gathering medicinal herbs for their brothers at Kelso, but this answer so displeased my master that he ran the monk through with his sword.

The rest of the friars ran for their lives but were soon chased down and killed by my master before they could retrieve their horses in the bushes. We were all astonished by Hotspur's rash thinking and callous action. However, he soon revealed the truth to us. None of us had noticed that the monks had no tonsures and that they wore riding boots under their habits.

Their discarded armour and a pile of stripped chicken bones beside the nearby fire proved they were the reivers beyond doubt, and in relief, we all laughed heartily at their mistake.

But my master remained morose. He drank another flask of wine from his saddlebag, cleaned his sword of blood and with a stern shout of, 'Avaunt!' dug his spurs hard into Parzival's flanks.

Our next destination was Fast Castle on the Northumberland coast. A journey which involved riding across lowland Scotland and braving the rugged country that in any hidden ravine might hold an entire Scots army. Hotspur increased the pace. It was a race against time and survival, especially for the beleaguered garrison that depended on us. The new Earl of Douglas was at large, and the Scots Earl of March, George Dunbar, had also been reported near Berwick. Any one of these powerful lairds might ambush us, said Hotspur, and to our horror, the ghostly horsemen on the horizon were still following our every twist and turn along the Tweed.

Fast Castle stood on a promontory of rock lashed by the winter swells of the North Sea. The garrison captain rode out to greet us as we approached and asked us our business. He said his castle was well stocked for the winter, that his soldiers were all fresh recruits and that he did not anticipate any unseasonable campaigning by the Scots until at least spring. Our horses were blown, and Hotspur complained that he had received word at Roxburgh that they needed help and arms urgently. The captain shook his head, and immediately we suspected another deception - although the captain made sure he was safely back inside the castle first.

When we heard the drawbridge rattle up and saw a Douglas flag hoisted above the battlements, we all knew what had happened. The fresh recruits and the captain were Scots. They had taken the castle already from the English garrison, and we set about wondering how we could take back to save face.

There were sheer cliffs on either side of the seemingly impregnable fortress, and a barbican and drawbridge protected the landward side of the peninsula. I thought it an impossible task to reverse the humiliating situation we found ourselves in, but Hotspur ordered our men to use the bows meant for the garrison and set light to two dozen arrows wrapped with sackcloth.

'Burn the bridge!' he ordered, and my master took another long drink from his flask of wine, bidding me sit beside him.

'You're my b-best squire Master Hardyng,' he said drunkenly, 'but you say little.'

'I'm your only squire, my lord.'

'Ha, so you are, and for a g-good reason. I hear you're a g-good scrivener?'

I nodded and saw the wooden drawbridge catch light.

'Then I'll g-give you something to w-w-write about,' he said ordering some of his men down another ravine that ran adjacent to the promontory.

Smoke was in our faces as we followed Hotspur under the barbican. A wall of rock rose before us with a crevice running through it, and this led to a small cave barely wide enough for a man to squeeze through. Beyond this we climbed upwards, aided by lighted torches and presently we found a staircase. My master told me that the previous constable had shown him the secret passage some years before and soon our small force emerged through a trapdoor in the castle chapel, much to the surprise of the Scots who were all trying to extinguish the burning drawbridge.

'Stay here Hardyng,' said Hotspur, as our men unsheathed their swords. 'And be certain to make a true r-r-record of my feats of arms.'

I had no time to answer, and I wondered why I could not protect my master in the time-honoured fashion by following him into battle. I was well versed in arms by now, but when I ignored Hotspur's words, I was severely scolded by him, and from that moment on, I became a bystander.

However, in a surge of energy, surprise and clash of arms, the fight for the castle was soon over. Some of the Scots were killed by us, some were wounded, while others were taken prisoner by the original garrison once released from the dungeons. We replenished the castle as planned and saved the grateful captain's reputation, who in thanks supplied us with fresh horses so that we could ride on to Berwick.

Hotspur refused the offer of a new horse and rode on with Parzival who never complained of ill-treatment. Jet black and fearless, we all wondered at his stamina and willingness to endure my master's tireless spurring. And our next mission was to speed an important witness to the March Day at Norham that afternoon; that is if the horseman still following us did not attack us before we got there.

The coastal road was always treacherous in winter, and we made even slower progress due to an icy blast that suddenly lashed us with salt spray. The wintry sea squall was unrelenting, but we soon sighted Berwick Castle in the distance, and my master pulled Parzival up sharply. It was well known to all of us that Hotspur refused to enter the town due to the prophecy served to him at Westminster, and in his place, Sir Robert Umfraville had acquired the responsibility for

Berwick for a term of five years. Despite my master's previous dismissive attitude to the curse, it had become a much more serious matter for him due to his father. Northumberland expected his son Hotspur to fulfil his duties as march warden and the embarrassment of non-attendance was a pressure that my master was reminded of time and time again.

So that afternoon we were all relieved when two men emerged from the gatehouse of Berwick Castle bearing the Umfraville banner. My master strained to see the identity of the second horseman as he was wearing a cloak and hood, but there was no doubting my master's icy stare at Umfraville as he drew near.

Sir Robert still bore inward scars of the fight at Otterburn, and even further back, the betrayal of Hotspur's trust when forced to tell the Earl of Northumberland about Thomas Crackenthorpe's death. To add to his woes, a few years previous Hotspur's injured younger brother Ralph had taken Umfraville's advice to seek a cure for his unhealed leg in the Holy Land. Ralph yearned for knightly service once more, and the rift between Hotspur and Umfraville had deepened when Ralph was killed by a band of Saracens who ambushed him near Jerusalem. The split between my master and his old companion was irreconcilable. However, there was a dutiful air of respect between the two knights as they parted company at Berwick and wished each other well.

As for our itinerary, we immediately rode west following the River Tweed with the identity of our hooded witness still shrouded in mystery. Lately, there had been a severe breach of the truce aimed at Sir Thomas Grey, the constable of Norham Castle. Archibald Douglas had accused Grey's men of plundering a number of his towns for nothing other than pleasure. It seemed that the constable of Norham was out of control, said Douglas, and Hotspur had the unenviable task of judging the case even though Grey was his father's retainer. Accusations and counter-accusations had almost led to open warfare with England. But thankfully our witness, whoever he was, had seen the plundering of Douglas's towns with his own eyes and this evidence had postponed hostilities until he could be heard in court.

I was told that our witness had a mutual desire to keep the peace on the border and to ensure that the business of March Law was smoothly and fairly dealt with on behalf of King Henry. The hooded man would speak on behalf of Grey, but it was debatable whether Douglas would accept the invitation to parley, and this might render the tribunal 'fouled' due to favouritism. Such were the workings of law between the two kingdoms, and at this point, we conjectured that our unidentified pursuers on the horizon might be Douglas and his men.

But when we reached Norham and ascended to the great hall, there was already a Scots presence inside. Lord Grey was upbraiding the ageing Archibald Douglas. Both sides had drawn their weapons, and despite the Scots having letters of safe passage, it seemed someone was about to be injured. However, my master soon put a stop to the argument by ordering servants to bring wine and food for everyone. It was an unconventional way of enforcing the law, but it had the desired effect by forcing each side to take their places at the meeting table.

Douglas was the first to put his petition forward, and Grey answered that neither he nor his men were responsible for the destruction of his towns. Despite his past conduct across the border - which he admitted was an oversight - Grey said that the Earl of Northumberland had restrained him. He then spoke about the reivers that had lately been pillaging lowland livestock and reminded everyone that he had not broken his oath even to oppose these outrages. Hotspur assured him that he had already punished the reivers and the Scots growled their disapproval. However, there were a few laughs from both sides when Hotspur explained what had occurred near Kelso that morning.

My master's head by this time was drooping from the vast amount of wine he had consumed during the day. The fire in the hearth was hot, he was exhausted, and worse, he seemed to have little control over the large characters embroiled in the feud. Diplomacy was never Hotspur's forté, and when the hooded witness was ushered into the hall, every Scot drew their sword.

'Traitor!' shouted Douglas.

All the Scots present echoed the charge, and when George Dunbar Earl of March threw off his hood, my master's jaw dropped. Dunbar was a famous Scot's laird and a veteran of Otterburn, but it was clear to Douglas and his followers that he had now openly defied his fellow countrymen. Dunbar's voice was steady, yet his thick-set frame quivered with hate and loathing for Douglas that no one could ignore.

'Twas ah that brent yer towns,' said Dunbar boldly, 'and ah will hae at thee for all the wrongs ye hae done to mah family these past years. From now on a'm King Henry's man Douglas, and this is mah big glove tae prove it!'

Dunbar threw down his metal gauntlet at Douglas's feet, and the clang awoke the sleeping demons in Hotspur. He had not realised what troublesome baggage he had brought with him from Berwick and now to act on anyone's behalf might start another border war.

Douglas and his men tore up their safe passages before our eyes. They stormed out of the castle casting food and drink everywhere, and before Hotspur could stop the inevitable from happening, the Scots charged the sentries and joined the ghostly riders waiting for them across the valley.

I argued that we should take refuge in the castle for the night. We had another two hours ride ahead of us, and I felt that it might be our last given the trouble Dunbar had caused. But Hotspur would not stay a moment longer at Norham. He upbraided Dunbar, dismissed the court, and quickly mounted Parzival who, despite his size and fortitude, was blown and barely rested.

With fear in our hearts, we rode east to Roxburgh at a furious gallop, and it was no surprise our horses began to snort heavily after only the first mile.

Further along the Tweed, our poor mounts began to sweat profusely, and soon they became nothing more than cart horses urged on against their will. But Hotspur was not deterred, and he increased our speed until we spied our troublesome pursuers following in the distance. We felt that Douglas would descend on us at any moment. We were outnumbered and too exhausted to fight or outrun them. But as another icy blast hit us in the face, we thanked God for its intervention. It was a miracle that we did not die on those bleak uplands, and it was all due to Hotspur's determination that we managed to reach Roxburgh safely before sunset.

Ralph, Earl of Westmoreland, was waiting for us patiently in the courtyard. He had a cup of wine waiting for my master, and Lady Percy was on his arm. However, Hotspur ignored their calls to join them, and half ran, half fell, towards the north tower. From here, he rushed onto the parapet to see if the Scots were still following us, but thankfully they had disappeared into the snow-driven whiteout that had covered our retreat.

Lady Percy cried out for my master to come and join the celebrations at once, but it was only when Neville eventually caught up with my master that I became fearful that all was not well in the world.

When I caught up with him, a stern expression had creased Hotspur's worried face. Ralph Neville's naturally cordial and friendly banter was absent. I heard my master raging at him, and then he let out a gut-wrenching cry that echoed across the courtyard and castle walls. It was only later I found out that the Earl of Westmoreland had brought my master terrible news from Yorkshire.

King Richard's reign had, at last, run its tortuous course, and he had been found starved to death in a corner of Pomfret Castle.

21

York 1400

'Then he went yn harvest-tyme, so unto Scotlande'

The common talk in England was that the son of the Black Prince had wasted away in prison. And although Ralph Neville later tried to cover up the truth of the king's death, saying that Richard had caused it himself, Hotspur was sure that King Henry had condoned his murder for purely personal reasons.

Richard had been too dangerous to keep alive, said Thomas Percy years later. Rebellious talk was in the air, and despite his broken oath, Lancaster's only option was to make Richard disappear. As for my master, he was sure his friend was the guilty one, followed by the Earl of Northumberland who had pandered to Lancaster's wishes and then confined himself to Alnwick Castle feigning illness.

Hotspur, as always, turned his attention to the sword. Staring danger in the face, he participated in more irrational border raiding, this time with anyone who would follow him into Scotland. And this included the turncoat George Dunbar who decided his clandestine military ambitions against Douglas now tallied with the Percys.

The north soon returned to a battleground, and when we penetrated Scotland as far as Hailes Castle, even Hotspur thought we had overreached ourselves. Without adequate supplies, our small force was soon beaten back by the Scots. Douglas's son, also called Archibald, chased us to Cockburnspath and Dunbar's attempt to dispose of him for purely selfish reasons ended in complete disaster. I was wounded in the leg by an arrow as we retreated, and most of our men were slaughtered in the running battle back across the border.

But even this reversal did not deter the single-minded Dunbar. We needed help urgently to stop the Scots ravaging Northumberland, and Hotspur rode through the night to reach York where the king was mustering a large army to teach the Scots a lesson they would never forget.

However, my master's intentions for meeting with his erstwhile friend were far more personal. He knew that Dunbar was an able Scot well versed in military matters, and Hotspur feared that the king might consider him a contender for march warden if there was a battle for control. My master also wanted to speak to the king face to face and know the real truth about Richard's death, or he knew his guilt would continue to haunt him and double the demons now plaguing his sleep at night.

But at York, my master's fears about Richard's demise were soon quashed by King Henry. He received Hotspur warmly as a trusted friend and showed him the thousands of soldiers, horses and canon that were being mustered to aid him against the Scots. He introduced him to his chief captains, saying that my master was, 'the glass that everyone should dress themselves in.' It was the latest quote from his friend Thomas Walsingham, the chronicler, and for a while, it seemed as if the past belonged to a different life.

'I will make King Robert pay homage to England just like the old days,' said Henry leading Hotspur by the arm through the camp, 'and you will be there to see it Harry.'

Hotspur forced a smile.

'Then my friend we will ship to France, and together we will teach them a lesson in chivalry that will make them surrender the crown.'

My master surveyed the vast array of tents stretching across the water meadows below York's ancient walls and the thought of riding with his friend again spurred his soul. But still, the conjured images of King Richard's starved body would not let him be.

'I need to know the truth, Your Majesty,' said Hotspur.

'You mean you want a fight?' laughed King Henry. 'That would be like the Harry I used to know—'

'So, did you kill him?'

'He would not eat Harry…what could I do?'

My master visualised Richard alone in the throes of abject hunger, even thinner and more wasted than usual.

'He would not let me be,' continued the king, 'and now I will be a king and succeed where Richard failed—'

'The Scots w-will not fight you like the old d-days' sire,' said Hotspur formally. 'They will b-burn everything before you. They will not try and charge you d-down like at Halidon Hill or Nevilles Cross. Richard tried and f-failed—'

'I am not like Richard or my father,' said the king, 'and now we have Dunbar's help, we shall prevail. He knows the country well, and more importantly, he has a feud with Douglas to set him on.'

'I trust it w-w-was you sire that sent him to parley at Norham?'

The king sighed. 'He is a betrayed man in every sense of the word. Douglas wronged his daughter, his family honour is slighted, and he will stop at nothing to restore his injured pride.'

Hotspur's shoulders tensed anxiously. 'I have seen that r-rage in Dunbar's soul sire. Some of my men were k-killed because of it. God knows I almost k-k-killed him myself for his boldness!'

'And I thought you might be evenly matched...' joked the king.

King Henry held my master's stare for a few moments. Two riders were weaving between the lines of tents, and they disturbed a flock of birds that had been feasting on a discarded carcass of meat. It reminded the king of another time and place; of a lead coffin and the bones of a dead king prepared for burial.

'He did starve himself to death,' said Henry frowning at the sight of the ripped flesh and bones strewn like sticks in the grass.

But my master said nothing.

'It took fourteen days for him to die. Waterton told me that in the end, he refused to speak to anyone. You know how thin he was without fasting. In the end, his legs and arms were like drumsticks.' The king sighed. 'He was difficult to the end, and now I have to live with that for the rest of my life. Everyone wanted me to execute him, you know, including your uncle

Thomas.'

'You swore to me that your lands w-would suffice—'

'That could never be Harry. You know that.'

'But the Mortimers, R-Richard's named heirs, they are next in line to the throne.'

Henry shook his head quickly. 'Then we would have another infant king to contend with. England would be weakened beyond recovery. The French are waiting for just such a mistake. And that rising at Epiphany…they almost killed me, you know.'

'I heard that sire, and I was aggrieved.'

Hotspur gazed at the English camp and the thousands of soldiers mustered in the king's name. The support for him had not wavered since Doncaster, and it was true, he was already acting like a man who was born to be king.

'Where have you been Harry?' said Henry offering his hand to my master. 'I need you now more than ever.'

The king went to embrace Hotspur, but the riders who had just disturbed the birds feeding dismounted and bowed to him.

My master knew the aged Sir Thomas Erpingham well. He was Henry's most trusted captain, but my master had rarely seen the king's son who was at his side. Harry of Monmouth was thirteen years old, and Hotspur said to me later that the prince immediately reminded him of himself at that age. He detected a wilful and single-minded kindred spirit that he could not place but identified with completely; even more so when the young prince shunned the king's embrace.

The king's son was a handsome, studious looking boy with chestnut cropped hair. His angular features were reminiscent of classical statues, or a young cleric, rather than that of a warrior in training. He wore fashionable clothes more suited to the late king than a son of Lancaster and when he beheld my master he was noticeably in awe of him. He stood before Hotspur carefully examining his armour and weapons with jealous admiration. Then he drew out his short sword and held it out for my master to examine. 'They only let me have a little one,' he said, glancing at Erpingham.

'There is a r-reason for that, Highness,' replied Hotspur.

King Henry and Erpingham laughed, but the prince's blank expression spoke volumes of what single-minded feelings he had against authority.

'Here…have this one,' said Hotspur, pulling his sword from its scabbard. 'Give me yours and let me see w-w-what Sir Thomas has taught you.'

As soon as the blades were exchanged, the prince struck home with lightning speed.

'He's better with the bow,' said Erpingham retreating to a safe distance.

But the prince ignored his henchman's words and swung again at Hotspur's undersize sword, narrowly missing my master's head. Hotspur's nimble sidestep saved his life, and he angled his 'toy' sword sideways, ready to attack the prince's exposed flank. Hotspur parried the prince's thrust easily, but it was only a feint, and my master switched hands and brought his blade down to within an inch of the youngster's head.

Erpingham gasped, but before he could speak, Hotspur flattened the blade on the prince's cropped hair.

'*Vous rendez-vous?*' said Hotspur.

The prince nodded, and his father stepped forward.

'There's clearly room for improvement,' said King Henry raising his eyebrow at Erpingham.

But the prince threw down Hotspur's sword in a temper and rushed over to his horse to retrieve his bow.

'You can have my sword to p-practice with,' said Hotspur staring at the prince as he braced the weapon against his foot.

King Henry shook his head at his son's immaturity, but the prince notched an arrow to the bow and loosed it within inches of Hotspur's head.

It was if a seasoned archer had taken the prince's place. When the arrow left the bow, it arched high into the air, and we soon lost sight of it over the sea of tents. But Erpingham's keen eye followed it, and when there was a yell in the distance, we feared someone had been struck by it. There was a commotion beside a large wagon in the distance, and we all rushed over to see who had been skewered by the prince's arrow.

Soldiers were running about aimlessly. Water was brought in a leather bucket, and it appeared that there was a fire somewhere close by. Some soldiers cowered away from a stack of barrels piled on the wagon. Yet others flattened themselves on the ground, and there were shouts that the camp was under attack by the Scots.

My master and I ran between the tents, followed by the king and Erpingham.

'Black powder!' cried Hotspur seeing the barrels on the wagon.

Erpingham immediately pushed the king to the ground, and when my master jumped on the wagon, I followed him.

'No Hardyng!' said Hotspur pushing me clear.

It was a tense moment, and when he retrieved the prince's arrow from the barrels, we still had our faces buried in the grass.

'All is w-w-well,' said my master holding the arrow aloft.

'I thought you said he was good,' said the king to Erpingham, 'even I could hit a wagon at that range.'

But when Hotspur climbed down from the barrels with the prince's arrow, he had another story to tell.

'I assure you sire your son is g-good. Either that or it was a lucky strike,' he said

The king growled his disapproval. 'He could have killed us all.'

'No sire, the arrow struck the b-banner,' said Hotspur.

It was true. My master said the prince's arrow had pierced the cross of Saint George on a small standard flying above the wagon, and Henry immediately demanded an explanation from his son who proudly strutted towards us.

'From now on, you will practice with the sword only!' said the king clipping the boy on the back of the head. 'How many times do I have to tell you that archery is for low born Englishmen...not princes!'

Thomas Erpingham winced at the king's remark and ordered his soldiers to disperse back to their tents. He knew his archers worth. On the battlefields of France, they could win the day even before men-at-arms came to hand strokes, and he congratulated the prince with a sly nod of his head.

'This is the future,' crowed King Henry tapping the barrels of black powder on the wagon, 'and while we tear down the walls of Edinburgh Castle with our bombards, my son will learn from the great Hotspur about knighthood and chivalry.'

And that is how Henry, the fifth of that name, became my master's pupil. During that summer he was toughened and trained in arms, taught how to skirmish and ride like a march warden. He learned the chivalric code, how to joust like a champion and when to stare death in the face even when the odds were great. Thomas Erpingham continued to teach the prince how the humble war bow deployed in large numbers could devastate armies compacted in the field. But above all this, my master now felt that he had a new purpose in life. He shunned wine and ale from that moment on, became the perfect knight once more, and in return, the young Prince became Hotspur's second son.

The next day the army marched north, and the prince accompanied us on our visits to some of the Percy castles. We even visited Paradise to see the chained library and the famous history that had spurred on my master's career. The English army stretched for miles along the great north road, and all the greatest nobles in the land had high hopes of success against the Scots. Even the 'sick' Earl of Northumberland arrived before Edinburgh to witness its fall.

But like all those other kings before him, Richard included, Henry's invasion of Scotland failed miserably, and their armies melted away before him as Hotspur predicted. King Robert paid no homage to the English 'like in the old days', and in the end, it was everyone's opinion that Henry had wasted a great deal of money for little gain.

It was a time of continually moving borders, and now to increase King Henry's fears yet another threat to his throne was rising in the west. Its leader was a Welshman that Hotspur had met before but never since. He would bleed King Henry's war chest dry and in the end estrange his son and famous friend in the face of defeat.

Owain Glyndŵr had observed the English well, and now he aimed to free his nation from years of oppression and servitude.

22

Wales 1401

'But Owayn wane him-selfe, eche day to great estate'

The revolt in Wales had been pursued for some time before my master met with the knight whose life he saved on the road to Berwick.

Glyndŵr had a deep-rooted hatred of Reginald Lord Grey of Ruthin who, amongst other misdeeds, had accused him of not attending the king's recent invasion of Scotland. This royal summons, suppressed by Grey, escalated their existing rivalry in the marches to intense hatred. Manors and farms were raided, men were killed on both sides, and Glyndŵr's audacity sparked a long-held passion amongst other Welshmen to take up arms against their English oppressors. Under Owain's direction, another grim border war ensued, and this forced King Henry to march west into Wales to put down the rebellion.

However, Welsh tactics closely echoed those of the Scots a

few weeks before. And when the Tudor brothers of Anglesey joined Owain's rebellion, they easily captured Conwy Castle; an affront that the king could not ignore. He summoned Hotspur to take the stronghold back at his own expense, it being then under his jurisdiction, and this resulted in a stream of official letters from my master to the king asking for help and above all money to continue the siege.

But the help never came, and my master gradually became aware that lack of capital was at the root of all Henry's troubles. The king's mismanagement of proper taxation in England had rendered his war chest almost empty, and his various attempts to stamp out the recent disturbances in Wales and Scotland made the situation worse. It was now up to Hotspur and the young Prince of Wales to keep order as best they could, and from their various strongholds at Chester, Shrewsbury and Denbigh the king's son would soon receive a military education from Hotspur that he would never forget.

After pardoning the Tudors, Conwy surrendered. But King Henry was furious with my master, and from then on, Hotspur operated independently in the Principality. The broad sweep of lush valleys and mountain ranges in Wales resembled the Scots border in character, and Hotspur was everywhere despite realising that the revolt was too widespread for him to handle. Without the support of a well-paid army and trusted garrisons, he sent another letter to the king warning that Glyndŵr's men would soon occupy vast areas of Wales. Even with the support of a few loyal English marcher lords, who had their own interests at heart, my master penned in the strongest possible terms to King Henry that the rebellion was out of control.

Faced with a war on two borders of his kingdom, the

king decided once more to lure Glyndŵr out into the open. With what little money he had left in the Exchequer, he raised another army to conduct a ruthless pillaging campaign through the Welsh hills - an act of barbarity that caused Welshmen all over England to join their kinsmen in revolt.

Soon Glyndŵr proclaimed himself *Tywysog Cymru*, Prince of Wales, as a direct slight on Henry's son. And this caused the king to pass several threatening new laws against the Welsh people: namely, prohibiting any man from buying land in England, from holding senior office, from bearing arms, from entering into mixed marriages, not to mention a host of other laws that wholly alienated the Welsh as a people. Henry even banned the Welsh language. However, none of this did any good, and when the king's army retreated through lack of finance, the rebellion fell once again on my master's shoulders.

None of us knew Hotspur's plans in those days. He fought fire with fire wherever the revolt surfaced, and had it not been for the Earl of Northumberland's coffers, England might have been invaded several times by the Scots. It was a time of crumbling borders and desperate measures. But in the spring of that year, as we entered Gwynedd and rounded a mountain known as Cader Idris, I feared we might never see the north again. Here on a low ridge teeming with wildflowers Glyndŵr and his men were waiting for us in ambush and we all wondered at Hotspur's carelessness.

The Welsh greatly outnumbered us, but my master seemed far from worried. He immediately spurred forward and consulted with the young prince who was already embattling Arundel's archers to face the Welsh threat. Even though he was barely fourteen years the prince, once taught, could recall instructions in the most incredible detail and he had the best military tutor in Hotspur who he now secretly admired above all men.

'What are your commands Highness,' said Hotspur reigning in Parzival.

The prince looked puzzled. 'To kill them of course.'

My master studied the deep formation of Welsh spearmen and archers berating us from a distance. 'What w-would you do if they charged us now, Highness?' he said.

'Shoot them down.'

'You have made a g-good show of our archers, Highness, but Arundel's men are few and no match for the W-Welsh. If we had a thousand Cheshire archers, then I w-would agree with you—'

'Then we should charge them,' said the prince.

'We could, b-but then our men w-would tire climbing that hill. Besides, G-Glendower outnumbers us three to one.'

The prince sighed. 'Then we should parley with him?'

'Ah, now you're thinking like a k-king. If you had read Vegetius, then you w-w-would know that there are several ways to skin a cat. And b-believe me Highness, Glyndŵr is a cat. He will stare at us all day until he sees a w-weakness, but today we have the advantage.'

'Advantage…what advantage?'

Hotspur checked his purse. 'Stay here Highness,' he said, tossing a gold coin in his hand. 'And if I d-die on this mountain today, then learn from it. Today we'll see how chivalrous this W-Welshman is.'

The prince nodded, and I rode forward with my master up the fragrant slope prudently carrying the blue lion banner against the Welsh and a bleak chance of survival. Soon we would be fair game for any Welsh archer who wanted to kill Hotspur and make a name for himself. Renowned for their use of the war bow, I gauged that in another furlong a hail of arrows would rain down on us. But a bowshot before we reached the Welsh ranks my master reined in Parzival sharply.

'Stay here Hardyng...' he said, drawing his sword.

I mumbled a warning, but when he patted Parzival on the neck and took a deep breath, I knew his mind. I felt the change in him, and before I could protest, he charged the Welsh line aiming for the red dragon fluttering above the wall of helmets and spears.

Using his speed to full effect, my master crashed into their archers first. He was engulfed almost immediately, and he rode down four men who were flung aside by Parzival's great hooves. The rest of the archers parted like a field of wheat before a scythe, and beyond that, Hotspur struck down two spearmen with the hilt of his sword. He parried the blades of several other Welshmen with similar ease, and for a moment I thought that Hotspur might emerge triumphant at the rear of Glyndŵr's ranks.

But then I saw Hotspur disappear in the crush of bodies. Parzival had fallen, I thought, and I spurred forward not believing what had just happened.

It was a suicide charge, and the fact that I had been saved from it made me spur my horse forward without thinking. Parzival and my master had sunk into the confused mass of bodies and weapons. I feared Hotspur was being hacked to pieces, and without a thought to my own safety, I came so close to the Welsh spearmen that I too was in danger of being killed. Above all, I was conscious that I had disobeyed Hotspur's orders, and when at last, I saw my master on his feet slashing about him in a whirlpool of broad strokes I did the same.

A breakwater had formed around him as if no one was brave enough to rush forward, and when a cry went up from a Welshman in a red cloak, the wave of willing assailants stepped back in fear.

Heaving fitful breaths of exhaustion, Hotspur rose to his full height before Glyndŵr. Regaining his senses, he rushed forward as if he had not yet finished with his sword. But this time his enemies ignored him, and he struck his groaning horse with a single merciful blow through the heart.

Now there was no escape for us, and as I cantered forward to see what I could do, our enemies closed in rattling their spears. Hotspur told me later that he never meant for his dutiful horse to die. When he knelt beside Parzival, he removed his gauntlets and stroked the motionless head with his hand. He said he remembered his father's constant rebukes about killing every horse he had ever owned, and after saying a prayer for his horse and himself, he flipped a gold coin in Glyndŵr's direction.

It fell in a clump of daisies at the Welshman's feet.

'What does Henry of Lancaster mean by outlawing our native tongue,' exclaimed Glyndŵr picking up the coin. 'Robbing our monasteries and selling our children into slavery. What kind of Christian knight is that?'

Hotspur threw down his sword in a rage.

'And who is that boy you bring against me?'

'He's the P-Prince of Wales.'

'No, I am that,' spat Glyndŵr. 'I am descended from the Prince's of Powys. Therefore I have the right of succession.'

Glyndŵr examined the coin in the palm of his hand.

'Richard's death aggrieved me,' he said, looking closely at the image engraved on the coin. 'Your new king has a lot to answer for—'

'Maybe w-we have something in c-common then.'

'Turning your coat will not save you now, Harry Percy,' said Glyndŵr. 'Look around you. My men could easily kill you and that false prince of yours with one sweep of my hand. And remember my men fight for their lives and families, not money. Our nation is sick of being herded around like cattle by the English.' There was a cry of agreement from Glyndŵr's men. 'Be assured Percy your ransom will cost Bolingbroke a small fortune. He'll not be able to invade Wales for a long time to come.'

'You are w-wrong,' replied Hotspur, 'the k-king will never pay my r-ransom. Nor pay for any marcher lord you might take hostage hereafter. I have no men left to speak of, as you can see. But b-believe me, Welshman, you would do b-better listening to my terms than talking of r-r-ransom.'

Glyndŵr seemed shocked at King Henry's penury and held up the gold coin to the sun. 'But your father has money. Maybe I will ask him to pay your ransom.'

'He'll pay if it serves his p-p-purpose, but that w-would not help your cause, would it?'

Glyndŵr still saw Hotspur as the young rash paladin that had saved him from the Scots near Edinburgh, but he could also smell a deal in the air, and he flipped the coin back to my master. 'That's for saving my life in Scotland,' he said.

Hotspur offered his hand to Glyndŵr and grinned. 'As I remember it, w-we both rode against a common enemy as friends.'

Glyndŵr stared through Hotspur like a man who had a

greater destiny tucked away in his purse. He whispered something into my master's ear as he took his hand, and then he threw his cloak over his shoulder and disappeared into the ranks of his men.

It was a miracle we were not killed or held hostage that day, and soon Hotspur and I were left alone on the mountain with his dead horse.

'What did he say, master,' I said.

'I told you to stay back Hardyng.'

'But master, it's my place to ride beside you.'

'From now on follow my orders, or I'll g-get another squire.'

'Yes, master,' I said, lowering my head.

And that was the last time I crossed swords with Hotspur.

We watched Glyndŵr's army melt away into the Welsh hills and buried Parzival where he fell. It was only much later that I realised that Hotspur's loyalty to his king was buried in that grave too. Spurred on by Glyndŵr's parting words, a much grander plan was fermenting in his mind, and in Hotspur's last confident letter to his king after the 'battle' of Cader Idris, my master was already thinking of leaving Wales forever.

For my part, Hotspur ordered me to return to Denbigh with our men, and as the trees shed their leaves that year, our meagre garrisons took refuge behind castle walls. Despite the season, no one in England knew what miracle had suddenly calmed the revolt and why Hotspur never again went on the offensive. The Prince of Wales assumed it was his mentor's courage at Cader Idris that stalled the rebellion. But after writing to King Henry yet again for money and soldiers, my master rode to Chester, where he met the prince for the last time in his life.

Chester was still a hotbed of support for the murdered

King Richard, and my master thought to collect archers there for service in the north. But when this plan failed, and no favourable reply came back from the king regarding his bad tallies, Hotspur flew into a rage. He received reports from his father that the northern border was under attack from the Scots, that the French were contemplating an invasion of the south coast, and that inwardly some nobles were turning the kingdom's woes to their advantage. My master's face spoke volumes of his lack of patience with King Henry, and soon his genuine love for the Prince of Wales became compromised.

He told me that their friendship became more strained due to the king's aloofness. And early one morning Hotspur bid me saddle his horse to ride north.

'Above all, seek help from my b-brother-in-law Mortimer,' said Hotspur to the prince who had followed him into the courtyard. 'If the W-Welsh rise up again, call upon Lord Grey to fight your b-battles. He has a p-personal interest in the marches Highness. Do not rely on your father for help, and above all, do not endanger yourself.'

'What do you mean?' exclaimed the prince.

'I have made a truce with Glyndŵr that if you k-keep the march lords from p-pillaging Wales, he will k-keep to his side of the b-border.'

'But Glyndŵr is a rebel. He must be punished!'

'He's g-given me his word.'

The prince set his teeth. 'Do you not think me worthy of my spurs?'

'Yes Highness I do, b-but I must go north.'

'Why?'

'I must. I fear your father has p-placed too much trust in George Dunbar. My father fears that Dunbar and the Earl of Westmoreland will usurp his p-p-power in the north. He needs my help.'

The prince shook his head. 'Go then.'

'You are much older than I w-was when I first tasted war,' said Hotspur recalling the past, 'I have sent for Erpingham and—'

'Erpingham!' The prince produced his dagger and thrust it towards Hotspur. 'You will stay with me here. I am the Prince of Wales, and you will obey me!'

Hotspur grasped the prince's blade with his bare hand, and the prince frowned when he tried to pull it from his fist.

Hotspur clenched the blade until it cut into his flesh. 'Give me the b-b-blade Highness,' he said calmly.

'Let go…I command you to let go.'

'If you move, I will not be able to serve anyone.'

Hotspur grasped the dagger tighter, and blood appeared between his fingers.

The prince saw droplets splash on the cobbles, and his eyes widened. He knew he was losing the only man that had ever taken an interest in him and he felt his guts churn with indecision.

'You will be k-k-king one day Highness,' said Hotspur not letting go of the blade, 'and I will serve you with every breath in my b-body if you release the dagger.'

'No.'

'Let it g-go Highness—'

'No, you are not my master!'

Hotspur let go of the blade and kicked the prince hard between the legs.

The searing pain rising in his body caused the prince to double over, and Hotspur caught a fleeting glimpse of his own brutal beating at Leconfield. He wanted to leave the prince amicably, but by the time two armed guards rushed towards him, it was too late.

'Let him go,' cried the prince to the guards. 'That's the last lesson...you teach me. You're lucky you still...have your hand.'

Hotspur stared at the open wound on his palm. 'I have suffered far greater w-w-wounds Your Highness.'

The prince punched Hotspur in the face savagely. 'Do not pretend to know me, Henry Percy. I have measured you these last months, and now I know your mind.'

Hotspur glared at his protégé. 'You may be w-worthy of your spurs Highness, but you still have a lot to learn.'

It was the last words my master ever spoke to the prince. And as we rode out of Chester, I knew their friendship was over. Thereafter the prince acted independently to prove his mentor wrong. He used his marcher lords to renew the war with Glyndŵr. And when the Welsh captured Lord Grey of Ruthin and Sir Edmund Mortimer in battle everyone in England was aghast; especially Lady Percy who immediately asked Hotspur to seek her brother's ransom with the king.

'You know how he hates him,' said Hotspur one day while out riding with her.

Elizabeth set her falcon free, and it circled the keep of Warkworth Castle. 'You should never have returned from Wales, my lord.'

'You know I had to Elizabeth.'

'And the Scots take precedence over my brother?'

Hotspur gave Elizabeth a morsel of meat. 'Place it on your glove, my lady.'

'If Edmund dies in Wales, there's only Roger's son left and if the king kills him...'

'Glyndŵr will k-k-keep Edmund safe,' said Hotspur, 'he owes me—'

'That Welshman loves only one thing.'

Hotspur pointed to the speeding bird. 'Look, here comes *Merlin!*'

The blue-grey falcon swooped low and set its claws at the meat on Elizabeth's outstretched glove. She sneered at the savagery of the bird as it tore away the sinewy raw flesh of the bait. 'Yes, eat up little friend, and then I'll set you on the king,' she said.

'The king is p-penniless,' said Hotspur untangling the bird's jesses, 'even Lord Grey will not be r-ransomed from Glyndŵr.'

'But the king will listen to you and free Edmund.'

'He thinks more of George Dunbar—'

'And yet you ride with Dunbar.'

'I must know his mind.'

'Maybe I should set *Merlin* on you, my lord?'

Hotspur drew Elizabeth toward him and kissed her full on the mouth. Her falcon flew free into the trees, and my master pulled his lady across him. 'I will ride to the k-king when I have d-d-dealt with the Scots,' he said frowning.

'As long as you ransom my Edmund—'

Hotspur kissed her furiously. But of course, my master knew it suited King Henry to keep Mortimer his prisoner, and when the king received news from his son the prince that Hotspur had deserted his post, he knew what he must do. Lord Grey was a personal friend, whereas Edmund Mortimer was his enemy and keeper of the boy who threatened his throne. The choice between the two was obvious, and the resulting meeting would not be Hotspur's first or last argument with Lancaster.

23

Homildon Hill 1402

'To Homyldon, where on holy-rode-daye, he met them yn stronge arraye'

Although my master often confided in me, I could never hope to be more to him than his squire. I was an orphan you see, and to my knowledge, my father was only a steward in the Percy household. However, when my father died, I was lucky enough to receive a good formal education at Leconfield and in time, the Percys rewarded me with the promise of employment. But in truth, I always wondered if I was more than just a servant or if there was another reason why the Percy family gave me such preferential treatment.

However, apart from serving Hotspur in arms, my talents sometimes extended to using the pen rather than the sword. I drew border maps for my master and even copied important documents that the Percys used on official business. There was a time when I also forged papers at the behest of the Percys too, which in time of war seemed justified, especially when the Scots under Archibald Douglas decided to invade England.

For instance, in the second year of King Henry's reign, I was tasked by Thomas Percy with falsifying a letter that we let fall into enemy hands at Nesbit Moor. Here my master and George Dunbar won a great victory over the Scots that secured the border and allowed us to conceal this same letter on the dead body of Sir Patrick Hepburn, one of Douglas's kinsman.

The forged letter contained a plot to deceive Hepburn's master into thinking that King Henry, the Earl of Northumberland and Hotspur were leading a large English army against the Scots then raiding the west march. The letter, once found, implied that the east march was completely undefended, except for a small garrison town under George Dunbar, which of course was not true. But the clever deception was so convincing that Douglas mustered a large army of many discontented Scots lairds to punish his enemy Dunbar and plunder England at will.

To avenge Nesbit Moor they burnt and pillaged as far as the River Wear, but on their way back to Scotland we closed the net and brought them to battle near Millfield on Holy Rood Day where there was great slaughter done by the English war bow.

As heavy rain clouds rolled in like boulders over the nearby hill called Homildon, our archers herded the retreating Scots up its slope like cattle, and they made a stand hoping to defy Dunbar and his new masters or die trying. Douglas and his army finally took refuge on the balding summit and formed a shield wall there to await the deadly hail of arrows that would fall on them from below.

Douglas, standing hawkish and proud on the hill, was determined to weather out the storm of wood and steel to teach the English a lesson in blind courage. Sir Alexander Ramsay was at his side along with many other famous Scots earls and knights who had sent their horses to the rear for safekeeping. They all knew a trap had been sprung, and it soon became apparent to Douglas who commanded the English archers advancing up the hill towards them. Dunbar's red standard impaled with a white lion was plain to see above the five thousand men with bows braced. Douglas's pallid face became red with fury when his foe blew a war horn in defiance of their blood feud. And Hotspur desperately tried to persuade his father that he should lead a mounted attack uphill instead.

Dunbar had advised the Percys to take up a position with the rest of the English men-at-arms on an adjacent hill called Herehope from which they would charge the Scots after the arrow storm had done its deadly work. It was a request that the prudent Earl of Northumberland willingly agreed to, but my master was possessed by his usual demons that day and warned his father that he wanted to face Douglas in a chivalric duel instead.

'Have no fear Harry,' said the earl, 'with any luck the Scots will kill Dunbar. Then we'll be free of that dotard forever.'

'I'll take care of Dunbar,' said Hotspur, watching the archers forming across the slope. 'I am the king's east march w-warden—.'

'No you must be prudent boy, Dunbar has the king's ear.'

'How do we know Dunbar will k-keep to his word? If he

turns those archers on us—'

'There you go thinking the worst again! You forget Dunbar has much to prove against Douglas and the king. So we will be prudent today boy and pray he dies while we sit on our arses and eat our dinner.'

Soon we arrived at the head of the English knights and men-at-arms who were drinking heavily on the adjoining ridge. Some had dismounted and were laughing at the humble archers as they hurried into formation. Other border lords were eager for battle and toasted the Earl of Northumberland who took a cup of wine from his squire Merbury ignoring Hotspur's mounting impatience.

My master knew what this aloofness meant, and he struggled to suppress the persistent voices chattering in his head. He rode back and forth along the ranks of knights, sword drawn, straining at the leash. We all knew his frustration, and I thought he might slam down his visor at any moment and gallop at the Scots schiltron like he did at Cader Idris. His face was pale and drawn, his eyes darkly ringed through lack of sleep. He had difficulty breathing, controlling his new horse, and each time it bucked and whinnied he tugged at its reins savagely secretly wishing his beloved Parzival was beneath his saddle.

Northumberland continued to stare at his son and consume more food and wine at his leisure. Sir Robert Umfraville joined him and even he looked dismayed at Hotspur's antics. He told me later that all the old memories of Otterburn came flooding back in a whirlpool of emotions. And when my master tried to sway him into attacking the Scots, Umfraville urged him to remember the twilight battle in the heather where his brother had been grievously wounded.

'There's no honour in this!' yelled Hotspur shunning Umfraville. 'See, those archers are stealing our thunder... Dunbar is laughing at us...'

But the gentle sound of banners flapping and harnesses rattling told Hotspur that the northern gentry still feared his father's overmighty influence. And for this reason alone it seemed like an age before the battle of Homildon began. The wind buffeted us and swept viciously down the slope flattening the long grass between our two armies. Overhead the dark clouds rolled in again as if heralding the gloomy prospect posed by the English archers, who had increased their threat by moving to within a bowshot of the Scots bristling schiltron.

A muffled order to halt from Dunbar caused his men to empty their arrow bags and plant their missiles point down in the ground. The next order was to notch their arrows. And when this was done, the Scots on the hill instinctively raised their shield wall ready to accept the wooden hail.

Then both sides waited for the inevitable cry of 'Loose!'

Hotspur's temper surged to breaking point. He could not hold back any longer and addressed the knights behind him. 'They will gain the g-g-glory,' he said, pointing viciously at the archers, 'we must attack now, or we w-will be disgraced!'

'We'll move when I give the order,' said Northumberland finishing a leg of mutton and throwing it in the heather.

'This is not chivalry!' cried Hotspur fuming.

But when everyone heard Dunbar's final order to the English, even Hotspur was silenced by it. The distant cry came from Dunbar's throat, and we all stared as the line of archers released their bowstrings in unison.

'God...' I heard someone shout behind me.

The arrow storm looked like a great flock of starlings climbing high into the heavens and descending on their prey. There was no sound until the arrows hit their target. Then a great clatter and moan came from their ranks that sent shivers up my spine. We were far from the mayhem but knew what slaughter the Scots were facing. And when several more volleys loosed in quick succession, I shivered again.

I saw the Scots formation shatter under the weight of falling arrows. Yells and screams drifted across the dale that separated us, and a trickle of fugitives escaped from beneath their shields only to be skewered to the ground. At the same time, I saw Scots knights running for their precious horses, and I thought they might be escaping too. But nothing was further from their minds. A few of Douglas's archers tried to cover their retreat, but more clouds of arrows soon cut them up and made standing in the open a deadly impossibility.

The battle was developing into a massacre, and Hotspur smiled broadly as the Scots knights wheeled around their crumbling formation and sped down the hill. Seeing Douglas was leading his men directly at the exposed archers, my master saw his chance and immediately slapped the reins of his ill-tempered horse.

'Hold!' cried Northumberland. 'Not yet!'

Hotspur ignored his father and looked back to see if I was following with his banner. Umfraville had dutifully snatched my reins, but in a few moments, our eager knights and men-at-arms swept forward in a wave of steel. Hotspur was now the focus of our attack, and as we charged after him, I felt my heart leap into my throat.

'Stay close Hardyng!' yelled my master.

I wheeled beside him.

He dug his spurs into the flanks of his horse. 'Don't stray, or I'll kill you!'

And I obeyed, feeling the wind howling past my helmet.

It was my first battle, and a short, bloody cull of men and horses was all I remembered of it. The flower of Scots chivalry fell that day even before we traded blows, and the dead included the Earl's of Angus, Moray and Murdoch of Fife. Several arrows also killed Sir John Swinton who fought at Otterburn, and Douglas was reported missing presumed dead somewhere on the hill. Hardly any Englishmen died during the Scots attack, and I later found myself lost in a daze, wandering the fields below Homildon, and trying not to step on the dead.

I cannot remember to this day what I did during that charge, or if I traded blows with anyone. When we chased the Scots into a river, it seemed that my mind left me. Hotspur seemed to be everywhere, and as the sun began to set on my first experience of war, I was drawn back to the moans on the battlefield.

Arrows in their tens of thousands had fallen on Homildon Hill, and several English soldiers warned me away from the place saying that some Scots were still at large hiding under the dead. The heaps were piled waist-high in some places, and huge undulating mounds of dead traced the first position of the Scots and their headlong charge down the hill. It was a great fellowship of death with arms and legs intertwined with fallen arrows, and I had not seen anything like it before. The English were cutting throats out of mercy they said. Men took on the appearance of hedgehogs, and the entire hill seemed to be leaking blood.

Sickened and exhausted by the sights and sounds I had

witnessed, I took our soldier's advice and staggered back down the hill. A wounded Scot called me out by name, but it seemed for a few paces I had even forgotten that. Although his wounds were many, I recognised the soldier immediately, and when I knelt beside his body, I faced a terrible choice.

'D'ye know...who I am?' said the Scot breathlessly.

'You are Sir Alexander Ramsay,' I said, recalling his heraldry and the many times my master had spoken of him.

'Ah want tae see yer master,' he moaned.

'If I move you, my lord, you will die,' said I, looking at the forest of arrows that pinned his body to the ground.

'Then ye must murder me,' he said.

I stood up quickly. Blood was pooling from Ramsay's mouth, and as he spoke, I thought he might choke, saving me from doing his bidding.

'Hae mercy...' he spluttered. The Scot held out a few coins concealed in his clenched fist. 'Here take this...dae it now...'

I assumed Ramsay would be dead soon without my help, but as if prompted by his pleas for mercy I saw Hotspur galloping up the hill. I could tell he was angry, and when he dismounted, he seized me by the collar.

'I thought you w-were dead!' he said, barely glancing at Ramsay. 'It's not your p-place to tend the dying.'

'Aye, ye will nae ransom me this time Haatspore,' joked Ramsay looking down at the wooden shafts impaling his body.

My master stared long and hard at Ramsay. He seemed numbed by the sight of his terrible predicament, and I wondered why the Scot failed to move Hotspur to tears.

'Dae nae think too badly o' mah master,' continued Ramsay, 'Douglas was after Dunbar, not the English.'

Ramsey's eyes rolled sleepily to one side of his head, and

when Hotspur followed them, he saw Douglas's body partially hidden under a fallen horse.

'Ah fear we're both dead men,' groaned the Scot, his whole body convulsing and racked with pain.

Hotspur gave me his dagger, but I shook my head. Even though I felt we should end Ramsay's life, I was shocked by my master's coldness. And when Hotspur folded each of my fingers around the hilt of the blade, I began to hate him intensely. My whole body flinched from the task. I shook my head pathetically. I thought to run away, and I wished myself somewhere else but failed miserably. It was no use, Hotspur was guiding my hand towards Ramsay's throat, and I could do nothing about it.

'You may have to do this for me one day,' said my master.

All my muscles tensed. I closed my eyes, and as both our hands slid sideways, I bit into my lip drawing blood.

Ramsay's last breath seemed to wheeze Hotspur's name, and when I opened my eyes, he was dead. Silence had fallen on the battlefield, and before we left Ramsay to the elements, we pitched a fallen Scots standard beside his body so we could find the place again when it came to burying him.

Staring down from the hill, we viewed the appalling slaughter caused by the simple bow and arrow, and I wished for the night to come quickly.

'You did w-well in the fight Hardyng,' said Hotspur.

'I have no memory of it, my lord.'

Hotspur examined Douglas's body further. 'You are alive, that's how I know you did w-well. I hope this will be your last b-b-battle John.'

'Somehow I think not my lord.'

Hotspur put his face to Douglas's mouth. 'You must stay

b-b-by my side at all times Hardyng unless you w-wish to die young,' he said frowning.

Douglas wore his finest black armour, but despite this, he had suffered multiple wounds to his body, one of which had ripped out his left eye. Hotspur believed him dead although he was too was exhausted to tell. He was sorely depressed and explained how much he had wanted to save lives that day, including Douglas, rather than cause needless slaughter. It was a quest of his that I was well aware of by this time, given he had always tried to shield me from harm rather than protecting himself. But as Hotspur and I talked, and the moon began to rise over the carnage, I became aware that Douglas was alive. His lips began to quiver as if trying to form words, and we quickly pulled him from beneath his horse and rushed him to a surgeon in the English camp.

Later, when Douglas had been tended and was feverous, Hotspur stood vigil at his bedside willing him to live. He assured the Scot he would be well treated as chivalry dictated and he would not be ransomed to the king, or his mortal enemy Dunbar. He would soon be free to return home to Scotland, said Hotspur. And they both made a pact between knights, although I was unaware of it then, that they would live in peace forever. Even the Earl of Northumberland was secretly pleased with my master's decision, although he later followed the king's orders to surrender all his prisoners from Homildon to the crown.

However, the trading of ransoms was a slight to Hotspur's honour that he could not ignore. My master was not about to revoke his recent oath to Douglas by pandering to the king, and this annoyed his father, the Earl of Northumberland, who refused to accept his son's cries of tyranny. It seemed that the bad tallies owed to the Percys by the crown, their sudden loss of offices, their support during Henry's usurpation, and even Hotspur's own friendship with the king had been ignored.

The chattering in Hotspur's head would not stop. He knew there had to be a reckoning with his friend to clear all that had gone before. If not, then honour meant nothing and true chivalry was dead.

24

London 1402

'The derest-bowght buffet that ever was yn Englande'

A little before Christmas I was summoned by Hotspur to accompany him to London. It was inclement weather and roads were awash and caked with mud, but my master determined to ride on despite the season. His mind was filled with questions that demanded answers, and I judged from his mood that he was spoiling for a fight.

He wished to know from the king why his brother-in-law, Edmund Mortimer, had not been ransomed from Glyndŵr along with Lord Grey of Ruthin. His wife Elizabeth was the reason for his angst, but I knew this was not Hotspur's only grievance. The core of his friendship with the king was at stake, and as we climbed the stairs to the royal apartments in the Tower, I was fearful that we might never see the light of day again.

Royal guards and the young Earl of Stafford accompanied

us to the throne room so great were the threats against King Henry's life at this time. Hotspur had learned that his friend was wearing talismans again and that several of his servants had died recently after tasting his food. The guards watched our every move, and Stafford, with drawn sword, checked every corridor for assassins before we entered. We had already been searched and disarmed much to Hotspur's consternation, but it was Stafford's confident manner that troubled us. He exuded an air of superiority, and when we entered the great hall, the king greeted him before my master.

Henry looked dishevelled and thin as if all the troubles of the world sat on his shoulders. As we bowed, he continued to dictate a letter to his clerk, and Stafford's harsh demeanour bid us go no further until the king had finished his work.

'Good day Harry,' said the king at last. 'I hope you're not here for a fight.'

'Fight? No, Your Majesty, but I need to secure w-wages for my men in the north. I beg that you might pay those b-bad tallies that my father and I w-wrote to you about in several letters b-bearing our seals.'

'Ah yes, by coincidence I have just authorised that payment,' said the king, passing Hotspur the order with his seal of approval.

It was apparent a clerk had prepared the document earlier for our meeting, and the king continued scribbling despite not seeing my master for over a year. 'You need not have come to London, my friend,' he said, 'and in such inclement weather.'

Hotspur read the authorisation and frowned. 'This letter says one hundred p-pounds has been g-granted to us.'

'Yes, a hundred pounds. What of it?'

'You…you owe us twenty thousand p-pounds or more, Your Majesty.'

King Henry peered beyond Hotspur into the corridor.

'Where's the Earl of Douglas?' he said frowning.

'Sire, my father released his p-prisoners to you during your last parliament. The Earl of Douglas is my p-prisoner. Therefore his r-ransom is mine to dispose of as I see fit.'

'Until you release Douglas to us, you'll not see a penny.'

'Chivalry d-dictates that I have the r-right to ransom Douglas myself, sire. It's not honourable for you to d-deny me this.'

The king hesitated. 'Then you can use Douglas's ransom to wage your men.'

'Sire, your northern b-b-border is in peril, and we have little money left to defend it. Also, why have you appointed John Neville Marshal of England and k-keeper of Roxburgh Castle, my tenants w-w-wonder who commands them.'

'You may wonder at my decisions, Harry, but I marvel at yours,' said the king. 'You desert my son and leave Glendower to pillage the Welsh marches, and now you threaten me with Scotland? I thought you were my friend. I never have this trouble from the Nevilles or Lord Dunbar.'

'That is b-because we bear the w-w-weight of the border on our shoulders sire.'

The king stood and eased himself onto his throne. His clerk handed him a letter, and Henry waved it in my master's face. 'I am surprised at your guile Harry, and that your father still calls me his Matthias.'

'You know he uses that term to p-prove his fealty and his love—'

'Love!' Henry's cry filled the chamber, and the Earl of

Stafford joined the king at his side. It seemed like a pre-arranged signal. 'Sometimes I wonder whose side Northumberland is on.'

'You forget, my f-father and I helped you to the throne, Your Majesty.'

The king shook his head. 'I knew you came here for a fight.'

My master's hand went to his empty scabbard, and when Stafford took a step forward to protect the king, Hotspur laughed and folded his arms defiantly. I also wondered why a man of Henry's martial prowess needed such an inexperienced youth to defend his person, and when the king waved him away, I marvelled at their playacting.

'The Percys are your true liegemen, Your Majesty,' said Hotspur gazing at Stafford. 'We have p-protected the b-border since the Conquest. Why do you now p-pay other nobles to do our—'

'Neville and Dunbar have received nothing from the crown,' said the king taking a cup of wine from a servant.

'But sire, you have g-granted Dunbar land adjoining the east march. Land that is ours to b-bargain with now that Douglas is our p-prisoner.'

'Dunbar has to win that land at his own expense.'

Hotspur thrust his fist into his hand. 'Then, I will oppose him!'

The king tried to answer my master, but at that moment, Thomas Percy entered the hall from an antechamber.

Thomas was troubled. His face contorted as he tried to smile, and as he bowed to the king, he looked small and insignificant. He seemed unsure what to say, his posture was hunched over more than usual, and my master reached out to support him, thinking he was ill and about to faint.

'Ah, Thomas, perhaps you can calm your nephew's famous temper,' said the king. 'He wants to fight me again, and I need an arbitrator to allay his fears about Neville and our Scottish friend George Dunbar.'

'Begging Your Majesty's pardon, I come here on a different matter,' said Thomas.

'What troubles you, my lord?'

Thomas eyed Stafford. 'I would rather speak with you alone sire.'

An uncomfortable silence permeated the chamber. Thomas was wary of young Stafford, and his overconfident stare caused the elder Percy to let out a frustrated sigh.

'Then let me be plain Your Majesty,' he said, 'I have heard a grave rumour that my lieutenancy in Wales is about to be ended.'

'That's a lie,' said the king.

'Lord Grey told me so himself sire. And to the point, he went out of his way to tell me first about his ransoming from Glyndŵr and then his new appointment in my place.'

The king leered at Thomas, and I saw his usually unruffled face burning with guilt. It was a thing I had never seen before, and no one knew why the Percys were being stripped of their titles so acrimoniously. When Hotspur recently lost his governorship of Anglesey, he had welcomed freedom from the responsibility, but when the king shrugged his shoulders that day even the previously quick-thinking Earl of Worcester was lost for words.

'So, if there is no more business...I have much to do,' said the king summoning his clerk to his side.

But Hotspur had not finished with his friend yet, and as he approached the throne, Stafford raised his sword. He followed my master's every move as he prowled before the richly ornamented chair, but a glance from him made the young earl nervous. His eyes shifted from my master, and I saw his hand tremble with fear.

'Sheath your sword, my lord,' said Hotspur to Stafford. 'That is unless you w-wish to run me through?'

Stafford turned to the king for help who calmed him with his hand.

'My lords, let us all be friends,' exclaimed the king, rising and embracing Thomas Percy. 'Stafford put away your sword, I know your worth, and Harry, you know how invaluable you are to me. My only wish is to secure the kingdom, and as your king, I must do this as I see fit. Don't you see my lords the kingdom is beset on all sides? Thomas, I am freeing you from your responsibilities in Wales to concentrate on the north with Harry. I know you are hard-pressed on the border, but the French are knocking at my door too, and I need other good lords who have local grievances to help my son against Glendower.'

'Then g-give Glyndŵr what he w-wants sire,' said Hotspur.

'Wales belongs to the crown; my son is the prince!'

'Then free Mortimer so he can help your son w-win it back.'

Henry's old fears and insecurities materialised in an instant. 'I will never pay a traitor's ransom. He covets the crown for his nephew!'

'But you have paid Lord Grey's r-ransom and made him your lieutenant.'

The king shook his head. 'There is no money left in my treasury…besides my spies tell me that Mortimer fell into Glyndŵr's hands by his own design and that he is betrothed to Owain's daughter.'

Hotspur turned to his uncle dismayed, and Thomas nodded in agreement.

'Then at least release my nephew into my w-wife's care,' said Hotspur.

Henry threw up his hands. 'So that the Percys can control him? Never. You can tell Lady Percy if she wishes to see her nephew again she can come to Berkhamstead to wet-nurse him!'

Hotspur lurched forward, but Thomas Percy pulled him back.

'As G-God is my witness, you're not the man I used to know!' growled Hotspur, shrugging off his uncle's hand.

'You are right, Harry,' said Henry throwing his head back. 'I am the king.'

'You are king b-b-because the Percys put you there!'

Henry reached out and seized my master by his mail collar. 'I am king by the grace of God because I am Edward's heir!'

'You murdered King Richard for it, what kind of k-king is that?'

Stafford stepped forward again to protect his sovereign.

But against all the odds the king punched Hotspur in the face.

The force of the blow took my master completely by surprise, and when he staggered back, I caught him as he fell. Thomas stared at my master, willing him to retaliate, but it was the first time that I ever saw any kind of restraint in Hotspur. As he wiped his bloody nose, a strange calmness came over him. 'Not here but in the field,' he whispered.

'What's that you say?' said the king angrily.

'Not here b-but in the field!' shouted Hotspur, throwing down his glove at the king's feet.

Stafford grinned. Thomas stared at my master, and we all backed away. It was the end of their friendship it seemed, and as Hotspur turned, I saw him glance back at King Henry failing to see the russet-haired boy he once knew.

Contrary to my earlier fears, we did get out of the Tower alive that day, but when Thomas Percy joined us on the road north, we knew that he too had severed all ties with the crown. He warned Hotspur that Stafford's men were following us. He said that he had a plan and that he too thought Edmund Mortimer should be king.

But my master was silent, and after only a few miles, we lost sight of him as he spurred northward alone.

He later said to me that if I wished to leave his service, he would understand. He warned me that the king's honour had been brought into question and that his failure to comply with Percy demands now threatened the family's survival. He said I should seek employment with Sir Robert Umfraville or some other trustworthy knight, but I refused. And then my master warned me that to stay could mean death. He knew that a duel *à l'outrance* was the most chivalric way to end such a quarrel between knights. But King Henry was no longer his equal, and no one would expect the king to stoop so low. Therefore there could be only war.

We are all carnivorous creatures by nature it seems, and soon many men would have to choose sides, including myself in the coming conflict. From the humble archer to the highest noble in the land, a life or death choice was speeding towards us like a comet in the heavens. And as for my master, he knew there would be no heroes if he took up arms against his king. This time if Hotspur drew his sword, there would be a civil war, and he would be the rebel.

25

Bamburgh 1403

'And these three shall ryse agaynst the Moldewarpe'

At Epiphany, everyone in England witnessed the *stella commata* that appeared in the heavens, and from that moment on, we all feared something was about to change in the world. As the comet's fiery tail streaked across northern skies, people believed that due to England's turmoil the falling star was a portent of doom. Soothsayers at city gates issued a stark a warning:

'A blasting star in the west whose flames are bold and bright, signify the Moldewarpe's fall and the Percys might.'

But it seemed the usually dismissive Earl of Northumberland was afflicted more than any other by the heavenly spectacle that night. He was a superstitious man and had survived thus far only because of his prudent nature. He had looked after his family well, everyone said, he was a good lord to his tenants and had served three kings of England faithfully in the north. The earl was still respected by all who served him, was feared by his enemies, and above all, he had the power to muster an army of thousands with a sweep of his pen. But now with the appearance of the comet, Percy saw his star falling. King Henry was ignoring his letters, his family was being stripped of titles, and the Nevilles were moving in for the kill. Everything was changing, he moaned, and he blamed all the reversals on his reckless son, the living *stella commata* that he had never been able to control.

However, Thomas Percy was unlike his superstitious brother. Second sons of the nobility either become members of the clergy, politicians, or soldiers and Percy had proved himself worthy of all three. As a soldier, he had served his country above and beyond the call of duty. Thomas had been a diplomat to kings, a lawyer to the house of Lancaster, and had even played god when Henry was unsure of how to dispose of King Richard. Now he must play the politician again, but this time to ensure his survival.

King Henry had committed perjury, and Thomas deemed it unlawful. He had already drafted a list of additional crimes that the king had committed. He knew he would need the support of his brother, the Mortimer's and Owain Glyndŵr to depose of Lancaster, but his nephew Hotspur would be the spearhead of the campaign and the sacrifice if needs be. My master would raise the Cheshire levies and then draw Henry out into the open. Even I would be party to the Percy rebellion by producing several forged documents to prove that King Richard was still alive and well.

It was a desperate plan by Thomas, but I soon realised that

it was the only one that might save us. Everyone had to be convinced that committing treason was the only way forward, and I was no exception. Hotspur had spoken up for me, and as *stella commata* hung precariously in the northern skies over Bamburgh Castle, I was invited to share the Percy's table to discuss my part in the plan. It was a great honour that I had not enjoyed before, and after listening to the conversation that evening, I knew that my artistic talents would not be the only skills needed in the battles ahead.

However, to all our dismay, it immediately became apparent that the Earl of Northumberland was not about to raise his northern retinues lightly. While Thomas read out his manifesto against the king, the great earl looked uncomfortable. He became agitated in his favourite chair as Thomas recited each of Bolingbroke's crimes, and his brother knew that, despite our involvement, it would be he alone that would carry the weight of blame if Thomas's plan failed.

But another person was squirming in her chair that night. It was her birthday and her demands at such a time, to my mind, were selfish and beyond reason.

'So my lords, where are my presents?' shouted Elizabeth over the monotone delivery of Thomas's manifesto.

Thomas paused mid-sentence.

'Why are you all being so secretive my lords?' she asked. 'Where are my gifts?'

Despite his fraught expression Hotspur took his wife's hand. 'Soon, my love,' he said. But Elizabeth quickly drew it back.

'Continue brother,' said Northumberland stroking his white beard. 'we need to know we are in the right, and that when the king reads your appeal, he will know our mind.'

Thomas eyed Lady Percy and continued to read. 'And that

when you entered England, you swore an oath to us that you would not claim the crown, but only your own proper inheritance, and that King Richard should reign during his lifetime governed by the lords spiritual and temporal... wherefore thou art perjured and false.' Thomas paused for breath. 'You also swore that you would not suffer any monies or taxes to be levied on the clergy, nor fifteenths on the people, nor permit any bad tallies to be withheld from your lords... wherefore thou art perjured and false.'

Northumberland's head cocked to one side.

Elizabeth yawned.

Thomas continued again. 'You also caused King Richard, traitorously within the castle of Pomfret, without the consent or judgement of the lords of the realm, by the space of fifteen days and so many nights, with hunger thirst and cold, to be cruelly murdered...wherefore thou art perjured and false.'

'There is no proof of that crime,' exclaimed Northumberland.

Thomas carried on. 'And that you extorted power and did usurp the kingdom of England unjustly and contrary to your oath from Edmund Mortimer, Earl of March and Ulster the true heir to the throne—'

'Enough!' cried Northumberland rising from his seat. 'The king will never submit to those claims Thomas, and if he does, he will accuse us all of treason.'

'I will not be b-blamed,' said Hotspur.

'Did you not convince Richard to leave Flint?' said Northumberland sourly.

'I was true to King Richard—'

'No boy, you are wrong. You will be blamed by association, especially now that you have quarrelled with Bolingbroke.'

'The k-king is unchivalrous.'

Northumberland set his teeth. 'Christ's blood chivalry again! I grow weary of such idle talk. You and your Neville ways…'

'I challenged the k-king to a duel so all this might b-be avoided.'

'Your blasted gauntlet will be the ruin of us all.'

Thomas shook his head at Hotspur. 'The king would never submit to a duel Harry you know that. His supporters would never allow it. Even a great jouster like the king would prefer a civil war to running the hazard with you in the lists.'

Hotspur stood and kicked over his chair. 'So be it then, we shall have w-war!'

'See, he will not be happy until my head is on the block,' cried Northumberland, gripping his neck with both hands. 'You have killed me Harry. My own flesh and blood has killed me!'

The earl circled the hall and waved his arms at the sumptuous surroundings of the castle. 'All this would have been yours one day boy. But Neville blood runs in your veins, and now you have killed the Percys with this…this bastard chivalry of yours.'

'We're not dead yet brother,' said Thomas calmly.

'But you will make sure my lords that after your battles are won, my Edmund is crowned king?' said Elizabeth.

'I have such a plan, my lady,' said Thomas, 'but first we must join with other lords against the king. Not to do this would court disaster.'

'Others?' said Hotspur.

'King Henry will come against us, Harry, have no doubt of that,' replied Thomas. 'He's a warrior just like you, and despite his bad debts and tallies, he has the power to raise commissions of array on pain of death. Therefore we must join with Mortimer and Glyndŵr in Wales, or we will be overwhelmed.'

'And what w-will they want in return, uncle?'

Thomas rose from his chair and staring at us all he paced the room. He knew that for all the wheels of his plan to move in harmony, he must appease everyone present. 'Henry will do nothing yet,' he said, thumbing his chin, 'he will marry his new queen soon and will not have the inclination, nor the means, to muster an army against us. This will give us time to prepare. But when he does come against us, he will use Westmoreland and Dunbar.'

Northumberland thumped the table. 'Then we must kill them both now!'

'No brother, we must put them to sleep. There will be time enough to deal with them later. Harry you will keep Dunbar busy on the border, then when the time is right, you will ride to Chester and muster the county in the name of King Richard. Master Hardyng will produce commissions in King Richard's name, commissions that have some grounding in fact. There are reports that a man claiming to be Richard has been seen in England—'

'Richard...alive?' gasped Northumberland, his eyes widening.

'No brother, I can assure you Richard is dead. I saw his corpse in London. But thankfully not all men saw it before burial, so the rumours abound that he still lives. No, brother, you will stay here and raise the north claiming that Henry plans to lead an invasion of Scotland in the spring. I know, on good authority, that the king is planning just such a campaign and that commissions have been sent out to the shires. If we are prudent, Dunbar and Westmoreland will be ignorant of our real purpose until it is too late.'

Northumberland nodded.

'I will go parley with Mortimer and Glyndŵr in Wales, then join Harry at Chester with all the men I can muster from the marches. And be assured,' said Thomas casting his eye towards Elizabeth, 'your concerns about Edmund will be satisfied too.'

Elizabeth nuzzled up to Thomas. 'And how will you make him king uncle?'

Percy was troubled by her flirtatious presence, but the next part of his plan would be so surprising to everyone that they would be struck dumb by its audacity.

He ignored Lady Percy's advances and set his gaze on the comet framed in the castle window. 'After the king is no longer king,' he said, 'and your nephew is in our safekeeping, we will proportion the kingdom accordingly like a great pie. Glyndŵr shall have Wales, Mortimer England, and the Percys will rule the North and Scotland.'

It seemed that Thomas had left nothing to chance, and he was so pleased with his words that in the weighty silence that followed he poured himself a cup of wine and drank it down without taking a breath.

'But my lords,' warned Thomas, pausing to savour its sweetness. 'I fear we must be prudent for a while longer. We must not act until all is in place, and the king is marching north with his army. When we are fully committed the king will mark us as rebels, and if any part of our plan fails, or we are captured, we—'

'We'll be hung, drawn and quartered,' said Northumberland.

Elizabeth ran to her husband and took his hand. She gazed into his eyes and stroked his cheek as if fearful of what might happen to him.

But my observation was wrong.

'So where are my presents, my lord?' she said.

Even my master was amazed at his wife's detachment, but he kissed Elizabeth on the mouth and clapped his hands together.

A trumpet sounded somewhere outside the chamber, and several servants entered carrying four large chests of unequal shape and size. Elizabeth rushed over to them excitedly as each one was carefully placed on the floor. She was so delighted that she danced around each one opening the lids, and hoping that the boxes might contain fine gowns, sweetmeats or some other expensive gift that accompanied the perfumed aroma coming from inside.

When they were all opened, Elizabeth saw each box was filled with flowers, and at first, she was confused until she began searching under the petals.

In the smallest box, she felt something hard and cold against her skin. She paused for a moment then frowning she pulled out a helmet so brightly burnished that it mirrored her puzzled face. Next, she opened the longest chest revealing a gilt-edged leg harness. In the largest box, she found a breastplate and arm defences of the finest Milanese steel. And so on, until she scattered a full complement of armour on the floor.

'Hardyng will help you arm yourself,' said Hotspur with a grin.

And I dutifully walked over to where Elizabeth was standing quite speechless.

She stared at her husband. 'You mock me, my lord. I need

no armour to protect myself. And do not think because I am a woman, I cannot do a man's work.'

'I thought you w-wished to be a soldier like me?' said Hotspur cheerfully. 'And unlike my harness, this one will adorn your p-pretty body in every way.'

Everyone laughed, but Elizabeth pushed Hotspur away and kicked the helmet across the chamber like a football.

'Just make sure my nephew becomes king, my lord,' screamed Elizabeth pointing at her husband, 'or you will have no support from my brother in Wales, or me in our bed!'

She stormed from the room, and everyone laughed except my master. He knew the grave danger we were all in and that most of us who had seen the *stella commata* that night might never meet again.

26

Cocklaws 1403

'That to Scotlande, agayne came he never'

Only three of us who stood before Cocklaws Castle knew the siege was a sham. But the fraud had a purpose, and for the moment Thomas Percy's plan was working.

Hotspur had freed Archibald Douglas without achieving his ransom, and now both men had joined forces to invest several peel towers in Teviotdale but with only one thought in mind. And that was to deceive everyone into thinking that they were not about to rebel against the king.

Three thousand soldiers swarmed beneath the walls of Cocklaws, and at first, the Scots inside braced themselves for a swift defeat. However, it soon became apparent, even to those inside the tower, that something about the siege was unusual; namely, that our half-heartedness was so spectacular that the real battle was not about how to capture Cocklaws, but of how to limit and postpone its destruction.

Before crossing the border, my master had asked King Henry for financial help once more, this time against the Scots, and predictably the king refused, saying that he was already planning an invasion of Scotland with all the money he could muster. The Scots regent, the Duke of Albany, was also reluctant to relieve such a paltry siege as Cocklaws. After Homildon Hill, some of his best knights had been killed or captured, and he needed time to gather a new army so that he could meet the English king. In truth, both sides had their motives, including George Dunbar and the Earl of Westmoreland, who had been put to sleep by the stalemate and were completely unaware of the planned Percy's rebellion.

However, when battering rams and catapults were rolled up to Cocklaws, the pretence of the siege became a more complicated matter. The eagerness to raise the castle to the ground and kill all those inside became so fervent amongst the English that Sir Robert Umfraville soon became suspicious of my master. He galloped up the hill with Dunbar and John Neville Earl of Westmoreland to know Hotspur's mind, and predictably Archibald Douglas was the first one to react. Even though he was still suffering from the ten wounds received at Homildon Hill, he took a large axe from his belt and threw it at Dunbar as he cantered up to our camp.

Predictably it was a wayward shot by the one-eyed Scot, who had not yet become accustomed to his impediment, and Dunbar managed to avoid the axe and charge his rival down. Neville tried to stop the two Scots from killing each other, but when Hotspur pulled Dunbar from his saddle Neville dismounted and hit Douglas over the head with his baton.

'You seem to be having problems, Harry,' said Neville using

his fist this time to concuss the Scot.

'No, not at all my lord,' replied Hotspur, striking Dunbar with his gauntlet.

Hotspur bid me tie Dunbar's hands and legs together so that he could not attack his foe again. 'Take Dunbar away from here, my lord,' he said to Neville, 'or w-when Douglas awakes he will k-kill him.'

Dunbar began to moan and tried to stop me from tying him up, but Hotspur knocked him about the head again until he was quiet.

'I will remove him when you tell me why you are besieging this worthless tower?' said Neville. 'I could knock it over with my left boot.'

'Why are you here, my lord,' said Hotspur, 'and with Dunbar, you know how Douglas hates him.'

'I hear that you Percys are planning to extend your lands into Scotland and I thought Dunbar should know about it.'

'King Henry has g-given me leave to contend these lands in lieu of w-wages.'

'I hear you fought with him.'

Hotspur grinned. 'Do you w-want a fight, my lord?'

'Maybe after you've toppled that heap of rubble over there,' said Neville pointing at the castle nestling in the hollow of the valley.

Umfraville was frustrated. 'One stone from my catapult will destroy that tower my lord, and yet we shower it with arrows every day.'

'I told you they have hostages inside R-Robert,' said Hotspur trying to cover up the fraud. 'I'll not see them k-killed for the sake of a few days siege?'

'Then allow me to batter the door down with my ram.'

'They will all be slain b-before our men set foot inside.'

Neville and Umfraville knew Hotspur well enough to see he was lying. His face contorted as if to avoid betraying his guilt. He shielded his face from view and girded himself for an inquisition.

'Very well,' sighed Neville at last, 'I will ask my kinsman, Lord Furnival, to take Dunbar back to Roxburgh provided that tomorrow you allow Umfraville to use his best catapult to pound Cocklaws to dust.'

'Are you g-giving me an order cousin?'

Neville threw Hotspur a knowing glance. 'I could have you arrested under March Law, for inciting border war.'

'Be about it then.'

'It was the same at Lyliot's Cross—'

'I was younger then.'

'And now I am the Earl of Westmoreland.'

'Then I w-will end this now,' said my master, seizing his helmet. 'Get your catapult ready R-Robert. I will speak to the constable.'

'Of Cocklaws?' said Neville aghast.

'What of it?'

'John Greenlaw is touched by madness,' exclaimed Umfraville. 'He thinks himself a great laird and above the law. Let me smash his little castle over his head!'

'Umfraville is right, you cannot reason with a man like Greenlaw, Harry,' warned Neville holding Hotspur back. 'He's not a chivalrous man.

Hotspur shrugged Neville off and called for his horse. 'That's w-what you all want isn't it...my death...then you Nevilles can r-rule the north?'

Neville seized Hotspur's bridle and hung on to it partway

down the hill. 'Whatever you think of me, Harry, this is not the way,' he said struggling. 'You are my cousin, and despite your father's contempt for my family, I've never wished you any harm.'

'Let go of my b-bridle!' shouted my master tugging his horse away.

Neville's face soured as he let Hotspur go. And as we watched my master and Umfraville gallop down the hill, even I wondered what was in store. It was as if Hotspur's demons had twisted their knives into his gut and he was riding to certain death.

'He's the greatest knight I've ever known,' Neville said to me watching him spur down the hill, 'but I fear he's lying through his teeth. Either that or he has become dim-witted like his father.'

I said nothing and ran to get Hotspur's banner. I hoped I could persuade him to stop, but others had already read my thoughts.

'Where's that damn Scot?' said Neville looking around anxiously.

Douglas had slipped away unnoticed. I looked for him in the camp, but when Umfraville blew on his horn and raised a white flag before Cocklaws, I saw the Scot galloping to join them. I wasted no time too, but I quickly found out that I had gone against Hotspur's wishes. He asked why I had disobeyed him and seemed uncomfortable with my presence. Douglas was still bleeding from his fight with Dunbar. He had lost his eye-patch in the fighting and looked more fearsome for it.

Hotspur glanced at me as Umfraville's men took up position. 'What did Neville say to you?'

'He said you were the greatest knight.'

Hotspur looked for Neville but could see no sign of him on the ridge. He seemed to shrug off my admiration for him, and I sensed he was only concerned with my safety - a thought that I had felt many times in his service.

'Ah will murder that caw-jacket Dunbar next time,' mumbled Douglas drawing his sword.

'That time may not come, my lord,' said Hotspur. 'If the Constable of Cocklaws is mad, and we cannot r-reason with him, then we must leave for Chester tonight and g-go against King Henry unprepared.'

'Dinnae worry about me Haatspore. A'm prepared for that. Look up there, that wee man o' the tower can hardly see over the parapet.'

It was true; when we saw the constable on the battlements, he was in the arms of two soldiers. And when he spoke to us, his voice squealed like a mouse.

'Who wants tae parley withe the laird o' Cocklaws?' he shouted.

'Open the gate!' ordered Hotspur seething with anger.

'Who are ye?'

'Sir Henry Percy and the Earl of Douglas!'

The constable laughed. 'Hae ye had enough then?'

Hotspur had heard enough. 'Open the g-gate, or we will b-break it down!'

The constable disappeared from the battlements, and when the gate finally creaked open, we dismounted and peered inside the dark hole in the wall. Sir Robert Umfraville was at our side in a moment sword drawn, but Hotspur took him aside. He spoke to him harshly, pointing to the tower and giving him instructions that made his brow furrow.

In the end, he shook his head.

'No!' growled Umfraville.

But my master ordered him back to the trenches to load his catapult.

'Dinnae worry,' said Douglas trying to calm us, 'Greenlaw's a wee man with a large opinion o' himself.'

'He's mad if he thinks w-we'll surrender to him,' exclaimed Hotspur.

But beyond the hole in the wall, we soon surrendered to the putrid smell inside Greenlaw's castle.

When our eyes adjusted to the darkness, we were met by such an incredible stench of rotting meat that I threw up. In the murky half-light, animal carcasses were piled up randomly or strewn on the sopping wet floor. Blood and guts were spread everywhere. Large intestines were hung from the rafters to dry, and a toothless sentry descended the moss-infested staircase and limped towards us. He escorted us up another spiral staircase to the next floor where soldiers huddled in small groups. Clutching their weapons anxiously, but barely noticing us as we passed, we sensed madness in the air. The smell of urine and sweat was overpowering, and before the dutiful sentry urged us on, he paused to drop his breeches and shit in the corner.

The squalor of a castle in siege is never a pretty sight, but when we reached the upper floor, nothing could have been further from the truth. Four armed Scots guarded a spacious landing, and beyond that, a barred door was hiding a wealth of opulence. Inside the chamber shone brightly with some of the best furnishings and draperies money could buy. Silver cutlery and gold plated cups were set out on a long polished table, and sumptuous hunting tapestries hung from every wall. The chamber reeked with scented candles and waiting for us impatiently on two thrones in a small alcove were the lord and lady of Cocklaws dressed in ermine and cloth of gold.

The lord of the castle, John Greenlaw, was a small man not five feet tall with fiery green eyes and hair to match. His legs dangled from his chair, and when we entered, he quickly jumped down, summoning his wife to do the same.

The 'lady' of Cocklaws towered above him and was a fat, buxom woman who immediately folded her arms as if waiting for a compliment. She wore a coronet on her great head and was eating a mutton pie balanced in her plump hand.

'Ah ye must be Haatspore,' said Greenlaw grandly, 'and welcome laird Douglas it's good to see mah humble tower has such a large English hoast afore its walls.' He ambled over to the window and peered through. 'And catapults too!'

'Good sense w-will tell you, Greenlaw, that we have not been serious in our siege,' said Hotspur furtively.

'Not?' exclaimed Greenlaw's wife.

'Hold yer tongue, wifie!' snapped her husband.

Hotspur peered through the window at Umfraville standing below us in the trenches. 'One well-aimed b-blow from my siege engine out there will smash your tower to dust G-Greenlaw,' said Hotspur. 'That is unless you submit to our plan.'

Greenlaw stamped his foot. 'Ah, will nae be told what t' do by you, or any other laird in Scotland!'

I handed Douglas a paper with the Duke of Albany's wax seal attached to it.

'Ye will read this Greenlaw,' said Douglas, 'and if yer wish is to be laird o' Cocklaws hereafter, then ye will sign it or make yer mark.'

Greenlaw joined Hotspur at the window to confirm the

threat from below his castle was real. A large English catapult was being moved into position by soldiers, and I saw the little man's lower lip tremble as the mechanism creaked back.

He rushed to the table, calling for his wife to bring him a pen quickly.

Douglas unfolded the treaty and Greenlaw made his mark casting us a sour glance.

'You w-will hold here for six weeks,' said Hotspur setting out terms, 'and then if you are not r-relieved, you will submit to my captain Sir Robert Umfraville. Your r-regent, no doubt, will see that you are well r-rewarded for your services.'

Greenlaw's wife rubbed her hands.

'You will also get p-p-punished if you fail to do our bidding,' added my master sharply.

Greenlaw clutched the signed paper and puffed out his chest. 'Haw, ye think me mad!' he said with a wry smile. 'This is mah hour o' victory. Ye should submit tae me instead. Ah have killed soo many o' ye English out there that ye now fear me. Or why would ye hae brought such an army of locusts to eat at mah sprig o' barley?'

'I think you better submit to them husband,' said Greenlaw's wife in good English, 'just how many Englishmen do you think you have killed today?'

'I couldnae count them mah dear, the number is sae large,' said Greenlaw scratching his head, 'Methinks Albany should make me an earl for all mah troubles.'

Hotspur gazed at Douglas knowingly, but from that moment on, we were careful not to turn our backs on the little man.

'Have it your w-way then. We will let Albany know your mind, Greenlaw,' said Hotspur at last. 'But for now, farewell…

But as far as Greenlaw was concerned, the conversation was far from over. The talk of lofty titles had muddled his brain, and he blew a small hunting trumpet concealed in his doublet.

His wife let out a shriek as several guards rushed into the chamber.

'Now you're mah prisoners,' chuckled Greenlaw producing a small dagger not fit for a child. 'And ah will make ye all mah hostages!'

Hotspur secretly threw something out of the window, and almost at the same time, we heard a dull slap of wood followed by a sudden rush of air.

We all sensed the danger coming, but when the deafening crash came, it numbed us all including Greenlaw who fell on the floor covering his head. The guards ran for cover, and all around us, there was a sound of falling masonry.

Greenlaw's wife screamed wildly at the hole that had opened up in front of her. Where the stone from Umfraville's catapult had hit a large opening had been blasted in the wall and the countryside beyond was plain to see. Hotspur was the only one still standing, and when Douglas seized Greenlaw by the hair, I barred the door trapping the fleeing sentries.

'Unless you let us go, Greenlaw,' exclaimed Hotspur, 'the next stone will destroy more than your wife's b-b-bedchamber.'

'Go...go now!' shouted Greenlaw's wife in floods of tears. 'I will make him see sense...now go!'

Douglas threw Greenlaw to the floor, and the little man scrambled to his wife's bosom. The guards had fled, but that said we had to fight our way out of the castle floor by floor to escape the maddened cries from above. Hotspur led the way and launched himself at a group of soldiers coming up the stairs. His speed so shocked the Scots that others behind turned and ran away. We made short work of the rest on the lower floors with our swords, and as we emerged from the castle, Umfraville's archers covered our retreat.

But Greenlaw had not had enough, and as we slid into the waterlogged entrenchments before the peel tower, a hail of arrows showered us, one of which grazed my hand.

Not for the first time in my life, I wondered at my lucky escape and how death was slowly closing in on me. The more I stayed in my master's service, I thought, the more chance I had of being killed. Hotspur was immune to danger it seemed, but I was not so sure of my luck any more. Even Douglas heaved a sigh of relief as we lay there in the trenches exhausted from our ordeal.

Umfraville scrambled along the ditch to join us, and while my master bound my hand, I feared there would be more questions about the pretended siege unless Hotspur told Sir Robert the truth. However, when Douglas passed Umfraville the treaty Greenlaw had signed, his face softened, and we hoped that he too might be taken in by my clever forgery.

'Lucky for you my captain was familiar with Cocklaws and saw your signal from the window,' said Umfraville reading the parchment. 'He has a keen eye and—'

'You saved our lives, R-Robert,' said Hotspur, 'and I am g-grateful to you. But we must continue with the siege here despite what Neville says.'

'Then tell me the truth my lord, you owe me that much,' said Umfraville staring at us hopefully. 'Why are we here at this wretched tower and not pursuing a more noble cause elsewhere?'

'I cannot tell you, R-Robert. Upon my oath, I w-wish I could.'

Umfraville gazed at me, hoping for an answer.

'Then I will have to ask your father,' he sighed. 'God knows I have been loyal to you and the Percys all my life. It pains me that I am not worthy of your trust.'

Umfraville took my hand and re-bound my wound tighter to stop the bleeding. The burning pain seared through my palm and up my arm like a knife. But thankfully, despite the discomfort and Hotspur's concern, it was only a flesh wound.

'And you squire Hardyng, what do you know of this?' said Umfraville, still not content with my master's secrecy.

I fumbled for words, but despite everything, I was sharp with an answer. 'I carry out my master's will, my lord. I trust his judgement.'

'Then you are a dutiful squire,' said Umfraville tying off his handiwork. 'I would expect nothing less myself if you were in my service.' Then he turned sullenly to Hotspur. 'I know you blame me for Ralph's death Harry, but I deserve some respect...'

'Ralph was his own master, Robert. You are not to b-blame.'

'But I suggested he go on that damn pilgrimage—

Hotspur took his arm. 'I b-bear the guilt myself.'

'And I'm truly sorry for that Harry...'

It was as if Umfraville was saying his goodbyes to each of us. We knew nothing could be done; someone had to keep up the pretence on the border until Hotspur could muster another army elsewhere. Time was running through the hourglass, and we had to act quickly, or Dunbar and Westmoreland might alert King Henry to our plans. Even Umfraville could not be trusted, it seemed, and I felt that now we were beyond the law. Soon we would be traitors in every sense of the word.

27

England 1403

'And Owayn also on Severne hym for to mete'

We rode from Cocklaws that same night with forty trusted men. Hotspur left his besieging force behind to keep up the pretence of border war, and my master never told Umfraville the real reason why we had departed in such haste. King Henry was somewhere in the midlands mustering his promised army for Scotland, the Prince of Wales was lodged with a small host at Shrewsbury, and we all prayed for God to favour us in the days ahead. My master knew his notoriety in Cheshire was the only thing that stood between victory and defeat, but Hotspur said that Glyndŵr and Mortimer would soon come to our aid, and this eased my mind as we came within sight of King Richard's former hive of support.

Chester's love of the former king was still recent history, and the town was still in rebellious spirit against Henry of

Bolingbroke. Hotspur was well-loved by the citizens for his forbearance three years before, and as we rode through the crowded streets, it seemed the whole of Cheshire had come out to greet us. My forged letter and numerous commissions from the 'newly resurrected' King Richard heralded our advance, and Hotspur was presented to the civic authorities as England's new saviour. Richard's urgent plea to the rebels became a common war cry in the shire, and even old men turned out in their kettle hats of former wars to join Hotspur's army so great was his fame. Farmers left their cattle and crops in the fields. They re-strung their war bows to strike a blow against King Henry's newly raised taxes. Townsfolk and local knights rallied to Hotspur's side like so many leeches craving the king's blood. Richard's trusted Cheshire archers proudly stitched white hart badges onto their quilted jackets once more. And above all this, the lord mayor promised everyone in the town that they would soon see their beloved Richard who would lead them to victory.

Cheshire had gone mad, and despite our recruiting success, our lies had become so uncontrolled that when Thomas Percy arrived at our camp with a contingent of Welsh archers, he was a worried man. His famous stone-face was animated with discontent, and he quickly waylaid my master in his tent.

'So Harry, tell me how in the name of Lazerus are you going breath life back into Richard's worm-eaten corpse?' said Thomas with an air of sarcasm.

Hotspur was gazing at a map I had drawn up for him during the Welsh campaign. 'Once our army is on the march p-pretence will not matter.'

'And what if that rabble out there learns the truth about young Hardyng's letters and decides to turn on us instead of the king? What will you say to them then?'

'I will tell the truth that Richard is dead and that B-Bolingbroke has murdered him. That way we can all be absolved of p-perjury.'

I felt another great weight lift from my shoulders as Hotspur spoke. I too wished for a speedy end to all the lies and forgeries, but I could tell Thomas was still displeased by his nephew's plan, and he slumped into a chair as two of Hotspur's captains blustered in.

Sir Richard Venables, a long-faced Lancashire knight, had previously served King Richard in his bodyguard and he spoke up first.

'My lord, I must beg you to speak to the Cheshire archers,' he said, trying to contain his anger. 'Or I will have them all flogged.'

Hotspur gave his captain a disdainful look.

Venables continued. 'They are ready to commit every sort of crime, my lord, and they even treat us, their chief captains, with contempt.'

His anxious companion Vernon nodded. 'They pillage and rob others of their provisions, my lord. They pay for nothing, not even the town whores. They are all rustics, tanners, shoemakers, and the like, and are not worthy of pulling our boots off, let alone fighting for us. No one dares stand up to them, and all because King Richard used to let them call him 'Dickon' or some other flippant name.'

'It's true my lord, they eschew any form of authority,' added Venables.

'But they can shoot,' said Hotspur calmly.

'That has to be seen, my lord.'

'And there are two thousand of them,' continued Hotspur,

'what do you w-wish me to do, flog them all?'

Vernon heaved a long frustrated sigh. 'That would be a good plan, my lord.'

'Once compelled to fight, they w-will have no time to thieve or p-pull your boots off,' said my master. 'Now go, I will speak to the army tomorrow and let everyone know our p-purpose.'

'Very well, my lord,' said Venables turning to leave.

'Also, my lord,' added Vernon with some urgency, 'my scourers have just come in from the east. They say the king's army is at Derby. Henry has sent out writs to the ports saying no one is allowed to leave the kingdom. And they also report that George Dunbar is with him—'

'Then the king knows our plan,' said Thomas getting to his feet. 'Dunbar will have guessed what your pretended siege at Cocklaws was all about.'

'What day did the king close the ports Vernon?' said Hotspur gazing at the map again.

'My scourers said yesterday—'

Thomas Percy snatched the map from Hotspur. 'Christ's blood Harry, the king has gained a march on us!' He traced his finger along the roads Shrewsbury. 'We must prevent him from joining his son or—'

Hotspur threw up his hands. 'Sir Richard r-r-rouse the army. We march tonight.'

We all rushed from the tent. I ordered servants to pull down the canvas as we left. Trumpets sounded in the distance and drummers beat a rapid to assemble the soldiers into three wards. Presently the whole camp was alive with noise and shouted orders. Dogs barked, and horses neighed as everyone rushed to their standards. But despite the might and power marshalling before us my guts churned. Only Hotspur seemed composed and, as usual, he was encouraging every soldier to move faster. He drew his sword and cut the tent ropes of those soldiers still sleeping. He reprimanded groups of archers for carrying empty arrow bags, and he made sure the baggage wagons were moving freely along the road ahead of us.

'I will send a messenger to Glyndŵr,' said Thomas gathering the reins of his horse. 'The Prince of Wales will close the gates of Shrewsbury and fortify the town so he cannot cross there. When I last saw the prince, he told me that he begged the king several times for men and money, but to no avail, so his garrison will be unwaged.'

'Good. Then that means the p-prince is at odds with his father.'

Hotspur nodded and mounted his horse.

'His men will flee when they see our fair array,' cried Thomas.

'And hope the k-king's army is slow-footed.'

'I will send word to Glyndŵr and Mortimer.'

'And will they fight?'

'When I met with Glyndŵr at Carmarthen, he told me how the prince's men burned his home at Sycharth. Be assured Harry he will come.'

'And Mortimer?'

'He wishes for nothing more than to see Lancaster destroyed and his nephew crowned King of England.'

'Then all is w-well uncle,' said Hotspur as a group of soldiers mobbed him. 'Perchance I should take the crown myself!'

Thomas nodded, and I noticed the thought excited him. 'Now you have an army at your back anything is possible,' he said.

Hotspur's young son had Plantagenet blood in his veins, but even I knew there was a forest of legitimate claimants standing between my master and the English throne. For years chivalric perfection had always been my master's goal, and his whole life meant being faithful to the code and his king. However, now I felt Hotspur had discarded this high ideal. Maybe now, after over thirty years of loyal service, he had seen enough of corruption and courted ultimate power for himself? His uncle's ambition was infectious, and it seemed, for at least a time, that the whole world had sided with us in rebellion.

In the crush of adoration, the crowd of soldiers pushed Thomas Percy aside. The Cheshire archers chanted Hotspur's name until they were hoarse, and even I marvelled at my master's renewed vigour. He was captain of a large army, hope was in the air, and as we left Chester behind us and took the road south, I wondered if Hotspur's demons had been exorcised - or were they just sleeping.

Our first forced march took us to Whitchurch where more men swelled our ranks hoping to see King Richard. Like all raw recruits, they were taken in by the thought that the king would lead them personally into battle accompanied by the Percys. But soon like all stories built on weak foundations, the deception became threadbare. We had heard nothing from Hotspur's father since leaving the north, and when our lie about Richard became too absurd to keep hidden, we formally declared him dead, murdered by the Bolingbroke.

Hotspur proclaimed that he now meant to set England to rights with his sword. He said that the Percys had made a terrible mistake by helping Lancaster to the throne and that he would now rectify this in battle. Edmund Earl of March was Richard's nominated heir, he said, and Thomas Percy had formal articles of defiance in his mailed fist ready to accuse 'Henry of Lancaster' of perjury. Renouncing his allegiance to the king, my master charged his former friend with usurping the throne. Henry had lied upon oath at Doncaster, and now Hotspur vowed with God's help to make good his error *in extremis*.

After my master's speech, there was an air of discontent in the ranks, but most men had been recruited by their masters under indenture and had no choice but to follow their leaders into battle. Feudal obligation is a strong mistress, and while ever Hotspur's chief captains and knights stayed loyal to him so would their men. However, this loyalty did not stop a balding militia captain called Ramkyn. He questioned my master's admission of guilt, and when this became common knowledge on the second day of our march towards Shrewsbury, I thought Hotspur's worst fear might become a reality.

Richard Ramkyn was a mercer by trade and a coward by nature.

'And who are ye that my men should help ye right the wrongs of this land?' he said as Hotspur made his regular visit to the campfires that night.

My master could tell Ramkyn's men were in awe of their local captain. 'I had hoped you would fight for good g-governance,' said my master, 'for your families sake.'

'And how do ye know that Mortimer will be a good king?' said Ramkyn shaking his fist at Hotspur. 'Ye have done us all wrong by bringing us thus far under false pretences!'

Some of Ramkyn's men cheered their leader and encouraged by this the mercer drew his sword as if to strike my master.

Hotspur easily kicked the sword from the mercer's hand.

Ramkyn smirked and picked up the sword again. I stepped forward to disarm him, but Hotspur was too quick for me, and with a sweep of his arm, he hammered the captain into the ground.

'You would do w-well to save that b-blade for the coming battle,' said Hotspur, helping his assailant up.

Ramkyn clasped his hands together in prayer. 'I were only speakin' up for others mi' lord,' he said, shuffling away. 'Weren't I lads?'

But his followers were already returning to their campfires.

They seemed surprised that Hotspur had failed to punish them more severely for their mutinous behaviour, and so did I.

'No amount of violence can change the future Hardyng,' he said, clapping me on the back.

'No, my lord.'

'And I w-will not let fear r-rule my cravings for it ever again.'

I nodded in agreement. But as we neared Shrewsbury a few days later a much greater fear gripped the army that was not so easily remedied.

The day before Saint Mary Magdalene's eve, our scourers reported that the king's army was encamped outside the town. Tents and pavilions were pitched beside the abbey they said, and worse still, the royal standard had replaced the prince's banner flying above the ramparts of Shrewsbury Castle. Henry was dining with his son it seemed, and the Severn bridges had been blocked with barriers and guards so that Glyndŵr could not cross into England. We were on our own. And the next day at first light we saw for ourselves that cracks were beginning to appear in our carefully laid plans.

'Now we are traitors,' said Thomas gazing at myriad plumes of smoke rising from the royal campfires outside the town.

Hotspur set his teeth. 'Then I must challenge the k-king to a duel. Ride with me uncle.'

'It will do no good, Harry,' shouted Thomas as Hotspur spurred forward.

'I will r-r-reason with him!'

We all rode after my master to gain a better view of the town and the royal camp outside the walls, but as we came closer, we heard trumpets alerting Shrewsbury to our presence.

'The king will not reason with you or take up your challenge, Harry,' said Thomas, 'he is in the right, and we are rebels.'

'Then g-give me Glyndŵr and Mortimer!'

Hotspur stood up in his stirrups and gazed at the royal standard flying above the castle. All his previous energy and optimism had drained from his face, and after Thomas explained how the ox-bow in the Severn enclosed the town on all three sides, he quickly realised Glyndŵr's crossing was impossible.

'Burn the fields and houses before the w-walls,' said Hotspur at last. 'We must g-gain the day we lost and find another place for the W-Welsh to cross. Scour the Severn. We must find a crossing b-before cock-crow.'

'Let me go, master,' said I.

Hotspur frowned. 'Very well Hardyng, but if there is no ford, then be sure to r-return to us post-haste.'

I knew perfectly well why Hotspur was so happy to let me go, and all my years of service with him raced before me like fortune's wheel. He wanted to keep me out of harm's way, and I felt a deep well of guilt filling up inside me again. I was trapped between the dual fears of cowardice and courage, but I wasn't alone.

'If there is a ford Hardyng we may all be able to cross over into Wales before nightfall,' said Thomas Percy thumbing his chin.

'And if all else fails, we will embattle our men to the north at dawn.' Hotspur gazed back up the Whitchurch road. 'I expect my father's army soon, and that is the w-way he will come.'

'I fear he is still in the north, Harry,' said Thomas lowering his voice.

'Then w-we will fight with Glyndŵr. If the ford is there, Hardyng will find it.'

Thomas's eyes widened. 'But without your father—'

'He w-w-will come!' raged Hotspur clenching his fist.

'But if Dunbar and Westmorland have arrested him—'

My master dug his spurs into his horse's flanks. 'We do no g-good here, uncle, arguing like small boys. Set fire to the houses as I bid, and Hardyng, find me that crossing or I will challenge the k-king man to man.'

It was all we could do, and when I rode past the Chester militia, sat eating their pottage on the Whitchurch road, I saw Richard Ramkyn preaching secretly to his men again. He was quietly spreading discontent among the ranks out of fear for himself, I thought. But then even I, God forgive me, was looking for a way out of the madness.

28

Hateley Field 1403

'Hys father fayled hym foule, wythout wytte or rede'

Some things in life are God's will, and often a man comes face to face with his destiny at a place he was once told to avoid. The workings of fate are a strange mistress, and often her all-seeing eye speeds us ever onward towards a conclusion that, by compulsion, leads to untold human suffering.

Now that our carefully laid plans were falling like dead leaves from a tree, every soldier in Hotspur's army feard the worst, and I was no exception. After leaving my master and the army marching east towards the Severn, I managed to find an old ford downstream that was used by farmers to drive their cattle to better pastures on the other side. A husbandman from a nearby village pointed the crossing out to me, but when I saw the river was in spate, my master agreed that crossing it at night with wagons and horses would be a disaster.

When I showed him the place, Hotspur even removed his armour to try and find shallower water. But the undertow was so dangerous that he was almost swept away. Also, the ford was so perilously close to the town of Shrewsbury, that Thomas Percy warned that even if the river was fordable by the next morning then the king's men, once alerted, would cut our army to pieces as we attempted to cross into Wales.

And so it was, that when dawn broke the following day, we struck our camp near a small village hugging the Severn and marched north to await the king's pleasure. The place chosen to embattle our host of ten thousand men was on good rising ground astride the Whitchurch road. Thomas Percy, always the careful planner, declared that by drawing the king's army out of Shrewsbury this might aid Glyndŵr's cause if he chose to cross the Welsh bridge north of the town. But sadly this was our only hope, and as our men climbed the slopes of Hateley Field, it was clear that some of our contingents were thinking of desertion - especially when they saw the banners of King Henry marching up the road to meet us.

It was the vigil of Saint Mary Magdalene, a Saturday, and the weather was hazy and humid as I recall. I felt a heavy stillness in the air as we watched the king's vaward unfold from the road and take up a position in the fields opposite us. Their ranks were thronged with archers, and the banner of the Earl of Stafford was flying above a multitude of burnished helmets and rustic bowstaves too numerous to calculate. Another column of soldiers was behind them displaying more colourful banners of knights loyal to King Henry. And behind this middle ward was the king himself, his household men, the Scot George Dunbar, countless other men-at-arms, and the Prince of Wales who was that day riding a white horse.

The breathtaking sight was a mixture of royal splendour and military might, and when I saw old Sir Thomas Erpingham's banner flying beside young Stafford's I knew we would be facing archers of proof who could ply their trade well.

Hotspur gestured for Venables to deploy our men to the fore quickly, and the men of Cheshire eagerly rushed together with their bows at the ready. They fanned out to the east and west of our sloping position and some, who clumsily fell in the tangle of peas before us, greatly encouraged Hotspur that our defence was a good one. Another shout, this time from Thomas Percy, bid his Welsh archers form up behind Ramkyn's town militia, as there was still some doubt about the mercer's loyalty. The last command was for Vernon to order all our men-at-arms, wearing crescent and manacle badges, to dismount so that they might fight in the English manner and send their warhorses to the rear out of bow shot.

When all this was done, Archibald Douglas placed his men in the centre of our army, and without warning, the Scots began to strike their shields in defiance of the king. Douglas then limped towards us using his huge battleaxe as a walking stick. He was still suffering from numerous wounds that never seemed to heal.

'Hae ye seen any sign o' that ball-bag Dunbar yet?' he said to Hotspur cynically.

My master pointed out his standard-bearer riding alongside the king.

'I'll hae that turncoat's head today,' cried Douglas raging. 'Sae don't be thinking ye can rule me Haatspore. I'll hae mah revenge for Homildon with or without yer help.'

'You are the most ungrateful b-brigand I've ever known my lord.'

'What's that ye say?'

'Perhaps I should have left you on that hill to d-die?'

'I'll hae at ye too!' spat Douglas limping back to his retainers.

His words were hardly a threat, and Hotspur knew the Scot respected him despite having old scores to settle with Dunbar and the English. It was as if all the ghosts of the past were revealing themselves, and when Douglas nodded that he and his men were ready, my master went to draw his sword.

'Get me the sword I w-wore at Homildon, Hardyng,' he said to me, unbuckling the one he wore for hunting.

I stared in amazement.

Our departure had been rushed that morning, and my first thought was that his favourite sword was still in a cart slowly trundling towards us. But before I could speak, there was a movement in the king's army. Hotspur pointed out two riders approaching across the fields, and soon an archbishop and Lancaster Herald raised a flag of peace as we rode out with Thomas Percy to greet them.

'How now my lord bishop—'

The archbishop cut Hotspur short. 'I have brought terms from His Majesty,' he said arrogantly. 'You would do well to read them and comply, or you will be charged with high treason and executed.'

Thomas Percy shook his head as Lancaster Herald read out each surrender condition to my master. Each of the herald's proposals was a death sentence. The archbishop tried to address the army in person, but Thomas stopped him by threatening to drag him from his horse. Hotspur had private words with his uncle, who in the end, produced his manifesto and gave it to the herald to take back to the king. He shook the parchment in the archbishop's face, briefly voiced some of the crimes that King Henry had offended in, and then he bid the royal emissaries leave to consult with their sovereign.

The threatening atmosphere grew more intense as we returned to our ranks. An exhausted rider had dismounted from his sweating horse, and above all this, I had to tell my master that he had most likely left his favourite sword where we had camped the night before. I could feel all eyes turning on me even before I spoke to him, but before I could utter another word, there was a great commotion in the army and Hotspur spurred his horse forward with Venables in hot pursuit.

Ramkyn and his men were running away. They were fleeing down the slope towards the king, and I saw other men breaking ranks to join them crying, 'Sanctuary! Mercy!' It seemed a terrible rumour had preceded the messenger that the Earl of Northumberland was still tarrying at Alnwick, and it took all of my master's skill and words of warning to keep our army together on the ridge.

Thomas Percy ordered his Welsh archers to shoot the deserters as they ran for the royal ranks, and when we saw Ramkyn fall, struck by several arrows in his back, we knew no one else would dare follow him. The Cheshire archers braced their bows in defiance and were unmoved by the killing of their countrymen. Richard's former bodyguard had already planted their arrows in the ground and were ready for a brawl, especially with anyone who had murdered their beloved king. It seemed no one would dissuade them from punishing Lancaster, and their enthusiasm steeled the hearts of our army, be it only for a moment.

'I will appeal to the k-king,' said Hotspur to his uncle.

Thomas Percy shook his head. 'No, Harry, I will go. The

king will listen to me, and if he fails to see our argument, I will buy some time for you to seek out Glyndŵr.'

Hotspur lurched forward. 'I will stop this now. I will challenge him man to man, *à l'outrance,* before G-God and our two armies.'

'I told you no,' said Thomas noticing the usual flame of mischief flickering in his nephew's eyes. 'The world has changed since the days of Roland,' he said peevishly. 'Remember what I told you many years ago. True chivalry is dead; there is only ambition or death. And both have set the king on his throne. Henry thinks nothing of chivalry, only that we threaten his crown.'

'No, you are w-wrong uncle, Henry is a chivalrous man—'

'But the nobles who follow him will not allow him to fight you. They are all looking for advancement, Harry, and this field is where they can get it.' Thomas recalled the evening at the Savoy when Hotspur had questioned chivalry. 'I should have told you why I lost faith in the code Harry,' his uncle continued, 'but, now it's too late—'

'This is a g-good day to die,' said Hotspur gazing at the steely sky.

'You must let me go to the king. Don't you see I have advised Lancaster for years, first Gaunt, then Bolingbroke, both as their lawyer and councillor? When I first served them, I was, like you, a chivalrous man…'

Hotspur was not listening to his uncle. He was staring into the firmament, beyond the thin wisps of haze, listening to the chattering voices in his head threatening to spiral him out of control.

Thomas seized my master's clenched fist. 'When my friend Sir John Chandos died,' said Thomas frowning at my presence, 'he was the flower of knighthood as you know. He was a good man, a wise councillor and a master of chivalry. But despite all his fame, I failed him foul.'

A flock of birds swooped overhead and settled in some isolated trees to the west. Hotspur followed their flight onward towards the Severn River, and again he lost interest in what his uncle was saying.

'Chandos was a melancholic man,' continued Thomas despite Hotspur's indifference. 'He spoke about how he was losing the war in France and how he had failed the king and his master, the Black Prince. His captains told me how he foresaw his own death the next day, and yet I abandoned him to follow my chivalrous ambitions in Poitou. The following day, as you know, Chandos was wounded by the French on the bridge of Lussac, and he died after a day and night of agony. His confessor said he called out my name several times when he was dying, but I failed him in that too.'

'You were not to b-blame uncle,' said Hotspur his eyes now fixed on the king's army awaiting orders to attack, 'Chandos knew death would someday take him. He met it honourably as I see it. It is how w-we meet death that matters.'

Thomas flew into a rage. 'No, Harry, you mistake me. Chandos was a great knight. He lived for chivalry to the point of devoting his whole life to it. He never married and took pleasure in male company. It was a mistake to assault that bridge, and everyone knew it. But don't you see I loved him, was spurned by him, and failed in my duty. I blamed chivalry for everything.'

Hotspur took his eyes from the threatening situation unfolding before us. For the first time in his life, he saw his uncle in a different light. After a lifetime of thinking the best of him, cracks appeared in his stone-faced exterior that he could not explain.

'So, you forsook chivalry b-because of Chandos,' said Hotspur.

'Worse, I was struck down with blind ambition. Who do you think contrived the plan to appeal to King Richard and plot his downfall? Ask yourself who arranged the execution of the appellants, including the Duke of Gloucester? And who do you think plotted to set Lancaster on the throne?'

'And Richard's murder?'

Thomas nodded.

A look of complete betrayal swept over Hotspur's face, and he felt for his sword again. 'Hardyng!'

I lowered my head. 'I fear your sword is at Berwick master.'

'Berwick?' exclaimed Hotspur.

'The village of Berwick my lord, where we encamped last night. Or perhaps it is at the ford where you waded the river.'

But my master's eyes had already widened in disbelief. His teeth clenched, and a fearful expression came over him that I remember to this day. I too recalled the soothsayers curse at Westminster that foretold Hotspur would not live long after seeing Berwick and I hung my head in shame for reminding him of it.

'Forgive me, my lord,' I said bowing low, 'I will retrieve it.'

'No matter,' sighed my master. 'I thought B-Berwick to be in the north, b-but it seems not...p-perhaps my hourglass has run its course.'

To my surprise, a look of complete acceptance softened Hotspur's blank stare. He forgot about the curse and pointed to several knights wheeling their horses around the flank of Stafford's archers. A brass fanfare sounded, and we saw the king and his son the prince riding along the ranks of cheering soldiers.

'God wills it,' sighed Hotspur. 'As you say uncle, we need to p-postpone this fight. Go to the king and use all your powers of p-persuasion to delay him.' Then he turned to me. 'Hardyng, scour the Severn again and g-gather news of Glyndŵr and Mortimer. We will see if curses cannot be b-broken in the name of chivalry. Now go!'

I took up the reins of my horse and thanked God my master had given me another chance to redeem myself. Berwick village was close at hand, and I could easily find the ford where Hotspur had tried to wade across it the night before. The river would be lower now, I thought, and I could be the first to bring news of Glyndŵr or Mortimer.

But alas, the soothsayer's curse was deep-rooted. It was cast against us all, and, for my sins, I thought to flee as I once more sped along the Severn River. My gut churned wildly as I rode, measuring my loyalty against the kindness the Percy family had shown me over the years. My eyes fixed on the sun's torturous course across the heavens, and its heat blinded me as I found myself back at the ford.

But instead of Glyndŵr, all I met at there was a farmer whose wagon was struggling to cross the river. He told me that he had been foolish against such a strong current, and had turned back when his oxen almost drowned. The sun was dipping in the west by this time, and as its long golden rays struck the fields like pointed fingers, I noticed a lone rider grazing his horse on the far bank. A twinkling from a burnished helmet caused my heart to leap. The farmer saw it too, but when he hurried off, I knew something was amiss.

'Who are you?' I shouted across the river.

The rider shook his head and put his hand to his ear.

'If you ride from Owain Glyndŵr then you must tell him to make haste,' I shouted. 'My master has great need of him against the king.'

My plea echoed back, carrying with it a strange finality. A chilling silence gave me cause to doubt my openness with the stranger and only the rushing water of the Severn stood between my hope and the awful truth the rider carried with him.

'Tell your master the Welshman's not coming, and Mortimer neither,' shouted the soldier, 'I've seen to that!'

My heart raced again, but this time with raw fear. 'You must tell me why? My name is John Hardyng, squire to Sir Henry Percy—'

'Ha, is that bastard Hardyng?'

My heart sank deeper. 'You—'

'I told you I would pay your master back someday for what he did at Radcot Bridge and now it seems someone else will kill him for me.'

'No!' I screamed. 'You must tell Glyndŵr—'

'The only reason I came here was to see Percy die like a dog. So, farewell Hardyng, and take my advice, flee yourself, remember us bastards should look to ourselves!'

Sir Thomas Mortimer laughed at me as he turned his horse into the blinding rays of the sun. I continued to shout his name, imploring him to seek out Glyndŵr, but soon the pounding of my horse's hooves equalled my beating heart. I churned up vast sods of earth as I charged back towards Hateley Field. I caught up with the farmer soon enough and to my surprise saw him gloating over Hotspur's jewelled sword balanced on his knee.

He yelled as I breezed past him and yanked the blade from his grasp.

'I found that by the river...it's mine!' he cried.

I stuck the sword through my belt and urged my sweating horse over obstacles and ridge and furrow. I looked back at the sun countless times, trying to judge how little time I had left to reach my master and stop the bloodshed.

Galloping for all I was worth, I thought I could somehow change everything with my news. But despite this, the sand in the hourglass had run its course. I knew in my heart it was too late for miracles. Even before I saw Hateley Field, black arrow clouds were gathering in the summer sky, and I reined in my horse transfixed by the sounds of fighting coming from beyond the next ridge. Countless yells of panic and rescue cried out in unison. It was as if the ground had opened up, and hell was swallowing up everything I held dear.

More than anything, I felt waves of panic and guilt flood my brain. The simple truth was that I had failed my master because of a single length of steel. It cut me to the core as I beheld the jewelled hilt of his blade flicker in the evening light; and now it seemed the battle had begun without me, almost as if Hotspur had willed it so.

29

Battlefield 1403

'After long trete, the armys began to fyght'

With a stave of Spanish yew, a handful of goose feathers, simple twine, and a tempered iron head fixed to a wooden dowel, archers of both sides had killed or wounded thousands of men in Hateley Field.

By the time I reached our former position on the slight ridge, the tangled crops had sprouted another deadly harvest. Each soldier without armour suffered multiple injuries, and I was trying hard to avoid the great heaps of writhing humanity. Dead and dying men littered the slope where the men of Cheshire had stopped the Earl of Stafford and his vaward. But the fight was far from over. Hotspur had followed up this initial victory by charging Stafford down and advancing against the king's men-at-arms.

A dust-filled haze shrouded the fighting, and from it came a sound like thousands of blacksmiths hard at work. Roars and cries of anguish filled the once tranquil meadows, and only distance dulled the horror of the carnage being wrought. I was mesmerised by the weight of men hurled to their deaths. If the dam burst, I too might be engulfed I thought, and when something seized my master's banner, the shock almost threw me from the saddle.

I saw a hand attached to the wooden shaft, and the great weight of whatever was attached to it warned me that I had strayed too near the fight. A voice shrieked out from somewhere between the stamping hooves of my horse. But it was only after jerking the pole away that I noticed what was clinging to it. The soldier was only half a man; a carcase of ripped flesh whose tangled insides spilt down his only remaining leg.

His mangled state held me transfixed until I saw Thomas Percy ride up and, without an ounce of pity, cut the poor soul across the head with his sword.

'Well Hardyng,' he said, barely acknowledging his butchery, 'what news of Glyndŵr?'

For a moment, I was struck dumb. 'None, my lord.'

Thomas wheeled his horse as a peppering of arrows struck the ground beside him. 'Ah, just as I expected, Mortimer is worried that King Henry will kill young Edmund if he joins us...and as for that Welshman—'

'You knew?' said I, avoiding another arrow.

Thomas lifted his shield above his head. 'A squire should never question his master Hardyng. Forget that, and you're no better than a servant at a table.'

Yet another arrow thumped into the ground, and I decided not the cross the Earl of Worcester.

With a nod, he shook the reins of his horse. 'Your master

is down there,' he said, pointing to the heaving mass of men that had somehow moved closer as we talked. 'And I expect he'll be missing that...' pointing at Hotspur's sword.

I wanted to kill Thomas Percy so many times during my master's service, but as I galloped off that day, I was glad to be rid of him. I decided he was the cause of all the ills that beset England, and when I saw him loitering on the slope, a detached observer to the carnage below, I wished him a cruel and bitter end. Thomas was directing men into the fray from the safety of the ridge, and I concluded this was one reason why some great lords lived while their lowly tenants perished in their place.

But as arrows flew around me, I had no time to ponder the fate of others. Time seemed to quicken as I approached the rear ranks of our army, and above all the tumult of noise and bodies heaving before me, I suddenly realised I could never hope to find my master amongst the mayhem. He had no banner to mark him out; it was still in my hand.

The clamour of weapons drowned out any rational thinking I may have had. But unlike Homildon, I saw every detail of the fight in a hellish tableau, worse than anything conjured up by a truculent priest in his pulpit. Soldiers were pushed into the conflict like sacrifices only to be thrown back out again fatally wounded as the battle moved back and forth. Space was limited in the continually moving ranks, and some men were suffocated even before they had a chance to strike a blow. To fall was to be crushed under a stampede of moving feet. The cries of the wounded, the breathless exertion from those still alive, and the screams of those being mutilated were all inhaled and dispelled like a great bellows before a roaring fire of hatred and fear. The stench of sweat, leather, urine and blood sickened me to the core. Bodies were boiling over in the heat of their armour and thick quilted jacks. Flesh and bone were hacked into chunks, and limbs fell to the ground like meat in a butcher's shop. Blood seeped into the parched soil and formed muddy pools where others slipped and pounced like demons. Herded together like lambs to the slaughter, I saw the front ranks fall only to be trampled to death by others pushed into the fight. It was only a matter of time before I became embroiled in the slaughter or one side yielded, I thought. And after a few minutes on the edge of the carnage, God forgive me, I decided to turnabout and flee the field.

But then I saw Thomas Percy watching and waiting in the distance. He had gathered a group of horsemen on the ridge armed with spears. They all eagerly obeyed his will to run through deserters, and I felt their menace when they began spearing those who were hobbling injured to the rear. Men like Thomas Percy expected others to fight for him and make the ultimate sacrifice. Only Hotspur was reckless enough to fight against convention, to expose himself to the same dangers as his men, and I was no better than Thomas it seemed. I was alone with my master's banner, a safe distance from the fighting and emptying my stomach like a sick child.

From that moment on everything before me became real and dangerous. I saw the glint of razor-sharp steel, the forest of slashing weapons, the red mists of expelled blood, and I even heard the last words of soldiers as they cried for their mothers. All around me, the battle was moving ever closer, but I seemed to be in another more heightened state of awareness. I remember thrashing about with Hotspur's banner at anything that came towards me. I drew my master's sword from my belt realising I was in danger. I grasped it in my right hand, but when I stupidly dropped the reins of my horse to save my master's banner from falling the animal reared, and I fell clumsily to the ground.

Through the fog of confusion, I used Hotspur's sword to lash out. I saw a severed head fall to the ground like a discarded cabbage. The shock made me turn away, and a mass of weapons prodded me into retreat. I fell over a dead body, collapsed in a heap with others on top of me, and found I was trapped. I was drowning under the weight, and I thought I might suffocate. I could neither breathe in nor out. But someone had seen my master's banner fall beside me, and I felt several hands pulling me clear of the fight.

When the fog cleared, I saw Hotspur holding my horse's bridle. Sir Richard Vernon and other men-at-arms were urging their men forward, and my master ordered him to hold the line at all costs.

'Glyndŵr and Mortimer have forsaken you, my lord,' I whined remembering my mission and passing my master his sword.

'I know Hardyng, but k-keep my sword you may need it. I swear I have slain three k-kings of England today in the same coat-armour,' he said, looking back over the fence of men and slashing weapons. 'Vernon stay here and p-protect Hardyng with your life.'

Vernon nodded, and Hotspur lifted his banner from the ground. 'God b-be with you, John,' said my master turning away.

'But my place is with you master,' said I, reaching out to him.

Hotspur shook his head. 'You can't serve me today Hardyng.'

I was lost for words. And with tears welling in my eyes,

Hotspur unfurled his *lion passant* banner and mounted my horse.

Then he reached down and took my hand.

'Long life John,' he said, before spurring back up the slope towards his uncle.

I tried to follow him, but Vernon held me back.

'He has seen the king,' said Vernon, trying to hold back his despair. 'We cannot stop him now Master Hardyng. He is resolved to break the line and kill him. It's our only chance.'

I was about to break away again, but at that moment we had to turn and fight for our lives. The Prince of Wales was pushing more men against us, and in a moment, cries of 'Flee!' and 'Rescue!' were on every soldier's lips.

As the moon took the sun's place in the sky, a great moan came from our ranks. Men turned their backs on the enemy and were hacked to the ground. Soon the moon loomed over the battlefield like a bloodshot eye. It seemed that God had decided to mimic the madness being perpetrated on earth using a celestial messenger. The lunar eclipse numbed us all, although we were busy trying to fight for survival.

I hardly remember the tide of battle sweeping over us. In a moment, I drowned under another heap of falling bodies. The world shimmered before my eyes, and for the first time in my life, I was aware of how fleeting life could be. My fitful breathing, the blood coursing through my veins, and the intense beating in my breast made me aware that I was about to die. Men were being crushed to death as others fell on top of them. Soldiers cried out for their loved ones as their souls were cut loose from their bodies. The blood of young and old empurpled the soil around me. It seemed I was a spectator to the carnage; that is until my legs turned to stone, and I believed they had been cleaved from my body.

At first, I was content to lie there. I was alive and not in pain, but knew if I moved then I might die. I closed my eyes and waited for the end to come. The battle raged above me like a storm. I posed no threat to those still fighting, and when the enemy moved on, a gap of reddish light opened up before me. It was a brief vision, but I was transfixed and saw with clarity my master and a handful of riders making a last desperate charge towards the king's standard. It seemed as if Hotspur's armour was glowing red, the fluted edges white-hot with stars and sunbursts of the purest light. His lance was a needle, his shield a burning blazon of azure lions, and his famous rowel spurs wheeled like firebrands at his heels. He had taken on a mythical appearance, I conjectured, and I believed for a moment I had a raging fever. But as God is my witness, I saw every moment as Hotspur charged down the slope with his uncle and Douglas at his back. It was a vision, yet it was reality, and stranger still, I had the feeling that my master was already dead; that his soul had somehow left his body before the king's men could destroy it.

The sight chilled my bones, and when Hotspur's body was engulfed in the crush, the unearthly vision was extinguished like a candle, almost as though it had never existed.

His uncle and men-at-arms stove in after Hotspur with cries of, 'Henry Percy king!' but as the moon further eclipsed, a hail of arrows descended on both friend and foe. The king's standard fell into a sea of bodies. There were eerie cries of, 'The king is dead!' My master's banner fell once more, and I hid my face in my hands, fearing the worst. I prayed that my master was still alive, but when I raised my head, the battlefield was snuffed out, and I feared my life was too.

As always, Hotspur's charge was rash and premeditated, but it was his only course. My master had saved my life once again, and somewhere in me, I felt the guilt of Hotspur's death pass through my heart like a lance.

Most rebel soldiers had thrown down their weapons and surrendered. Survivors were roaming the field dazed and broken in both mind and body. Some were trying to help others staunch bloody wounds while others limped from Hateley Field to die in secret far away from the scavengers who would soon be out searching for loot. No one was taking any notice of the rebellion anymore. Most men were trying to survive as best they could, and one of these was Archibald Douglas who stumbled by me as I lay there half-buried under the heap of bodies.

Douglas's face was deathly pale. He was breathing heavily, staggering without his great axe for support.

'My lord Douglas!' I croaked, trying to raise myself from the mound.

Douglas put a finger to his lips. 'Hah ye seen mah horse?'

I shook my head, and he fell to his knees before me. His jupon was soaked with blood, and he showed me where a blade had broken through his mail and ruptured him.

'You will bleed to death, my lord, unless you seek ransom from the king,' said I.

Douglas reached down under his armour and caught a handful of gore in his hand. 'I'll nae be taken by the English again Master Hardyng?'

'You must look to that herald over there; he will help you my lord.'

I called out to the young official who was stepping carefully between the blood and bodies. He tried to ignore me at first by taking notes of the dead, but when Douglas showed himself and the herald saw his livery, his priorities changed. He knew he could make a name for himself by handing over Douglas to the king, and after putting his notebook away, he was glad to help us.

I enquired after Hotspur, and the herald shook his head. His body had not been found on the field, he said, and after pulling me from the carnage, he went to find a surgeon.

Douglas made sure the herald was gone. 'Wi luck they won't find yer master, he's —' The Scot became faint through loss of blood. He groaned as he held the weight of his body upright. But then a spark of life returned to his one good eye, and his words seemed to glow with pride.

'Ah never saw anything so glorious in all mah life,' he said. 'Ah bide with Haatspore as long as ah could, but then an arrow struck his head. His horse reared up. I held 'im in mah arms for a moment. Then ah saw that the arrow had stove in his visage. His skull wah no more...'

Douglas clenched his fist and cursed George Dunbar several times.

'But ah sware Haatspore looked at me Hardyng...he...he...'

I caught the Scot as he toppled over.

'...but then he wah gone.'

I felt my world had ended, and after making sure Douglas was safe, I wandered the battlefield for some hours in search of the man who had saved my life so many times. My mind was utterly confused. It was the end of everything I knew. I had served the Percys all my life, and my master had been my world since before I could remember. What would become of me now, I moaned, and what would become of the Percys now that Hotspur was dead? In truth, I wished for death also.

But I was cowardly, and when I finally found my master's broken body at the very edge of that bloody field of peas, I sat in the ditch and wept for both of us.

As I saw it, I had only two choices. I could run for my life and wait to be hunted down like a common criminal or I could throw myself at the king's mercy. And it was only after I wrenched Hotspur's fallen banner from his mailed fist and saw my master was finally at peace that I decided to beg King Henry for my miserable life.

30

Shrewsbury 1403

'Hys uncle dere, sew hym there dedde'

Sooner or later, everyone sits down to plot their revenge. But I was content to trust in God and not dig graves for my enemies, or myself.

After the battle, I was imprisoned by the king in Shrewsbury Castle along with many other rebels awaiting trial. Like the dead still being cleared from Hateley Field, the common soldier had been released from his martial obligations without charge, and those captured were set free to return to their homes unmolested. King Henry was magnanimous in victory, and only those men of note were taken prisoner. My torture was that I was neither notable nor a commoner, but I was known for being my master's squire, and this notoriety grieved me beyond words.

However, my greatest fear was that King Henry might recognise me as the unscrupulous forger that had aided the

Percy rebellion. This crime, if anything, was far worse than serving Hotspur, I thought. But on the second day of my imprisonment, my fears redoubled when guards led Thomas Percy into the dank undercroft of the castle where we were all held captive.

Thomas was a ghost of his former self. It was clear he had not slept, and his hair was still matted with grime and dried blood from the battlefield. In this state, it was difficult to imagine Thomas as the once all-powerful Earl of Worcester who had been the puppet master of all that had gone before. His face was crisscrossed with battle-scars, his undershirt was torn and bloody, and despite being acknowledged by Sir Richard Venables, he sat completely alone in a corner of the dungeon deep in thought.

'The king will soon free us, Master Hardyng, have no doubt of that,' whispered Venables turning from Thomas and forcing a smile.

'I fear we are all dead men,' said I.

Venables shook his head. 'No, the earl says men are being pardoned. The king needs friends, not enemies, to secure his throne.'

But that same afternoon Venables and Vernon were taken away by guards, and I now know both were executed in Shrewsbury market place on the king's orders. Their bodies were hung, drawn and quartered on the insistence of the Prince of Wales, who had miraculously survived the disfiguring arrow wound on his face due to a surgeon named Bradmore.

But I was especially fearful of the prince for other reasons and was mindful that my jaw was still pounding from the swipe he had given me on the battlefield. Everyone knew that the prince hated my master for abandoning him in Wales. Yet at the same time, I knew he held him in such high regard as a soldier that he was ashamed to admit it. I was tarnished with the same crime in the prince's eyes, it seemed, and now I too feared the worst kind of punishment for my part in the Percy rebellion.

Later that day, our numbers in the dungeon diminished further, and I sunk into a deep depression. All my clothes stank of death, and I became so anxious that I yearned to die peacefully in my sleep. But that evening, Thomas and I were roused and taken to another chamber in the castle where our guards gave us something to eat and drink. The room was sparsely furnished, but servants provided us with fresh clothes and a bed to sleep on. And for the first time in my life, I was thankful for the great earl's company.

We spoke until the morning sun streamed through the windows of the chamber, and my spirits raised somewhat. Thomas reminded me of my home at Leconfield and spoke fondly of the place, his life there, and of how my master had been the perfect knight worthy of all the chivalrous books in Paradise. He assured me that we would soon see Leconfield again. He was certain we would serve King Henry and the prince faithfully once more, chiefly because he was the architect of all Lancaster's plans thus far. As soon as his elder brother, the Earl of Northumberland, was apprehended the king would free us, he said. And then he finally spoke of my early years. I never saw him in such a good mood, and presently all my fears were dispelled in a revelation from the past that for a brief moment detracted from the situation I found myself in.

'So, did you not know you were a Neville, Master Hardyng?'

he said, picking at a morsel of bread from the night before.

'I...no, my lord.'

'Then believe it. You are a bastard of course, but a Neville none the less. I knew your father, Solomon. I employed him at Leconfield as my steward. He had a good keen eye for figures and drawing plans for building work as I remember. I knew your mother too, but that's another story—'

Thomas broke off mid-sentence as a key turned in the lock. 'And I have a feeling that tale will have to wait for another time,' he said, getting to his feet and straightening his doublet.

Armed guards entered the chamber, and he smiled knowingly. He adjusted his jacket again, donned a red felt hat he had been given to wear and waited for the guards to take him to the king.

'The king assured me that he would move us today,' said Thomas confidently. 'He told me that the Earl of Westmoreland captured my brother fleeing for his life and that Sir Robert Umfraville is arriving today to escort us to York so that we might give evidence at Northumberland's trial.'

'Then we are to be spared?' said I shocked.

'Aye, only to denounce my brother, of course. Someone has to carry the blame for the rebellion, and my brother knew it would be he.'

But as we descended the tower staircase with our escort and made our way into the courtyard below, I had a feeling something was deeply wrong. Umfraville was not there to greet us and instead a large unruly crowd had gathered beyond the castle foregate. They jeered as we passed by them. Rotten food was thrown in our faces partway down the street, and I felt one of the guards tighten his grip on my arm as they hustled us into the busy marketplace.

There was no market that day. The stalls had been cleared away, and I imagined Umfraville leading horses into the square to save us from the angry citizens. But instead, more soldiers filed in from between the houses and lined the perimeter of the square; in the centre of which, propped up by two great millstones, was a strangely familiar carcase of rotting meat.

My master's limp, yellowing body was covered in blood and filth. It had been manhandled many times and was covered in soil as if it had been exhumed from a grave. The remains of the arrow that had killed him still protruded from his skull, and at first, I failed to reconcile the butchery with the man I once knew. I thought the sight unreal and that I had inadvertently fallen asleep in the castle. I consoled myself that it was a dream or a night terror perhaps. But that thought was soon dispelled when I saw beside Hotspur's remains a bundle of straw, a large block of wood and a hooded executioner shouldering an axe.

I felt my knees weaken as Thomas was roughly seized from behind and led forward. A group of officials appeared, and a priest gave Percy absolution for his sins.

I remember seeing Thomas's eyes fall first on his nephew's body, then on King Henry and the prince who had arrived in the marketplace to much applause. By this time, I was shaking and sweating under a blinding sun. A statement was quickly read out by an official accusing Thomas Percy of treason and of conspiring the destruction of King Henry, the Prince of Wales, and the whole realm of England.

And it was then I knew we were both about to beheaded.

The crowd yelled again; their noisy approval of the death sentence was unanimous. Like wild animals, they jostled for a better view of the earl's butchery. The executioner removed

Thomas's felt cap, grinned, pushed his head firmly onto the block, heaved the axe, and without further ceremony, severed Thomas's head just as he was about to confess.

Then my world spiralled into darkness.

I had succumbed to exhaustion, and just as I began to feel reconciled with my fate, I was revived by a splash of water in the face. I had fainted in the heat and now found myself before King Henry and the Prince of Wales. They were both sat at a large dais in the great hall of Shrewsbury Castle, and when a guard dragged me forward, I fell heavily onto the cold stone floor.

'You say little John Hardyng but do much,' said King Henry at last. He was thumbing through a pile of papers and maps on the table before him. 'And you have done much to anger your king.'

'Yes sire…I crave…mercy Your Majesty,' I said breathlessly.

'Ah, but do you agree that like your master you now have to answer for your crimes?'

'But sire I am innocent, I only served my master…'

The king held up his hand. 'All your comrades served and are dead Hardyng. Others soon will be, so do not tell me that you are innocent.'

'Then I humbly beg your forgiveness sire.'

Up until that point, the Prince of Wales had said nothing, and when he stood up and strutted confidently towards me, I feared he would strike me again.

The side of his face was caked with blood, and his cheek was utterly destroyed. The Cheshire arrow had done its work well, and Henry's once handsome profile had paid the price of a surgeon's rudimental pincers, cauterisation methods, various herbal potions and six large purple stitches. On one side of his face, he was still the handsome, courtly prince I once knew, but on the other, he was a disfigured monster. And when he spoke to me, I felt all his pain was aimed at his former mentor Hotspur and everything that had ruined their friendship.

'You were in your master's service for what, thirteen years Hardyng?' said the prince at last.

'I was brought up in the Percy household from birth, Your Highness.'

'And what did you learn from Hotspur in those years?'

I was feeling faint and felt myself drifting as I spoke. 'He was the greatest knight who ever lived—'

The prince laughed. 'He was the greatest rebel!'

My hand stopped me from falling to the floor, and the king gestured for a servant to pass me a cup of wine.

'So Hardyng what did you learn? And beware you speak the truth,' said the king not waiting for me to recover.

The warmth and bitterness of the grape revived me instantly, and for a moment, I had no fear and regard for my life. 'I learned much about the Scots, Your Majesty,' said I, taking another sip from the cup.

The king held up two maps of Scotland. 'Is this your work?'

'Yes, Your Majesty.'

'Good…good…very detailed,' said the king looking at it closely. 'And is this your work too?'

The prince seized the documents I had forged bearing King Richard's signature, and when he stepped from the dais, he threw the papers into my face. 'So, how do you explain these Hardyng?'

I said nothing and the prince unsheathed his dagger.

'And at whose bidding did you falsify these documents, Hardyng? Was it the Earl of Northumberland?' said the king.

'No, it was the Earl of Worcester your grace.'

'But his brother agreed to it,' added the prince trying to egg me on.

The king rose stiffly and limped towards me. 'I know none of this was wholly Hotspur's fault Master Hardyng. We all know that Thomas Percy conspired against us and persuaded your master into raising battle. But we must know the truth or others will rebel in his place.'

When I raised my head, I saw that the king was not only scarred from the battle, but his expression betrayed a measure of grief. He had tears in his eyes.

'He was truly chivalric,' said the king, 'and I bemoan, like your master did, how others have disregarded the codes we once held so dear in our youth. Some men curry favour, others ambition, those who wage war do it under the guise of being true knights. But we must guard against such men at all costs Hardyng. And when we weaken we must all look in the mirror where Hotspur once dressed himself and ruminate on what he might have done differently.'

'Yes, Your Majesty.'

The prince shook his head. 'But we need to know if Northumberland is a traitor father. They must all be punished, or we will never have any peace in England!'

'I think we all know who the true rebel was Harry.'

'Then we should execute Hardyng too,' said the prince, raising his dagger.

But the king caught his hand deftly. 'And then where would we be,' he said gazing at me, 'like my cousin Richard?'

The reference to the dead king silenced the prince, and he managed to hold back his anger from me and direct it at his father. In his eyes, I saw all the old father-son frustrations mirrored at the very highest level, and I gave thanks to God that I was only a humble squire.

'The Earl of Westmoreland and Sir Robert Umfraville have spoken up for you Hardyng, so you are free to go,' said the king at last. 'But do not stray too far as I may call upon you to do more work for us in Scotland. You will make maps and spy for me there until England has peace on all its troubled borders.'

'Yes, Your Majesty,' I said quickly.

It took all of my strength to rise and thank the king for my life. I also gave thanks for the new day and how I had almost not seen it. Henry would not be the first or last king I would ever thank, but he was the most like my master, and I admired him for that. As for the prince, I would have to earn his trust, and I feared he would never forgive me for rebelling against the crown or being Hotspur's squire.

As for freedom, after acquiring a horse, I rode straight to Leconfield and climbed the tower my master's feet had ascended so many times before. The castle was deserted, and the little chamber called Paradise was gloomy as usual. But I did manage to find the only book Hotspur ever loved waiting patiently for me on the shelf, and soon I began writing a new chapter in it telling the world of my master's life.

31

Kyme 1461

'That if John Hardyng bee a trew-herted Englysheman'

And what became of that soldier I once was? The moon is no longer eclipsed. The fields near Shrewsbury are ripe with yet another crop of mature peas waiting to be harvested, and now only ghosts inhabit the place where once thousands died.

It is late summer, and birds fly across Hateley Field. Arrows no longer darken the sky, and a small chapel has been built where once mass graves marked the site of Hotspur's battle. Priests pray for the souls of the Shrewsbury dead, and relatives weep for lost loved ones, and even ancestors, who fell like autumn leaves. A few old soldiers who return to the battlefield come to mourn their comrades - and I am no exception. I am in my eighty-third year, a new king is on the English throne, and the kingdom is once more at war. History repeats itself, and I still marvel at how little things have changed in the world since I was Hotspur's squire.

But I am a fortunate child it seems, and because God has granted me the privilege of a longer life than most, my only joy lately has been to see some of those who once opposed my master die before me. I still regularly wake at night to the sound of metal striking metal, and the cries of dying men continue to haunt my dreams, although I have tried desperately hard to consign them to history. Writing, I have found, is a good cure for a troubled heart, but I can still feel the ghost of my master wherever I go, and the shadows of those who brought about his death.

Years after the famous battle at Shrewsbury, I learned the true story of what had been said between Thomas Percy and the king before the battle began. It seemed Hotspur's uncle had not finished with Lancaster, and when he arrived at King Henry's tent, he made clear in the strongest terms that the king was a liar just like his father. He read out the Percy manifesto once more, but this time at length, much to the king and prince's annoyance. He was raging by the end of the document, and Henry railed against Thomas's 'lying lawyer's tongue' despite his willingness to find a compromise. In the end, King Henry tried to save Hotspur and those who might give up their arms. He said he did not want a battle and asked to parley with his friend alone. But Thomas said what had been done by the king could not be undone by words, only swords, and stormed from the tent.

Thomas was the opposite of my master in every way, and years later in the library at Leconfield I read of an ancient Percy prophecy which said that someday the cast-off beast, would carry away the two horns of the moon. A passage that wholly described King Henry, his exile, and the conflicting intentions of Hotspur and his uncle. It spoke of how two opposing ambitions of the same whole could court disaster, and this was certainly true of the Percys; a dynasty that would soon be involved in yet another civil war.

After learning of Thomas Percy's betrayal of Hotspur, I never visited his grave in Shrewsbury again, and soon after being set free by King Henry I willingly took up service with Sir Robert Umfraville in the north. My former master was the true guardian of the east march, but Umfraville was a worthy successor. I prospered in his service, and when rumours spread that Hotspur and Thomas Percy were still alive, I felt that Umfraville was hopeful of a reconciliation. He questioned me about what I had seen in Shrewsbury marketplace that day, and it was not until my master's decaying remains were removed and displayed above the gates of several English towns, that Umfraville truly believed Hotspur was dead.

As for the sickly-frail Earl of Northumberland, he was spared execution for his treason such was his standing with the king and his followers in the north. I bore witness to his trial in York, where he claimed his son and brother had acted without his consent. As prudent as ever, he lied through his teeth. And I must confess the earl's outpouring of grief failed to move me when he was forced, in the pouring rain, to stand and view his son's weathered head spiked over the city gate.

Later that month, I was tasked with collecting my late master's decayed remains on behalf of his wife, Elizabeth. Hotspur was to be buried in York, and I had the pleasure of Lady Percy's horror when I placed my master's head and limbs in the self-same boxes that had once contained her armourial birthday presents from him. After that, I never saw

Elizabeth again. She married Lord Camoys soon after, and the Mortimers never achieved the English crown, although some nobles since have tried to claim it on their behalf.

Rumours circulated in the years following the battle of Shrewsbury that Sir Thomas Mortimer had died in Scotland soon after Bolingbroke's usurpation of the throne. However, I know now that Thomas was taken in by the Mortimers and then Glyndŵr after King Richard's death despite being declared a traitor. His betrayal of Hotspur is not widely known, and when Glyndŵr received news of Shrewsbury, Thomas ran for his life. Estranged from his family, his country and his wife he died a miserable death in the Highlands. But that day at the ford crossing the River Severn I will never forget.

All my master's enemies were falling by the wayside it seemed. And in the eighth year of King Henry's reign, the Earl of Northumberland tried one last time to remove the man he had helped to the throne. After failing and fleeing into Scotland, he returned to England in a desperate attempt to win back his confiscated estates. He tried to fulfil his brother's dream to divide the kingdom, but when the revolt ended in Wales, and he was killed in battle at Bramham Moor, the Percy family paid dearly for his selfishness. The Nevilles became rulers in the North, and Ralph Earl of Westmorland enjoyed a long association with King Henry and his son in place of the true hereditary keepers of the northern marches – the Percys.

As for King Henry's demise, he died like his father eaten away by his own body. He was beset with illness for most of his life, but I also thought his ordeal against Boucicant at Saint Inglevert contributed to his death in the end. He was the greatest jouster of his time, but not the greatest English king. Plagued by his own usurpation, and the death of King Richard at Pomfret, his dreams of an untroubled reign were never realised. His perjury at Doncaster tortured and gnawed away at his soul, and after Shrewsbury, he never spoke of his friend Hotspur again, although he did build the chantry and college where his throne had been saved. Henry died in the Jerusalem chamber at Westminster aged forty-five years, and when he was near death I was told that he imagined he was leading a crusade to the Holy Land, but then he was the most crusader-like knight of his age.

When his son Henry, the fifth of that name, came to the throne I was in my Lord Umfraville's retinue when he decided to invade France. Near the village of Agincourt, I once again saw arrows darken the sky and the French nobility laid low by the 'lowly' English archer who even today knights fear and belittle so readily. Thereafter Henry was acclaimed king of England and France, I was made constable of Warkworth Castle and later visited Rome where I found the passion for studying and writing history. Serving the young king, I like to think I gained his trust by acting as his chief spy in Scotland. I laboured busily on both sides of the border in those days, charting distances between towns, defining what roads could be used by invading armies, and what land was ripe for plunder. I reported the strengths and weaknesses of border castles, and I also acquired documents supporting England's claim to Scotland if ever it were needed. But I fear the king never used my information about the old enemy to any great advantage. Henry, like his father, never trusted me, and he could not easily reconcile my good service with that of being a former rebel. However, when he died in fourteen hundred and twenty-two, he said that his victory at Agincourt would never have been won if not for the memory of Hotspur who taught him all he knew about the French and the folly of being reckless in battle.

As for the turncoat, George Dunbar Earl of March, he returned to Scotland soon after Shrewsbury where he lived a long life, dying in his eighty-second year. Once released by King Henry, Archibald Douglas was reconciled to his former enemy against all the odds, and in return for those lands he had previously lost in the marches both he and Dunbar promised to live in peace together despite their differences. Nicknamed 'The Loser', Douglas resumed his wardenship on the border, and the English never managed to achieve his ransom despite taking many hostages. He died fighting on the French side at Verneuil in Normandy so great was his hatred of the English.

So much for being a soldier.

Lately, two earls of Northumberland have met with violent deaths in the wars between York and Lancaster, including Hotspur's son, and I am forever thankful that my armour is well and truly rusted over. I have served many kings of England, but the latest, Henry, the sixth of that name, is the weakest monarch that England ever had. His overthrow in the north led by yet another usurper king claiming the throne through Mortimer blood is the saddest history I can recall, and I fear the kingdom may be torn apart again for his sake for many years to come.

Thank God I traded armour for monkish robes long ago. Now I can only admire Hotspur's sword above my mantle, rather than wield it, and wonder what he might have achieved had he lived to realise his dream of limiting violence in the world. His sword is my prized possession. I hid it in the ditch where he died before my capture, and in remembrance, I still visit the chapel near Shrewsbury every year to give thanks to God for not being killed alongside him.

Here in the chapel, and among the fields of peas that still cleave to my weary heels, I can find some small measure of peace in the world. In the nearby hospice I seek a cure for my night sweats, and by chance during one of these pilgrimages to that place, and adjoining chapel, I learned of a much greater truth that even today I find hard to accept.

Early in the reign of the present king, Hotspur's only daughter, Elizabeth, wished to know where her father had perished. And a little before her death she visited the chapel and hospice with her husband Ralph Neville, the second Earl of Westmoreland, to seek a cure and pay her respects to my master's memory.

I too was there praying for his soul, and after I had lit a candle to his name and mine, I was surprised to see their small entourage file passed me in quiet contemplation. Elizabeth looked in poor health, and when she fell before the altar weeping, I was moved to see if I could help her. The little girl, who I had schooled in archery when my master was alive, was now a pale and frightened middle-aged woman. She seemed consumed by some sad illness that I could not see, and as I stooped to console her, the Earl of Westmoreland immediately demanded to know who I was.

Thankfully his grave expression changed when I told him my name, and when he took me by the hand and shook it furiously, I thought my bones might break.

'Are you truthfully John Hardyng?' he said enthused.

'Yes, my lord, I knew your grandfather.'

The earl nodded gravely. 'Yes, he loved your master, but as

I see it, he failed him foul by not supporting his cause.'

Ralph helped his wife to her feet, and when she lifted her veil, I was shocked to see Hotspur's exact likeness pasted across her ghostly face.

'This is squire Hardyng, my dear,' said the earl slowly to his wife. 'Do you remember him?'

The countess shook her head, but then, almost as if a curtain lifted between us, a fragment of memory shone through. 'Yes,' she said. 'My mother called you some other name though…'

She turned to her husband for help.

'No matter my dear,' said the earl trying to cover his wife's frailty. Then he turned to me. 'We have come here to pay our respects before…well…before it is too late. It was good to meet you Hardyng at last.' Ralph shook my hand again, less forcefully this time. 'As someone who knew and fought with the famous Hotspur, you must have many stories to tell.'

I bowed. 'Yes, thank you, my lord.'

'Was he as chivalrous as men say?'

'He was the greatest knight.'

'If he had been a Neville instead of a Percy then perhaps this present civil war would never have happened. The Percys have always been a rash and overmighty breed, quick to take revenge, especially on my family. And now we shed each other's blood in English fields and streets instead of killing our natural enemies in Scotland.'

'I fear, my lord, you confuse my late master with his father the earl.'

Westmoreland frowned. 'How so?'

'My master always held the Nevilles in high regard. The Lord of Alnwick was a great man loved by his tenants and feared by the Scots, but I fear he was a difficult man to fathom—'

'You are a testament to that Hardyng,' said the earl turning to go.

At first, I was confused by this remark. That is until the earl's wife bid me farewell too.

'Good day,' she said, replacing her veil, 'bastard Neville.'

My eyes widened, and I felt the presence of Hotspur's wife in the chapel. A shiver coursed through my body. I was struck dumb. And I remembered that Elizabeth had used my name in such a way before in France.

The earl of Westmoreland carefully folded a comforting arm around his wife. He was clearly embarrassed by her outburst.

'I'm sorry for that Hardyng,' he said, 'for one so constant to your late master you deserve better. My wife is ill at ease as you can see, and lately, she only recalls the past with any clarity.'

'But mother...she used to called him that...' cried Elizabeth pulling away from her husband.

I nodded and smiled at her kindly. 'I have heard that name before my lady, but to this day I have no idea why Lady Percy called me it. I may be a bastard child, for I never knew my mother, but as I see it I was only ever loyal to the Percy family.'

Westmoreland smiled and thumbed the stubble on his chin. 'Then you really have no idea about your lineage Hardyng?'

I shook my head and looked eagerly at the earl for an answer.

Westmoreland sat down in a choir stall opposite me and rested his hands on his knees. I sat down too and waited for him to marshal his thoughts though I could see he was desperate to leave the chantry due to his wife's infirmity.

'You are a Neville, Master Hardyng,' he began, scratching his head. 'My father told me before he died that you caused all the bad blood between the Neville and Percy families.'

'I don't see—'

'I expect you know that Hotspur's mother died in childbirth?' said the earl.

I nodded.

'Well, you were the child that was pulled from her womb.'

I was dumbstruck again. 'Then, I am the Earl of Northumberland's son?'

'No, your father was the steward at Leconfield Castle. You are the bastard child of Margaret Neville, the Earl of Northumberland's wife, and you were taken in by the family to be raised in their household at Thomas Percy's request. Your conception and birth so angered the Earl of Northumberland that he had your father killed by his henchman. I forget the man's name—a man with a limp as I recall—and forever after my family blamed Percy for his part in abandoning his wife and causing her to seek comfort elsewhere.'

I felt the past suddenly overwhelm me.

'I too felt the earl's hate,' said I, 'even though he never spoke of it. But I was ignorant of the why and wherefore.'

'You know how overmighty the Earl of Northumberland was. How he thought he was a king and blamed all my family for the ill will between Percy and Neville? Now you know the truth. The earl had many mistresses in great families you understand, and his association with John of Gaunt was infamous at the time. It was not long before Hotspur's mother tired of his constant fornication, and while Percy was pursuing ultimate power and favours with younger women in the Lucy family, your father gave Margaret comfort and love.'

I was exhausted by the earl's revelations.

'And did my master know this, my lord?' said I.

Westmoreland nodded. 'Hotspur told my father once that he had no greater companion than you Master Hardyng, although, in truth, he wished for you to follow a life of peace and contemplation rather than that of war.'

Tears welled in my eyes, and after shaking my hand again, Ralph said that if I ever needed his help, he and his family would aid me in any way they could. Silence returned to the battlefield chapel. It was becoming late, and as the earl turned to go, his wife stopped and waved at me dreamily.

I may have been a humble soldier, but as fate would have it, I was Hotspur's brother-in-arms in more ways than one.

THE END

About the Author

Andrew Boardman is a historian with an established readership in non-fiction. His published work includes *Towton: The Bloodiest Battle, The Medieval Soldier, Blood Red Roses, Hotspur: Henry Percy Medieval Rebel* and *The First Battle of St Albans*. He lectures on historical subjects and has been a consultant on many TV documentary series including Secrets of the Dead (Channel 4 & Sky One), Towton 1461 (BBC Yorkshire), and Instruments of Death (Yesterday Channel). He lives in Yorkshire.

You can connect with me on:
- https://awboardman.com
- https://twitter.com/wotroses
- http://linkedin.com/in/awboardman

Subscribe to my newsletter:
- https://historymondays.substack.com

Printed in Great Britain
by Amazon